Beetles in the Boxcar

A
Mystery Novel

by
Joyce Oroz

CHAPTER 1

The snow-capped Sierra Mountains had become a faraway blur as my mud-spattered pickup bounced along Highway 41 to the beat of "She Loves Me, Yah, Yah, Yah." Riding shotgun was my Aunt Clara, who didn't care for music by the Beatles or commercials and frequently turned the dial. Protesting would not have helped. Aunt Clara had a mind of her own, not to mention a stubborn streak that stretched all the way from her home in Oakhurst to mine in Aromas, from one side of California to the other.

We had been on the road heading west for less than half an hour when she suddenly demanded I stop at a restroom. We had already passed Coarsegold. Why didn't she say something then? I knew why she had her sweatpants in a twist. It was because she had to leave home in a hurry with me instead of her own daughter. Candy was on a cruise in the Bahamas with her third husband, Brent, celebrating their first year of marriage.

"Can you wait till we get to Madera?"

"No," she snapped, fanning herself with a ropy freckled hand. A minute later, she asked to be forgiven for her impatience.

"Not a problem, Auntie. I'm sorry things aren't going well."

"Never mind that, Josephine. Get me to a restroom—a bush—something!"

"All I see are orchards and that shack up ahead. Must be a fruit stand."

"Pull over," she pointed to the one-room shack surrounded on three sides by bare fruit trees.

Brakes squealed as we jerked to a stop in front of "Facelli's Fresh Fruit," boarded up and deserted for the winter. Clara jumped out of the truck wearing a gray sweat suit and clear plastic rain boots. She plowed through the mud, ducked behind the old shed and minutes later returned with a better disposition. "Thank you, dear," she said as she hoisted herself into the cab.

The turnoff to Highway 145 caught my eye just in time. We had about ten more miles to Madera and then another 120 miles to my home in Aromas, positioned just one hill shy of a perfect view of the Pacific Ocean.

"Goodness, now Felix has to go!" Aunt Clara pulled a scrawny yellow cat out of her over-sized knitting bag. "When he squirms around like that, it's time."

I pulled off the road onto an unpaved shoulder near a double set of railroad tracks paralleling the highway. The pickup idled as Clara cuddled the old cat, climbed out of the truck and set the animal on the ground. Felix jumped a foot into the air when a semi roared by, giving my truck a good shake. Aunt Clara held him close for a moment and they tried again.

Fortunately, Felix was able to complete his mission before a freight train appeared in my rear view mirror. We traveled alongside the train most of the way to Chowchilla where we stopped for a fast food lunch. My aunt and I ended up with mustard stains down our fronts. Travel was like that, or maybe it was just us. After all, we were not neat little girly girls...or queen bees like Mom. It was astonishing to me that Mom was Aunt Clara's older sister. Clara was a fanatic when it came to mucking around in her extensive flower and vegetable gardens, while Mom babied a couple of rose bushes and belonged to the Senior Garden Club. Mom was active, kept her hair styled and knew how to dress for every occasion. She owned the latest in hiking boots, wetsuits, tennis togs and a red sari, while Aunt Clara's socks didn't match and her white hair billowed.

Aunt Clara and I had the same wavy, shoulder-length hair, except mine was still auburn with a white hair creeping in now and then, which I would immediately yank out. Clara's green eyes were twenty-five years older than mine but still had plenty of sparkle.

"You're awfully quiet, dear," Aunt Clara said, as we roared up Pacheco Pass.

"I was wondering what it was like for you growing up with my mother."

"Kind of like it is now. She was so busy with all her friends and activities. Couldn't slow down if she tried. I wasn't like Leola. I was quiet, always had my nose in a book and not very good at making friends. Leola used to haul me around to parties and football games; but it took years for me to come out of my shell, marry Roger and 'find my voice' in the world." I figured she was talking about her poetry—the published ones in particular.

"Aunt Clara, I'm glad you're going to stay with me so don't get me wrong, but why did you have to leave in such a hurry? The mudslide only affected the backyard."

"Josephine, you remember the Bass Lake fire last summer in the mountains behind my house?" I nodded, remembering the scary images shown on the news. "When the trees are gone, there's nothing to hold the earth in place. It's November and we've only had two rains. The mud is already at my back door. A construction crew is coming next week with bulldozers and such, and they'll scoop out the mud and build a retaining wall . . . that is, if they're allowed into the area. Cross your fingers it will be enough to hold back disaster." Clara stared at her muddy boots while she stroked Felix. "Besides, my neighbors and I were told to evacuate."

"How long will the work take if the crew is allowed into the neighborhood?"

"Depends on the weather. Our winters are colder and wetter than yours."

Aromas had gone six months without rain, which was typical, and then it poured on all the little trick-or-treat goblins and witches. Clara stopped turning the radio dial when she heard classical music and left it alone for almost an hour. Conversation was minimal until an advertisement for termite abatement flashed over the air waves. She quickly snapped it off.

"Don't you just hate commercials?"

"Ah, yeah. Auntie, I'm afraid I won't have much time to spend with you after my new job starts Monday."

"That's OK, dear. We can spend Saturday and Sunday together," she smiled as she dropped Felix back into her knitting bag.

"What is your new Wild Bush job? Painting, I presume."

"Yes, my Wildbrush Mural Company is scheduled to paint murals in the new Watsonville library. We're doing a thirty-foot mural in the children's story room and another one on the rounded entry wall."

"Won't you be a distraction to the folks in the library?"

"Only if we don't finish before December 15th, when the new building opens to the public. We have exactly five weeks to paint two large murals depicting changes in California over the last three hundred years. I've researched the subject and my sketches got us a decent contract."

"Do you still have people working for you? Alice and the college boy—what's his name?"

"Yes, Alicia and Kyle are still working for me. They're wonderful. Alicia lives in Watsonville, about ten miles from my house. Kyle lives about a half hour away in Santa Cruz." I smiled, picturing Kyle, the tall, skinny redhead decorated with tattoos and piercings.

"That's a gas station up ahead. Pull over," Clara said. As soon as the wheels stopped, she jumped out. I waited for my turn, standing outside the restroom door, shivering in the weak afternoon sun. I figured we would have to stop at least one more time for poor old Felix and maybe another for Clara.

In spite of all of Aunt Clara's pit stops, we made it to my house in time for me to search the fridge for an evening meal. Clara had settled herself on the sofa and seemed happy to be eating dinner in front of the TV.

Solow, my dear basset hound with a backside the size and shape of my coffee table, barked at Clara's knitting bag. She pulled the old cat out and placed him on my new tasseled throw pillow, a froufrou fiftieth birthday present from Mom and Dad.

"Does he chase cats?" she asked.

"Do bears live in the woods?" Clara smiled. I told her about Fluffy, David's cat next door, and how Solow loved to chase her. "She always runs circles around him," I said, watching Clara's eyes light up when I mentioned David.

"How is Mr. Galaz, dear?" She must have heard about him

through the Leola grapevine.

"David's fine...very fine, actually." My cheeks felt hot as Clara gave me a knowing smile. "We usually go to the pancake breakfast at the grange on the last Sunday of the month. Maybe you'd like to go with us next time."

"Thank you, dear, but I'll be staying with Candice and Brent by then." I secretly wondered if Candy would find time to be with her mom now that she had a new husband to break in and a flower shop to run.

Clara was bushed by nine thirty. She and Felix slowly climbed the old wooden stairs to the loft where I had put a new spread on the lumpy bed I inherited from my paternal grandmother. I heard the mattress coils squeak as she sat down to catch her breath. The only other bed in the house was mine and I vowed to keep it. On the other hand, I would have been more than happy to share my five acres of weeds, wild lilacs and oak trees. In fact, I hoped Clara would have time, weather permitting, to plant a few bulbs or bushes or just take care of my dehydrated marigolds in the window boxes.

Out of habit, I stayed up for the ten o'clock news. But after driving all day, I had a hard time keeping my eyes open. It seemed like KPUT ran the same old news stories day after day, year after year. Only the names changed. They were people I didn't know so I didn't have to feel their pain except in a distant sort of way. But when the reporter talked about a man who was found dead on the railroad tracks, I quickly turned my head away. That one made me shudder.

I turned back just as a photo of the man's face filled the TV screen. According to the reporter, the elderly man wasn't carrying identification; and people were asked to call the local sheriff's office if they recognized him.

I heard a sigh coming from the loft, followed by a loud thud plus an angry yowl from Felix. I looked up at the little three-sided bedroom. Clara's arm dangled in midair between the railing spindles that substituted for a fourth wall.

"Auntie, are you all right?" I shouted, as I leaped from the sofa and took the stairs two at a time. All kinds of things ran through my head—heart attack, stroke, spider, fear of heights?

"Josephine…it was like seeing a ghost." She lifted her head and tried to pull herself up. "Joey is dead, but there he was on the TV, run over by a train. I couldn't believe my eyes," she moaned. I helped her to her feet and held her arm as she stepped back a few steps to the bed. She sat down, hugged her shoulders and blinked back tears as she stared at the redwood ceiling beams. Felix watched us cautiously from the other side of the bed.

Finally, Aunt Clara turned her head, looked up at me with wet eyes and apologized for the meltdown. Felix crept closer as her voice softened. I sat down beside her, causing the bed to creak and the mattress to flatten even more.

I had never known Aunt Clara to be emotional or even close to it. She was just as calm, sound-minded and logical as I. In fact, people always remarked about how similar we were and how strangely alike Candy and my mother were. Sometimes I entertained the idea that Candy and I were mistakenly given to the wrong mothers at birth.

"Can I get you anything, Auntie?"

"I'm OK, dear. I must be mistaken. Joey died a long time ago…and I'm over it. I know, you want to know what Joey was to me, right?"

"Sure, if you want to tell me." I wondered why she wanted to unload her story on me, but I was willing to listen. She took a deep breath and let the air out noisily.

"Joey lived next door to your mother and me when we were growing up in Santa Cruz. The Gianelli sisters were all grown up and starting their own families when Joey was born, so he was like an only child. His parents had raised four girls, and then they got this clever little boy who grew up taking apart clocks, radios, toasters and all kinds of things and putting them back together again. I used to help him reassemble appliances before they were missed."

"Were you two the same age?"

"I was a month older."

"Were you good friends?"

"Oh yes. In fact, I grew up thinking I would marry him someday. But Joey went off to the Air Force Academy in Colorado and I started college. I said 'started' because before the first year was up, I was engaged to Roger Ramsey. I married Roger, and as you know, he passed away six years ago. A few months after my husband died, I made a visit to Santa Cruz to see your folks and to see what Joey was up to. You know, see if he was still married and that sort of thing."

"So you two hadn't kept in touch over the years?"

"No. He came back from the Air Force and married Darla, a new girl in town. I never met her," Clara sniffed. "Anyway, while visiting in Santa Cruz, I found out from Myrtle, your mother's neighbor, that Joey had recently died in a plane crash...his own little airplane...sniff. Myrtle gave me the details."

"I'm so sorry, Auntie." I put my arm around her shoulder and felt her shiver. "Were his remains found?"

"Not really. The plane went down off the coast...according to the authorities. All I know is what Myrtle remembered from the newspaper story."

"So you don't think the face on TV is Joey?" I asked, getting a creepy feeling in my stomach, like termites in the basement.

"It's been so many years, how would I know what Joey looks like? I don't know why I reacted like that. It was obviously some bum, I mean, who else walks along the tracks at night?"

"Can I get you anything before you lie down?"

"No dear. Felix and I will be fine. Goodnight." I padded down the stairs and turned off the lights and TV. I went to my room, closed the door and called David.

"Hi, Josie, how was the trip?"

"Fine, if you don't mind half a dozen pit stops; you know—old plumbing, nervous bladder. Poor Aunt Clara was all shook up tonight when she saw a picture on the news. It seems this old man was hit by a train...."

"Yeah, I saw that."

"Well, she thought she knew who he was. She thought it was Joey, an old childhood friend. She fell to the floor in a puddle. I helped her up, but it wasn't easy."

"So she knows who the guy is?"

"No, because Joey died about six years ago in an airplane accident. Are you coming over tomorrow to meet Aunt Clara?"

"Is she a good cook?" I could almost see his rascally grin through the phone.

"David, you're awful. I guess she can cook. She loves to eat. She and I haven't seen much of each other in the last twenty years, but we seem to have a few things in common." I pulled the blankets up around my neck and drank in David's deep voice.

"Are you still there, Josie?"

"I'm here, getting sleepy though." I heard the crinkling of paper from David's end of the phone.

"Josie, I found the train accident in the Sentinel on page two. They estimate the guy was about seventy-five years old and he had a scar on his chin. He was five-foot-eleven, about 130 pounds, wearing western clothes and cowboy boots—no jacket."

"Sounds underclothed and undernourished to me. If he was a homeless person, he would have been wearing everything he owned, especially since we're going into winter," I yawned.

"Guess we'll never know," David yawned. "We should be yawning in the same room."

"I know. By the way, Aunt Clara thinks she's going to move in with her daughter as soon as Candice gets back from a cruise with her husband."

"And you don't think so?" David said with another yawn.

"Nope, it's just a hunch I have. Are you coming over for dinner tomorrow?"

"Now that you've invited me, what can I bring?" he asked.

"Bring Fluffy so we can see how she gets along with Aunt Clara's cat, Felix."

"So, Aunt Clara has a cat. Any other animals?"

"No. You can bring over some of your homemade salsa. I have a bag of corn chips."

David had learned how to cook out of necessity after his wife, Susan, ran off with the preacher ten years ago. Since he was in his early fifties, retired and had plenty of time and money for hobbies, he took cooking seriously. He had perfected a few savory favorites such as his apricot salsa. It was one more way to use up the surplus apricots from his orchard.

"OK, I'll bring Fluffy and salsa. See you tomorrow, sweetie."

We hung up way before my smile faded. Even my ears were smiling. There's nothing more adorable than the image of a man wearing an apron in the kitchen. That night I dreamt about a very skinny old man wearing a big white apron. I watched him fall out of an airplane and sail in the wind like an aimless kite while sharks gathered in turbulent water below.

CHAPTER 2

Either a Brahma bull found its way into my living room or Aunt Clara was up early Saturday morning, tripping over things and slamming doors and drawers. I tried to ignore the commotion but eventually rolled out of bed and pulled on my robe. A brilliant sunrise backlit panels of forest green poplin stretched across the east window. I scratched my head and stretched, noticing that Solow's bed was empty. Aunt Clara peeked in from the hall.

"Oh, Josephine, you're up. I've been dying to talk to you about an errand I want to run, with your help, of course. I hope you don't mind, dear."

"I don't mind at all. My truck and I are at your disposal," I yawned as I shuffled down the hall to the kitchen.

"I'm so glad," she said in a somber voice. "You see, I didn't sleep very well last night. Joey was on my mind and I even dreamt about him."

"Yeah, me too." I remembered sharks and the old man wearing an apron.

"I just have to see the body for myself," she said, "or else it's going to keep me awake every night." She sat down at the kitchen table and took a sip of coffee from her mug.

"OK, Auntie." I leaned against the fridge with my hands cupped around a mug of hot coffee. "They said the accident happened a mile south of Watsonville, right?"

"Yes, I believe that's what the reporter said." Her eyes were dry, but without the sparkle.

"So that makes it Monterey County. Where's Solow?" I asked, looking around.

"Oh, dear, I hope I did the right thing. He wanted to go outside awfully bad so I let him out."

"That was the right thing to do. You just saved me the trouble." I watched Felix jump into her lap, circle a couple of times and curl up for a nap. The cat looked quite comfortable until Solow barked at the back door. Felix jumped to the floor and bolted, his yellow hair standing straight up. Clara called him, but the cat had quickly rounded the corner and gone into hiding. As soon as I opened the door, Solow dragged himself inside and collapsed under the kitchen table, panting. "Now you know what happens to my dog after a Fluffy chase."

I excused myself, took a shower and returned to the kitchen wearing a green angora sweater that matched my eyes, Levis and black, one-inch ankle boots which I enjoyed wearing because they brought my height up to five foot eight, just a titch taller than Clara. My hair had been moussed, dried, and fluffed. Lipstick and mascara made me feel five years younger.

"More coffee, dear?"

"No thank you, Auntie," I failed to mention how dark and bitter the brew was. "I'll start breakfast. Do you want your eggs scrambled?"

"That would be lovely. I'll make the toast. Just show me where you keep the bread." I pointed to the loaf of sourdough lying on the counter. I pulled a can of orange juice out of the freezer, reconstituted it and scrambled the eggs while Clara carefully scraped black soot off our toast with a butter knife.

After breakfast, I rinsed the dishes and Clara called the Monterey County Sheriff's Office. She was referred to a number in Santa Cruz. After the second call, Clara put the phone down.

"They told me the "John Doe" was taken to the morgue in Santa Cruz at the County Hospital on Emeline Street. It seems the Salinas facility is full." She raised a hankie to her nose.

"I know where the hospital is, but I wonder if the morgue is open on Saturdays."

"They're not exactly open, but the Coroner will meet us there at nine. He sounded anxious to get an identification. And while we're in Santa Cruz, we can stop and see your mom and dad."

"If they're home," I added. By nine o'clock, we were cruising through the County Hospital parking lot, reading signs on six different buildings, each built in a different style over a period of sixty years. Finally, I saw a small wooden sign for Sheriff-Coroner posted on the grass in front of a nondescript, two-story building with an extra-wide green door. Parked at an angle near the green door and windowless wall was a white car with a "Santa Cruz County Coroner" decal on the door. It was the only car around. I parked next to the official vehicle and cut the engine.

"They said he would meet me here," Aunt Clara said as we climbed out of the truck and walked a few feet to the green door. She knocked. I suddenly got cold feet and told her I would wait in the pickup. I watched the green door open. Clara disappeared inside and a minute later it started to rain.

I sat in the cold cab wondering if Solow and Felix were getting along and wished I were back in my warm kitchen, sipping a cup of tea and listening to the rain on the roof. The word "morgue" gave me the creeps so I continued to think about other things until I saw Clara close the green door behind her. She held a handkerchief to her nose. Her pale face was wet with rain but she seemed not to notice.

I watched Aunt Clara try to catch her breath as tears and raindrops streamed down her soft cheeks. I opened the door, jumped down from my seat and hurried to her side. She leaned into my arms, quivering with each sob. It was all I could do to hold back my tears as I helped her into the cab. She hiccupped her thanks as she buckled her seatbelt.

I turned the truck toward Walnut Street, and we traveled in silence to Mom and Dad's house. The rain and the tears had stopped. Clara's red-rimmed eyes dried as the sun peeked through the last of the fast-moving clouds. Aunt Clara's face spoke volumes, but I was dying to hear what really happened to Joey. Finally, as I parked at the curb, she told me she had seen Joey at the morgue and talked about the scar on his chin, a childhood souvenir from a fall out of a tree.

"Are you OK, Auntie? We could go home...."

"I'll be fine, except I need to know more about the supposed airplane crash. But we'll let that go for now." Mom opened Clara's door for her. They hugged.

"Why didn't you tell me you were coming, Clara?" Mom asked. "Are you all right?"

"I'll be fine," Clara said and sniffed.

"I didn't think to call ahead. Sorry, Mom. Glad we caught you at home." She gave me her usual sumo-wrestler hug, and we proceeded to the front door. Mom and Dad were just three birthday candles short of eighty, but their health was good. Mom explained that Dad was at the Bowl and Bowl with his bowling team, practicing for the semi-finals.

"Have a seat, Clara," Mom said, pointing to a chair at the kitchen table. "I saw the strangest thing on the news last night…oh my, is that why you're in town? Joey?"

Aunt Clara nodded. "I saw him at the morgue a few minutes ago."

"You don't really think it was Joey Gianelli?" Mom covered her mouth with her hand and then stared at me. I gave a slight nod just before a tear escaped and ran down Clara's face.

"I don't understand it myself," Clara said, "but we'll get to the truth, won't we?" She looked at me, probably sensing my curiosity in the matter, not to mention the availability of my trusty old truck. Unlike Mom, Aunt Clara had never learned to drive.

"Mom, I need your phone book."

"Over there, honey," she pointed to a drawer by the phone. While Mom and Clara talked about the old days, growing up next door to Joey and all his shenanigans, I searched for Gianelli in the phone book and found three: Dominick, Jamie and Sal, but no Darla.

"Did Darla remarry?" I asked. Clara shook her head while Mom nodded.

"Darla remarried?" Clara said. Mom nodded again. "Who did she marry?"

"A friend of Bob's. Actually, they're on the same bowling team. His name is Wayne something. Bob said the man sold his locksmith shop years ago but still likes to tinker around."

"Leola, call Bob and get Wayne's last name, would you,

please?" Clara said.

"Sure, I'll get it for you." Mom picked up the phone and dialed. After a brief conversation, she wrote a name on the phone
book cover. "It's Wayne Bracken. I could barely hear Bob over the
racket at the Bowl and Bowl."

I grabbed the phone book, found one listing under Bracken,
Wayne B., and jotted down the phone number and address on a
scrap of paper for Clara. She tucked it in her purse. Mom brought
out the cards, and we played a lively game of Hearts.

"I was just thinking, wouldn't it be nice to meet Darla?" I said,
at the end of our third game. "Before Wayne comes home?" Clara
looked ready to go and Mom looked mildly interested. Without a
word, we stood, grabbed our purses and headed for Mom's Subaru parked at the curb behind my truck. It was a short drive to
Gross Avenue on the east side of Santa Cruz. The modest, well-
kept old neighborhood was a haven for seniors and young yup-
pies.

"That's it, 1550, right there, the white stucco with a red door
and gray shutters," Clara said, her voice climbing higher than
usual. "Park over there, sis. Never mind the hydrant. We'll be back
in a jiffy." We climbed out of the car and charged up the sidewalk
to the front door, our hearts pounding with anticipation.

"Ring the bell, Clara," Mom said, but Aunt Clara's arm was
frozen in mid-air. I reached around her and pushed the doorbell.
"I hear someone coming," Mom said, as if her sister and daughter
couldn't hear as well as she. The door opened a crack.

"Sorry, I'm not interested."

"We're here to see Darla," Mom said, since Clara's lips seemed
to be frozen shut.

"I'm Darla Bracken, but I don't want to buy anything." She
tried to close the door but my foot happened to be in the way. She
sighed and opened the door a little more. The wrinkled lids over
her pale blue eyes blinked fast from the sun's glare.

"Mrs. Bracken, my husband is Bob Carl, a bowling friend of
Wayne's. My name is Leola and this is my sister, Clara, and my
daughter, Josephine." Darla stepped back inside and motioned for
us to enter. She was a petite woman in her early seventies, wearing

a heavily pilled cardigan over her retro, purple polyester pantsuit. She leaned against the far wall.

"Won't you sit down? Wayne should be home soon...ah, he bowls."

"Yes, dear," Mom said, "with Bob Carl, my husband." I noticed that my mother and her sister were smiling, trying to appear casual. I had pasted a smile on my face too.

"This is a very cozy room. What do you burn in the fireplace that smells so good?" I asked.

"I collect pine branches from the hillside behind the house," Darla said, "but they burn awfully fast. My son, Jamie, brings us scraps of wood from his cabinetwork when he remembers. He's only fifty and already forgetful." She looked at her feet and shook her head.

I cleared my throat and looked at Aunt Clara sitting opposite me on the saggy tweed sofa next to Mom, staring into space. Mom finally spoke to the wispy little lady in purple.

"Darla, my sister and I grew up in Santa Cruz next door to the Gianelli family. Clara and Joey were the same age and very good friends."

"You're talking about my first husband, aren't you?" Darla said, her eyes widening. "What is this all about?"

"We were wondering if you saw the news last night," I said. Darla shook her head.

"No, our TV's on the blink. Wayne and I would rather play scrabble anyway. Is there something I should know? You didn't come here without a reason, did you?"

"Right," I said, looking at Clara, hoping she would answer Darla's questions. Mom played with her wedding ring, crossed and re-crossed her legs and finally finished my sentence for me.

"If you had watched the news, dear, you would have seen a picture of Joey after his recent accident," Mom said, looking at her ring and then back to Darla.

"You mean a picture of him six years ago after the plane crash?" She cocked her head.

"No," Mom said, "a recent picture from a train accident. The police were asking people to call in if they knew who the man was.

Apparently he wasn't carrying identification." Darla's mouth tightened as she squinted her glassy eyes behind wire-rimmed glasses.

"I'm sorry, dear. I hope I haven't upset you," Mom said.

"I don't think you're talking about Joey Gianelli. He died years ago," Darla shot back.

Clara's eyes were filling up. I hoped she could hold it together a little longer.

"Darla," Clara sniffed, "Joey was my closest childhood friend. I was with him when he fell out of the walnut tree and split his chin open, and I saw the scar in person today…at the morgue." A couple of tears leaked and ran south. Mom put a hand on Clara's arm.

"I really don't know what this is about or why you're telling me this nonsense." Darla stood up, ready to escort us out of her house. Mom pulled herself up from the sofa and approached the frail-looking woman.

"We aren't trying to be mean, Darla. You have to understand that Joey meant a lot to my sister. She just wants to know more about the airplane crash." Mom patted Darla's bony hand. We jerked our heads around when we heard a door slam in the kitchen, followed by heavy footsteps and a gravelly voice.

"I'm home." Darla barely noticed her heavy-set, balding husband as he tramped through the kitchen from the back door wearing a shiny gold bowling shirt.

"Why do you concern yourselves with the plane crash?" Darla asked, looking at Clara as if she were an unwelcome rodent. "You know very well Joey died six years ago. Why are you telling me this pack of lies? Why should I believe anything you say?"

"Because it's true, honey," Wayne said, as he entered the room. "I heard the guys at the Bowl and Bowl talkin' about the man with the scar on his chin. One of the guys knew Joey a long time ago." Suddenly Darla's thin face turned alabaster white. Wayne grabbed her arm and helped her into a well-worn wing chair.

"Honey, Sal came lookin' for me at the Bowl and Bowl today. He said he saw a picture of his dad on TV last night, so he and Jamie went down to the morgue today at noon. They identified their dad, but they were worried about you. I told Sal I'd take care of everything."

"I still don't understand…Wayne, water…pill…." Darla's head fell back against the high back chair, and her eyes rolled upward until they were as white as her pasty skin. Wayne rushed around the kitchen gathering water and medicine. He leaned over her, pushed a pill between her thin lips and steadied her glass of water as she took a sip.

"Oh, look at the time," I said, motioning to Clara to get up off the sofa. "We really have to go now." Mom and Clara funneled out the door as I said a quick goodbye to the Brackens and handed Wayne my business card. I closed the front door behind me, hurried down the sidewalk to Mom's car, snatched a little pink note from under the wiper and jumped in.

"Did I get a ticket?" Mom growled, turning to look at Aunt Clara in the passenger seat.

"It's an advertisement for the Pizza Rut," I said, buckling up in the backseat. "Poor Darla looked more stunned over Joey's second accident than we are. Let's see…she's remarried, obviously not rich and still believed her husband died six years ago."

"Last year Bob told me Darla had been ill and the Brackens were having tough times financially, so all the guys pitched in to pay for Wayne's bowling shirt. Actually, he's the best bowler on the team by far," Mom said. It was easy to imagine him rolling a super fastball.

The first thing I saw when we entered Walnut Street was Dad's new, pre-owned silver Buick. The Buick had been on Dad's bucket list for turning eighty. I was pretty sure that turning eighty wouldn't have much effect on him or his driving since he hadn't even begun to slow down.

"OK, everybody out," Mom said, "I'll call for some pizza," she waved the pink coupon in the air as she walked toward Dad. He stood half in, half out of the front door.

"Good grief, I almost forgot!" I sputtered. "We need to get home before six. David's coming over for dinner." Mom and Clara made eye contact and smiled.

Dad stepped onto the front porch. I hurried up the walk and

gave him a big hug. Clara marched up the sidewalk with arms out and gave him a warm hug with a quick explanation of why we were leaving right away.

Once we were traveling in the direction of Aromas, Clara shut down. Rather than cry more tears, she slipped away into her own thoughts as Ray Charles sang "Georgia on My Mind." I busied myself trying to remember, word for word, the conversation that had taken place at 1550 Gross Avenue. The Brackens seemed like a decent couple, struggling to make ends meet and obviously not living on a life insurance settlement. I felt sorry for Darla, going through Joey's death all over again. But, I also hated to see Aunt Clara suffering a second time.

We motored south to Watsonville and then ten miles further to the Aromas exit. It was already dark when I drove into the hills half a mile and turned left on Otis. We rolled up my long gravel driveway and parked next to David's cute little black Miata. There were no streetlights or sidewalks on Otis; so even with a flashlight, the four hundred feet of uneven ground between our houses was difficult to navigate after dark.

"Is that David's car?" Clara asked. I nodded. She climbed down from her seat and stretched her arms. "It's a pretty little thing."

"Yeah, and look at the smoke," I said, pointing to the little round chimney on top of my house. "David built a fire, bless his heart." I opened the front door and immediately felt the warmth. My little freestanding, overachiever woodstove usually had me opening windows to cool things down; and sure enough, David was pushing a kitchen window open as we entered. Solow stood up, howled and wagged his whole body.

"Sorry we're late, David." He left the window and joined us in the living room. "This is my Aunt Clara."

"It's nice to finally meet you, Aunt Clara. I heard you came here with a cat, but I haven't seen him yet." David scratched his head of thick graying hair and looked around the room.

"Here comes my baby, my little Felix." Felix cautiously eyed Solow. Clara bent down and scooped the old cat into her arms.

"Where's Fluffy," I asked, looking around.

"She was acting cranky this afternoon, and this evening she refused to get out of the car," David said. "I plan to go out later and get her when she's in a better mood."

"What's cooking, David?" Clara asked.

"When you girls didn't answer the phone all day, I decided to make something new I want you to try." I was excited because David's cooking was always divine.

"That black smoke seems to be coming from the...." I stammered. David was already heading for the kitchen. He grabbed a potholder, opened the oven door and quickly slammed it shut. His shoulders caved as he turned the dial to the off position. I think it was his first big failure in the gourmet cooking department and my opportunity to give him a reassuring kiss for his efforts. And a second kiss because he looked like a little boy with a popped balloon.

"Don't feel bad, David, I can't cook either," Clara said. "Where's the peanut butter?"

CHAPTER 3

I slept soundly for a couple of hours Sunday morning after a night of tossing and turning. Feeling a lick on my cheek and whiskers tickling my chin, I finally opened my eyes halfway. I looked into Solow's droopy and perpetually bloodshot peepers. He whined.

"Need to go out?" I pulled on my robe, stepped into slippers and trudged down the hall to the kitchen. As I let Solow out the back door, I heard the rustle of paper and noticed Clara sitting at the kitchen table copying information from the phone book.

"Good morning, dear."

"Morning. What are you doing, Auntie?"

"I'm working on a bus schedule, and I just finished looking up names and addresses pertaining to Joey's accident," she said. "I pondered his death all night and came up empty. I sort of finished off your ice cream while I pondered." We were a lot alike, my aunt and I, including the extra fifteen pounds we each carried around. At least my pounds were twenty-five years younger and firmer than hers.

"That's OK, Aunt Clara. I planned to go grocery shopping today, and I want you to come along and point out some of your favorite foods."

"Thank you, Josephine, but remember, I'll be leaving soon so we won't need much." Clara looked more put-together than usual in her mint green sweat suit and faux fur-lined boots.

"I just want you to enjoy yourself and eat well while you're staying with me, Auntie. Any places you'd like to see today? Is that clock right? Can't be."

"It's eight o'clock all right. I thought you would never wake up. On our way to the store, let's stop for breakfast somewhere, my treat."

I gulped some lukewarm coffee-sludge, charged down the hall to the bathroom and took a quick shower. I came back wearing Levis, a yellow sweater and my favorite shorty boots.

"I let Solow in and fed him," Clara said, smiling. "He was a sorry-looking pup after that prissy ball of white fur got through with him."

I heard Solow snoring under the table, his muzzle resting atop Clara's boots. "Where's Felix?"

"I let him out," she said. "He's good about staying close to home. I think he's insecure."

"That's not Solow's excuse. He likes to stay close to food and his bed. Besides, he's too lazy to go very far." After I buzzed through a few last-minute chores, Clara put Felix back in the house; and we drove to Watsonville where we found sustenance in the form of Sausage Egg McMuffins and coffee.

"Was that enough food for you?" Clara asked. I nodded.

"Where do you want to go before we shop?" I asked.

Clara pulled a list out of her shiny black plastic purse. "I copied down Sal's and Jamie's addresses. Let's start with Sal over on Morrissey Boulevard."

Because I grew up in Santa Cruz, I was able to drive straight to Morrissey, the main entrance into the east side of town. "Ok, what's the number?"

Clara checked her list. "2240. Keep going. Should be riii...ght there. You can park behind the black Mercedes."

"Wow!" I said, looking up the sloping lawn to a 1920s-style, two-story home at least five times bigger and nicer than Sal's mother's home on Gross Avenue.

"Sal seems to be doing all right," Clara said. "Shall we go for a visit?"

"Why not?" I grabbed my purse. "Don't you just love old-growth trees like these. Is that a lawnmower I hear? Must be in the backyard."

We bypassed the wide stairs leading to the front porch, followed a stone path to the left around the house, and Clara unlatched the gate. We followed the meandering walkway through an immaculate garden encompassing a large oval lawn. The young man behind the mower saw us and cut the engine. He cocked his head full of shoulder-length blond hair as we walked toward him.

"What can I do for you ladies?" He tossed strands of damp hair out of his eyes.

"We thought Sal was back here, but you aren't Sal...are you?" Clara asked. He laughed.

"Sal's my dad. I'm Patrick."

"It's wonderful to meet you, Patrick. My name is Clara Ramsey and this is my niece, Josephine Stuart. Your grandfather was a dear friend of mine." I watched Patrick's smile fade as his deep blue eyes wandered to the back door of the house.

"I guess you know he's...dead," Patrick said, his voice softer than before.

"Yes, dear, and I'm so sorry for your loss. I was hoping to talk to your father. Maybe another day," Clara's eyes followed Patrick's stare. I saw the back door slowly close.

"Will there be a memorial or funeral service for your grandpa?" Clara asked. Patrick squinted into the sun.

"Dad said, no. We already did that six years ago."

"OK, ah, we'll stop by another day, dear."

"Yeah, another day." He fired up the mower and went back to work, making tighter and tighter circles, moving toward the lush green grass in the middle.

We stood for a minute in the pale dappled sunshine next to my truck. "Good looking boy, don't you think?" I said. "Must be an athlete."

"Yes," Clara said, "but no resemblance to his grandfather. He doesn't have the distinctive Gianelli nose." She shook her head. "And blond hair?"

"Well, he was very cute," I said. "I wonder who owns the Mercedes." Just as I said the words, the car moved forward into traffic. All I saw through the tinted windows was the back of a blond head. The mower droned in the distance as we climbed into my truck.

"Now, Auntie, where to?"

"First the grocery store. After that I want to go to the railroad tracks where Joey died, and after that we'll see where Jamie lives."

"Really?" I blurted. "I mean, if that's going to be closure for you, Auntie, it's fine with me."

"More like curiosity," she mumbled, as we headed back to Watsonville and my favorite market. I parked near the cart corral where Robert wrestled a long line of unruly baskets. The short, pudgy, freckled young man wearing a big blue apron looked our way and grinned. I introduced Clara, grabbed a cart and the three of us walked to the market entrance.

"What's new, Robert?"

"Did you hear about the guy run over by a train?" he scrunched his nose up as if he smelled a skunk. "I listened to KPIG this morning. They say it was murder."

"Yeah, it looked suspicious to me," I said. "Is that all you know about it?"

"They know who he was, Joseph Gerelli, Gimelli ... or something like that," Robert said, just before he was called back to his check stand.

Clara pushed the cart up and down the aisles while I loaded it. I decided not to buy ice cream since we had more stops to make, and it would be soup by the time we got home. When the cart was full, we pulled into Robert's checkout lane behind three other shoppers with full baskets.

"Josephine, that line is shorter," Clara pointed to the right.

"I know, but I like to pick Robert's brain," I said. Aunt Clara rolled her eyes, but I had the feeling she understood. She listened to every word Robert said about Joey's case. He was still talking as he closed his lane, pushed the cart outside and loaded our groceries into the truck.

"Thanks, Robert," I fired up the engine. "Where do we go now, Auntie?"

"I need to see the railroad tracks; you know...where Joey died."

"I understand your curiosity, but how are we going to find the exact spot?"

"I called KPUT TV this morning...told them I was doing a

story for the Times. The gal on the phone was very helpful until she got suspicious and cut me off. Luckily, she had already told me how to recognize the spot. She said she was there yesterday with the cameraman doing a story." Clara smiled smugly.

"So, which way?" I asked, looking up and down Riverside Drive.

"Let's go that way," Clara pointed to the left. I hoped she wasn't just guessing. We merged into traffic going east, crossed the Pajaro Bridge onto San Juan Road, and cruised through the little town of Pajaro. Eighty-year-old farmhouses, decrepit barns and rusty metal packing sheds dotted the agricultural landscape. Acres of salad material, five kinds of lettuce, some spinach and three types of cabbage thrived under a weak winter sun. About three hundred yards south, two sets of railroad tracks paralleled San Juan Road. Dozens of empty freight cars, defaced with graffiti, sat on a side rail.

"Now what?" I asked.

"We look for San Marcos Canyon Road. Oh, on your right," she said, tapping the dash nervously with her fingers. "Turn, turn…there." I yanked the wheel to the right. We proceeded one short block up San Marcos Canyon Road and parked in a wide spot just short of the railroad tracks and twin red and white striped arms at rest. The only building in shouting distance was a large, beige-colored metal packing shed the size of Costco, located on the other side of two sets of tracks. Spread out behind the shed were two or three acres of potted trees and bushes standing in neat rows.

"Now what?" I asked. Clara didn't hesitate.

"The gal I talked to on the phone told me to go west, down the tracks, past the packing shed about fifty yards to a little yellow flag," Clara said. "A sheriff's deputy put it there." We climbed out of my warm truck and began our trek along the tracks. I looked and listened for a train. The twice-a-day run obviously wasn't coming, but a cold northwest wind haunted us. It blew across our faces, cancelling out any warmth the weak sun might have provided. Aunt Clara shivered.

"Guess we should have worn our jackets," I said with chattering teeth. But Aunt Clara was on the move a few yards ahead of me and didn't seem to be concerned with the cold.

"I see the yellow flag, Josephine, over here." Clara climbed up the sloping three-foot embankment onto the steel tracks. I caught up to her as she examined the little yellow flag attached to a metal shaft stuck firmly in the rocky ground halfway between two sets of rails. I saw a smear of dark brown on the metal by my foot. I ignored it.

"Clara, do you feel better now that you know where Joey died?"

"No, but I would feel better if I knew how and why he died. It was no accident. Even a bum wouldn't be caught this far out of town, in the dark, on the tracks, in the winter without a jacket. And Joey was no bum, at least not when I knew him." She bent down and touched the flag lightly with one finger. A sad smile crossed her lips.

"Auntie, do you see those marks in the dirt...over there?" I pointed to a long swath of black dirt between us and a zillion rows of decapitated lettuce plants.

"Oh, I see what you're looking at. Let's go down and see." Clara gripped my elbow as we made our way down the slippery gravel incline and then out about ten feet to the first row of lettuce. In the soft black dirt, I saw a set of tracks obviously made by small narrow tires. A large wagon or small vehicle with a wheel span of about three feet had marked the earth all the way back to my truck. At times, mysterious footprints mixed with the tire tracks.

"What do you think of these footprints, Auntie?"

"I can't tell if it was one person or two, but some are coming and some are going. Probably male because the prints are pretty big," she said. "One thing I'm sure of, these footprints start at the road and head west until they line-up with the yellow flag. That's no coincidence. What do you think, Josephine? Why are you going back?"

"I'm going back to the flag to see if the prints cut over to the tracks." Aunt Clara came up behind me, breathing hard. After careful inspection, we decided someone had swept the area between the yellow flag and the long row of foot and tire prints. I figured someone had brushed the ground with a hand or foot or article of clothing, but not perfectly, because we were able to find a few traces of wheel tracks.

"Look, Aunt Clara, a button." I held it out for her to see. "Probably came off when he tried to get rid of the tracks in the dirt." She nodded and searched the ground for more clues. I heard voices and looked up.

"Don't look now, Auntie…." A green sheriff's car had parked behind my truck, and two uniformed sheriff's deputies were coming our way. The rangy blond wore her hair pulled back in a tight bun. The second sheriff was the same height, but heavier, mostly bald and African-American. I immediately recognized the pair from a previous encounter.

"Ms. Stuart, what are you doing here?" Deputy Lund asked with a hint of annoyance in her voice as she walked closer to us with her hands on her belt full of deadly weapons. Deputy Sayer stood beside her.

"You folks have business out here?" he asked.

"This is my Aunt Clara…Ramsey. Auntie, this is Deputy Sayer and she's Deputy Lund." Clara smiled politely.

"We just came out here to say goodbye to my friend, Joey Gianelli," Clara said, wiping a tear from her cheek. Deputy Sayer bit his lip.

"Ok, folks, this is a crime scene. Let's move along now," Deputy Lund said with no sign of emotion. "By the way, what was Mr. Gianelli to you, ma'am?" she asked Clara.

"We were best friends growing up. I hadn't seen him in fifty years, but he was always right here," she put a hand over her heart. I was on the edge of tears but Officer Lund didn't flinch.

"Ms. Stuart, what was the deceased to you?" Deputy Sayer asked me on the way back to our vehicles.

"My favorite aunt's best friend, of course."

"Sorry, you need to go now," he said. We climbed into my pickup, glad to be out of the wind and away from all the questioning. I fired up the truck and we bumped across the tracks, heading toward the hills. Clara asked about the officers.

"I've run into those two before. They mean well. Are we going to Jamie's?"

"Yes, just stay on San Marcos." She checked her notes. "Look for Bonita Lane. It should be coming up...right there, on your right," she pointed. I turned onto a narrow dirt road heading away from the lettuce fields. The dusty lane was short and lined on each side with a couple of dozen identical one-story wooden houses painted beige. No garages, not even a carport, just a variety of old dusty cars and trucks parked willy-nilly up and down the road. Each home had a tiny plot of dirt where a front lawn should have been. Number four had an old Ford pickup parked on the weeds near the front door.

"That's it, number four. Not exactly like Sal's house, is it?" Clara said, pointing to the boxy house with a United States flag sticker in the lower corner of the front window. I noticed the truck had a similar sticker on the back window. I parked behind the Ford but took my time climbing out. The sun had disappeared behind fast-moving clouds and the chilly breeze cut right through me. We slipped into our jackets and made our way up a short concrete sidewalk to the front door. I rapped on it a couple of times.

"Coming, hold on, I'm coming...ah, ladies?" The man looked puzzled.

"Jamie?" I asked. He nodded, looking a lot like a fifty-year-old Al Pacino.

"That's me. Are you here about the piano?"

"Piano? No, I'm Josephine Stuart and this is my Aunt Clara from Oakhurst," I babbled, still thinking about Jamie's resemblance to the actor.

"I have a piano for sale...never mind, how can I help you?" he asked, leaning against the doorframe. Clara stepped closer to the open door as we gazed into Jamie's thick-lashed brown eyes.

"I'm sorry about your father, Jamie," Clara said. "I was a close friend of his years ago. May we come in? It's freezing out here. I would love to talk to you about your dad?"

"You mean about the train accident?"

"Yes, that, and the airplane accident," Clara said.

Jamie stepped back awkwardly. We followed him as he limped across the tiny living room and plopped into a worn-out Lazy Boy. He motioned for us to sit on the old sofa by the front window.

From where I sat, it looked like the house had one of everything—one bathroom, one bedroom, one piano.

"Do you play, Al...I mean, Jamie?" I nodded toward the old piano.

"Sometimes." He reached down to his right knee, grabbed his pant leg and pulled his right leg up onto the footrest next to his left leg. He caught our stares from across the room. Without a word, he lifted his pant leg a few inches above his boot, revealing a metallic calf.

"Were you in the service?" I asked.

"Nope, motorcycle." As soon as his condition had been explained, Aunt Clara asked about Joey's airplane accident. Jamie stared at his brown leather work boots.

"Dad took off from the Watsonville airport in his Piper Cub alone. He usually flew with company, like me or my brother or his old friend from Santa Cruz. He loved to circle the whole county pointing out and naming stuff like mountains, buildings, crops, rivers, everything. He loved flying. I wasn't crazy about flying, but I loved being with him."

"I guess he didn't crash into the ocean after all," Clara said softly.

"Guess not. I don't know what to think." Jamie rubbed his hands together. The room was cold and I wished he would turn up the heat. As I looked around for the furnace, I heard a click and noticed a portable heater plugged into the wall. The coils turned red and a fan broke the silence with a dull whirr.

"So you don't know why he disappeared?" I asked.

"Nope, Dad was my best friend. He wouldn't have left us if he didn't have to."

"Who was your dad's friend in Santa Cruz?" Clara asked.

"Benny, Ben DeWald is his name. I'm not sure where he lives now, but he used to live in Santa Cruz. He also had a place up in Boulder Creek—a whole mountainside with an old cabin and a barn. He and Dad spent lots of time up there fishing and stuff." Clara was wide-eyed.

"Benny DeWald. I remember him from high school," Clara chirped. "He was a little scrawny guy with buck teeth."

"Not any more," Jamie said. "Ben's a good six feet tall and two hundred pounds and his teeth are straight. Last time I saw him he had long gray hair in a pony tail."

"I remember Benny playing some kind of horn in the school band," Clara said. She was smiling at her memories, thirty miles and sixty years away from the moment.

"He played the piano and drums too," Jamie said. "Taught me how to play the piano. He was a lot of fun, but I haven't seen him since Dad disappeared."

"Are you sure Ben and your dad didn't fly away together?" I said. Jamie squirmed in his chair as Clara leaned forward waiting for an answer.

"All I know is that I personally haven't seen Ben in six years."

"Do you have any idea why your father was on the tracks in the middle of the night?" Jamie had a dark cloud of gloom hanging over his head so I quickly changed the subject. "Your mom said you work with wood."

"Yeah, sometimes. I'm a finisher, you know, cabinetmaker. Trouble is—there are lots of finishers around. I was doing pretty well with my own business until the motorcycle accident. My wife left me and took her half plus half of my half of everything we owned."

"Sorry to hear that," I said.

Aunt Clara stood up and stretched. "We should be going now. It was nice meeting you, Jamie. Thank you for answering our questions." He stood up and walked us to the door. We climbed into my truck. Clara waved goodbye to Jamie, and we headed back to San Marcos Canyon Road with lots to think about.

"Next stop, home sweet home. Jamie's house was way too cold for me," I said. Clara agreed. "What was your impression of Jamie?"

"He has it, the Gianelli nose. Jamie looks a lot like his dad. I wonder if he can afford to heat his little house. And those houses . . . they look like rentals for migrant workers. I had a chicken coop bigger than Jamie's house."

"I didn't know you raised chickens, Auntie."

"Thirty years ago we had chickens. I'm too old for that nonsense now." She laughed as we passed through the two blocks of downtown Aromas. "Oh, look at that stud," she pointed up the hill.

"Mr. Ortega, or the bull?" I asked.

"The bull, of course, but the man doesn't look too bad either. About my age, wouldn't you say?"

"Yeah, but there's a Mrs. Ortega waiting for his return," I said as we passed the sturdy, gray-haired man walking his impressively large black bull up the street on a leash. "Somewhere in the neighborhood an amorous cow waits." Half a mile later, I turned up my driveway and parked beside David's Miata. He opened the front door for us and helped carry in the groceries. Fluffy and Felix napped on the couch as the three of us hustled groceries into the house with Solow at our heels.

"David, are you cooking again? It smells so good in here," Clara said, setting her bag of groceries on the kitchen counter. David nodded, wheeled around and was already heading for the front door and a forty-pound sack of kibble waiting in the back of the pickup.

I wanted to make sure David's food didn't burn so I pulled the oven door open just before he yelled, "noooo!" from the living room. I watched as his beautiful soufflé collapsed in the middle. He hurried back to the kitchen to see for himself.

"David, I'm sorry. Is there a way to fix it?" He groaned and wrapped his arms around me.

"Josie, I think your oven is bad luck. Aunt Clara, breakout the peanut butter."

CHAPTER 4

The phone beside my bed rang its obnoxious ring again and again. I was somewhere between sound asleep and barely awake when I picked up the receiver. "Hello?"

"Jo, are you awake?" Alicia asked, cautiously. She knew I was not an energetic morning-type person. I loved to sleep late and could become grumpy if provoked. Time and a stiff cup of coffee usually improved my disposition.

"I'm awake. What's up?"

"Did you get your messages yesterday?"

"What messages?"

"That's what I was afraid of. I left a message for you because the foreman called me after he tried all day to get hold of you."

"Foreman?" I let the word circle my brain for a minute. "You mean, Atwater, the foreman of the library project?"

"Yes. I bet you're awake now."

"You're right about that. What did he say?"

"He said the walls haven't been painted yet because the plaster wasn't dry because the weather has been so cold and damp." She took a long breath.

"What do they expect? It's November. We've had cold wet Novembers before. Somebody didn't plan very well."

"Hey, you're preaching to the choir, Jo. Anyway, he said it would be a week before everything's ready for us. That means you can sleep late. No work today," she laughed. "I already called Kyle and he's OK with it."

"Thanks, Allie."

"How about coming to my house for dinner tonight? I want to meet your Aunt Clara. Bring David, too." Alicia asked me over for dinner at least once a week. Besides being my best friend, she knew how much I loved her whole family, not to mention her wonderful cooking.

"Aunt Clara and I will be there, but last night David said he plans to go to Modesto for a few days. Monica's nanny was arrested during a protest march over the weekend, so Harley decided he wants to upgrade the sitter. Unfortunately, he's having trouble finding one. You know how David dotes on his son and granddaughter."

"Harley needs a wife," Alicia said.

"I know, but he's always working and doesn't get out much. His insurance office hired two women but they're too old. Besides, I think he's still a little nervous after his last marriage. I know how he feels. It's been seventeen years since Marty was run over by an eighteen-wheeler and I'm still nervous about remarrying, not that anyone is asking."

"Jo, you know very well David would marry you in a nanosecond if you let him."

"Maybe, but I'm not going there…yet."

"Is six o'clock OK for dinner?" Alicia asked.

"That would be great. Thanks, Allie." I hung up the phone, rolled out of bed and pulled on my robe. Solow followed me to the kitchen where Clara sat with the Yellow Pages flopped open on the table. She leaned over the book, concocting another list.

"Good morning, Auntie."

"Good morning, dear. Since you're not working today, I thought we might run a few errands."

"Sure, Auntie, but how did you know I'm not work…?"

"I ran your messages this morning. Leola wants you to call her."

"Where are we going?"

"I haven't been to Boulder Creek in at least thirty years. Wouldn't it be fun to go?"

"Yeah, I guess, but it's pretty cold and damp up there in the winter." I shivered just thinking about the high, forested mountains and the valley with its little rustic towns, narrow roads and cliff-hanging cabins.

"I found DeWald in the phone book," she said, "but he's not in Santa Cruz. It seems Benjamin DeWald lives on Tinker Ranch Road just off the Big Basin Highway about seven miles north of Boulder Creek." She pulled a computer-generated map out from under the phone book. "Seven point two miles north, turn left at Tinker Ranch Road, one mile and there it is."

"You make it look easy. Where did you get the map?

"Your computer."

"Wow, I'm impressed. Maybe you can teach me how to do maps sometime. When do you want to go?" I asked, feeling less than enthusiastic and wondering when my aunt became computer-savvy.

"I'll buy us a nice breakfast in Watsonville as soon as you get dressed and drive us down there."

I let Solow out the back door, shuffled down the hall and grumbled to myself for twenty minutes while I managed to complete my shower and personal beauty chores. I reappeared at the kitchen table dressed in my warmest turtleneck sweater, blue jeans and wool socks squeezed into shorty boots.

"Don't forget your jacket, dear," Clara said over her shoulder as she hoofed it over to the front door. "I let Solow in and he's been fed. Felix went back to bed . . . oh, don't forget your umbrella. Looks like it might rain today."

"Probably already dumped ten inches on Boulder Creek," I grumbled, but Clara didn't hear me. She hummed as she wiped moisture off the windshield with the Sunday paper. We slid into our seats and headed west to a fast food breakfast. Hot coffee and Egg McMuffins filled the empty, growly spaces. From Watsonville, it was usually a fifty-minute drive to Boulder Creek, except in a downpour.

"Can you believe this rain? I can hardly see two feet ahead," I said, leaning into the dash as we surfed the highway at thirty miles per hour.

"Dear, we can do this another day if you think driving is too difficult…."

"No, no. I'm OK, Auntie, and I understand your need to know what really happened to Joey. I've been thinking about it a lot and none of it makes sense."

"I know what you mean," she said.

I thought about the cost of gas and the fact that I wasn't working or getting paid for a whole week. Fortunately, I had a small rainy-day fund tucked away. Alicia would be fine since her number one job was wife and mother. Kyle might have to forgo a few dates but nothing rash. His parents helped out with the necessities of college life.

"OK, we made it to Ben Lomond," I said, eyeing the local shops. "Ten more minutes and we'll be in Boulder...wow. Hold on!" I yanked the wheel as we skidded off the shoulder and bump, bumped to a stop in a parking lot. We were puddled up to our bumpers in muddy water. "Did you see that? He cut right in front of me!" Clara didn't answer but her eyes were as big as cucumber slices. The offending vehicle, an Evergreen Nursery delivery truck, sloshed through the parking lot and parked in front of a weathered little flower shop attached to a nursery building.

"Any restrooms around here?" Clara asked, pulling a clear plastic bonnet over her head. "I'll just check out the flower shop."

She opened her door and dropped one leg into a foot of water. "Oh my," she squealed, yanking her leg back inside the truck.

"I was going to warn you, Auntie."

"Guess I'll have to wait a little longer for a restroom," she fumed.

"Those galoshes are too short for Ben Lomond puddles," I said as I cranked up the heat and put the fan on high. She pulled the boot off, dumped water back into the puddle and slammed the door. I heard something and whipped my head around. The young, dark-eyed truck driver who cut us off had his face at my window. I hesitated, then rolled the window down.

"Sorry, I didn't mean to cut you off. Are you ladies OK? I almost overshot my turnoff and didn't see you back there," he said with an impish smile, running a handful of fingers through soaking wet black curls. "Name's Gabe." He looked boyish, somewhere between Hispanic and Polynesian.

"Don't worry about it, Gabe. We're OK," I said, keeping it short as I pulled back from the window, trying to escape the rain.

I rolled up the window, backed out of the puddle, slipped my truck into drive and merged into the flow of traffic heading north on Highway Nine.

"He was cute, don't you think?" Clara smiled as she draped her wet sock over the dash.

"You just like guys in uniform, even if it's green overalls," I teased.

"If I were fifty years younger..." she smiled.

"At least he was polite when he wasn't driving. Looks like the rain is letting up a bit." I turned the wipers down a notch as we rolled through the historic lumber town of Boulder Creek and then turned left onto Big Basin Highway.

After passing five miles of redwood forest sprinkled with country cabins positioned close to the highway, we came to a golf course, a meadow and several clusters of two-story condominiums. Clara was in complete slack-jawed awe. "Josephine, I remember when all this was just forest. This is unbelievable"

I was impressed but not completely taken by surprise since I had driven the windy road to Big Basin State Park a couple of years earlier. We admired the stone structures nestled at the edge of the forest like jewels on a crown of evergreens. I switched the wipers to the slowest speed.

"Two more miles...look for Tinker Ranch Road," Clara reminded me for the tenth time. "Sorry, dear, it's just that I'm looking forward to seeing Ben. Imagine, after all these years. Do you think he'll recognize me?" I sincerely doubted it.

"The question is, Auntie, will you recognize him? Long grey hair? What else has changed?"

"There...turn, turn," she said. I yanked the wheel to the left, crossed the empty oncoming lane and crunched up a narrow gravel road sandwiched between redwoods as tall as skyscrapers.

At the end of the curvy mile-long road, we were 500 feet above the main highway, facing a grassy meadow the size of two or three Wal-Mart parking lots.

"Look, Aunt Clara, to the west," I pointed. "See, at the end of the meadow."

"Yes, I think I see a building of some sort," she said.

"It's a large barn painted forest green. It blends so well into the trees I had to look twice." Closer to us, an ancient weathered sign attached to a chain-link fence announced the Tinker Ranch and the sign next to it said, "No Trespassing."

"Not very welcoming, is it," Clara said. The fence followed the contour of the land as far as we could see in both directions, until it was swallowed up by forest. Beyond the meadow and in every direction, the mountains were covered in redwoods, tan oaks, laurel and madrone. The taller, farther-away mountains had their heads in the clouds. Boulder Creek was notorious for its sixty to eighty inches of rainfall every winter; but for us, the rain had stopped and the sun peaked out from billowy clouds.

"This place takes my breath away. It's so beautiful," I gushed as Clara forced her bare foot into a wet tennis shoe and pulled on the clear plastic boot. My little ankle boots were designed for sidewalks, not walks on spongy meadows or in mulchy forests, but I had a feeling they were about to venture into some real muck.

"Honey, don't just sit there. Honk the horn. Let Ben know we're here," Clara said, fluffing her hair in the mirror. She smacked her lips together, spreading a fresh coat of ruby-red lipstick over her wrinkled lips. Finally, she lowered herself to the ground and slammed the door. I rolled my eyes, let my head fall on the horn once and climbed out of my mud-spattered Mazda, sitting in muddy water up to its armpits. I circled several puddles as I hurried to catch up with Clara. She struggled with a rusty chain.

"Auntie, let me help you." We stood in the muck, wrestling with the long heavy chain looped a couple of times between the gatepost and the gate. A rusty padlock hung at the end, rusted in the open position. The chain finally fell to the ground and the gate squeaked open. Clara zipped back to the truck faster than any seventy-five-year-old I'd ever seen.

"Now what?" I said, firing up the engine.

"Just follow the road to the left, up there." She pointed to the barn. I pushed the gas pedal down, wheels spun, gravel sprayed and we rounded the gate. The tires dropped into a deep rut filled with water and climbed out slowly, only to sink into another puddle. All the ruts were full of water, making it impossible to judge how deep the potholes were. With a lot of slipping and sliding, we worked our way slowly up the hill.

Halfway to the barn I tugged the wheel to the right, dodged a menacing puddle, and accidentally discovered it was easier to drive on meadow grass. A little slippery, but with steady pressure on the gas, we went from snail-speed to turtle-speed. As we approached the giant green barn, I pulled the wheel to the right. I cut the engine on a flat grassy area beside the vintage building. Ahead of us was nothing but forest bordered by a single row of bare fruit trees. A rusty tractor sat between two apple trees.

"Wonder why he didn't park the tractor in the barn," I said, watching for any signs of life.

"Maybe you should honk again."

"Auntie, I don't see anyone, not even a cabin or a car or anything."

"Guess we should look around," Clara said as she hopped down from her seat and slammed the door. I followed her to the front of the barn where two giant doors were padlocked together. I pressed an eye to the minuscule airspace between them, but the inside was dark as night. We rounded the barn, found a little back door and I tried the doorknob.

"Locked. Now what?"

"Where do you think that goes?" she pointed to the other side of the barn where a dirt road headed northwest up a hillside. It was obviously an extension of the rutty driveway we had already experienced. "Let's see where it goes," she said. I knew she would insist, so I didn't argue. We slogged our way back to the truck and headed up the hill.

"One more sharp turn and I'm going to be sick," Clara announced, looking a bit pale.

"Look, there's the top of the hill, Auntie, and someone's white pickup truck."

"And who's the old man with the rifle?" she asked as if she didn't know. I braked and shut down the engine. "He's coming closer. Is my hair OK?"

"You look fine, Auntie, but don't forget, we're trespassing." I rolled down my window.

"Ladies, are you lost?" the man asked, leaning on his rifle.

"Actually, we're looking for a certain gentleman, Ben De-Wald," I smiled. He smiled back. Clara's mouth was locked in the off position, but her eyes were all over the handsome senior.

"I'm Ben. Who are you? Didn't you gals see my 'No Trespassing' sign?"

"My name is Josephine Stuart and this is my aunt...."

"You look familiar." He looked past me, his eyes locked on Clara. "Do I know you from somewhere?" Clara's eyes sparkled, but her tongue seemed to be tied in a knot. Finally, a croaking sound crawled up her throat and out of her mouth. She drew in a breath.

"Benny."

"Cat?"

Clara scrambled out of her seat as Ben dropped his gun, rounded the front of the truck and met her with a hug. She laughed, teared up and sniffled. He held her and stroked her hair. Ben wiped his eyes and then hers and his again. He held her shoulders back and examined her flushed face.

"I remember when you were the prettiest little green-eyed girl in pigtails. You wouldn't give me the time of day. Cat, you grew into a beautiful woman."

"And you're a sight to behold, Benny. How are you, my dear?"

"You mean, besides being old as dirt?" he laughed.

"Benny, you look great. I wish Joey could be here too." Ben's face froze. "Did I say something wrong?"

"Guess you're here about Joey, right?"

"Well, yes. I'm very confused about the airplane crash...."

"Guess we'll never know what happened." He shrugged his shoulders and looked away.

"Benny, may I use your powder room?"

"Well, it's no powder room. See that little shack with the moon cut in the door?" he pointed to the little wooden lavatory twenty feet from the cabin. "I'm sorry, Cat. It's all I have. Never got around to putting in a real bathroom. It's not even a real house, it's just a cabin. Now that I live here, I plan to get going on the remodel." Clara had gone and come back before Ben finished his rambling history of the cabin he inherited from his grandfather.

"Would you ladies like to come in for a cup of hot tea?"

"That would be lovely," I said, welcoming a chance to warm up. Ben ushered us into his old-time country kitchen. He stoked the fire in the cast iron stove, filled a kettle with water and set it on the stovetop. Ten minutes later, the whistle blew and three mugs of tea were served. I let my eyes wander around the large room featuring redwood walls, two windows facing west, a white enamel sink from the twenties and wall cupboards with transparent beveled glass windows showing off blue and white patterned china.

We sat on high-backed chairs pushed up to a very old, round oak table. As Clara and Ben caught up on the last fifty-five years of their lives, I heard Ben say he had been married for forty years to a nurse he met when he was in the Army. She died from a rare blood disease when she was sixty-five. They had no children. I decided to join the conversation.

"So, Ben, when was the last time you saw Joey?"

"Ah..." he scratched his chin, stood and walked to a window. "About six years ago we fished for trout down at the gorge...where the river runs through my property." Ben came back, sat down and rubbed his thumb up and down his cup, his eyes focused on the intricate golden grain of the tabletop. Clara's face was still aglow as she savored every word he spoke, but I heard a new stiffness in his voice.

"Sounds like you two were close friends."

"Yeah, we were. I guess you saw the news Friday night." He stood, crossed the room and came back with more hot water. Clara got a refill so I held my cup out. Ben filled my cup with a shaky hand and dribbled hot water across my pant leg. I jerked and dumped half the tea on the wood floor.

"So sorry. Are you all right?" he asked. I assured him I was fine even though my leg was on fire. "This whole Joey thing has me as nervous as a beached guppy."

"Yes, I know what you mean," Clara said. "I'm not myself either. I was the first person to identify poor Joey at the morgue. I wonder why he was so thin."

"So, Ben, what do you keep in that big old barn of yours?" I asked.

"Tractors, that sort of thing," he said over his shoulder as he rummaged through the fridge and pulled out a birthday cake with one candle and two pieces missing.

"Would you girls like a piece of my birthday cake? It's chocolate. My birthday was last Thursday and my friend thought I needed a cake."

"Sure, Benny, we would love to celebrate your birthday," Clara beamed. Ben cut and served the cake while we took a break from the Joey subject.

"I have one question, Ben, why do you call Aunt Clara, Cat?" They smiled at each other.

"Your Aunt Clara was always getting into things that were none of her business, tagging along with Joey and me, getting into our stuff. You know, curious, like when curiosity killed the cat. We always called her 'Cat.'" He winked at the blushing old woman who, at that moment, looked much younger than her seventy-five years.

CHAPTER 5

Aunt Clara wore a whimsical smile as we cruised through Boulder Creek, Ben Lomond and Felton. I wore a smile of my own, but it had nothing to do with Ben. I was hungry, and we were heading south toward Watsonville and Alicia's home cooking. The rain had stopped hours ago. We were full of birthday cake, tea and stories of Ben's grandfather living on the property before there were light bulbs, radios and TVs.

"At least Ben has a TV," I said, remembering the fourteen-inch black and white television set, dwarfed by a twelve-foot, two-man saw hanging on the wall above it.

"I wonder if he gets lonely way up there in the woods." Clara cocked her head, raised an eyebrow and then answered her own question. "I think he does get lonely. Even I get lonely sometimes, living five miles out of Oakhurst. I have lovely neighbors, but we all keep to ourselves for the most part. Ben is very attentive, don't you think?"

"Yes he is," I thought about the four-hour conversation between old schoolmates. I knew Joey had been Clara's best friend, but what was Ben? I had noticed it was getting dark outside the cabin, but when I checked my watch and told Clara the time, it was like trying to talk sense to Solow when he has Fluffy in his sight. I didn't blame her for being smitten. The guy had aged well. He was still tall and strong with plenty of silver hair pulled back in a ponytail. His blue eyes shone and his smile was disarming. I wondered if he dated. Clara must have read my mind.

"Do you think he has a girlfriend?"

"No, but he might have a lady friend," I said.

"He makes me feel like I'm twenty again. The women around

here are probably knocking down his door." Her voice was soft and distant.

"You mean women knocking on his door like us? That gun had me scared, but he sure changed his tune when he recognized you."

"Josephine, stop here. All that tea . . . and that terrible little outhouse."

"I understand, Auntie." I parked near the back of the Shell station she pointed out. She dashed into the restroom while I watched a young man wearing dark green overalls pump gas into a delivery truck with a picture of a large potted fern painted on the back. My cell phone rang.

"Hello . . . David, what are you doing?"

"I'm playing 'dolls' with Monica. Wish you were here, Josie."

"I bet you do. What's the matter? Don't you know how to play 'dolls'?"

"How was your first day painting at the library?"

"We didn't go because the walls aren't ready, so Aunt Clara and I took a little drive up to Boulder Creek."

"Kinda' cold and wet up there, isn't it?"

"Yes, but the rain stopped and we had a good time. Now we're on our way to Alicia's for dinner. She invited you too."

"Sorry to miss it. Monica's calling me, talk to you soon." I hung up as Clara climbed onto her seat. One mile later we entered Highway Seventeen, turned south onto Highway One and half an hour later pulled into Alicia's driveway. A full yellow moon hung over the housetop.

"For rush hour, we made good time," I said. Clara nodded. The porch light blinked on as we hustled up to the front door. I rang the doorbell and Alicia's ten-year-old son, Trigger, opened the door. We hugged and I introduced Aunt Clara to my favorite juvenile. He took Clara's hand and led her inside to an iron bench in the entry. Trigger's little sheltie, Tansey, joined us, twirling around my ankles as I tried to pull my boots off. Trigger offered to pull off Clara's boots.

"That's all right, dear. I just unsnap them like this, and they come right off," Clara grunted. Mine weren't so easy and the crusted mud crumbled onto the tile floor. We pushed our footwear under the bench and followed Trigger and Tansey to the kitchen in stocking feet.

"Mom, this is Aunt Clara," he said proudly. "Oh, and this is Alicia, my mom." Alicia wiped her hands on her apron and gave Clara a warm hug.

"Nice to finally meet you, Alicia. Alicia is one of my favorite names."

"So nice to meet you, Clara, and the man behind you is my husband, Ernie." Clara spun around and received another welcoming hug. Alicia turned back to the stove.

"We've been looking forward to meeting you, Clara," Ernie said as he pulled out a stool for her from the breakfast bar. I asked Alicia if she needed help.

"Jo, you have perfect timing. Everything is ready to serve." She pulled a large bowl of green salad out of the fridge and took it to the dining room table.

"I'll carry the tamales to the table for you. This sauce goes too?"

"Everything goes. Trigger already set the table and Ernie will take care of the wine." We made a few more trips back to the kitchen for rice, beans, tortillas and hot sauce. Ernie opened a bottle of wine and Alicia said "grace." I felt so happy to be sharing the Quintana family with Aunt Clara. Trigger substituted for the child I never had. Ernie, the biologist, was a real family man and Alicia was a true friend. Aunt Clara took to them like a kid to bubble gum.

"Is that water I'm looking at?" Clara asked as she settled into her chair at the table and stared out the large window.

"It's Drew Lake, Auntie. See the reflection of the moon? They have a big lawn that ends at the edge of the water and a dock for Trigger's pedal boat.

Tansey yipped. "Was that the door?" Alicia asked. I nodded and she headed for the foyer with the fluff ball at her ankles. She came back to the table a couple of minutes later with another guest for dinner, a young man about five-foot-eight, stocky, with dark eyes and a head full of black curly hair. My mouth dropped open

44 Joyce Oroz

when I recognized the kid in green overalls. Ernie stood up and shook the young man's hand.

"Ladies, like you to meet...."

"Hi, Gabe," Clara chirped. Alicia looked confused so Clara filled her in on our encounter with Gabe and the Evergreen Nursery truck. Gabe grimaced as Clara recalled every detail. "It takes a real man to apologize after a mistake like that," she smiled.

Ernie set a place for the newcomer next to Aunt Clara, and she made sure Gabe had enough food on his plate at all times. She rambled on about her gardens in Oakhurst. Gabe didn't offer much in the way of botanical knowledge, but Clara talked apple trees to zinnias, from salad to dessert. Gabe left as soon as he finished his sorbet, saying he had to get the truck back to the warehouse. I heard him fire up the engine and drive away.

"Allie, how do you know Gabe?"

"We've been buying plants and trees from the Greenhouse Nursery for years. Gabe is the owner's nephew and main deliveryman. He just delivered a bare-root pear tree I ordered, and our house is always the last stop of the day. Maybe he plans it that way because he likes my cooking."

"Doesn't everyone? Allie, I'm afraid we need to get on the road. We have a dog and two cats waiting for their dinner." We hugged and Trigger walked us to our boots.

The air outside was crisp, and the inky sky was flecked with stars. Halfway home, as we rolled along San Juan Road, the headlights glommed onto a boxy truck leaning to the right with two wheels stuck in a drainage ditch. I took my foot off the gas.

"Did you see that truck, Auntie?"

"What truck?"

"Back there, in the ditch. It had a fern painted on the back like Gabe's truck."

"Oh dear, do you think it might be his?"

"Yep. How many delivery trucks are out at this time of night?" I found a farmhouse and turned around in the driveway. Clara was on the edge of her seat biting her lip. We headed back down the road toward flashing yellow emergency lights.

"There it is, Josephine. Stop...OK, you can park here," Clara said. My truck was still moving when she unsnapped her seatbelt and opened the door. She was halfway across the two-lane road before I turned the ignition off. I hurried after her, hoping it really was Gabe and not some criminal hoax. Being female, unattached and afraid of the dark had made me mindful of my surroundings.

"Josephine, sure is nice of you to stop," Gabe said. "I need to call a tow truck, and I left my phone at the Quintana's." I remembered seeing a silver cell phone next to his wineglass.

"How old are you, Gabe?"

"Huh? I'm eighteen."

"Old enough to work," I smiled, and not old enough to drink, I thought, wondering if the dinner wine had contributed to his truck swerving into the ditch. I would mention it to Alicia.

"Here, use my phone."

"I was just about to walk to the warehouse when you came along." He dialed. After a brief conversation, he handed the phone back to me. "My uncle's calling for a tow."

"Your warehouse is way out here?" Clara asked.

"Just down the road. It's on San Marcos Canyon near the tracks." I instantly pictured the beige-colored metal warehouse just fifty yards from the spot where Joey spent the last minutes of his life.

"So, Gabe, have the police been asking questions at the nursery about the train accident?"

"I think so, that is, I'm usually out delivering stuff, but my uncle said something about it."

"Guess we're done here," I said. Clara reluctantly followed me back to the truck. "What's the matter Aunt Clara?"

"He's just a boy . . . I'm wondering how long it will take for him to be rescued."

"Rescued? Isn't that a little strong for needing a tow?"

"You know what I mean. I wonder if his mother is worried," she muttered.

"Auntie, he's eighteen. He has a job. Yes, he's a lousy driver, but he'll learn."

"Two accidents in one day," Clara fussed. "Maybe he's working too hard." I rolled my eyes.

"Maybe he had too much wine at dinner."

"I saw him drink two glasses. Do you think that's too much?"

"Yes," I said, "especially for anyone driving. I can only handle one, and I noticed you had one glass. Did he explain how he ended up in the ditch?"

"No, I didn't ask because I didn't want to embarrass him."

"Auntie, you need a man in your life." Clara laughed.

"I thought so too, dear. Why do you think I came looking for Joey six years ago? There's San Marcos Canyon Road. Maybe we should talk to Gabe's uncle." Clara leaned into the windshield. I slowed the truck, and we careened around the corner and rolled up to the warehouse. Moonlight glanced off the roof of a lone car parked between the building and the tracks. I pulled in beside the old Firebird. In front of us was a large metal door, the first in a row of three. I grabbed my flashlight from the glove box and caught up to Clara.

"What are you looking for, Auntie?"

"Just looking to see if this place is open. How's Gabe going to get in if it's all locked up?"

"This old Firebird is probably his, and I bet it's not even locked." I tried the door handle, setting off a very obnoxious alarm. We walked away from the noisy car, looking for a way into the building. I pointed the light at the first large metal door, but there was no door knob to try. I finally gave up when I figured out that all three roll-up doors opened electronically.

I walked to the back of the building to snoop a bit, since we were in the neighborhood. I found a dumpster, a rusty barrel and something sparkling in the moonlight near my right foot. I picked up a button and dropped it in my pocket. Clara caught up to me.

"Shine that light over here, Josephine. I can't see a thing." She tripped along the side of the building.

"Stand next to me, Auntie. I'm going to look in here."

"What on earth for? It's a stupid barrel."

I aimed the light into the fifty-gallon drum, all the way down to the layer of ashes at the bottom. An icy breeze fluffed my hair and froze my ears. I straightened up and pointed the light at rows of potted trees standing at attention, resembling a division of soldiers protecting headquarters. I suggested we go home and Clara instantly said she was ready.

Back in the truck, I cranked up the heat and we roared up the road into the Aromas hills. We stopped at David's house to feed Fluffy and made it home just before nine. I opened the front door. Solow and Felix bolted past us, took care of business and were back begging for food in no time. I was blessed with a dog that never did his business in the house, but what was that acrid smell coming from the far side of the living room. It was stronger near the stairs. Clara sniffed the air.

"Felix, you naughty boy," she said over her shoulder as she sniffed the rug under the stairs. Felix slunk around the corner and down the hall.

"Clara, don't worry. I'll get some soapy water and vinegar. Felix couldn't help it if we were gone all day and half the night." I hoped soap and vinegar would be enough. After lots of scrubbing, vinegar became the dominant smell. I turned my attention to the answering machine while Clara fed Solow and lectured Felix. I listened to messages from Alicia, Mom and David, but first I answered a call from Wayne Bracken.

"Hi, Wayne, this is Josephine. How's Darla feeling?"

"Is this Bob's daughter?"

"Sure is."

"Darla is having a hard time with this train thing. I just don't think she's up to having any more visitors. I'm not trying to be rude, but I'd appreciate it if you would leave her alone."

"Don't worry, Wayne, we won't come over unless you say it's OK. Take care." I hung up, and Clara asked for the phone.

"I'm going to thank Benny for the tea and cake," she said.

"Auntie, it's nine-thirty. Kinda' late, isn't it?"

"Actually, I want to know if he stays home at night or goes out on dates." She climbed the stairs to the loft and took a couple of deep breaths at the top.

"You're acting like a teenager...." She leaned against the rail and looked down.

"I know! Isn't it fun? I haven't felt like this since...."

"You spent four hours in the man's house. That must have

been some crush you had in high school," I said. Her cheeks flushed and her eyes danced. She had memories all right. I pulled my cell phone out of my purse and dialed David.

"Josie, hi. How was dinner?"

"Fabulous as usual. Too bad you missed it." I heard Clara laughing upstairs, silence and more giggles. "David, you should hear my aunt cracking up on the phone like a silly teenager. She's talking to Ben DeWald, an old crush from her school days."

"That name sounds familiar."

"Really?"

"Yeah, but I don't know why," David yawned.

"You're tired. I'll let you go. Goodnight, David."

"Goodnight, Josie." I hung up, turned on the ten o'clock news and stretched out on the couch. At 10:30, I looked at the clock and heard more giggles from upstairs. I hoped and prayed Ben had played no part in Joey's disappearance, but the idea had rolled around in my head more than once. After the Ten O'clock News, Solow and I trundled off to bed.

It was normal for me to have vivid Technicolor dreams just about every night, but that night they were over the top weird. I saw myself slogging barefoot through knee-deep pink mud wearing a yellow pantsuit and a clear plastic bonnet. After much effort, I made it all the way to a giant green shed with a knitted sock mounted on the roof. The sock was filled with air and pointed south. I found a doorknob on the shed door and started to pull. The round glass knob fell off the door into my hand, leaving the impression of a buzzard stamped on my palm.

CHAPTER 6

Aunt Clara subtly roused me out of my bed by vacuuming the hall at 7:30 in the morning. She glanced into my room, caught me with one eye open, and shut the machine off.

"Good morning, Josephine. Did you sleep well?" she asked, not giving me time to utter a word. "I thought I'd take you to breakfast." My stomach lurched. "We could visit your mom, go to Sal's place, whatever you would like to do. By the way, Benny is meeting us for lunch at the wharf." She pushed a button and vacuumed her way down the hall before I had time to open my mouth.

Clara was true to her word. She bought me an Egg McMuffin and a cup of coffee. By nine we had already met up with Mom, exchanged my truck for her Subaru, and headed over to Sal's house on Morrissey. Mom looked great in her simple sage-green pantsuit, fur-lined mini-boots and matching gloves. Clara and I made louder statements in our clothing choices with lots of color.

"Right there, Leola. 2240, see it printed on the curb? OK, pull in behind the Mercedes," Clara popped open her safety belt. Mom and I looked at each other and then at Clara, wondering where all that energy was coming from.

"What's the big hurry?" Mom asked. "Do you think Sal knows what happened to Joey?" Clara shrugged, climbed out of the Subaru and rang the doorbell before Mom and I had time to climb the stairs leading to a spacious front porch. The door opened. We watched as a young woman's smile melted away.

"Hello, dear, my name is Clara Ramsey…I'm an old friend of Joseph Gianelli, and this is…" she turned her head and waited for us to move closer to the door, "…and this is my sister, Leola Carl, and my niece, Josephine Stuart." The young woman smelled like herbal shampoo. She had wet stringy hair, fair skin and a little pointy nose. She stood on the cold tile entry, shivering in her bare feet and knee-length green t-shirt with a yellow UCSC slug mascot on the front.

"I'm Angela. What do you want? I'm not really supposed to let people in...."

"We understand, dear," Mom said, "but we have to talk to your father. Your father's name is Sal, right?" The young woman nodded. "Good. Is he here?"

"I'm not really supposed to let anyone...." Angela backed up a few steps and started to close the door. A tall, rather bulky gentleman with fair skin and receding blond hair walked up behind her. He squinted his blue eyes against a brief show of pale sunlight.

"Ladies, are you looking for someone?" He wore a white polo shirt with a small company logo embroidered on the front and grey Dockers. The man didn't look anything like Jamie. They didn't seem to have much in common in the way of money, looks or lifestyle. Sal's two-story house, with its picture windows, generous wood moldings, mahogany floors and oriental rugs, was not even on the same planet as Jamie's tiny abode. Clara stepped forward and cleared her throat.

"Are you a friend of Sal's?" she asked.

The man laughed. "I am Sal."

Clara looked confused. "Really—well, I guess you take after your mother. Anyway, we wanted to tell you we're sorry for your loss." She introduced us, and we all moved into the living room where a giant grandfather clock tick-tocked in the corner next to a healthy-looking fern potted in an ornately decorated Chinese fish bowl. Subtle smells hinted at the house's age and the quality woods that went into its construction. The front room was like a page out of American history, except for the recent issues of Time, Sunset and Hobby Planes magazines spread out on the antique coffee table.

"Please sit down, ladies, and tell me what's on your mind." We sank into overstuffed chairs circling the dark walnut coffee table. Clara picked up the hobby magazine and placed it in her lap while she told Sal about her friendship with his father. She fumbled through her purse, pulled out her glasses and carefully positioned them on her nose.

"Looks like you have something in common with your father, Sal...airplanes."

"My son, Patrick is the model airplane enthusiast, not me. I fly when I have to, on business, but it's not my favorite thing to do." From the corner of my eye I saw Angela watching us from the top of the elegant "Gone with the Wind" staircase.

"Sal, your home is lovely," I said. "What did you say you do for a living?" He paused, and reset his pasted-on smile.

"I didn't say. I'm the business manager for a large firm in San Jose. I'm taking some time off right now, but normally I drive thirty-five miles each way, five days a week." Sal tilted his head, shoulders up and palms facing the ceiling in resignation, possibly looking for a little sympathy. He didn't get any from me. He was one of thousands of Santa Cruz commuters who drove over the mountain daily to San Jose, where the jobs were. Sal looked about forty-five. He could handle it. I continued to ask questions.

"Sal, I know this is difficult for you, but my aunt is trying to find closure. She was very close to Joey. Can you tell us what you know about your father's plane crash?"

"I don't know any more about it than what was printed in the Sentinel six years ago. All I know is my dad was good to my brother and me...but I never understood why he left Mom with a mortgage and a lotta' bills. I eventually took over the mortgage. Mom married Wayne and moved into his place. This is the house I grew up in and now it's mine. I just wish Dad was here," his voice cracked. "He had everything to live for...his family, a pension and time to fly his little Piper Cub."

"Do you think Ben DeWald had anything to do with his disappearance?" I asked. Clara squinted her eyes at me and Sal shook his head. "You say there was a mortgage on this house."

"Yeah, Mom and Dad refinanced the house about ten years ago. They invested the money in a local business."

"We met your son, Patrick," I said. "Nice kid. I guess he's at school today?"

"No. He starts at Arizona State in a couple of months. Right now he's surfing."

"Where does he like to surf?" I knew that Santa Cruz surfers had their favorite beaches.

"Steamer Lane," he said, closed his eyes longer than a blink and then told us he needed to make some calls. Mom stood up and hooked her purse on her shoulder.

"Sal, it's lovely to meet you. We must be running along, right, girls?" Clara and I stood up and everyone traipsed across the imported rugs to the front door. Thunder rumbled, wind tugged at my coat and I felt a sprinkle on my face as we gingerly made our way down the steps and along the wet concrete to the curb. I crawled into the back seat of the Subaru and looked up at the front door just as Sal disappeared inside. He hadn't once mentioned his wife, if he had one.

"We have an hour and a half before we meet Ben at the wharf, and Patrick is surfing in that area. Maybe we should check out his style," I said. Mom and Clara were agreeable. Fifteen minutes later, we were parked above the high cliffs of Steamer Lane. We watched six rows of waves enter the bay, grow larger, curl and break onto the sandy beach. Water and foam quickly receded back into the ocean as new waves matured and crashed in turn on the shore. The waves were pretty average in size, nothing spectacular, but every wave had at least three black-suited surfers riding their boards, standing or crouching, back to shore. At the end of the ride, they turned around and paddled out to sea, hoping for an even better ride.

"Look, pelicans." Mom pointed toward the prehistoric-looking birds gliding over the mile-long wharf jutting out from Cowell Beach where most surfers ended their ride.

"Do you see Patrick?" Clara asked, squinting at the water.

"It's starting to rain again," Mom said, "and I can't see the surfers very well. They all look like little black sea lions from here." My eyes were younger and I did see surfers instead of sea lions, but all thirty of them looked like Patrick, a bunch of sun-bleached blond heads atop black wetsuits. The clouds suddenly opened up and dumped rain all over Clara's plastic bonnet, Mom's umbrella and my bare head. I jumped into the car and slammed the door. Two more slams and we were on our way to the wharf.

"We have a few more minutes before lunch," Clara said. "Let's go to the fish market."

"Yes dear. I'll park over...."

"Right there, Leola, on your left. Careful you don't scrape that pickup. It looks like Benny's. He must be planning a trip to the dump with all that junk in the back." Clara sounded out of breath. I was afraid she would hyperventilate. "Oh, there he is, looking over the fish. I wish I liked fish so I could talk about fish with him." Mom looked at me and rolled her eyes.

"I know, Mom, she can't help herself. Look, she's already over there and she'll probably faint from the smell of fish." We watched Ben give her a hug and then he pointed out a few choice items featured in the open-air market. As Mom and I scurried across the street, a misty rain cooled our faces. We stood behind Clara and Ben and studied the piles of fish and squid displayed in stainless steel bins full of chipped ice. Ben looked great in white slacks, a white shirt and a light blue pullover sweater. He looked over his shoulder.

"Josephine, nice to see you again."

"Ben, this is my mom, Leola." A slow smile blossomed on Ben's clean-shaven face.

"Clara's older sister. I remember the last day of school when you and some other cheerleaders were caught...."

"That was a long time ago," Mom snapped, looking at me like I was still a child and shouldn't hear about her teenage mischief. "Girls will be girls," she laughed. "Your teeth straightened up real nice, Ben. Is that your real hair?"

"Yep. Is that your real hair color?" he asked. Mom's face reddened and puckered into a squinty scowl as Ben continued. "Your teeth turned out fine too, if they're real."

"Benjamin DeWald, these are my real teeth and you could use a haircut and some manners."

I felt my cheeks burn. I hadn't seen my mother that upset in forty-four years, not since I set fire to Dad's tool shed when I was six years old. Ben countered with a remark about how many squirrels it took to make Mom's fur boots, and she came back with how big his feet had grown. Ben finally cracked a smile and then Mom's face softened. The next thing I knew they were in a real friendly hug, laughing at me, as I stood with my mouth open.

"Anyone hungry?" he asked. Clara raised her hand and the good mood continued all the way through the clam chowder, crab salad and dessert. The visuals were as good as the food, since the restaurant windows faced Steamer Lane and West Cliff Drive.

"Ben, can you pick out Patrick Gianelli from the other surfers out there," I asked. He took a long look and shook his head.

"Sorry, they look like a bunch of sea lions to me."

"Patrick looks like his father and Sal doesn't even resemble Joey," Clara said. "Now, Jamie has the nose, you know, the Gianelli look. What happened to his brother?" she asked.

"There were rumors," Ben mumbled. "So what are you ladies doing after lunch?"

"Playing hearts at my house," Mom said. "You're welcome to join us."

"I have lawn bowling at two. Maybe some other time," he said and paid the check. We walked outside, crossed the parking lot and watched pelicans and seagulls fight over bits of fish guts tossed into the water by fisherman as they cleaned their catch. I inched over to Mom and ducked under her umbrella. Clara and Ben stood a few yards away watching a fisherman reeling in his line. The seagulls squawked and fought with each other in midair over who would get the next offering.

"Mom, let's sit in the car. I'm cold." We climbed into the Subaru and a couple of minutes later Clara joined us.

"Benny turned out to be a real gentleman," Clara said as she clicked her seat belt.

"Yes," Mom said, "but he really had me going there for a minute. You know, Ben and I were not the best of friends in high school." She gave the car some gas, caught up to Ben and followed his truck to the tollbooth at the other end of the wharf. Mom was handing over the parking money when Ben stepped on the gas. He bump-bumped over a speed bump, his tailgate flopped open and a plastic bucket rolled over the edge, falling on the street in front of us. Ben turned left into Beach Street traffic, never looking back.

"I'll be right back," I said, opened my door, scooped up Ben's bucket and jumped back in the car. "OK, let's go. Maybe we can catch him at the bowling green." Mom turned off the wipers and cruised through town at old-lady speed while I pulled stuff out of the bucket.

"Should you be going through his personal things?" Mom asked.

"Ben's obviously throwing everything away, and this is my chance to look it over while he's not around. I'm looking for something connected with the Gianelli case. You know, something that will clear Ben of any involvement." I watched Clara do a hard squint with one eye. "These aren't Ben's clothes. They're too skinny." I checked the measurement tag on a pair of navy blue slacks, size 30-36. I had Ben pegged for size 36-36. "And this old Air Force cap...and this denim shirt." The last item was a dirty old windsock.

"Are you seriously thinking Ben had something to do with Joey's disappearance?" Clara demanded, cranking her head around to glare one more time. I shrugged and she turned back around, mumbling at the windshield. "Oh, dear, it looks like he lost something else. Pull over Leola, right there by that silver pickup truck...not so close, you want to hit him?" I saw Mom's face in the rearview mirror and it wasn't happy.

"I'll get it," I said as I leaped out of the car, grabbed a bent fishing pole and an old rusty coffee can and tossed them in the car. The pole took three tries. Finally, I angled it into the back seat with one end dangling between the two front bucket seats.

"Are you sure those are Ben's?" Mom asked, letting the car idle.

"I'm sure," I said. "I saw this junk in the back of his truck right after the bucket rolled out over the tailgate." I yanked the plastic top off the coffee can and pulled out a greasy rag, several beat up photos and a few fishing lures. "Oh my God, look at this." I held up a picture of Ben and another man holding strings of fish they had obviously just caught. "I wonder who took the picture." But I didn't wonder long because in the next picture the unidentified man had his arm around a woman. In the third picture, the senior couple stood in front of Ben's cabin, holding hands.

"Let me see that," Clara said and plucked the picture from my fingers. "It's Ben and Joey in this one. Look, Leola. Joey was a nice-looking man, a bit thin, but not bad for an old guy." Mom leaned over for a look and nodded.

"Yes, not bad. Who's the lady in this one?" she asked. Clara put on her glasses.

"I don't know…unless-s-s-s…it's Benny's little sister. What was her name?"

"Beverly, wasn't it?" Mom said as she snatched the last picture from my hand. A horn sounded. We turned our heads toward the red-faced driver of a beefed-up Ford 350 pickup who was pointing a finger at us. Clara rolled down her window.

"Keep your pants on," Clara shouted.

"Aunt Clara, you can't do that. He could run over us like a speed bump."

"Well, I have a temper too," she said as Mom hit the gas and we moved into traffic. Clara studied the photos all the way to the bowling green, which was located near the San Lorenzo River, in the heart of Santa Cruz. Mom parked at the curb. Clara handed me the pictures, and I stuffed two of them into the can. The third went in my pocket. A glimmer of guilt crossed my mind; but after all, it was all junk that Ben was obviously throwing away.

As we walked by Ben's pickup, I noticed the tailgate was up. I took a quick look at the junk at the top of the heap, like the three-legged chair, a bulging black garbage bag, some rusty wire fencing and a box of old canning jars.

"Are you coming, Josephine?" Mom asked. I hurried down the walk and caught up to them just as they approached the benches near the lush green, 120-foot-square, perfectly level, bowling lawn. Ben sat on a bench along the sidelines changing his shoes while other senior bowlers mingled and chatted before the game started. He saw us and waved.

"Did you girls come to watch the game?"

"Actually, we're returning some items that rolled out of your truck," I said.

"Thanks. When I parked the truck, I noticed the gate was down. Everything's going to the dump, but thanks anyway." He smiled and introduced us to a couple of his friends who wore white hats, white sweaters and white slacks—even white shoes.

"Cross your fingers it doesn't rain." He picked up a small black bowling ball and waited his turn. The little gentleman ahead of Ben rolled a smaller white ball to the far side of the "rink." Another man rolled his black ball just short of the white one and then Ben took his turn, side-swiping the second man's ball. Ben's black ball stopped just two inches shy of the white one. I heard a quiet cheer. Was that the equivalent of a home run? It was all Greek to me.

"It's cold under these trees," Clara said. "Maybe we should go start our own game."

"Hearts it is," Mom said as we took our leave. Back at the Subaru, I gathered up the bucket, coffee can and fishing rod and delivered them to Ben's truck bed. I felt eyes watching me from a grassy knoll ten yards away. A homeless man wearing a jacket over his primary jacket sat on his heels beside a shopping cart full of bulging garbage bags. As soon as I returned to the car, he shuffled over to the back of the truck and peeked in. Mom drove down the block, and I looked back at the man rummaging through Ben's stuff. I didn't worry about it because Ben said it was all destined to go to the dump. In fact, I hoped the man found something he could use.

I couldn't help noticing the contrast between the clusters of unkempt homeless people relaxing on the grass between rains and the men wearing white at the bowling green half a block away. I wondered what my retirement years would be like and decided I didn't fit into either category. Halfway to Mom's house, Clara had an idea.

"I read in the paper about a big sale at Macy's."

"Am I imagining things or did you just suggest we go shopping?" Mom said.

"I just thought we might look around…you know, for the fun

of it."

"Clara, you sound like you really want to go." I was shocked. "I think I want to buy something pretty to wear...." she tried to stifle a giggle. Mom and I teased her ruthlessly all the way to the mall. Clara had more help finding things than she really needed, but Mom and I had fun and Clara bought two lovely outfits and a new pair of rubber boots. I hoped Ben was an honest guy and worth the effort.

CHAPTER 7

Clara and I had agreed to stay home Wednesday, get some housework done and save gas by not going anywhere; but even the best of plans can be undone when you're single and a certain gentleman from Boulder Creek calls. Clara grabbed the phone in the kitchen.

"Ben? Benny DeWald?" she asked. I rolled my eyes. "Actually I don't know that many Bens. I just wanted to be careful, you know, because of the things I read in the paper and the way men prey on mature women these days." I decided to take Solow for a walk before I had to listen to another insane word from my favorite aunt's mouth.

"Solow, let's go." He jumped up from his nap under the table, followed me through the house and out the front door. I attached a leash to his collar so we could practice our walking skills and manners. Solow pranced, sniffed and pranced until he caught sight of a squirrel, and took off like a basset on a mission. I ran to keep up, but he pulled hard on the leash, jerking it out of my hand. A few minutes later, he was back, dragging his leash. I laughed at him with steamy breath.

"Shall we go home?" My icy fingers gripped the leash as we turned and headed back. Ominous clouds were reflected in the puddles left over from the last rain. We hurried down the road in free-form, short-legged basset style. Even as we finished our run, a bank of dark clouds had moved across the sky from the west, obliterating the sun.

It had been six days since we heard the bad news about Joey, and still no one seemed to know what had happened to him. Why was he on the railroad tracks at night without a jacket, and how did he and his airplane manage to disappear for six years after a simple flight over Monterey Bay? Someone had to know the answers, and we needed to find that someone. I opened the front door and heard Clara laughing in the kitchen.

"I don't mind helping, really I don't," she said. "I have nothing to do around here and Josephine loves to drive. See you soon, Ben," she looked up.

"What's new with Ben?"

"He's redecorating his cabin and he needs a woman's opinion on colors to paint the walls. Men don't see color the way we do. The only colors they indulge in are blue, black, brown and gray."

"Unless it's a pink bikini they're looking at," I said.

"I think Ben is old enough not to be swayed by bikinis."

"Yeah and Popeye wears a tutu," I said, shaking my head. "So what's the plan?"

"If you don't mind a little ride up to Santa Cruz...we could meet Ben at the paint store, collect some color chips and see how they look on his walls. But if you're too tired or busy, I'll understand." She knew I wasn't tired or busy and that left me without an excuse. The gas stations were making a fortune off me, and I wasn't earning a dime.

"I'll take you to the paint store and then Boulder Creek if you'll do one thing for me."

"Of course, dear, anything," she said as I pulled various hardware items out of the kitchen junk drawer and deposited them in my purse which was stretched to the limit and heavy as Solow's backside.

"I want you to keep Ben busy at the cabin while I go for a little walk and check out the barn."

"I'll do that for you, but I think you're wrong about Benny. He's a good man and he wouldn't do anything wrong."

"I'm sure he is a good man, but he might have wanted to help Joey in some way," I said. "The pictures of Ben, Joey and Beverly were taken five years ago according to the date stamped on the back." Clara's jaw sagged. I pulled the photo of Joey and Beverly out of my jacket pocket and showed Clara the date printed on the back. "It's possible the pictures were taken a year or two before they were actually printed, but we don't know that. We just don't know."

"That's right, Josephine, we don't know and I'm beginning to think we're better off not knowing."

"You don't really mean that, Auntie. You want to know the truth as much as I do."

"I suppose you're right. We owe it to Joey to find the person responsible," she said in a softer voice. She picked up Felix and put him outside. I said goodbye to Solow and apologized for not taking him with me as in "pre-Clara" times when we went everywhere together. I grabbed a light jacket and my purse full of lead, ducked outside and climbed into the pickup. Clara hiked her senior body into the passenger seat.

"I'll buy lunch, Josephine," Clara offered. "Ben is expecting to meet us at the paint store at one o'clock." She had the whole day timed perfectly, and all I had to do was stay on schedule. But I had to admit to myself I wanted to search Ben's barn almost as badly as Clara wanted to spend time with the old stud muffin.

The miles flew by. It was a typical Wednesday and most people were at work or school instead of cluttering the highways. Only the geezer generation had time to drive around and foul up traffic, which they did according to a KPIG radio news report. It seems another old fool had hit the gas instead of the brake and smashed through the display window of a Santa Cruz flower shop on Ocean Street. A second report involved a seasoned citizen who ran over a water hydrant and flooded Pacific Avenue. Clara shook her head slowly.

"How do these old people expect to keep their driver's licenses?" she asked, never mind the fact she didn't have a license of her own. "I guess some people age faster than others, don't you think that's true, Josephine?"

I hardly heard Clara's remark, but I nodded. She pointed out the off-ramp to Soquel Avenue and proceeded to tell me we were getting close to the Double Doggie Drive-in and I should slow down. We stopped at the drive-up window, collected our hot dogs and fries plus a few mustard stains and continued down the avenue.

As I drove, I thought about ways to pick a lock using scenes from old mysteries on TV and the hardware in my purse. My private thoughts didn't last long because Clara kept reminding me we were getting close to the paint store and I should signal for the turn. She pointed to Ben's pickup and suggested I park next to it. What a refreshing idea. I shut my mouth and did what I was told.

"You don't have to park there if you don't want…."

"I'm fine with this parking spot, Auntie. Here comes Ben." He looked like a real mountain man in his sheepskin jacket, worn Levis and work boots. He leaned over to Clara's open window.

"Ladies," he smiled. I imagined Clara as a cube of butter pooling on the seat.

"Ben, is this where you usually shop for paint?" she asked.

"Nope, I usually don't buy paint. Not since my wife died and I moved into the cabin. How do you women do it…always talking men into home improvements and such?" He opened the passenger door for Clara and gave her a hand getting out of the seat. She took his hand as if he was Sir Benjamin and she was Lady Clarissa. It was not one of those times when she leaped out of my truck before I had time to turn off the engine.

As we rounded Ben's empty truck, I noticed he had made it to the dump. The three of us trouped across the parking lot and into the paint store.

"Over here, the color chips are over here," Clara motioned for us to join her at the "hundred thousand colors" carousel. Beads of perspiration formed on Ben's forehead. He seemed to be somewhere between scared and stupefied.

"Don't worry, Ben, its only paint," I said. He forced a smile while Clara spun the color carousel, searching for the perfect shade of the perfect color. "Don't forget, anything you pick will look darker when you paint it on an inside wall."

"I'm going to paint the outhouse," he said.

"Outhouse? Inside walls or outside walls?"

"Inside."

"What else are you painting?"

"That's all I'm committing to for now." He looked over Clara's shoulder at the dozen or more color chips she held in her hand as if she were in a card game, and pointed to a blue one.

"What did I tell you?" she looked at me. "Blue, black, brown, gray...dreary colors," Clara pulled the blue chip out of the fold. "The color should be cheerful but understated, friendly but chic."

"Auntie, he's not painting the Taj Mahal. He's painting the outhouse."

"Why don't you girls sort it out, and I'll meet you over there by the brushes and rollers." Twenty minutes later, we were down to seven chips, seven possibilities.

We walked outside into a blustery wind under fast moving clouds. Ben studied the sky. "I'll get a fire started as soon as I get home. See you there." He climbed into his manly truck outfitted with mud tires and a winch on the front bumper.

"We'll be right behind you," Clara purred. I fired up my truck and followed Ben into traffic.

About ten miles later I noticed another menacing bank of dark clouds hanging low over the San Lorenzo Valley just a few miles north of our position and getting closer. The further we went into the valley, the darker everything got. We were halfway through Ben Lomond when the sky opened up and dumped copious amounts of water on my pickup, making it difficult to see even a few feet ahead. I slowed the truck to a crawl and Clara searched the airwaves for a weather report.

"Auntie, why do you need a weather report? It's raining."

"We don't know how long it will rain or how hard. What if it turns to ice or snow?"

"It's been known to happen...about every five or ten years," I said sagely, remembering a dusting of snow the year before. "The valley had a little snow last year so chances are...."

"Josephine, isn't it weird how the rain is coming down slowly. It's half rain and half snow."

"You're right. It's collecting on the side of the road." It also collected on my windshield where the wipers didn't reach. Suddenly my thoughts went to mittens, knitted caps and long underwear, and I wished I had worn some of those items.

"I'm glad I brought my warmest jacket. Yours looks a little thin, dear." I thought so too, but it was too late to go home and get my warmest jacket that I almost never wore because it didn't snow in Aromas. My clothes were not suitable for icy weather and my plan to take a walk down to the barn had probably just been nixed, which meant my whole day would be centered around picking a color to paint the inside of a stupid outhouse.

"I don't see Ben's truck," Clara said, leaning against the dash, her nose to the windshield. I slowed my truck a little more, but the back tires swished side to side as I maneuvered through an extra tight turn on the slush-covered pavement. The San Lorenzo River had long ago carved a path through the valley and the narrow two-lane highway paralleled the raging waters.

"Maybe Ben made it through before the snow started," I said, hoping he hadn't slipped off the road into the icy water a hundred feet below. We passed through Boulder Creek and turned left onto Big Basin Highway. It was only two-thirty but dark enough to be five. The headlights were on and the wipers kept a fast beat.

"Josephine, just a couple more miles, but how are we going to know where to turn? Everything is covered in white and it's so dark out. Oh, there's the road, right there on your left. Turn…turn. OK, good, this is the one, I think." I wasn't sure either until we came to an open gate strapped with a familiar "No Trespassing" sign. I rounded the chain-link fence and pushed on the accelerator. The truck fishtailed up the slippery meadow. I followed Ben's tire tracks all the way to the barn, carefully avoiding the "rutty road turned rushing river." From there, we motored up the steep, curvy driveway toward Ben's cabin. As we approached the last turn, we heard a loud ripping noise followed by a crashing thud, which bounced my truck like a pingpong ball. Automatically my foot stomped on the brake and froze in that position.

"What was that?" Clara's eyes bugged as she turned her head and looked behind us. She couldn't speak. I looked in the rearview mirror and almost fainted. We had just escaped being flattened by a giant redwood tree which had done a face plant across the driveway, roots and all. Two seconds slower and we would have become part of the cycle of life…the dead part. We sat in stunned silence. I felt dizzy and imagined I heard voices.

"Are you all right?" Ben asked, knocking on my window with

his bare knuckles and gulping air. I rolled the window down and sucked in some arctic oxygen.

"I don't know. Clara looks like she's in a state of shock and my heart's beating double-time." He hurried over to her side and opened the door.

"Cat, are you OK?" Clara blinked and turned her head.

"Benny, where did you come from?"

"I ran down here as soon as I heard the thud. I was in the cabin when I heard something that sounded like thunder and then the house shook." His face was as white as the thin layer of snow on the ground. "I never figured that tree would go. It's only a couple of hundred years old. It should have lasted another fifteen hundred years." He held Clara's hand and babbled on about how redwoods live for thousands of years and this one was just a two-hundred-year-old baby. Once our teeth stopped chattering and our heartbeats slowed from a polka to a waltz, we padded down the road about thirty feet and stood next to the suicidal tree.

"Looks like you could build a dozen cabins out of this thing," I said, "and by the way, where is the other road down from this mountain?"

"You're lookin' at it, one way in, same way out. Sorry." The sorry word must have been for me because Clara's cheeks were pink and her lips curved up as she leaned against Ben.

I shivered and told Clara to get back to the truck before we froze to death. She and Ben obediently trudged back to my truck, slipping, sliding and laughing. I didn't think anything was funny. I wanted to go home, sit by the fire and snuggle up with David. Just the thought of David shot some much needed warmth through my body, and just in time because I was feeling like my next job might be posing as an ice sculpture at a senior's convention.

"I'll see you at the cabin," Ben said, giving my truck a pat on the hood. He leaned forward and trudged up the slippery drive. As soon as Clara settled herself in the passenger seat, I put the pickup in drive and quickly passed up our host. He was breathing hard when he finally made it to the top of the mountain. We dashed into the cabin without ceremony. Ben started a fire in the stove and another in the fireplace.

"No furnace, no forced air heat?" I asked. Ben smiled, shook his head and ducked outside for more wood. I would have helped him, but my feet were frozen to the floor...almost. Clara wrapped herself in a crocheted lap blanket she found on the old sofa.

"Looks like we're here for the night, don't you think?" Clara said.

"Yeah, and I need to call David. If he's not coming home today, I'll have to call someone else to feed Solow and the cats."

"Oh my, you're right. Do you have your phone?" she asked.

"It's right here in my purse...somewhere. I pulled out two screwdrivers, a small hammer and a pair of pliers before I found the phone. I dialed David.

"David, my phone sounds funny. Can you hear me?"

"I hear you stuttering and a lot of static. I'm on my way home just passed through San Jose. What's up?"

"It's what's down, I'm afraid. It was really awful, David." I took a breath, but my upper and lower teeth would not stop tapping each other like a typewriter with a deadline. "We're at Ben's house in Boulder Creek and we can't leave because...."

"Are you there? Josie, Jo...."

"Great, that was the end of my battery charge." I dropped the useless phone into my purse.

"I think he heard enough. He'll know to feed the animals," Clara said.

"Actually, I'm more worried about us than the animals." The back door slammed and Ben tramped through the house, dropping off small logs beside the kitchen stove and larger ones at the big river-rock fireplace in the living room. He looked at my pile of tools and scratched his head. Next to my tool collection sat an old black telephone. I picked up the receiver. Nothing

"Lines are down again," he said. "The phone was dead this morning. I'm sure there are lots of fallen trees." He turned and headed back to the woodpile. I flipped a few light switches but nothing worked. In the dim light from a window, I fumbled around the living room until I found a stash of matches, three candles and a hurricane lantern.

"Are you warming up, Auntie?" I asked as I lit two candles and the lamp.

"I'm fine, dear."

Just before Ben dropped more wood beside the fireplace, I gathered my lock-picking tools and dropped them into my purse.

"Benny, don't you have any pets?" Clara asked. He brushed his gloved hands together to get the wood chips off and smiled.

"I had a dog once. Does that count?"

"What kind of dog?"

"Guess you could call him a double mutt. About twenty years ago, Joey's mutt and Ed's mutt got together and had little mutts and I got the runt. He was good company, old Runt."

"You named him, Runt?" she said, frowning.

"I wasn't going to sugarcoat it. He was what he was, a good old dog. Now I have squirrels, raccoons, opossums and woodpeckers to keep me company." He tipped his big felt cowboy hat and headed out to the woodpile. We waited till he was out the door and then chuckled and ruminated over good old Runt. Clara looked more relaxed and I felt better too.

"Is it just me or is it getting darker in here?" I said. Clara agreed it was hard to see in the dim light coming from the living room windows. There were no drapes or blinds to open, just panes of very old blurry glass between us and the snowy scene outside. Even the candles weren't much help. Very little daylight penetrated through the towering redwoods, which ringed three sides of the house. The kitchen window faced the driveway and an open view to the west, featuring one mountain range after another. On a clear day with perfect eyesight and good binoculars, I wondered if one might be able to see the Pacific Ocean.

I used the poker to encourage more flame and warmed myself in the process. Clara fell asleep sitting on the sofa. I went to the kitchen, worked with the stove fire for a while and put the teakettle on. Ben and I had tea and some of his old chocolate birthday cake. He had me laughing so hard I got a stitch in my side listening to stories about Clara, Joey and Ben growing up in the old Santa Cruz neighborhood. Mom wasn't mentioned until I brought up the subject.

"So Ben, what is it between you and my mom?"

"Nothing. I just thought she had an uppity attitude...you know...could do no wrong. When we were about eight or nine, Joey snitched a cigar from his grandpa's stash. We hid in the alley behind the backyard fence and took turns puffing, turning green and coughing our brains out. Leola watched us through a knothole and told Joey's mom, who came down hard on him. Poor guy couldn't sit down for a couple of days."

"Sounds like you were typical kids."

"Yeah, I guess we were. Had a lot of fun we weren't supposed to have," he laughed. "Leola turned out OK. In fact, she's a lot more fun now."

"I'm glad you two can finally get along." I sipped a second cup of tea. "Anything I can do to help with dinner?"

"Hope you gals like beans."

"Sure. No problem." I watched Ben pace the floor. "Anything I can do?"

"I'm thinking. Sorry, Josephine, but I gotta figure a way to get you gals out of here. This has never happened before. I'll probably have to walk to the golf course tomorrow and use their cell phone, call a couple of buddies and hope we can cut a section out of the tree...unless you have a better idea."

I shook my head, wondering what it would be like to spend the night in a little cabin in the redwoods with no forced air heat, bathtub or indoor toilet. If only I could call David and explain what happened, tell him not to worry and say "goodnight." Why did I always appreciate him more when he wasn't around?

CHAPTER 8

I sat up, slowly worked the kinks out of my neck and looked around. Light poured in through the bare window to my right, and the smell of coffee streamed through the doorway to my left. I was already dressed from the day before; so all I had to do was slip on my boots, run fingers through my hair and I was up for the day. I was happy to leave the drafty little spare bedroom with its narrow bed, thin blankets and mothball odor.

I shuffled by the empty sofa where Clara had spent the night and took in the view from the windows—early morning sun on sparkling snow. No footprints, just a few inches of snow everywhere and the sound of machinery far away. I scratched my head and entered the warm kitchen where Ben and Clara chatted quietly.

"Good morning, dear. Do you smell mothballs?" I nodded. "Care for a cup of coffee?" Clara stood up wearing the same celery green sweat suit she had worn the day before. Her hair billowed, but somehow she looked younger than she had earlier in the week and her green eyes were clear and bright. I wished I could feel bright in the morning.

"I'd love some coffee. Thanks." I sat down at the table and warmed my hands on the cup.

"Did you sleep well?" Ben asked. I nodded, not wishing to go into detail about all the spooky noises that kept me awake until after midnight, or about my cold feet refusing to warm up even though I wore socks all night, not to mention a frigid trip to the outhouse.

"What's that noise outside," I asked.

"It's a bulldozer." Ben went on to explain that he had already walked two miles to the golf course, made some phone calls and one of his friends was clearing the road with a dozer.

"What time is it?" I checked my watch and answered my own question. It was eight. Ben must have been up since five. There was a noticeable silence.

"Sounds like the dozer stopped. I'll see you gals later." He pulled on his jacket and slipped out the door carrying the two-man saw I had seen hanging above the TV in the living room. Clara reheated part of an overcooked omelet she had made earlier. Apparently, Ben hadn't eaten much. I took a bite and understood why.

"Have any salt?" I asked. Clara handed me the shaker, but salt didn't help. I should have told her to stay away from cooking if she wanted to impress Ben, but I couldn't bring myself to say the words. Clara bustled around the kitchen cleaning every inch of counter, floor and table space. I held my plate in the air while she scrubbed the tabletop.

"What's that noise? Sounds like a chainsaw," I said.

"You're right, it is a chainsaw. Ben said his friend was bringing one to cut off the branches."

"Now that he's busy, we can take a look at the property. You know—the barn and stuff."

"Josephine, why are you so obsessed with that old barn?" She didn't wait for an answer. She stepped into her boots, took a last sip of coffee and pulled on her heavy jacket. I grabbed my purse and had my lightweight jacket zipped before we left the cabin.

Our eyes watered as morning sun glanced off the snow, almost blinding us. The driveway was full of surprises, like potholes full of water covered over with a thin layer of ice and topped with slushy snow.

I heard bird songs as we rounded a turn in the driveway and realized the chainsaw had gone silent. We stopped about five yards from the gigantic horizontal redwood and watched the two men work. The pesky lower branches had already been sliced off with a chainsaw and stacked in a pile. Using the two-man saw, Ben and his friend made a small slice in the trunk—the equivalent of a termite's first bite into a two-story house.

Ben stood with his back to us. His friend, a forty-year-old

Native American, was at the other end of the saw, standing on the downhill side of the frosty tree trunk. Ben pushed downhill and the younger man pushed his end uphill, back and forth with all the force they could muster. Rhythmically, they pushed and groaned, pulled and groaned until beads of perspiration covered their foreheads. They had already shed their jackets as if it were a warm day in June. Unfortunately, the bar on the chainsaw was way too short to do the job.

Snow edged the driveway, adorned the trees and turned to slush under our feet as we carefully made our way around the up-ended, twelve-foot-high circle of roots. The men didn't look up as we hiked past a parked bulldozer and continued down the road. "Hold on to my arm," I said. Clara grabbed hold just before we both lost our footing and landed on the damp ground laughing. We listened for a moment to the two-man saw chewing through thick redwood bark and then the red-ringed flesh. After a short rest, we continued down the windy driveway until it flattened, straightened and ran behind the barn.

"I'll just...sit here for a minute," Clara said as she plopped down on a wooden apple crate, breathing hard. I felt bad. I should have gone alone. My poor aunt would never make it back up the hill, but there was no time for should-haves. I rummaged through my purse, pulled out a couple of screwdrivers and carefully examined the back door. I poked a screwdriver at the center of the knob, but the slot was too tiny. I stared at the sky, scratched my head and finally sat down beside Clara.

"Are you sure it's locked, dear?" I rolled my eyes and walked back to the door. Clara must have been psychic. I turned the knob and stepped inside. The first thing I noticed, looking across the interior, was the snowy view through the extra-large, wide-open double doors at the far end of the building. I found a light switch and after a few seconds, a fluorescent light hanging over a workbench flickered on. Clara was right behind me as we moved through the cluttered workshop area into the expansive and nearly empty barn.

"I wonder what's up there," Clara said, her head tilted back as she pointed to the ceiling.

"Since when do barns have ceilings?" I asked. She shrugged and pointed to a set of narrow stairs that ended suddenly at a padlocked square panel in the ceiling. I took the stairs two at a time, feeling an adrenalin surge.

"Auntie, what if it's locked?" I asked, grinding my teeth when I discovered the padlock was locked and I had no clue how to open it. I tried various number combinations until my arms ached from reaching above my head and I got a crick in my neck. I finally gave up and found Clara in the workshop area studying some old black and white photos pinned to a panel of corkboard.

"This must be Benny's father, don't you think? Looks a lot like Ben."

"Yeah, and maybe this was his grandfather?" I pointed to a middle-aged man standing proudly next to a shiny new, old-style tractor. "Wow, the meadow used to be an orchard."

"Look, Josephine, this plump little lady must be his grandmother showing off the apples they grew. I wonder if she made apple pies," Clara smiled at the thought, but my stomach growled as I conjured up the smell and taste of freshly baked apple pie. I remembered baking pies during the three years I was married, before Marty died. After that, I had no interest in culinary achievements.

"I can't help wondering what's being stored upstairs," I said. "The space is 2,000 square feet if it's an inch. But it would have to be small stuff that would fit through the trap door. I guess that doesn't include airplanes."

"Josephine, what are you babbling about?"

"Oh, nothing." I sat on the crate for awhile, letting the sun warm my face, wishing we had found some piece of evidence that would help us unravel the Joey mystery. Clara sat beside me, her breathing back to normal. I marveled at her strength and hoped I would do as well at her age.

"Do you hear something, dear?" she asked. The engine noise increased and suddenly the little bulldozer rounded a turn in the driveway, straightened and stopped ten feet short of the crate. The husky, dark-complexioned driver flashed his white teeth as he hailed Clara.

"You want me to climb up there?" Clara yelled over the engine noise, and then walked up to the machine with rear wheels up to her chin. "Where do you want me?" He pointed to a small space behind his seat and gave her a hand. I pushed from behind. Finally, she stood up behind him, leaned forward, grabbed the back of his metal seat and arranged her feet facing forward.

"Hold on tight," he said and slowly turned the one-seater machine around. The scraper was in the up position as black smoke poured out the little stack next to Clara's head. They powered up the hill and disappeared around the turn. I decided to hike as far up the hill as I could, and if he came back for me, so much the better. My fascination with the barn was over. All I wanted was to go home, but as I climbed the hill and finally caught sight of the suicidal tree, I realized we weren't going anywhere soon.

Clara's driver was back to pushing and pulling the two-man saw with Ben doing his share on the other end. Their rhythm had slowed and looked more labored than before our trip to the barn. The men stopped to wipe their brows and laugh at me as I dragged myself up the steep driveway with my jacket tied around my waist. At first, I felt like a fifty-year-old slug; but I had to admit I felt flattered that no one thought they needed to drive down the mountain to rescue me.

Clara looked happy sitting on Ben's red plaid Pendleton shirt, which was stretched over a pile of freshly cut limbs sawed into two-foot logs. Her eyes followed Ben in his white t-shirt, soaked with sweat and covered in sawdust. I walked up to her.

"Scoot over, Auntie," I said and let out a sigh. Ten minutes later, after a rest, I encouraged her to hike back to the cabin with me. I didn't know how much more of the manly workout Clara's heart could take. We trudged slowly up the hill, commenting on the beautiful snow scene as we walked. The sunshine was intense, the clouds were gone and it would be only a matter of time, maybe hours, until all the snow melted.

"Wish I'd brought a camera," Clara said. I told her I would look for one in the cabin. She scowled. "Josephine, didn't your mother teach you anything. You can't go looking around in someone else's house."

"Afraid of what I might find?"

"No, not at all," she said just before she turned left and entered the outhouse. I welcomed the opportunity to be by myself and began poking around the cabin. I decided to search the built-in drawers and bookshelves behind the ancient horsehair sofa. I bent down and began pulling the old furniture away from the wall.

"What in the name of Polly's pickles are you doing?" Clara startled me. I jerked my head around and the corner of the sofa slipped out of my grip. The front leg fell off and the sofa dropped down like a camel on one knee.

"Darn! Now what are we going to do?" I said, picking up the fancy leg. "The leg has a nail poking out of the wood."

"Let's fix it before Ben comes back," Clara said.

"Good idea, but how?" I looked around for an idea. "I know. We position the leg with the sofa resting on it. We stand on the couch and jump up and down until the nail goes in."

"Not me, Josephine. I know my limits." She crossed her chest with both hands.

"That's OK, I can do it." I held the corner of the sofa up while Clara slipped the leg into its original position. I lowered the sofa, dragged a chair across the room and parked it at the corner of the couch. I pulled off my mini-boots, stepped up onto the chair and from there, gingerly stepped onto the sofa cushions. After two awkward jumps, Clara bent down and checked the leg.

"It's only halfway in."

"I'll try again." I jumped three more hard jumps and Clara checked the leg. She straightened up and giggled nervously. I saw something out of the corner of my eye, turned my head toward the kitchen and was shocked and mortified to see two large men standing in the doorway, eyes big, mouths gaping.

"Mice…I thought I saw a mouse," I blurted, blushing from my head all the way down to the bunion on my big toe. I stepped onto the chair and then down to the rustic floor planks. Ben put the chair back in its original corner and asked if we were all right.

"Oh, don't worry about us," Clara said. "We know about mice. We live in the country too." The mouse-panic faded as we turned our focus on lunch. Ben rummaged around in the kitchen gathering ingredients to construct tuna sandwiches.

I began mixing together tuna, mayo, chopped onion and pickle. I quickly spread the mixture on slices of bread and added lettuce leaves before Clara had time to help. She put the kettle on for tea, and our host found a beer for his friend and one for himself. I piled the sandwiches on a platter and everyone helped themselves. The men looked like they were starving but almost too tired to eat. However, they managed to eat twice as much as we girls, and I was sure their sandwiches would not stick to their thighs or anywhere else. Ben spoke between bites.

"My friend here, Gibbs, and I are halfway through the first cut. We'll have a couple more guys helping us tomorrow. You OK with that, Cat?" She swallowed a bite of tuna and smiled.

"I guess we stay another night," she said. "It's nice to meet you, Gibbs."

"If you really have to get home, I can ride Gibb's dozer down to the golf course and call a taxi for you."

"That won't be necessary…" Clara said. "…You see, Josephine has already arranged to have someone feed the animals and we will be just fine." I imagined we would have beans again for dinner and noticed Clara had slowed her tea consumption, just as I had. We dreaded our trips to the outhouse. My bath would come from a bowl of water and a washcloth on the bureau in my bedroom I shared with Clara.

The men went back to work. Clara stoked the fires and I carried in more wood. When all the chores were finished, we gratefully sat down at the kitchen table.

"Think we should look at the colors for the outhouse?" Clara asked. I nodded.

"But not if we have to be in the outhouse. I can pick one from right here in the kitchen."

"Yes, we'll just imagine we're in the…or just pick a pretty color," she said, pulling the color cards out of her purse and arranging them on the table like a winning poker hand. She picked out her favorite green, a light yellow and a pale, peachy orange. Out of those, I pointed to the green, and she set the sample aside for Ben to look at. Our work was done.

Time passed quickly thanks to shelves full of good books to read. I pulled out one of my favorites, *To Kill a Mocking Bird*, and as I opened the book, a small white envelope fell from between the pages.

"What's that, Josephine?"

"A little note inside…says, 'Happy birthday, love, Bev' and then a lipstick kiss." I slipped the note back in the envelope and tried to decide what to do next.

"Josephine, you're not thinking of keeping that?"

"It's not Ben's. Bev is his sister, right? And sisters don't give lipstick kisses to their brothers. This note was Joey's."

"We don't know that and yes, Beverly is his sister, but it's Benny's house so the note belongs to him." I set the book on the coffee table with the note in it and began searching through other books. Clara's jaw was set and her eyes didn't look friendly.

"OK, I'll just read a book," I said, pulling out the first one I could put my hand on which happened to be titled, *Dynamite*. It was about a rodeo cowboy from Colorado—not my usual read. After three pages, my eyelids felt heavy so I set the book down, curled up on the sofa and closed my eyes. When I woke up, still wearing my jacket and boots, I heard voices. The room was dark except for flickering light from the fireplace. I stretched, yawned and trundled into the kitchen. Clara and Ben sat at the table with my favorite book between them and Ben held the note from Bev.

"Josephine, did you sleep well? Clara asked. I nodded and looked at the clock on the wall.

"Oh…it's almost six?"

"It is. You slept almost three hours, dear." Clara stood up. "Now that you're up, I'll make dinner."

"No, no Auntie, let me. After all that sleep, I should make my-self useful around here." First, I had to shake the cobwebs out of my brain. I started to notice things, like the fact it was dark outside and I needed to use the outhouse. I grabbed the flashlight hanging on a nail by the door.

"You won't need that, Josephine," Ben said as he pointed to a light switch next to the flashlight. "Flip the switch and you'll have plenty of light." That was when I realized the kitchen light was on, illuminating steam from the kettle.

"How about the phone?" I asked. Clara smiled.

"Help yourself, dear. I called Candice, but I guess they aren't home yet."

"I'll be right back to make dinner, and I'll call David later this evening." I stepped outside and instantly appreciated the light over the back door and the one ahead of me, attached to the out-house roof. An owl hooted just before a critter flapped its wings above my head and disappeared into the black night. I walked cautiously over slick, uneven ground. The snow had turned to slush and then to ice.

When I got back to the kitchen, Clara was telling Ben that his bathwater was ready. He picked up a big tin pot of hot water by its handle and walked through the house to his bedroom, floorboards creaking under foot. She followed him carrying a blue enameled pitcher of cold water. I guessed a sponge bath was better than nothing, especially after a man has worked hard all day. Personally, I'd rather wait for a shower or bubble bath. Clara wandered back to the kitchen.

"I don't know how he manages way out here in the mountains," she said, shaking her head. "He acts like he's a young cowboy. Thinks he can live in this old cabin the way his ancestors did with no decent plumbing. It's not civilized."

"So, Auntie, you would never live in a place like this?" I put a pot of leftover beans on the stove.

"I didn't say that. But if I lived here, there would be some major changes." Clara meandered into the living room, flopped into a soft chair and asked me if I had seen the remote control for the TV.

"I don't think there is one," I said from across the room. "The TV looks forty-years old at least." She grumbled something, walked up to the screen and turned a knob. Suddenly we had black and white technology, snow included. The picture wasn't fuzzy—it was a local snow scene on the six o'clock news. The pictures had obviously been taken earlier in the day before the snow began to melt.

"It's just like those Currier and Ives pictures," Clara swooned.

"I wish David was here...that reminds me, I forgot to call him." I picked up a black receiver at the end of a curly cord, which only allowed me to walk three feet in any direction. I dialed David's number and heard his comforting voice.

"I hope you didn't worry about us, David. We're fine."

"I thought so. What have you two got yourselves into now?" he laughed.

"We're in Boulder Creek visiting Aunt Clara's friend, Ben. We were almost to his cabin when a giant redwood fell across the driveway, just a few feet behind us. There's only one driveway and no other way out."

"Did he call a tree service?"

"Ah, no. Ben and his neighbor have been cutting on the tree all day. Tomorrow a couple more guys are going to help. If all goes well, he thinks we can go home tomorrow night."

"Solow and Felix are fine, and I miss you."

"Miss you too. Oops, I smell burnt beans. Bye."

CHAPTER 9

Thursday night, Ben set up an old canvas cot next to my bed shortly after our blackened bean dinner. I gave Clara my bed and stretched out on the WWI relic. My limbs hung off the edges on three sides. The cot would have been worse for Clara—after all, she was seventy-five years old and sounded like Gibbs' chainsaw when she snored.

I kept reminding myself that it could be worse. We could have been flattened under the tree, but instead we were living the "Little House on the Prairie" adventure. I shivered under a musty-smelling quilt that refused to keep me warm. After a couple of hours of trying to fall asleep, I crawled out of the pseudo bed, pulled on my boots and jacket and tiptoed to the living room.

A few embers glowed red in the fireplace. I stirred them up and added a couple of logs. I checked the kitchen stove, added more wood and a kettle of water for tea and opened the fridge to claim the last piece of birthday cake. I felt I deserved the last piece since I had given up my bed and spent two torturous hours on a collapsible cot.

I settled onto the sofa with a book, tea and cake, a little lamp-light and a warm fire. I opened a hardback copy of Michael Crichton's, *Jurassic Park*. Loopy handwriting on the inside cover caught my eye. It was the flowery style I recognized from the birthday note to Joey. The note read: "Happy birthday, Joey. Love, Bev." I figured they were at least friends, maybe more. I heard something, stiffened, turned my head and saw a tall shadow moving across the far wall.

"You look comfortable, Josephine," Ben said, shuffling into the room and settling into the overstuffed chair next to my resting place. "I didn't think you'd last long in that old cot."

"It's no reflection on your hospitality, Ben. I never was a very good camper."

"How's the book?"

"Just opened it and read this little note." I handed the book to him. He smiled, but it was a sad smile. He looked away. "How well did Joey and your sister know each other?"

"I'd say they were lifelong friends, soul mates maybe," he muttered, studying his sister's handwriting. "She died two months ago."

"I'm so sorry." A lump formed in my throat. Ben suddenly looked older as his shoulders caved and his sad eyes focused on things I couldn't see and knew nothing about. He had obviously been close to his sister. "Where did Beverly live?" I asked after a very long silence.

"She lived here after her husband went to prison…white-collar crime, you know. Anyway, she had Alzheimer's for about ten years and died here."

"You mean in Clara's bed?" He nodded. "I won't tell her. She's a little touchy about things like that." Actually, I was too, but I put it out of my mind. "Was she younger than you?"

"Yeah, three years younger. Prettiest redhead…looked a lot like my cousin, Sarah," he said, handing the book back to me. Minutes later I had some serious stereophonic snoring going on, Clara down the hall and Ben just six feet away with his head back, mouth gaping. The "handsome cowboy image" temporarily faded, but I had had a peek at Ben's softer side and admired him for taking care of his sister. I stretched out on the sofa with the lap blanket over me, propped up my book and began to read.

◆ ◆ ◆

Friday morning, I awoke to annoying rays of sunshine pouring through the east window. I opened one eye at a time. Ben's chair was empty and I smelled coffee. Like a mindless robot, I entered the kitchen wearing the same clothes and mustard stains for the third day in a row. I ran fingers through my hair, pulled a bentwood chair out from the kitchen table and sat down.

"You might think about getting some little pillow seats for these chairs, Ben."

"And a good morning to you, Josephine. Sleep well?"

"Yes. Did we talk last night…or did I dream…?"

"We had a nice little talk last night," he chuckled and poured a cup of coffee for me.

"Where's Aunt Clara?"

"Outhouse." We quietly sipped our coffee in the warm ambiance of the retro kitchen where time and hectic life styles had no place. If it weren't for the modern clock hanging on the wall, I might have thought I was living a hundred and fifty years ago with pioneers, trappers and such. Gradually I remembered the conversation I had had with Ben in the middle of the night.

"Ben, when was the last time you saw Joey?"

"I don't remember exactly…." We looked up as Clara opened the back door and walked inside rubbing her hands together to warm them. Ben pulled a chair out for her. Her whole face smiled. I wondered if Clara was going to want to leave once we were able.

"Good morning, dear. Were you comfortable sleeping on the sofa?"

"I guess so. I slept pretty well." I said nothing about the snoring that had echoed through the house from two directions.

"You were still sawing a few logs when I got up," she said, smiling. I bit my tongue. I noticed plates in the sink and realized they had already finished breakfast. Ben stood up.

"Time to go to work. See you ladies at noon." He pulled on his jacket, gloves and the familiar cowboy hat. The door snapped shut behind him. I was sure he would be shedding his jacket and gloves real soon, like a lizard in spring. I trimmed the mold off a couple of pieces of white bread and arranged them on top of the cast-iron stove. When they were toast, I smeared on some peanut butter and washed them all down with more coffee.

"I'll wash the dishes and you can make the beds," Clara said. I folded the lap blanket and placed it on the sofa. From there, I turned the corner and walked down the short hall to Clara's room. When her room was straightened, I crossed the hall to Ben's room, an ordinary bedroom except for the moth-eaten cougar head on the wall and the rifle hanging over the little closet door. I pulled his quilt up, straightened it and looked around, wondering what he kept in the closet.

"Josephine, what are you doing in Ben's closet?" I jumped.

"Just straightening up things," I said as I shoved a shoebox full of junk back into its place on the shelf above the short rack of shirts. I tugged on a long string hanging from the middle of the ceiling, and the room went dark.

"Find anything?" Clara asked with a hint of sarcasm.

"Actually, I found some ribbons and medals from the Air Force. Was Ben in the service?"

"No...but they could have been anybody's. Now, let's go for a walk." We gathered our jackets, left the house and decided to explore an inviting path heading north, away from the driveway and fallen tree. The narrow path was fairly level until it eventually sloped downward, following the contour of the mountain. We zigzagged around towering redwoods but always headed down and to the left. The trail took us across a stream with the help of an old footbridge and then left again onto flatter ground.

"Auntie, did you know that Ben's sister had Alzheimer's?" We were both breathing hard and had shed our jackets.

"You don't say. How sad. I only knew her as a girl, but she was a very pretty redhead. Everyone thought so."

"Even, Joey?"

"She was younger than we were. I don't know if he noticed her," she said, leaning against the crusty trunk of a tree. A blue jay sounded an alarm from a nearby branch and another jay repeated the message with an indignant squawk. Just what we needed—birds with attitude interrupting our conversation. After a few minutes of rest, we continued our nature hike. I was becoming very concerned about the return trip and our energy levels, especially Clara's. I began hearing things.

"Josephine, do you hear that?"

"What? Oh, that. It sounds like men sawing wood." Even as I said the words, the path ended abruptly at the edge of Ben's driveway about ten yards up from the horizontal redwood. We watched as two young men pushed and pulled on the two-man saw, and Ben and Gibbs sat on the ground resting. All four men were covered in sweat and woodchips. The younger two-man team groaned with each push and pull, but the rhythm was faster than the day before. With any luck, the ten-foot section would be free and rolling down the hill well before the sun went down.

Ben saw us, spread his flannel shirt on the ground and motioned for us to sit down. Clara held onto my arm as she carefully worked her way down to a sitting position on the shirt. One sleeve was left for me to sit on. We relaxed for half an hour and then it was time for the men to switch places. Just before Ben and Gibbs left us, Ben suggested we go to the golf course and buy sandwiches for everyone. He handed Clara a wad of bills and Gibbs threw me his set of keys.

"Can you drive a pickup?" Gibbs asked me.

"You better believe she can," Ben said.

"OK, it's the white Dodge," Gibbs said as he walked with us around the upended roots. We watched him grab his end of the saw and push. The rhythm had begun all over again.

Three pickups were parked along the driveway and the dozer was gone. I pushed Clara up into her seat in the white truck that made my Mazda pickup look stunted. Unfortunately, I had not owned or driven a stick shift vehicle since I was eighteen.

"What's the matter, Josephine?"

"Just trying to remember some things, like how this clutch pedal works. After a minute of locating all the important knobs and levers, I adjusted the mirrors and fired up the powerful engine. Gibbs snapped his head around at the first sound of grinding gears. I worked the clutch pedal, gearshift and brake until the truck jerked and then quietly moved backwards. I slowly, carefully, backed down the road, around several turns, all the way to the flat area behind the barn, which was the first place big enough to turn around. Once we were facing forward, the driving was easy. Clara sucked in a long breath and color came back to her face. Two miles later, I turned right into the golf course parking lot.

"Right there, Josephine. Pull in next to that Lexus." I followed her instructions, being careful not to wing the black beauty with our four-door, four-wheel-drive, mega-truck. We were slightly early for lunch, but a young woman gave our order to the chef— twenty minutes later, we paid for the burgers, fries, milkshakes and a grilled cheese sandwich for me. My stomach and I were singing a happy tune.

◆ ◆ ◆

A mere four hours after lunch, with some light still in the sky, the ten-foot section of tree trunk had been freed by a last exhausting cut of the saw. Twenty tons of tree trunk thundered down the driveway, rolled over a bank on the first turn and went airborne, coming to rest at the base of a group of three giant redwoods. All six of us were jumping up and down, cheering and clapping. The exhausted men had suddenly shed their fatigue. I hiked up to the cabin, grabbed our purses and drove my truck down to where Clara and Ben were hugging and saying goodbye.

"Come on, Clara, just walk away. You can do it," I thought to myself.

"Ready, Auntie?"

"Yes, I suppose I am," she murmured. She climbed into her seat and we waved to Ben. I flipped on the headlights and turned my attention to the road ahead, rolling through the San Lorenzo Valley at the speed of slow traffic. I had called David earlier, letting him know we would stop for dinner and be home around eight. Since we had not bathed or changed our clothes in three days, we ate fast food in the truck and then headed home.

"Clara, I'm curious, did Ben and his wife have any children?"

"No. He said they couldn't." She stared straight ahead. "My husband, Roger, wanted a boy, but I had to have a hysterectomy when I was only twenty-four," her voice was soft as she lowered her eyes. No one spoke for a couple of miles.

"What did Ben do for a living?" I asked. Clara laughed.

"He was a very successful contractor." We glanced at each other in the dark and then laughed some more. "Don't ask why he doesn't build a bathroom. I don't understand that part of him."

I was still mulling over Clara's words and Ben's occupation

when I parked next to David's Miata in front of my house. Home had never looked so inviting, especially the plumbing, heating and David. He greeted me with a hug, took Clara's arm and helped her inside. Solow was just waking up from his early evening nap, saw me and howled with every inch of his giant lungs. His tail slapped my calves and warmed my heart. I suddenly realized how blessed I was.

"I'll take your jacket, Aunt Clara," David said, helping her out of the second sleeve. He took mine too and asked if we needed anything. He looked wonderful in his Dockers and light green sweater. We must have looked like yucky stuff the cat dragged in, and smelled worse.

"Where's Felix?" Clara started to get up from the sofa, but David motioned for her to stay put, picked up Felix and set him down on her lap.

"David, I'm surprised he let you pick him up," she said as Felix circled a couple of times, purring like a motorboat.

"Seems like all I do is feed and talk to animals around here," he laughed.

"David, I slept on a tiny cot, ate burnt beans and the bathroom was an outhouse. You have no idea what my aunt and I have been through."

"But I'm sure you two will tell me," he smiled.

"And don't forget the mice," Clara winked and we laughed.

"By the way, your boss called—something about working on Monday. Better give him a call tomorrow. And you have messages." He pointed to the answering machine.

"Later," I said. "I'm too busy enjoying my home and the bubble bath I'm about to have."

CHAPTER 10

I woke up Saturday morning with a smile on my face and stars in my eyes. I stared at the open-beam ceiling, feeling warm under my comforter, thinking about the night before. I had taken a luxurious bubble bath right after Clara finished hers. I dried my hair, brushed my teeth and dressed for bed. I heard voices and wandered out to the living room where David sat on the sofa trying to teach Solow to roll over. He was trying, but Solow wasn't getting it.

"Give him a treat," I said, "he'll do anything for food."

"Yeah, next time," David laughed and stood up.

"Wow, Aunt Clara's out cold," I whispered. "I remember that snore so well." David put his arm around my waist and guided me down the hall. We spent some quality time together, and then David gave me a "goodnight kiss" and drove home.

I dreamt David was a cowboy, I was his lady and our little baby boy's face reminded me of Solow.

◆ ◆ ◆

"Josephine, are you awake? A Mr. Atwater's on the phone." Clara opened my door a bit more and leaned in.

"Tell him I'll be right there." I pulled on my robe and raced to the kitchen phone, the old-fashioned type with a cord, but thirty years newer than Ben's black phone.

"Hello, Mr. Atwater?"

"Ms. Stuart, as you know we're a little behind schedule, but I'm sure your people can make up for the time lost. We'll see you Monday?"

"We'll be there…." Click, he hung up. Great, he probably expected us to put in long hours. What most people didn't understand was that mural painting is very taxing on body and mind. After seven or eight hours of balancing on a ladder, the artist is standing on legs of jelly.

Later that morning I called Kyle and Alicia to make sure they would be on the job Monday morning. Alicia was more interested in finding out where I had been for the last three days. As soon as I finished telling her my Boulder Creek story and hung up the phone, Mom called.

"Honey, it's as if you and Clara disappeared off the planet," she said. My mom didn't usually worry or keep close track of my schedule. Actually, I think she was more concerned about Clara, probably still thinking of her as her little sister. I repeated my Boulder Creek story and then asked if she would like to get together with Clara while I worked.

"Of course I want to get together with my sister. I'll take her to the garden club Monday afternoon and Tuesday I have tennis…."

"Just take it a day at a time, Mom. Aunt Clara is kind of funny about what she likes to do."

"Yes, I think you're right. I tried to call her last night, but the line was busy for over an hour."

"Tell me about it," I groaned. "Now she's in the bathroom trying to style her hair."

"Benny?"

"Yep, I gotta go, Mom. Love you." I hung up feeling hungry. Hungry enough to sample Clara's burnt toast and coffee sludge. I tossed Solow a piece of crust. He let it fall to the floor and walked away. Maybe he was smart enough to learn to roll over after all.

Clara stepped into the kitchen wearing her hair in a French twist. She poured a cup of coffee and sat down. "Candice called this morning." Her eyes were fixed on the mug in front of her. "She asked me to help out at the florist shop. It seems someone ran a car through the front window."

"I remember hearing about that accident on the news when we were driving to Boulder Creek, but I didn't think it was Candy's shop," I scratched my head.

"She had the big window replaced right away and her employees are putting the store back together, but there's a lot to do."

"Where's Candy?" I asked, trying not to sound judgmental.

"They won a free week at the Sheraton in Jamaica," she smiled. "She was always lucky, except with love. Maybe this time…." her voice turned to a whisper. "Anyway, if you aren't busy…maybe we could drive to Santa Cruz and lend a hand. But if you have plans…."

"Don't worry Auntie, I have plenty of time." I thought about David and realized we would have lots of time together once Clara went back to Oakhurst. "I'll call Mom and we can meet for lunch." Half an hour later, we were on the road with Santa Cruz in our sights.

"What did your mother say when you called?"

"Oops, I forgot to call her. We'll just give her a call from Candy's shop. Maybe Dad will join us too." Clara nodded. The sun was out and traffic was minimal all the way to Santa Cruz. We rolled into the parking lot behind the one-story building just before nine. I parked next to a white delivery van. Three businesses shared the old stucco building. The florist shop was sandwiched between a barbershop and a paint store. We rounded the building and walked past a line of men and boys queuing up for haircuts. At the opposite end of the building, people hustled in and out of the paint store. I banged on the front door of the florist shop with my fist.

"Maybe they're not here yet," Clara suggested.

"Somebody's coming." The door opened and a squat old woman with dyed red hair frowned at us, asking what we wanted.

"This is Candy's mother, Clara. I'm Josephine and we're here to help put the shop back together." Suddenly the suspicious little woman understood, relaxed her puffy white face and invited us in.

"My name is Maureen Wise. Call me Maurie," she chuckled nervously as she wiped a tissue across her forehead. "Candy said you were coming. I'm so glad you're here. I've been working since seven o'clock trying to push these shelves into place, but I just don't have the muscles to do a proper job."

"My dear, this is too much to expect from one small woman,"

Clara said. Maureen smiled. We dropped our purses behind the counter in the back and followed Maureen's instructions.

"We'll start on this shelf first," she said. We did as we were told and put our backs into the work. Two hours later, all six units were in place and wiped clean.

"So, Maurie, where are the other employees?" I asked. She pursed her lips.

"There were three of us, but the driver can't be located and the manager quit yesterday; so I guess that makes me the manager. I only wanted part-time work to supplement my Social Security." She plopped down on a bench and sucked in some air. "I'm expecting a delivery this morning and then we can stock the shelves."

"Someone's pounding on the back door," I said, carefully stepping around the gazillion potted indoor plants and silk flower arrangements sitting all over the concrete floor. I made it to the door before Maureen's tired derriere could leave the bench.

"Hey, Josephine, what are you doing here?" the dark, curly-headed boy laughed.

"How are you, Gabe? We're here because Clara's daughter owns this store."

"No kidding. Like, it's a small world," he laughed. Clara heard his voice and galloped over to the boy, arms outstretched for a hug. I halfway expected her to pull adoption papers out of her pocket. "I got half a truckload for you, just sign here." Clara scribbled her name on the invoice without hesitation.

"Can I help you carry things in…?"

"Auntie, it's his job," I said, reaching for her arm. Gabe turned and disappeared out the door. A couple of minutes later, he pushed a dolly piled high with potted plants packaged in bubble wrap into the shop. We unloaded and unwrapped everything while Gabe made half a dozen more trips to his truck. We were having trouble finding floor space for all the plants, so Maurie began arranging them one by one on the shelving units we had set up earlier. Gabe said he was leaving so I followed him outside.

"Gabe, how do you like working for your uncle?" I asked.

"I don't know…never thought about it. My uncle raised me,

and I started working at the nursery when I was ten."

"It's just you and your uncle?"

"Yeah. I'd like to join the Marines, but he won't let me."

"How can he stop you? You're eighteen."

"Actually, I'm almost seventeen." He glanced at his feet and then looked up into my face smiling. "Most people think I'm older." He turned and climbed into his delivery truck.

"Yeah, because you tell them you're eighteen," I laughed.

"I have a delivery in Ben Lomond and a couple in Scotts Valley. See ya later." The truck belched smelly exhaust and lurched toward Ocean Street. I entered the shop and began loading merchandise onto shelves. The phone rang.

"Are we open for business?" I asked Maureen. She nodded and I answered the phone. "It's for you, Maurie." She grumbled something and took the phone. After that, the calls kept coming. By one o'clock, she had several arrangements promised. I grabbed the phone and called for reinforcements. Mom answered. She and Dad were available, offered their services for the afternoon and arrived carrying a bucket of Kentucky Fried. The smell alone had me swooning.

When the chicken had been consumed and only naked bones remained in the bucket, Maurie instructed us on stocking the shelves. She wished us luck and retreated to the backroom where the deep, stainless steel sinks and long counter tops accommodated the cutting and arranging of flowers. In the next three hours, she managed to complete the first six orders, plus answer the phone and take down three more orders. By five o'clock, she looked like Old Mother Hubbard's grandmother after a full day of babysitting.

Our work wasn't too bad, except when Maurie had to take the clippers away from Clara by force because she wanted to even-up the limbs on a miniature potted maple, and she had to pour kitty litter on the floor where I accidentally dropped a bottle of fish emulsion. By five, we were all pooped and ready for a nap when Maurie cornered Aunt Clara.

"Who's going to make the deliveries?" she asked, wiping her brow.

"Ah, ah ... I think Josephine and I can do it ...." Clara said, looking at me for a sign of willingness on my part.

"Yeah, we can do it," I said. "What do you want us to do?"

"You probably saw the white delivery van parked in the back. We load it with arrangements and you deliver them," Maureen said, pointing to the row of flower bouquets she had just finished as she smiled sweetly. "And this is the list of addresses."

Clara took the list. Mom nudged Dad with her elbow.

"Honey, we have a reception at the gallery and it's almost six o'clock." Dad nodded and said they needed to go.

"Thanks, everyone," Maureen said. "I need to catch my bus. Good luck with the deliveries." She handed me the keys to the van, and we all shuffled out the back door carrying flower arrangements. We placed them in the back of the van and went back for more. Mom's Subaru took off with Maureen in the back seat, saving her a bus trip.

Clara crawled into the van's passenger seat and dropped her head back against the headrest. It was already dark when I clipped the list of addresses to a clipboard on the dash, and set out for the west side of town. The first house was the easiest. They were home, answered the door and loved the arrangement. For the next half hour, I delivered flowers all over town.

"Where are we, Josephine? I think I must have dropped off for a minute."

"We're on the east side of town. One more stop in this neighborhood and all the rest go to Dominican Hospital. We cruised up Morrissey Boulevard and stopped in front of number 2240. The porch light was on.

"I know where we are. This is Sal's house," Clara chirped as she popped her seatbelt and climbed out of the van. The night was brisk and full of stars. I carried the bouquet of red roses up the stairs, across the porch and rang the doorbell. Angela opened the door wearing a huge smile, which quickly diminished in radiance when she recognized us.

"Oh, hi, roses for me? Why?" she sputtered.

"I'm just delivering them. They're from someone else." Her smile returned as she reached for her flowers. Sal walked up behind her.

"Mr. Gianelli, how are you?" Clara asked.

"Just fine, thank you. Would you like to come in?" he asked, running fingers through his hair. Angela stepped back into the foyer. We followed her inside where tantalizing hints of Italian cooking drifted our way. My stomach growled.

"We were just about to have dinner…ah, would you care to join us?" Sal asked. Clara smiled.

"That would be lovely, thank you, my dear. May I sit for a moment?" Sal took Clara's arm and led her to the sofa. Once she was settled, I wondered if she would ever move again. I sat down next to her. Angela trotted upstairs with her roses, passing Patrick on his way down.

"Hi, ladies. Dad, I have a game at eight."

"Dinner is ready," Sal said. "You can start eating and we'll join you in a few minutes." I thumbed through a magazine and tried not to look at the pictures of food.

"So what brings you ladies out tonight?"

"We delivered Angela's roses and a whole host of other arrangements because Aunt Clara's daughter's florist shop is short-handed," I said and Clara nodded. "Is there anything I can do to help in the kitchen?" I sincerely hoped there wasn't. Sal shook his head.

"You two look exhausted. Stay right here and I'll bring you a bite to eat." He turned and walked away. Minutes later he came back with a full tray and set it down on the coffee table. There were two plates of spaghetti and two salads. Nothing ever looked or tasted as good. Sal joined us minutes later with his plate while Angela and Patrick ate at the kitchen bar.

"Is this your cooking, Sal?" I asked.

"Yep, Dad taught me how to cook—Italian, of course."

"Speaking of your dad, do you mind if I ask you a silly little question?" Sal shrugged. "Do you remember the name of the business he invested in? Sorry, questions pop into my head and drive me nuts," I said. Clara rolled her eyes.

"Mom and Dad never told us the details. When Dad died—I mean disappeared, I was shocked to find out there was a half-million dollar mortgage on this house. Mom couldn't keep up the payments.

Too bad he didn't have insurance."

"Are you sure he didn't have any insurance?"

"Pretty sure," he said under his breath.

"Did you know Benny's sister, Beverly?" Clara asked. Sal swallowed.

"I knew he had a sister but I never met her. Can I get you something to drink?"

"We're fine," I said, scraping my plate for the last drop of spaghetti sauce. "The dinner was excellent. Thank you so much. We have one more delivery to make and then we can go home." Clara and I carried our plates to the kitchen, said goodbye to the kids and then said goodbye to Sal at the front door.

"Oh, one other thing," I said. "How long has your mom known Wayne?"

"How long do you think?" he said sarcastically. Like a smack on the forehead, I suddenly saw the resemblance and was sure he read my expression, especially the red hot cheeks. I think I was ten times more embarrassed than he was. I thumped down the stairs, caught up to my aunt and helped her into the van. I looked back at the empty porch as the front door closed.

"Wasn't that a lovely meal?" Clara asked. I felt too tired to answer, but nodded, started the engine and merged into traffic. Just a few miles later, we parked at Dominican Hospital. Clara carried one large flower arrangement, and I carried a dozen pink roses and a potted azalea with a big yellow bow. We handed over the merchandise at the front desk and hurried back to the van. It was like playing Santa Claus except that exhaustion had whittled away some of the fun.

"Well, that's done," Clara said. "I guess I'll be working at the shop Monday. Maurie certainly can't do everything by herself."

"What if you hired someone?"

"I don't know if Candice would want me to. I suppose I should, that is, if I knew someone who wanted a job. Maybe Leola can help out temporarily." Clara rubbed her chin thoughtfully. "I just hope Maurie shows up for work Monday. She's old and tired, poor thing. Speaking of old and tired, what do you think about Darla? Sounds like she cheated on Joey."

"Yeah, I didn't know you picked up on that, Auntie. No wonder Sal is blond and blue-eyed. He looks like a younger version of Wayne, don't you think?" Clara nodded as I parked the van next to my truck. We traded our warm seats in the van for cold ones in the Mazda. By the time we passed the city limits, the interior was toasty warm and I felt like having a nap.

"Are you crazy?" Clara snapped. "Roll up that window."

"I just need a little air. Sorry, I'm trying to stay awake." She immediately rolled her window down halfway.

"Why didn't you say so?"

"I just did. What do you think about Sal and his kids. Seems like they're taking a long time to warm up to us, or is it just my imagination?"

"Maybe it's those intrusive questions you're always asking."

"Kind of like your questions?" I said. She chuckled. We passed the time guessing who had sent flowers to the not-very-friendly Angela. Finally, the headlights struck the front of my house where a porch light welcomed us. David had obviously turned it on. Hopefully he let the animals out for a potty break. I was too tired to wonder where he was.

I followed Clara into the house. Solow and Felix were curled up together on the old braided rug, keeping each other warm. They looked up and Solo's tail pounded the floor.

"Our contented animals barely know we're alive," I said, feeling disappointed with the reception. Clara picked up Felix and cuddled him against her body, calling him every sweet name she could think of. I scratched Solow behind his ears with one hand and flipped on the 10:00 o'clock news with the other.

"Josephine, look! They're showing a picture of Jamie!"

"I know. Oh no, he's a person-of-interest in the killing of his father? How can they even think such a thing?" I kicked the sofa.

"He's missing," Clara said. "He's a nice boy. The sheriff is dead wrong and I hope they don't find him."

"I agree." I yawned and minutes later I was sound asleep, still sitting up. I dreamt about brigades of potted trees with stunted limbs. They stiffly marched into the back of my truck, following orders from someone I couldn't see but sensed was standing in the shadows. I drove them to the railroad tracks, dropped them off and tried to turn the truck around. The wheels stuck to the rails. I heard a train whistle getting louder. I panicked, jerked my eyes open and looked around the dark room trying to figure out where I was. I heard Clara's familiar snores drifting down from the loft. My heartbeat slowed. All seemed right with the world as Solow and I left the couch and trotted off to bed.

CHAPTER 11

*E*ven Aunt Clara slept late Sunday morning. Eight-thirty, we met at the kitchen table over coffee, still feeling the after affects of Saturday's hard work. And even worse, I couldn't get Jamie off my mind. Where had he gone?

"Clara, we need to shop for groceries and I thought we might...."

"Look around Jamie's neighborhood?" Clara grinned. I nodded and dropped a couple of frozen waffles into the toaster. After breakfast and a hot shower, I felt alive again. Clara looked pretty good for a senior citizen who had pulled a nine-to-nine shift the day before. Solow pouted by the front door, sensing that we were leaving him behind. Felix had had the time he needed outside. I left a note on the table for David, thanking him for feeding the animals the night before.

"Don't forget to bring a jacket," I said over my shoulder as I headed for the truck. A minute later, we were backing down the long driveway. Suddenly David's Miata turned the corner and stopped a couple of feet from my bumper. He walked up to my window.

"Hello, Aunt Clara, Josie. Looks like you're leaving again."

"We're going grocery shopping. Will we see you later this afternoon?" Clara asked.

"Sure, I'll be around." He winked at me and strolled back to his car, looking good in my rearview mirror. Clara watched me watching him.

"Why aren't you married to that good-looking man?"

"He hasn't asked me and I'm in no hurry," I said, hoping to stop the inquisition. Clara was beginning to sound like Mom.

Actually, all the old folks, including Myrtle, couldn't wait for me to remarry after seventeen years of living alone. Myrtle lived alone, but no one harped on her. I decided to take Clara's comment as concern for my well-being and concentrate on driving.

"There's San Marcos…."

"I see it, Auntie." We made a sharp left, drove one block, crossed the tracks and followed the road to Bonita Lane. It was our second visit and for the second time, it struck me how the name of the street was such a far cry from the real neighborhood with its shabby little houses and old rusty cars strewn everywhere. I parked in the empty dirt patch in front of number four just as a nosy neighbor across the street closed her ragged drapes, except for a couple of inches to peek through. We walked up to Jamie's front door and Clara knocked. I stepped a few feet over and leaned my face close to the window, noticing right away that the piano was gone.

"No one's home," Clara said.

"Not even the piano," I said. "Let's go to the back." We tramped over rocks and weeds, rounded the corner of the house and tried the back door. "Locked! Aunt Clara, hold my purse." I pressed my face to the little window encased in the upper half of the door and saw a bowl of cereal on the kitchen table—soggy and uneaten. I gave up trying to open the door and moved on to a window with its screen slightly ajar. I jiggled the screen loose and dropped it on the ground. As it happened, the bedroom window opened easily when I pried the bottom edge with a nail file from my purse. I handed the file back to Clara.

"Josephine, is this really necessary?"

"Just tell me if someone's coming…." and then, out of the corner of my eye, I saw a young Hispanic woman standing ten feet away, hands on hips, looking grim.

"Hi, aah, we're looking for Jamie. Have you seen him?" I tried to look casual with my leg stretched up and my foot caught on the window sill. Clara finally came to my rescue, lifting my foot an inch higher, releasing it from the window's grip. The woman put a hand across her mouth, trying to stifle a laugh.

"You know Jamie?" she asked.

"Sure do," Clara chirped. "He's my childhood friend's oldest son."

"You're not family?"

"No," I said, "just friends. We heard he was in a little trouble and wanted to help."

"Yes, I think he is in trouble," she said, "but he is innocent." She blinked back tears. "He had to go on a trip, you know, business, I think."

"Dear, do you have any idea where he went?" Clara asked, moving closer to the woman and handing her a clean tissue from one of the purses she carried. "I'm Clara Ramsey and this is my niece, Josephine Stuart."

"My name ees Mary. I live next door."

"What happened to Jamie's piano?" I asked. Mary blushed.

"He gave it to me because he had to leave, you know, on business. I must go now." She turned to leave, but before she could go, I gave her my business card.

"Please call us if you hear from him," I said to her back as she retreated to the house next door. "Do you get the feeling she's afraid of something?"

Clara nodded. "It sounds like Jamie isn't coming back to his house. What do you think, Josephine?"

"I think you're right. But I think he will contact Mary before anyone else." I decided Mary probably wouldn't call the police, and convinced Clara to give me a shove once I had one leg in the window. She pushed me up and I landed on my feet in a tiny bedroom, the only bedroom in the house. Hanging in Jamie's little closet were a few shirts and one pair of slacks. Below the shirts was a laundry basket piled high with dirty clothes. I bent down and gingerly sorted through the shirts and pants, checking all pockets. I pulled a folded piece of paper from a pants pocket, studied it and stuffed it into my pocket.

"He must have left in a hurry," I said to Clara as I opened the back door so she could enter the house. She shivered when she stepped into the cold kitchen, a small alcove off the living room. "Look at this stove, Auntie, only two burners. Can you believe it?"

"I wonder why he took the time to tell Mary she could have his piano," Clara said. "Let's go, it's freezing in here." I agreed, took a quick look at the modest little bathroom and then followed Clara out the front door. I held a hand to my forehead, shielding my eyes from the bright, but not-so-warm sun. Clara let out a little squeal.

"What's wrong…?" I asked as she came to an abrupt stop and I walked up the back of her boots. "Sorry." My eyes watered like crazy. I wiped them with my sleeve and was finally able to make out a couple of familiar shapes standing in our way, dressed in uniforms, holsters and somber faces. Deputy Sheriff Denise Lund spoke first.

"Ladies, here for a visit?" Her face looked like an impenetrable glacier, or maybe it was just the contrast of Deputy Sayer's warm brown skin and softer features next to her cold blue eyes.

"Yes, as a matter of fact we were here for a visit," Clara said. "We came to see our friend, Jamie, but it seems he's not home right now."

"You two entered Mr. Gianelli's house even though it was locked, and he isn't here to let you in," she said in her usual flat tone. I took a step forward.

"Our friend, Jamie, told us to come in and make ourselves comfortable any time. Friends do that," I smiled, "and Jamie is a good person and a good friend."

"OK, we get the point," Deputy Sayer said, "but this house is not at your disposal. See that you don't enter it again. I think you ladies are aware of the fact that Mr. Gianelli is wanted for questioning." I glanced at my shoes and kept quiet. We walked a few steps, climbed into the truck and quickly left the two deputies behind. I drove in the direction of the Watsonville market. Clara suddenly got a case of the giggles.

"What's so funny?"

"You, with one foot stuck in the window. Even Mary couldn't keep a straight face. We should visit her some time."

"I was planning to stop by and see her on our way home," I said. Clara smiled. "Look at this, Auntie." Clara took the folded paper I pulled out of my pocket. She opened it slowly, stared at it for a moment and then looked at me, confused.

"This is a pilot's preflight check list? What's that about?" she asked.

"I found it in the pile of dirty clothes in Jamie's closet. See the initial in the top right corner? It looks like J. G. to me."

"Jamie Gianelli...so what?" she said, frowning. "Jamie is a pilot?"

"I don't think Jamie likes to fly," I said, stuffing the yellow paper into my pants pocket. "Remember when he told us he just liked to be with his dad? But it could belong to...."

"Joey!" Clara's eyes were big and she was still nodding her head as I pulled into the market parking lot. "You think it's Joey's, don't you? The year and month are around the time he took his last flight. I wonder...."

"I wonder if Myrtle can remember the date. She's pretty good at stuff like that," I said and climbed out of the truck. We walked up to the store entrance and paused. "But if it is Joey's, how did Jamie get it? And why would he be carrying it around in his Levi pocket?"

"You searched his pants?" Clara asked as Robert fell into step with us. He looked more than curious but kept his mouth shut.

"Hi, Robert. You remember my Aunt Clara."

"Sure. How are you, ma'am?"

"Fine, thank you. Would you be a good boy and fetch me a big bag of Kitty Krinkles?" Robert was the kind of guy who lived to serve his customers. He took off for the pet food aisle without complaint. "He's a nice boy when he minds his own business," Clara said. I told her Robert was a lot like us, always curious, loved a good mystery and was usually a fountain of information, although I didn't see how he could possibly shed any light on our current problem. Finding Jamie wasn't going to be easy.

"That was fast. Thank you, Robert." Clara checked the bag of cat food for tears and then dropped it into the cart. Robert smiled politely, turned his head to look at me and rolled his eyes. I squelched a giggle as he answered a page from the intercom to please open lane three. Clara and I cruised the aisles, found what we needed plus a few calorie-loaded items we didn't need, and headed for Robert's register. Ahead of us, an elderly woman bent over her checkbook, filling in the blanks with great care. Finally, the transaction ended and she shuffled out the door, trying to keep up with the teenage girl carrying her groceries.

"You should have a special line for old people like that," Clara said. Robert and I looked at each other trying not to laugh. Clara enjoyed good health and vigor but was older than she would admit. If there was such a thing as an old folk's register, she was perfectly qualified to go there.

"Josephine, look at the lovely plants," Clara pointed to the floral display at the front of the store near the briquettes and other BBQ necessities. "I have a maidenhair fern like that one but not as green. And those azaleas are beautiful, especially the white one." I agreed and Robert said he liked the cactus with the red flower on top.

"The plants are local. Evergreen Nursery delivers once a week…every Sunday," he said.

"Is Gabe the delivery boy?" Clara asked.

"Yeah, how did you know?"

"He's everywhere, hardworking fellow, you know."

"Uh-huh. He came in this morning wearing a real shiner, black and blue and a cut under his eye," Robert winced at the thought, finished bagging and dropped the loaded sacks into the cart. Clara bit her lip.

"Maybe he tripped over a potted plant," I said. "He's a big boy. He'll be all right." But I knew Clara would worry, I just didn't know how much. Robert usually walked me outside and loaded my groceries into the truck, but it was an extra busy Sunday. No time for my friend to go missing from his check stand. I loaded the truck, climbed in and fired up the engine.

"Dear, if you don't mind, I'd like to stop at…."

"Evergreen Nursery." I said. She almost smiled. Ending each other's sentences was becoming a habit. "I noticed a couple of delivery trucks in front of the building when we were on our way to Jamie's. He might be out delivering plants by now."

"All we can do is try. Oh look, San Marcos Canyon. Turn, turn," she said, both hands patting the dashboard. "I see one truck. Isn't that him? That's Gabe, loading the truck. Park over there." She was out the door before I could put on the parking brake. She galloped across the lot as fast as her elderly body would take her.

From the opposite direction, a thick middle-aged man holding a clipboard emerged from the nursery's main entrance. He wore a frown as he headed toward Gabe's truck. I caught up to Clara, and we both greeted Gabe just before the frumpy fellow in green overalls arrived.

Gabe peeked at us from under a Giants baseball cap. He put a hand up as if to shield his eyes from the sun. His smile faded quickly when the older man arrived by his side, asking what was taking him so long.

"Uncle Mo, I'd like you to meet my friends, Clara and her niece, Josephine."

"Ladies, the name's Morton. Now, Gabe, what's holding you up?" he asked as his unattractive features turned red. He handed Gabe a clipboard, wheeled around and marched back to his building...out of hearing range.

"Where's your first delivery, Gabe?" Clara asked. He glanced over his shoulder.

"A flower shop in Aptos, but if you need to talk to me, I can meet you up the road at the berry farm." He pointed his thumb south, shoved the last two leafless potted trees into the back of the delivery truck and took off in a hurry. We were right behind him when he turned into the empty berry farm parking lot. In the summer, on any given day, two dozen or more big rigs would be lined up, waiting for a load of strawberries, blackberries or raspberries. Gabe walked over to Clara's open window.

"So what's going on with you two?"

"We heard you were in a fight," Clara said, reaching out and lifting his cap a titch before he could object.

"It wasn't really a fight, just one lucky punch."

"What does the other guy look like?" I asked.

"You just met him. He can be a jerk at times, but I can handle him. What are you ladies doing today?"

"Actually, we're looking for a friend, "Clara said. "Do you remember our conversation at Alicia's house? I told you about Joey Gianelli, my childhood friend." Gabe nodded. "Well, his son is in some trouble, but we can't find him."

"That would be Jamie," Gabe said. I was stunned.

"You know Jamie?" I asked. He nodded. Clara finally closed her gaping mouth and almost smiled. "Did you know the police are looking for him?" Gabe nodded, jerked his head around as if he heard something and scanned the parking lot again.

"A couple of sheriff's deputies came snooping around the nursery last night asking questions. I guess Mo decided to put them on Jamie's trail. He told the deputies Jamie hated his dad for deserting the family by pretending to be dead for six years. Then Mo told them he caught Jamie stealing, and that did it. Deputy Lund looked ready to string him up right there."

"As soon as the deputies left, I confronted Mo with the lies he told. He turned red, hauled off and hit me. He's my uncle so I didn't fight back, but I wanted to." Gabe's jaw tightened. He screwed his head around and searched the lot one more time.

"So what happened to Jamie? Where is he?" Clara asked, reaching up to touch Gabe's cheek. He let her. Suddenly I saw Gabe as a motherless boy who had just gone up against the only family he had, a jerk named Morton.

"Jamie used to help out at the nursery when he was between cabinetry jobs. Mo treated him like he was a one-legged cockroach, always on his case to hurry up. Gilbert, the old foreman, usually stuck up for Jamie. Jamie's smart, knows a lot about plants and trees, but he doesn't get around fast enough for my uncle. Anyway, Jamie was sitting in the back of my delivery truck when the deputies arrived."

"Why was he in your truck?"

"Because we had just pushed his old pickup over a cliff in another county. I had to check in at the nursery before I could take him where he wanted to go, and that's when the officers showed up. When the cops left, Mo hit me and I took off in the delivery truck with Jamie hiding in the back. My eye was really hurting and I was steamed, but my uncle had given me a good reason to get out of there in a hurry. Later, Jamie and I laughed about the stupid cops. They couldn't find him when he was only a spitting distance away. I couldn't believe we got away with it. When I got home that night, Mo didn't say a word."

"Where is Jamie now?" Clara asked.

"He's fine and that's all I'm going to tell you so you don't get into trouble, and something tells me you two aren't shy about getting involved in stuff like this." He winked. "Ouch! I shouldn't do that." He put a hand over his eye.

"Does Jamie know who murdered his father?" Clara asked, her voice soft as butterfly wings.

"He thinks he knows something, but he won't tell me what it is. Maybe someday I can help him figure it out…you know, like a detective." He smiled, "Ouch."

"When is your next delivery to the Ocean Street florist?" she asked.

"Tuesdays and Saturdays, unless there's a special order."

"I'll see you Tuesday," Clara said. He tipped his hat, turned and walked to his truck. "Life is so unfair. I wish I could help those poor boys."

"Don't worry, Auntie, we'll do our best to help them." Actually, Jamie was about Morton's age and far from being a "boy" at fifty years of age, but to Aunt Clara he was a boy in trouble. She would have made a wonderful but over-indulgent mother given the opportunity.

That evening I slipped the flight plan between the pages of Computers for Dummies, located on a bookshelf in my bedroom, and slept well.

CHAPTER 12

My alarm went off, signaling an impending sunrise and the need to prepare my body and soul for work. I had already loaded my truck with ladders and paint the night before, but images of miscellaneous items, such as camera, level, tarps, tape, etc., popped into my brain, begging to be bagged and loaded into the truck. I tiptoed around the house collecting supplies, put them into large canvas bags and parked the bags near the front door.

Squeaky bed springs alerted me. I looked up at the loft where Clara stood in her floor-length flannel nightgown. "What's all the racket down there?" she leaned against the rail and yawned.

"Just me getting ready for work, Auntie." I headed back to my bedroom closet for a portable electric heater I thought we might need at the library. I carried it to the front door with Solow at my heels, his way of trying to convince me I couldn't get along without him, and could he please, please go to work with me. Somehow, he always knew when I was leaving. New construction was no place for a dog, but I don't think he understood my explanation. "Don't worry, dear, I'll take Solow for a walk later. I don't need to catch the bus until 8:30."

"Auntie, you're walking to Aromas to catch the bus?"

"Certainly, Maurie needs me at the shop," she said, stumbling down the stairs.

"It's far! It's hilly and it's already eight o'clock." Personally, I never walked to town because I wasn't sure I would have enough energy left to walk back home, and Solow would never make it. A mile isn't much on the flat, but flat didn't exist in or around Aromas.

"If you hurry and get dressed, I'll give you a ride to the main bus stop in Watsonville. It'll cut your bus ride to Santa Cruz in half." I dropped a shoebox full of pencils, chalk and large erasers on the pile by the door. "I'll take this stuff out to the truck while you decide if you want to go with me." After three trips, Clara had had her coffee and decided she would like to hitch a ride with me. I took Solow for a short walk while she dressed. Once we were on our way, the "new job" jitters subsided.

Clara talked about Jamie and Gabe all the way to Watsonville. I told her we would work on finding Jamie later. In the meantime, I needed to be focused on creating murals at the library.

"I'll pick you up after work around five-thirty...at Candy's shop," I said, braking at the curb. Clara climbed out and joined a colorful group of spike-haired youth sitting and standing on public benches as they waited for the Santa Cruz County Transit Bus. She turned and waved to me just before a couple of shaved-headed teens behind her mimicked the "Queen's wave."

I drove one block and parked next to Alicia's green Volvo station wagon on the ground level of the library's nearly empty, three-story parking structure. Kyle roared to a stop, dismounted his yellow Honda motorcycle and pulled off his yellow-flamed helmet exposing spiked red hair, several piercings, tattoos and a shy smile. He wore black-leather everything accented with spikes and chains. I guessed it was his way of fitting in as a talented artist in his second year at the University of California, Santa Cruz.

"Hi, Kyle, old buddy. Let's carry a few things inside." I pointed to two large canvas sacks full of tools, rags and empty recycled containers. He yanked the sacks out of the truck bed and headed for the building. I followed him, carrying my purse and a folder of sketches.

"Excuse me, ma'am, this building is...oh, you must be Joan," Mr. Atwater said, staring at my outfit dappled with paint smears. He stepped back and held the door for us.

"Josephine. My name is Josephine," I smiled, trying not to look at the white blubber spilling out from under his too short t-shirt. "This is Kyle, one of my artists."

"Great," he said, "and there's a woman inside waiting for you."

"That would be Alicia, my other artist."

"I'm off to our wharf project." He wheeled around and headed toward a cluster of carpenter's pickups, easily identified by their built-in mega-toolboxes. I watched him pass by the trucks and squeeze his large body into a dirty white compact car.

Kyle followed me through the doorway and across the first floor to the main entrance. We passed by a persimmon-colored wall on our left, a fuchsia wall on our right and a celery-green wall behind the black metal railing of the staircase. Alicia met up with us as we examined a twenty-foot-long, thirteen-foot-high convex entry wall. It was our primary challenge and the wall visitors would see upon entering the building.

"Hi, guys," she said. "I've been all over this place. The upstairs reading room is especially nice. I love the giant windows and views of the city. They're installing the shelves today." We looked around. No shelves on the first floor—not even a carpet.

"Like what's all that noise upstairs?" Kyle asked.

"Guys with hammers and saws," Alicia laughed. "Shall we empty your truck, Jo?"

"You two go ahead. I need to study this wall—you know, placement stuff." I set my purse on the floor. Alicia and Kyle brought in a steady flow of ladders and equipment while I tried to concentrate on measurements and dividing up the work according to my sketch. When the truck was empty, we spread tarps and arranged our supplies. I sectioned the wall into four, five-foot-wide by thirteen-foot-high spaces. Alicia mixed up four shades of gold.

I assigned the space at the far end to Kyle. He filled the penciled-in area with a pale gold background while Alicia painted the space next to his with a slightly darker gold and I did the next one a shade darker. Kyle trotted down to the other end and finished the fourth section with the deepest gold. The wall needed to dry, giving us a perfect opportunity to break for lunch.

"There's a nice little Mexican restaurant down the street...." I hadn't finished the sentence before my painters dropped their brushes in water and headed for the back door. I hurried to catch up. We rounded the building, passed by the post office and a couple of shops and found ourselves at the end of a line. The restaurant was packed and the waiting line spilled onto the sidewalk. My phone rang.

"Hi, David. What are you doing today...and why are you laughing?"

"I'm at the post office. I looked out the window and saw some people I know rushing down the sidewalk. One of them looked like you," he laughed, "and then I remembered your library job started today."

"We're waiting for a table at the Mexican restaurant. Why don't you join us? Oh, they found us a table...." I tried to keep up with my group as we wove our way through the noisy dining room and out the back door, ending at a table on the patio.

"Are you still there, David?"

"I'm two minutes away," he said. Minutes later he joined us on the breezy patio. I would have preferred a table inside, but we didn't have time to dawdle. Between the spicy hot food and David's elbow touching mine, I wasn't too concerned about the cold weather.

"Josie, what have you and Aunt Clara been up to? You're never home," David said.

"Aunt Clara and I were home yesterday, mostly. Where were you?"

"I drove up to Modesto to spend a little time with Monica and Harley. Harley had some studying to do so I took Monica to the park. They have this little train she loves to ride—that is, when she's not chasing squirrels or picking up caterpillars." He smiled when Alicia and I harmonized with one long "a-a-aw."

"What is Harley studying?" I asked.

"Driver's test."

"Oh-h-h," I smiled. Alicia cocked her head to one side. "Harley has to take the test every year because he has too many traffic tickets," I explained. I could have said speeding tickets, but I wanted to spare David.

"Isn't he the insurance salesman?"

"Yep." I rolled my eyeballs and David looked ready to change the subject.

"Josie...how is Aunt Clara? Any news on her house in Oakhurst?"

"She left a message with her contractor Friday, but he hasn't called back. All we can do is keep our fingers crossed and hope it doesn't rain for awhile."

"What's the soil like, clay or sand?"

"Clay, I think."

"In that case it will probably take some time for things to dry out," he sighed.

"How's your snoop...I mean investigation going?" David asked as Kyle's eyes widened.

"Like, what are you investigating, Jo?"

"My Aunt Clara is looking into the murder of her friend, Joey Gianelli, that's all."

Kyle cringed, "the guy on the railroad tracks?" I nodded. "I didn't know it was murder."

"There are circumstances that point to murder," I said. "Even the police think so." David looked up at the clouds and Kyle bit into his burrito. Alicia wanted to know if we had any idea who murdered Joey. I had several suspects in mind but didn't mention them. Instead, I told my audience about our three days at Ben's cabin in the woods with no actual bathroom, bathtub or color TV. Alicia was shaking her head, looking confused.

"Jo, didn't you just tell us that Ben is a contractor? Why doesn't he build a bathroom?"

"Maybe he feels he's too old to start a new project. I don't know. Burr!" I shivered. We had ignored the sun's disappearance behind dark clouds until a slap of cold air lifted our paper napkins and plastered them against a lattice ten feet away. We quickly took our last bites, paid the bill and scurried back to the library, which seemed reasonably warm compared to the restaurant patio. I gave David the nickel tour of the place before he left us to our work.

We drew several meaningful historic icons on each of the four sections of wall, arranging them like a collage instead of a realistic scene. We copied our subjects from pictures ripped out of magazines and downloaded from the internet. The pictures of galleons, explorers, missions, and Native Americans would be copied onto the first two golden rectangles. The third and fourth sections would feature miners, railroads, vineyards, cattle, oil wells, Hollywood and Disneyland.

"Like, where are the strawberry fields?" Kyle asked me.

"Did I forget to tell you about the second mural? When all four panels of this mural are finished, we paint another mural on the other side of this wall for the children's story time area. That mural will feature agriculture, famous local people like Steinbeck and things like the Santa Cruz wharf and boardwalk." Kyle seemed satisfied, so I assigned each of us to a section, but I planned to rotate the assignments each day so our various drawing and painting styles would commingle into the bigger picture. The rotating began earlier than I had planned.

"Jo, you have a miner and his mule in this sketch. I'll draw the mule for you if you draw the mission for me," Alicia said, and so it went. We moved from section to section and finished about fifty percent of the drawing by four-thirty. We disbanded and went home or, in my case, to Candy's store in Santa Cruz. Clara beamed when she saw me coming through the back entrance and gave me a warm hug.

Josephine, you're early, but that's wonderful because we have deliveries to make." She let go of my arms and pointed to a row of arrangements standing shoulder to shoulder across the long counter top. Maureen finally looked up from her work at the sink. "Josephine, just the person we need. You gals go ahead and load the van. I'm almost finished with these roses." The poor woman looked frazzled as usual. "How about a lift to Laurel Street?"

"No problem. I'll drive you home and come back for Aunt Clara." Maureen added baby's breath to the yellow roses arrangement and handed it to me. I took it outside and set it in a box on the floor of the van. As I pulled my hands out of the box, a thorn caught my wrist, tearing the skin. "Ouch!" but no one was around to hear me.

"I'm ready," Maureen said, collapsing in the passenger seat. Her eyes were glazed and her wrinkly face drooped as she handed me the keys. I listened to her directions, drove ten blocks and parked the delivery van at the curb on Laurel Street in front of a modest apartment house. I looked up at the second floor window where a faint light backlit the crooked blinds. I jumped out to help Maureen, but she was already standing on the sidewalk, one hand on a light pole for support. Her eyes focused on my arm.

"You're bleeding, Josephine. Look, there's blood on your sleeve...and on your jeans, or is it paint?" I checked my arm under the streetlight; and, yes, there was blood. I wasn't sure if the blotch on my pants was paint or blood. Could one little thorn do all that? "Come along with me, dear." It sounded more like an order than an invitation so I followed her into a stuffy little entry drenched in yellow light from a forty-watt bulb overhead. We climbed a narrow metal staircase to the second floor where she inserted her key into the first door on the right. She pulled me inside, mumbling something about infections and tetanus shots. Surprisingly, her toasty warm apartment smelled like popcorn with a hint of oranges.

"Over here, Josephine," she said as she opened the door to the bathroom. She quickly cleaned and bandaged my arm and then walked me back to the front door. I got the impression she wasn't alone and wanted me to hurry up and leave so she could rest, or something.

I thumped down the stairs, dodged a couple of skateboarders screaming down the sidewalk, grown men actually, and jumped into the van. The drive through downtown Santa Cruz was slow. Pedestrians took their time crossing the street as panhandlers mimed and musicians strummed guitars. To the untrained eye, it could have been a holiday celebration, a street fair or a protest gathering. But I knew it was just the usual cast of characters. Block by block I made my way up Pacific Avenue to Water Street and finally turned left on Ocean. I parked behind Candy's shop and hurried inside. Clara's head popped up when she heard me.

"Well, don't you look comfortable in that rocking chair?" I laughed.

"I don't know why I'm so tired," Clara said, yawning as she stood up and hooked her purse over one arm. "Maurie gave me this list of addresses." She read the first one out loud as I fired up the delivery van and we headed into traffic. Minutes later I located the first address, grabbed the bachelor buttons neatly arranged in a ceramic bootie and handed them to a first-time father who could not get his grin under control. I was starting to enjoy the work as we took off for the next delivery.

"By the way, Josephine, how did you like Maurie's apartment?"

"It was OK, I guess. I'm not an apartment person. I'm used to having land and privacy, you know?" Clara agreed. "She keeps the furnace and lights on all day and I smelled fresh popcorn." My last words fell on deaf ears as Clara checked the delivery list and then pointed to a sign for Columbia Street.

"Turn at the next corner," she said. "Now, look for 3250…there it is, pull over." And so it went for the next five stops, leaving Dominican Hospital for last. We finally arrived at the hospital, hoofed it across the half-empty parking lot and up to the main entrance. We entered through the automatic doors, handed over two large arrangements to the volunteer "pink lady" at the front desk and turned to leave. I glanced into the lounge area where a half dozen people were waiting to visit their loved ones. A familiar-looking young woman, sitting slumped in a chair, caught my eye.

"Auntie, sitting over there, isn't that Angela?"

"Her head's down, but I think it's Angela." We walked to the other side of the room where the chairs were empty, except for one. "Angela, dear?" The girl looked up through red puffy eyes and smears of mascara. Clara dropped into the chair next to her and put an arm around the young woman's quivering shoulders.

"What are you doing here?" Angela asked, sniffling.

"Josephine and I are working, you know, delivering flowers. Now, tell me what's wrong, dear." Angela wiped her nose with her shirt sleeve and then stammered a couple of syllables. "It's OK, just spill it out," Clara said, handing Angela a tissue from her purse.

"There was blood everywhere. Like, all over his head and his face," her voice cracked.

"Whose face? You can tell us."

"My boyfriend and I…oh God, he's hurt and it's my fault," her head dropped down. She sniffled and wiped her eyes with the back of her hand. "I don't want to call Dad. He doesn't like

Duane." I scratched my head, Clara looked puzzled and Angela sighed.

"Like, I wanted to get married, but Duane wouldn't commit. We were arguing when he drove over the center line. Someone hit us coming the other way…there was a terrible noise and scraping and the car rolled over. I'm OK because I had my seatbelt on, but…." The tears began to flow again.

"What have the doctors said about his injuries?" I asked. She looked puzzled, as if she were seeing me for the first time.

"Have the doctors told you anything, dear?" Clara asked. Angela buried her head in Clara's soft shoulder. "It's going to be all right. Josephine will find out how he's doing." She waved for me to get busy and find the doctor. I felt like I had been running marathons all day, but I managed to trot over to the main desk, hoping to talk to the pink lady. Unfortunately, she was delivering the flowers we had dropped off. I looked around and then hurried down a wide hall, stopping at the first nurses' station.

"Excuse me. Can you tell me how to get to the emergency room?" Two out of three nurses looked up.

"All the way to the end of the hall, turn right through the double doors and follow the signs."

"Thank you." I fast-walked what seemed like a mile, zigzagging to the rear of the hospital. I finally found a nurses' station and asked about a guy named Duane who had been in an automobile accident.

"Are you family?" the nurse asked, sweetly.

"Not exactly, but…."

"I can tell you this much, once the doctor cleaned him up, all he needed was a few sutures. He's in X-ray right now. Just a precaution," she smiled. I thanked her and headed back to Clara and Angela. I found them chatting away like old friends, or like a grandmother and her granddaughter, which reminded me how lucky I was to have Aunt Clara in my life. Angela dissolved into Clara's arms when I told her the good news about Duane. Her flood of happy tears left a wet spot on the front of my aunt's jacket.

"Angela, would you like a ride home?" I asked.

"Yes…thank you, but I'm awfully hungry. Like, we were on

our way to dinner when…."

"We're starving, too, aren't we Auntie?" She nodded enthusiastically. We hurried outside to the van. Angela rode in the back on the floor between empty crates, and Clara pointed the way from the passenger seat. I drove a couple of miles to a sandwich place. Soon we were filling our bellies with hot corned beef, pickles and chips.

"Josephine, do you have a husband…or something?" Angela asked.

"I guess you would say David is my boyfriend. He's my neighbor and a very good friend. My aunt has a boyfriend too." Clara blushed like a thirteen-year-old but didn't offer any information about Ben. After we dropped Angela at her home and traded the van for my truck, I asked Clara why she hadn't talked about Ben.

"Benny's my dear friend, but I don't know how he feels about me. Until he adds on a real bathroom to his house, I'm not sure how I feel about him." I tried putting David and myself into Clara's predicament, but it didn't change the way I felt about him.

CHAPTER 13

Clara seemed to enjoy helping out at the florist shop, especially since Maureen was teaching her how to create some of the simpler arrangements. My mural at the library had several finished icons and was beginning to take shape. Alicia and Kyle were excellent artists and our styles blended together nicely. Things were going well, except when it came to finding Joey's murderer. As I drove Clara to the Watsonville bus depot Tuesday morning, she told me about her neighbor in Oakhurst who had lusted for her and her three acres. She didn't care for the old man but had considered selling her property to him. That was before the mudslide. She wondered if he still wanted to buy her land.

"Auntie, since you don't like your neighbors and it's hard to get someone to drive you into town, not to mention the cost of repairing the back of your house...."

"I know what you're going to say. Why don't I sell to my neighbor and move down here. It all sounds so simple, but I'm an old woman and I adjust to change slowly."

"I didn't think you did anything slowly," I teased, stopping my truck at the curb. "I'll see you at Candy's shop after work." She waved and joined the mixed crowd waiting for a bus ride to Santa Cruz. Minutes later I parked at the library and entered the building. I had arrived a little early and took the stairs to the second floor to see how it was progressing.

"Joann, good morning," Mr. Atwater said, halting his battery-operated screwdriver for three seconds. A couple of carpenters looked up from their hammering. I waved a couple of fingers and told the boss my name was Josephine, but he had already fired up his screwdriver. I rolled my eyes and headed back down the stairs.

Alicia and Kyle met me at the bottom.

"Hi, you guys."

"Good morning, Jo. How did Aunt Clara like working at the florist shop yesterday?" Alicia asked.

"Good enough to go back again today. Maurie is teaching her how to arrange flowers." The three of us congregated in front of the mural, critiqued our work and decided what to paint next.

"I'll paint the galleon...that is if you want me to," Kyle said.

"Wonderful. I have a volunteer. What would you like to paint, Allie?"

"The mission—I can have fun with that, now that you drew it out for me."

I decided to paint the gold miner and his donkey. We split up, Kyle to the first panel, Alicia to the second and I immersed myself in the third. By noon, we had finished our assigned depictions of California history. After lunch, we moved on to Father Serra, Shasta Dam and the Golden Gate Bridge. The average vignette, within a panel, measured approximately fourteen inches across, give or take. Mr. Atwater joined us in the late afternoon.

"I'm impressed," he said. "Looks like you'll finish this project before the deadline."

"If all goes well," I said and kept painting, hoping to apply the last touches to my bridge by four o'clock. I felt Atwater's eyes on my back. "Ten or eleven days should do it for this wall and a dozen more days for the other side."

"What about graffiti when you're finished?"

"We have a special clear coat for that," I said, wondering what kind of vandals target indoor walls in libraries. I painted in the cables on my bridge and added a hint of orange reflection to the choppy water below. I dropped my brush in water as Atwater walked away. Alicia and Kyle finished up and went home. It was only four when I decided to run over to Walnut Street and see if my folks were home before I joined Clara at the shop. I parked behind Mom's Subaru, hurried up the walk and raised a finger to the doorbell. Before I could press it, Mom burst through the doorway.

"Hi, Mom. What are you doing out here? It's cold."

"Sorry, honey, your dad's taking a nap in his recliner. You see, our hiking group met at Big Basin Park this morning and then we hiked down to the ocean."

"Mom, I can't imagine hiking that far...."

"That was only the beginning. When we arrived at the meeting place along Highway One, Wayne and the minibus weren't there."

"Wayne was your driver?"

"That's right. He would rather drive than hike. Anyway, we waited a long time and several people tried to call Wayne on their cell phones, but he didn't answer. After an hour of waiting in the cold windy parking lot, with only one bench and a trash can, your father decided to walk to Davenport and hail a ride for us. One of our younger members volunteered to go with him. Well, they headed south and half an hour later, Wayne showed up with the van.

"Did the guys make it to Davenport?"

"Not even close. And they were exhausted when we picked them up. I think Bob will sleep another hour. Are you going to pick up Clara at the shop?"

"Yep. Want to go with me?" Mom said she would love to, so we clambered into the truck. Two blocks from Mom's house, we passed by Maureen's unremarkable apartment building just as a delivery truck pulled out from the curb in front of us. I hit the brakes and the horn simultaneously. Mom didn't miss a beat, just kept talking as we skirted around the downtown area, and ten blocks later, fell in behind the same delivery truck with a potted fern painted on its backside. The driver parked near the back door of Candy's shop.

"Mom, have you met Gabe?" She said she hadn't, climbed down from her seat and introduced herself to the delivery boy. Gabe off-loaded his dolly full of plants and Mom followed him inside. Maureen greeted them and signed for the merchandise. Clara looked up from her arrangement, saw Mom coming and put down her shears.

"Leola, look what I'm making," Clara beamed.

"Clara, it's lovely! I didn't know you knew how to do that. I especially like the marigolds and lavender with the eucalyptus. Do you think the lilies go…?"

"Maurie wants me to be creative and that's what I'm shooting for. But I might pull out the lilies. What do you think?"

"Yes, I can picture it without lilies. Try some baby's breath," Mom suggested. Clara never liked being outdone by her older sister so she pulled out the lilies and substituted ferns. "Oh, that's perfect, dear," Mom said, "or you might try baby's breath." Clara pretended not to hear the last comment, turned and gave me a wink.

"How's the mural coming along, Josephine?"

"Fine, I think. Are we making deliveries this evening?" Maureen looked up from her work at the other sink.

"Only one delivery so far," she said.

"Good, I'll use my own truck instead of the van." I noticed Gabe heading for the door and walked him to his truck. "Have you heard anything from Jamie?" I asked. Gabe's jaw tightened as he kept his eyes focused on his delivery truck.

"Why would I hear from him? He's none of my concern." Gabe climbed into the driver's seat, fired up the engine and squeezed into the flow of traffic. Back inside, Maureen, Mom and Clara were yakking away in the backroom, unaware of a customer looking for help. I walked past the "old ladies' gossip klatch" to the front of the store.

"Can I help you, sir?"

"I'm just looking, thank you." The man moved away from me and down the aisle where he carefully examined a flowering cactus growing out of a ceramic boot. The man obviously didn't want attention, but he would stand out in any Santa Cruz establishment clad in his three-piece suit, polished shoes and precision-cut hair. I watched him leave the shop and climb into a white Crown Victoria parked at the front curb. I reasoned that undercover cops probably had mothers and wives and needed to shop for flowers like the rest of us.

My mind wandered back to the special times when David had sent flowers and times when he delivered them in person. He had raised the bar in so many ways with his thoughtfulness. I was still smiling when Mom found me.

"Thinking about David?" she asked.

"Mom, I think about lots of things...and David."

"Honey, your father and I were listening to KPIG news today on our way home." She paused and focused her eyes on her fingernails for a moment. "They reported that Jamie Gianelli was spotted in Santa Cruz last night, but the police lost him in the crowd downtown. Did you know there's a fifty-thousand-dollar reward for information on his whereabouts?"

"No, I didn't know." Suddenly I remembered the undercover cop, as my face flushed.

"What's the matter, honey?"

"It's just that Jamie's a nice guy, and Aunt Clara and I think he's innocent." Mom followed me down the aisle as I straightened a row of miniature roses and then checked my watch. "Wow, its five-thirty, time to close up shop." I turned the lock and the deadbolt on the front door and flipped the "Open" sign to "Closed." Maureen turned off all but one of the lights. She climbed into the back of the van and sat down between the rows of empty plastic crates. Mom climbed into the passenger seat. I delivered the ladies to their respective homes, circled back to Candy's shop and parked near the back door.

I unlocked the truck and Clara climbed in, still sleepy from her interrupted nap in the rocker. When she was settled in her seat, I handed her the unusually large arrangement of eucalyptus, lavender and miniature marigolds. It balanced in her lap and completely blocked her forward view.

"Wow, that thing smells. Where do we take it...and the sooner the better," I said, wondering whether I should turn right or left on Ocean Street.

"That "thing" is my arrangement. I made it for Angela."

"That's very sweet of you, Auntie, and it's very nicely put together." My sinuses were suddenly clear. I imagined the powerful botanical smells at work peeling paint off my truck.

"Now, you know where we're going," she said, relaxing her shoulders and then her eyelids. By the time we reached Morrissey Boulevard, she was sawing logs, big ones, as the arrangement teetered side to side on her lap. I parked two doors past Sal's house in front of three black luxury cars.

Clara grumbled when I shook her shoulder. I hurried around the truck, opened her door and took the bouquet. She slowly stepped down to the sidewalk and moved like a slug to Sal's front door. I sidled up to the door and pushed the bell with a free finger. A moment later, Patrick greeted us holding a half-eaten piece of pizza in one hand and napkins in the other.

"Patrick, how's it going?" I asked.

"Those must be for Angela, right?"

"Right...from my Aunt Clara. Is Angela home?"

"Yeah, but she's grounded," he said, trying hard to keep a straight face. "I'll give it to her." He reached for the flowers, but I held on as I peered inside.

"Looks like you have company tonight," I smiled. He didn't smile back.

"Dad's meeting with some lawyers...."

"Concerning your Uncle Jamie?"

"Yeah, I gotta go." Patrick pulled the basket of flowers out of my hands, ducked inside and shut the door.

"I wanted to talk to Angela," Clara pouted.

"Next time, Auntie." And if I knew my aunt, there would be a next time. "What would you say to tacos for dinner?" I asked as we settled ourselves into the cab.

"Bueno!" she laughed as we roared down the boulevard toward the nearest purveyor of tacos and such. We ordered tostadas and ate slowly, glad our day was winding down. I asked Clara what it was like to work in the shop all day.

"It was the strangest thing," Clara said between bites. "This man came into the shop twice, good dresser, looked around and left. The second time he even went to the backroom and watched Maurie cut flower stems. Every time I asked if he needed help he would say he hadn't made up his mind what he wanted to buy." She twirled her straw and sucked up some tea.

"Was he a little over six-foot, blond, about thirty?"

"Sounds like you know the man. Who is he, Josephine?"

"I think he's working in undercover law enforcement."

"So why would a detective hang around a florist shop?" Clara rubbed her chin.

"He might be looking for Jamie. Maybe because of Gabe or Maurie?"

"Maurie? What does Maurie have to do with any of this?" she asked. "Did I tell you I invited Gabe over to your house for a home-cooked meal? I gave him directions, but he said he didn't know when he would have the time. Mo keeps him busy everyday and half the night, poor dear," Clara sighed, bagged up our garbage and dropped it in the trash can on the way out.

We headed back to my truck wearing matching salsa stains. By eight-thirty, we were crunching up my gravel driveway. The headlights tagged Solow as he raced to meet us. David stood under the porch light holding Felix in his arms. Clara took the cat, carried him inside and gushed over him like all the other males she knew, while I enjoyed a long warm embrace from David. And then it was Solow's turn for lots of attention.

"You had a couple of visitors," David said as we settled into the sofa. "I think they'll be back." A vertical crease formed between his eyebrows, triggering a splash of stomach acid to wash over my tostada.

"Deputy Sheriffs?" I asked over the noisy western on TV.

"Lund and Sayer," he said, clicking to another channel and squelching the volume. I heard Clara in the kitchen on the phone with Ben, describing her "work of art" bouquet in great detail, giggling from time to time, sounding embarrassed at his praise. She finally joined David and me as we watched a movie about a sweet but wild and crazy dog that runs his master's household, grows old and dies. By the end of the movie, Clara and I were bawling. David yawned and went home.

I was startled by a knock at the front door. Solow stood up, tucked his tail and howled. The howls turned into barks. I followed him to the door holding his collar and cracked the door open.

"Oh, I thought you were...never mind." I said, opening the door wider and pulling Solow back so that Gabe could step inside. He quickly closed the door behind him and greeted Clara. Solow backed off his security duties, probably sensing the young man was a friend.

"Gabe, this is such a surprise," Clara said, crossing her hands over her chest. "What brings you out here late at night?" Her smile faded when she became aware of his dour expression. "Sit down, dear. Would you like a cup of....?"

"Not really," he said, sitting down on the sofa next to her. I sat in the rocker.

"What's up, Gabe?" I tried to act casual as my rocker gained a little speed.

"I came here tonight because I don't know what to do with...ah, Jamie," he whispered. He watched our faces and bit his lip.

"Don't stop now. You know where he is, don't you," I said. Clara's mouth hung open and her eyes didn't blink.

"He's close by. Like, I need to find a safe place for him. Santa Cruz is crawling with cops and if I take him home with me, Mo will turn him in for sure. In fact, my uncle is the whole reason they're looking for Jamie. He told them all kinds of lies."

"What about David's house?" Clara asked. I shook my head. "He's not going to break the law, not David." My rocker rocked and Clara cleared her throat.

"Dear, I've been thinking about staying with your mother for awhile. She invited me, you know. That would leave room in the loft for...."

"Gee, that's nice of you, Clara," Gabe said. "I'll go get him." He started for the door. I stood up and the rocker whacked me behind the knees.

"Gabe, are you saying Jamie is here...now?" I said, staring at the front door.

"Yep, out there in my delivery truck. Actually, he's been in the truck since five o'clock this afternoon. Jamie was staying at Aunt Maurie's place, but he almost got caught last night. Besides, I didn't want her to get in trouble if they found him." Apparently, Gabe didn't worry about me getting caught with a fugitive in my house. Even worse than that, what would David think about a man my age, who looks like Al Pacino, living in my house. I suddenly had serious doubts about helping Jamie. Clara cornered

Gabe at the door.

"I'll need a ride to Santa Cruz tonight if you leave Jamie here."

"Not a problem. Uncle Mo doesn't care if I'm late getting home. I'll get Jamie."

A minute later there was a light knock. I opened the door, grabbed Jamie's sleeve and pulled him inside. A crooked smile spread across his face, then faded. He looked disheveled and exhausted from bouncing around in the back of a delivery truck all day and half the night. I worried about what David would think if he discovered Jamie. Would he call the police? Since I couldn't think of an alternate plan, I helped Clara pack, hoisted her into the passenger seat and waved goodbye as the Evergreen delivery truck backed down the driveway.

As I entered the house, Jamie stifled a yawn and asked if I needed help with anything. I shook my head and marched up stairs. I spread clean sheets on the old bed in the loft while Jamie slowly hobbled up the stairs. He arrived in time to tuck in the last corner.

"Thank you, Josephine," he said as I turned, thumped down the stairs and grabbed the phone on the fourth ring. It was David.

"You sound out of breath, Josie."

"Yeah, I'm trying to catch up on my chores, making beds and stuff." My cheeks flushed with guilt. We talked almost an hour and I never mentioned Jamie.

CHAPTER 14

Wednesday morning was no different from any other morning except for the kah thunk, kah thunk, kah thunk reverberating through my house as a prosthetic foot tapped along the hardwood floors. I began to perspire, remembering I had a fugitive hidden in my house. I couldn't decide which would be worse, the deputies or David finding him. But the smell of bacon and fresh coffee wafting my way helped to transport my mind to a better space. I threw on a robe and padded down the hall.

"Good morning, Josephine," Jamie said, wearing a cautious smile.

"Morning. Did you sleep all right?"

"Sure did. The bed was great after spending two nights on Maurie's couch."

I couldn't believe my ears. He thought the old springs were OK, not to mention the lumpy mattress which I refused to replace because I didn't want visitors to get comfortable and forget to go home in a timely fashion. But I had to admit I enjoyed having Clara around the house.

"I thought I'd help out with breakfast," Jamie said, obviously trying to fill an uncomfortable silence. I wrapped my robe a little tighter and retied it. If only he didn't look so much like Al Pacino. "I'll give you the house rules, Jamie. You can cook anything you want as long as you don't let anyone know you're in my house. This secret could hurt me too, so please be careful. Don't take my dog for a walk or even stick your head out the door, OK?

"OK…ah, you don't want me to walk the…."

"No!" I poured myself a cup of coffee and popped a piece of crisp bacon in my mouth. "You can really cook!"

"I like to cook, especially for other people. Most of the time I'm by myself." While the bacon and eggs were still hot, I served up two plates, setting one in front of Jamie. I dropped bread in the toaster and poured more coffee. After a hurried breakfast, I rinsed my dishes and put them in the dishwasher. Jamie ate slowly, chewing each bite a zillion times like my grandmother used to tell me to do.

"Jamie, that was a lovely breakfast, but don't forget to put everything away when you're finished. My neighbor, David, has a key to my house, which I hardly ever lock; and he feeds Solow and Felix, brings in the mail and stuff like that. I don't want him to know you're here."

"I'll be careful." He crossed his heart and took another bite of toast. "I really appreciate...."

"What's that noise? Go, go!" I whispered, pointing to the hall. Jamie stood up, swiveled awkwardly, kah thunked across the kitchen and down the hall to my room. I heard a familiar tapping on the back door just before it swung open. David stepped into the kitchen, his face breaking into a smile as he twitched his nose.

"Smells good in here." He looked at the plate on the table. "Bacon and eggs—what's the occasion?"

"I just felt like having a nice breakfast, that's all."

"Where's Clara, still in bed?"

"Ah, she's staying with Mom for awhile," my cheeks burned. "David, if I knew you were coming, I would have cooked more food. I'm afraid I have to get ready for work now." I glanced at the clock on the wall for effect.

"Actually, I just came over to get the drill I loaned you a couple of weeks ago. My bookcase fell over during the night. Scared the stuffing out of Fluffy. I'm thinking we must have had a small earthquake. I've been meaning to screw the shelf to the wall ever since I bought it." He moved down the hall to the multi-use closet where I kept the vacuum, ironing board, a couple of folding chairs, toolbox, tennis racket and everything else that needed a place to be.

"Watch out...!" Too late. A basket full of ribbons and wrapping paper tipped off the top shelf causing a small avalanche.

David groaned, rubbed his forehead and began picking things up and arranging them on the top shelf.

"David, don't bother. I'll take care of that stuff after work." I said, squeezing past him.

"Am I holding you up? Go ahead and get ready for work. I'll let myself out." He gathered up an armload of candles, placemats and hand towels and arranged them on the second shelf between a pile of tablecloths and a stack of old photo albums.

I hurried through my shower and beauty routine, figuring David would be gone when I came out of the bathroom, but he had only finished organizing three shelves out of five. I rushed down the hall to my bedroom and shut the door. A little squeak popped out of my mouth when I realized I wasn't alone.

"Everything OK?" David asked.

"No worries," I yelled out, frozen and listening for David's footsteps. I finally relaxed enough to pull a pair of Levis and a paint-smeared shirt out of my dresser drawers. I stood beside the bed and motioned for Jamie to go into the closet. I closed the door behind him and quickly changed into my work clothes. With pounding heart and sweat trickling down my back, I tied my shoes, opened the door and sashayed down the hall, trying to look calm. David sat on the floor organizing the bottom shelf.

"David, the closet looks half empty now."

"That's how it's supposed to be—that way nothing will fall on your pretty head." He stood up and wrapped his arms around me. After a couple of kisses, I pulled away explaining that I needed to get on the road before traffic became unbearable. He said he understood.

"David, do you mind if I stop by your house after work?"

"Mind? I'll be looking forward to seeing you. I'll have dinner ready. Seven or eight?"

"Yeah, OK, I'm not sure what time because I'll probably have to deliver flowers…with Aunt Clara, of course."

"Don't worry about Solow and Felix," he said, shoving the ironing board into place and closing the closet door. He picked up his drill and ducked out the back door. I went back to my room and found Jamie sitting on the bed. I told him the coast was clear, but David might be back to feed the animals.

"Thank you, Josephine, for trusting me." I gave him a nervous smile and left. Soupy fog had me driving at a modest speed, straining to see ordinary things like an empty white car parked on Otis. I was listening to KPIG news when I heard the most ridiculous announcement. I couldn't believe my ears.

The reporter said, "Our sources tell us Mr. Gianelli will be in custody before the end of the day. Officers are warning citizens not to approach the fugitive as he may be armed and dangerous." I flipped over to a music station.

"What a ridiculous news report," I thought. Nobody knew where Jamie was. As I drove through the little farming town of Pajaro, I checked the mirrors to see if anyone was following me, but all I saw was fog. I told myself to stop stressing over the KPIG news report and get a grip. Finally, I arrived at the library and parked next to Kyle's motorcycle. He tucked his helmet under his arm; and we strolled across the parking lot, our faces acting as blotters, collecting the cool mist.

We entered the library. It was unusually quiet as our wet rubber soles squeaked across the concrete floor. We found Alicia studying sketches in front of the mural. She looked up when she heard us.

"Good morning. You two look a little damp around the edges. Isn't that fog something?"

"Why is it so quiet today?" I asked.

"It seems Atwater had to send his guys to the 'restaurant at the wharf job'…something about finishing the roof before it rains." Alicia pointed to a picture of the state capital. "This is what I'd like to paint today." I told her she had my blessing, and then assigned a cattle ranch to Kyle while I painted a vineyard. I was relaxed and lost in my thoughts when Mr. Atwater walked up behind us and examined the mural.

"I stopped by to see if you folks need anything…like pizza. I'm ordering pepperoni, Hawaiian and chicken pesto. That OK with you guys?" he asked.

As soon as we let Atwater know how much we liked pizza, he pulled a phone from his breast pocket and ordered. The last of my new-job jitters disappeared. Our boss liked our work, and he seemed to like us as well. We dropped our brushes in water and headed to the back of the library where the employee's lunchroom was located.

"Where is that country music coming from?" Alicia asked.

"Must be coming from the lunchroom," Kyle said. We turned the corner and stepped into a kitchenette filled with chrome and plastic chairs and Formica tables, illuminated by long florescent lighting tubes. It was very "retro" if you were old or "new and original" if you were a young person. Against the back wall stretched a countertop with mini-sink and microwave oven. A guy with a blond ponytail sat alone with his back to us. He heard us, turned his handsome head and smiled.

"Chester!" I said. Alicia and Kyle chimed in, still looking surprised to see our old friend.

"It's great to see you guys. Atwater told me you were working here," he said, beaming.

"Chester," Alicia said as we crowded around him, "it's lovely to see you again."

"Yeah, same here. I told Atwater I knew you guys, and he thought we should celebrate with pizza. I told him about the last three jobs we worked together," Chester winked at me, "and he said if he ever needs a detective, he'll call you, Josephine. Run into any murders lately?" he laughed.

"Actually, she's working on one," Alicia said. Chester shook his head in disbelief, but she insisted it was true. "Do you remember a couple of weeks ago, the man who was hit by a train?"

"Yeah, so what?"

"It was murder," I said, "and the victim was a friend of my aunt's. She won't rest until she finds out who put Joey on the tracks that night."

"Looks like you're in it as deep as your aunt," he said. I nodded.

"Like, when's the pizza coming...oh, never mind," Kyle said as he poured himself a Pepsi. Atwater set three boxes of pizza on the closest table. Chester shoved a second table against the pizza table, and we all sat down with plenty of elbow room for food and drinks. Kyle wasn't bashful about rummaging for the pepperoni pizza in the bottom box. Between the five of us and a couple of electricians who dropped by, the pizzas quickly disappeared. Only an occasional sliced olive or pepper survived. Alicia dropped the empty boxes in the garbage and wiped down the tables as we discussed past projects and Atwater told us about his wharf job.

"Chester's my subcontractor. His work is pretty good when he's not playing hooky."

"Hey, man, I've been working pretty hard on that restaurant of yours. But this library stuff is easy," Chester said. "I can install shelves with my eyes closed."

"I wouldn't do that if I were you," Atwater said. "This ain't your crumby old barn, ya know." Everyone had a good laugh. Suddenly I realized the country music coming from Chester's boom box had turned into a KPIG news bulletin. I choked on my iced tea when I heard the report.

"...apparently got away when the house on Otis was surrounded by officers." I giggled nervously, looked around at my friends and realized I was the only one listening to the report.

"Jo, are you OK?" Alicia asked. "You look like you need some fresh air." She pulled my arm. I stood up like a zombie, and she guided me out of the room. We walked around the corner to the staircase and sat on the bottom step. The walls swirled around my head.

"Jo, you look so pale. Was it the pizza?" I shook my head, wanting to tell her everything. She had always been a friend I could trust, so I decided it wouldn't hurt to tell her about Jamie, especially since, according to KPIG, I was no longer hiding him in my house.

"Did you hear the KPIG news report a minute ago?" I asked. She shook her head.

"I was listening to Chester's story about...no, I didn't hear the news."

"It seems my house was surrounded by police, but Jamie Gianelli got away," I whispered. "He was sort of staying at my house."

Alicia's jaw dropped. "What are you saying? What about

David? What's going on, Jo?" She looked so worried, I decided to explain everything.

"There's a fifty-thousand-dollar reward for information leading to the capture of Mr. Gianelli. They call him a 'person of interest' and say he's armed and dangerous. I think they want to pin the murder on him because of some lies Gabe's uncle told. Anyway, Gabe arranged for Jamie to stay at my house with Aunt Clara's blessing." Suddenly I remembered leaving Solow and Felix in the house with Jamie. Were they OK?

"Alicia, I have an errand to run."

"Can I help?"

"Actually, I need to check on Solow and Felix. You two go ahead with the pictures we discussed and I'll join you later." I hurriedly grabbed my jacket and purse, assured Alicia for the third time that I would be fine and dashed out the back door. Drizzly rain had replaced the morning fog, making for better visibility and speed until I was pulled over by a grouchy, rain-soaked, Highway Patrol Officer on a motorcycle. If my mind had not been racing through a dozen different scenarios, I might have seen him before he saw me. He came to my window. I rolled it down.

"Did you know you were doing seventy, ma'am?" Should I say yes, no, I'm sick, I just dropped off my cat at the veterinary hospital and he might not live, I was distracted by a UFO? Oh Lord, what do I say?

"Ma'am, have you been drinking?"

"No, but I dropped my chap stick." I pointed to the floor.

"Get out, please."

"It's raining."

"Yes, ma'am." I climbed out and stood in the rain. The officer ordered me to walk the line he had just drawn with his boot in the damp dirt. I walked it straight as a broomstick and he let me off with a warning.

I checked and rechecked my rearview mirror and speedometer all the way home. Minutes seemed like hours. Perspiration covered my forehead and my neck was stiff as a pair of new leather shoes. I drove up my driveway and parked next to a green car sporting a rack of lights on top and a sheriff's insignia on the door.

Officer Sayer greeted me at my front door, the door he was propping up with both hands.

"What happened to my door?" I growled, suddenly realizing a show of anger might cover up my actual fear, guilt and embarrassment.

"County Maintenance is coming to re-hang your door, Ms. Stuart. You can let go of the door, Officer Lund," he said. I had difficulty keeping my fierce expression because the whole scene struck me as something out of a Three Stooges caper.

My door hung by one hinge, the bottom one, with Sayer outside and Lund inside holding it up. Officer Lund stepped back as Officer Sayer lowered the door to the floor, as the bottom hinge made ugly noises, twisted and finally ripped the screws from the frame. Sayer smiled meekly.

"We have a few questions for you, Ms. Stuart," he said, brushing his uniform with his hands as if he had just performed hard labor. I walked across my flattened door and Solow greeted me on the other side. Felix looked down from the loft.

"Why are you in my house?" I asked as if I didn't know anything about the raid.

"We received an anonymous tip that a murder suspect was in your house," Officer Lund said. "A friend of yours, actually—a Mr. Gianelli." My mouth dropped open in feigned disbelief. I figured I deserved an Oscar for my exaggerated looks of shock, dismay and, finally, indignation. Unfortunately, Officer Lund wasn't buying it.

"Ms. Stuart, have you seen your friend, Mr. Gianelli, in the area?" she asked, her cold blue eyes squinty-sharp. I let my eyes roam around the room as if I were trying to remember.

"Are you telling me a criminal was in my house?"

"Actually, no. But we did receive a tip," Officer Sayer said. "The county will take care of all damages...."

"You mean there's more damage in my house?" My hands moved to my hips and my voice grew colder than snow cones in December. Solow took that moment to point his nose to the ceiling and howl like a bloodhound. I heard wheels on gravel outside and figured the county people had arrived. The officers made a quick exit as the maintenance crew stood by my flattened front door and politely rang the bell. I told Curly and Moe to come in. We toured the house together, discovering a broken window in my bedroom.

"Not a problem, lady," the bald guy said while Moe measured the window. "We'll send someone out with the glass."

"So, do you guys need me for anything?"

"No, ma'am," Curly said. And I was sure he meant it. The thinking and working would go much better with me out of the way, so I dashed out to my truck and climbed in. Instead of turning right on Otis, I turned left on a hunch. Otis was a dead-end road, cutting through all kinds of secret places to hide. Wild lilac bordered long stretches of road and most of the modest homes were set back far at the end of long driveways.

Light rain had started up again. Through my wipers, I saw a soggy fellow at the side of the road. I recognized his awkward gait about the time he recognized my red truck. I pulled over and motioned for him to climb in quickly. He slammed the door, and we roared over the wet blacktop, glancing at the rearview mirror every two seconds. My heart pounded in my ears as I circled around the cul-de-sac and headed toward Aromas. I already knew where we were going.

"Pull your cap down…and slouch down in the seat…put your collar up and pretend you're Harrison Ford in 'The Fugitive.' That's better. Now, what happened? Who tipped off the police and how did you escape?"

"I don't know who called the cops…not yet anyway," he growled.

"OK, what about that Houdini escape of yours?"

"It was the weirdest thing. This big old hawk flew smack into your kitchen window. It made the biggest thud and your dog was barking like crazy. I didn't see the bird hit the window and thought someone was out there so I hid for a while. Nothing happened so I looked out the window and saw this beautiful red tail hawk lying on the patio."

"You went outside?"

"Yeah, but I left the dog in the house like you said. I was thinking maybe the bird wasn't dead. I checked and it was dead so I decided to bury it. I found a shovel in the shed and dug a hole near the top of the hill behind the house. I was covering it up when I saw a couple of cruisers park down on Otis. Then a couple of black SUV's arrived and another cruiser. I started moving up the hill and then down the other side."

"I'm glad you didn't listen to me about going outside," I laughed. "I checked all the rooms and there wasn't anything anywhere to indicate you had ever been in my house."

"It was a close call, but what now?" he asked, shivering. I turned up the heat and headed north on Highway One.

CHAPTER 15

The afternoon showers had turned into a deluge—cats, dogs, and the works. At least Jamie and I were warm and dry in the cab with music and occasional news bulletins to keep us alert. San Juan Road stretched out before us, but we could only see two car-lengths ahead. Breaking the monotony was the occasional strand of lightning. Jamie squirmed in his seat.

"Where are we going, Josephine? You're not turning me in, are you?"

"Don't worry about a thing. We're going to visit Ben DeWald."

"But I haven't spoken to Ben since before Dad died...except for one phone call. Ben didn't even go to the funeral."

"Look Jamie, we don't have a choice at this point. I don't know what else to do with you."

"Just drop me at my house...."

"Are you crazy? I'm sure the police have your house staked out. We'll be lucky if we make it to Boulder Creek without getting pulled over, but if you're ready to give yourself up to the police, I'll drop you at the station."

"Ah, Boulder Creek will be fine...but it bothers me that Ben didn't go to Dad's funeral."

"Don't forget, your dad wasn't dead. Maybe Ben knew something you didn't know." I had surprised myself with the possibility, but my train of thought was interrupted by a steady stare from Jamie. "What's wrong now?"

"I haven't told anyone, not even Gabe, but I need to tell someone...."

"Hey, I really want to help you and Aunt Clara find the murderer," I said. "We need to share what we know."

"It's like this. For about five years now, I worked for Gabe's uncle whenever he needed extra help at the nursery. I did labeling, packaging, paperwork and stuff like that. Anyway, I was helping out last week, getting the paperwork ready for a big shipment of acacia and cypress trees.

Morton opened the office door and one of the inventories I was working on blew onto the floor. I bent down under the desk to get it and saw something way back against the wall…that I recognized," his voice had turned to a whisper.

"What do you mean, something you recognized?" I asked, swerving into the right lane before it was too late to exit the freeway. We were entering the San Lorenzo Valley where rain was as prevalent as taxes and that day the storm was a real gully-washer. Jamie's voice strengthened.

"It was an old leather backpack Dad used when he flew. He kept stuff in it like a jacket, his log and a few Snicker bars. Anyway, Morton saw me looking under the desk. Before I could stand up, he yanked my chair back and sent it rolling across the room. I never got a chance to look in the pack. His face was red, looked like he would pop a vessel, ya know? He told me I was wasting time and money, paid me for the day and I left.

"A few days later, when the deputies came around asking questions about the train accident, Mo told them lies about me. Gabe said he told them I stole money and hated my dad." Jamie made a fist and punched his other palm.

"Obviously Morton lied because you found the backpack, but how did he get your dad's pack in the first place? Did Joey and Mo know each other?"

"Yeah, they were in a business deal together a long time ago." Jamie scratched his head and then rubbed his forehead as if he had a headache. "I don't know how Mo got the backpack. It should have been in Dad's plane, wherever that is. Like I said, he always took the pack with him."

"Coincidentally, the train hit your father within spitting distance of Mo's nursery." I didn't believe in coincidences and Jamie looked like he didn't either. He swore to me he would find whoever killed his father if it took him the rest of his life.

"Is your brother actively looking for the killer too?"

"I haven't seen Sal since we went to the morgue together, except for a few minutes at the gravesite. Everyone there was shook up, kind of angry and sad and quiet." Jamie stared at a frayed hole in his well-worn Levis. "We barely talked."

"Jamie, I've been meaning to tell you something…about something I found, ah, in your house." He finally looked up in my direction. "Aunt Clara and I wanted to talk to you. You weren't home, but we were sure you wouldn't mind if we entered your house and that's when I happened to see this folded paper. It's a flight plan with the initials, J. G."

"I guess you want to know where I got it," Jamie sighed. "It was on the floor next to Dad's backpack. I grabbed it just before Mo slammed my chair into the wall. I don't think he saw me put it in my pocket." I was listening intently and almost missed the Scotts Valley exit. Then came Felton, Ben Lomond and Boulder Creek, all up to their knickers in rainwater.

"The last time I talked to Patrick, he said his dad had some lawyers working on your case."

"You really get around don't you? I guess Sal thinks I'm guilty," he dropped his head again.

"Maybe he thinks you're being wrongly accused. All your friends are behind you, like, my aunt and Gabe and Mary." He smiled slightly when I mentioned Mary's name.

"Mary seems like a nice lady. She said you gave her your piano."

"Yeah, she'll probably sell it. It's hard for her to keep food on the table. She has a couple of kids and a sick mother to take care of."

"Did you tell her where you were hiding?"

"If you think it was Mary that tipped the police, you're wrong. I didn't tell her anything," he said. "I wanted to tell her…."

"So, if Mary didn't call in the tip, who did?" I asked, as we turned left onto Big Basin Highway. Jamie just stared through the wet window at the endless, shoulder-to-shoulder redwoods lining the curvy road. We passed the golf course and a couple of minutes later made a left on Tinker Ranch Road. I stopped at the gate, dreading Ben's driveway with its rivulets of muddy water gushing down the hill like a broken water main. Jamie was immediately soaked head to toe as he unwrapped the chain and pulled the gate open. He hopped into the truck, and we charged up the slick mountain at a slippery speed.

Ben's pickup was parked beside the barn. "He's probably inside," I said, trying to sound cheerful for Jamie's sake. He just grunted, staring out the rain-streaked windshield. We climbed out of the truck and hurried to the open door. Ben was bent over his workbench. He looked up and smiled. He had to be surprised but did not show it.

"Jamie, good to see you. Hello, Josephine. I was just trying to glue this lamp base back together." He wiped his hands on his Levis and shook hands with Jamie. "Say, aren't you in some kind of trou…?"

"Yeah. They think I'm a 'person of interest.' If you don't want me on your property, Ben, I totally understand."

"My best friend's son is welcome anytime." Ben slapped Jamie on the back. "How have you been? You've been through a lot, I know. I'm real sorry." I checked out the broken lamp while the men caught up on the last six years. It sounded like they had been pretty close, years ago.

"Ben, I was wondering if Jamie could maybe stay here for awhile. Think about it before you answer. It's risky." Ben flipped his ponytail back over a shoulder and glanced outside.

"Who else knows he's here?"

"No one."

"Then we have no problem. If Gibbs or anybody comes over, we just stick you in the basement," he said, giving Jamie a pat on the shoulder.

"I didn't know you had a basement," I said.

"It's pretty well hidden. I think my grandfather made hooch down there. I store things in it."

"What about the barn? Isn't that a good place to store things?"

"My problem is that I have too much room and tend to keep too many things. I've been slowly sorting through stuff in the barn and taking some of it to the dump. I found this old lamp and decided to fix it rather than send it to the junk pile. See what I mean? I want to save everything. How's Clara doing?"

"She's fine. Making friends everywhere she goes."

"That's my gal. She thinks your mom has all the friends, but people really like Clara. She's a real 'kick in the pants,'" he laughed.

"What you see is what you get. That's my aunt."

"Where are you going now? I can make some tea," Ben said, following me to the door. I wished I had time to stay awhile and relax.

"I have to go to work," I said. Ben checked his watch.

"It's four o'clock...."

"Yeah, but I still have to deliver flowers with Aunt Clara. See you guys later." I climbed into my pickup, made a u-ie and slip-slided down the driveway to Tinker, then onto Big Basin Highway and south on One. Rush hour traffic was the worst, with wild weather, a couple of smash-ups and lots of stop-and-go conges-tion. I walked into Candy's shop a little after five, feeling like Wednesday had already been three days long.

"Josephine, here, sit down," Clara said, pulling a chair my way. "You look so tired, dear. How's Jamie?"

"He's fine. Have you been listening to the news at all today?"

"No, we haven't," Maurie said. "Is there something we should know?"

"No, nothing. Do you have anything to drink around here?" I asked. Maurie toddled over to the walk-in fridge where the flow-ers were stored, opened the door and grabbed a soda.

"Thanks. Looks like you two had a busy day."

"The two arrangements over there are mine," Clara said, pointing to a basket of mixed flowers and then to a vase shaped like a wine barrel, loaded with red, white and blue carnations which I imagined would be presented to a one-legged octogenar-ian at the VFW Hall.

"You can take me home first and then make the deliveries," Maurie yawned. We piled into my truck and took off, leaving Clara to keep the rocker warm.

"That was nice of you to let Jamie stay at your apartment, Maurie."

"Gabe is my son's nephew and the closest thing I have to a grandson. But when I finally found out who Jamie was, I told Gabe to come and pick him up. I don't need that kind of trouble," she crabbed. I thought, yes, she was definitely Mo's kin. He had Maureen's low forehead, dumpy build and short temper. But she had always been decent to my family and me, and I hoped it would stay that way. I dropped Maureen at her apartment and hurried back to the shop. I couldn't wait to get the deliveries over with so I could spend quality time with David.

The rain subsided into a heavy mist. Moisture magnified the yellow halo of light emanating from a city pole at the corner of Candy's parking lot. I loaded eight arrangements into the back of the van. Once we were underway, Clara volunteered to take the carnations into the VFW Hall. I delivered everything else, forging a trail around the city to avoid the downtown area. We ended on Walnut Avenue in front of Mom and Dad's house. Clara snorted, blinked her eyes open and looked around. She finally recognized the neighborhood and opened her door.

"Josephine, I want you to know how much I enjoyed staying with you."

"You can come back anytime. Jamie's gone...."

"What? Did you say he's gone?" She whipped her body around and scooted back into her seat. "Is he OK?" Where is he?"

"He's fine; and I'm not telling anyone where he is, not even you—so don't ask."

"I would like to come back to your house. Would tomorrow be all right?"

"Of course, Auntie. I'll pick you up after work."

"It's just that Bob and Leola are going up to Sacramento for four days. Bob's bowling team made it to the senior semi-finals," she said as she opened the door and climbed out.

"See you tomorrow. I'm glad you'll be coming back with me." I waved, waited for her to enter the house and drove away feeling a strong connection with an important member of my family. I drove south, checking the rearview mirror periodically, keeping track of the white Crown Victoria behind me. As I passed a row of Watsonville streetlights, I noticed the white Ford was still tailing me. He followed me through Aromas and onto Otis Road, but kept going straight when I turned up David's driveway.

I parked in front of David's house, hurried through the mist to his front door and walked straight into his open arms. Solow howled and whacked my calves with his tail.

"Josie, you're shivering." He pulled me close. "I almost gave up on you."

"Sorry, it's been a long day," I said with one last shiver. "I'm glad you thought to bring Solow over here. What time did you go get him?" I wanted to ask if he met up with the county maintenance people, but decided to keep still.

"I think it was about six. Isn't that his suppertime?"

"Yep. Can I help you in the kitchen with anything?"

"You can sit and relax. Everything's in the oven. Glass of wine?" I shook my head, knowing that half a glass would put me to sleep. I yawned as I collapsed into a captain's chair at the kitchen table.

"Have any tea?" I asked. He immediately put the kettle on and then pulled a well-done roast and two baked potatoes out of the oven. Next came a green salad from the fridge. The kettle shrieked and he made tea. The man could do everything and look good while he did it. I smiled as I watched him carve the roast. He looked up.

"What's so funny?"

"You remind me of my dad when you carve the meat. My Mom would tell him to cut across the grain and he would say he was and she would roll her eyes...lovingly, of course."

"You came from a happy family, didn't you?"
"Yes, I guess I did, and now I'm getting to know my Aunt Clara. You should see her flower arrangements. They're very original and she's so proud of them. Earlier this evening she marched into the VFW Hall carrying a red, white and blue bouquet spiked with a dozen or more miniature American flags and little green umbrellas."

"Umbrellas, sounds like a drink."

"I don't get it either," I shrugged. David loaded my plate while I babbled on, skirting around everything of real importance, like my house being raided by the police. He insisted on doing all the clean up after dinner while I stretched out on the couch in front of the TV. Next thing I knew, an hour had passed, David was sitting in his recliner reading the paper, the ten o'clock news had just started and I saw the front of my house, ringed with officers, on the TV screen. All my blood shot up to my face. David's chair sprung to the upright position as his jaw dropped.

"That looks like…."

"I know, my house," I said, "Sounds like you weren't home this morning."

"No, I wasn't." David jacked up the volume and gaped at the screen. I sat up straight, trying to think of a nice way to tell him what I should have told him much earlier. He cleared his throat. "I went shopping in Gilroy this morning." He turned his head in my direction.

"It's a good thing you weren't here, I mean, I'm glad I wasn't home," I mumbled.

"Josie, this is serious stuff. What are you involved in now?" he said, making it sound like I always hung out with guys on the lam.

"I'm not very involved. It's just that a friend dropped off his friend at my house because the man had nowhere else to go. Actually, he had already left my house to bury a dead bird by the time the police got there." I knew I wasn't making any sense and I wanted to keep it that way. But David kept the questions coming. "What was the 'person of interest' doing in your house?" he asked, eyes drilling into mine. I looked around the room. "Josie, I need to know."

"David, I told you, it was a friend who needed a place to stay." At that point, he gave up, shaking his head in disbelief and not wishing to hear any more explanations. We agreed to drop the subject, but when he purposely turned the TV to a wrestling match, I took Solow home.

I had hoped for quality time with David. Quality time with David was like warm sand between your toes, diving into cool water on a hot day, melted marshmallows on a stick, a kiss under the stars and all things warm and cuddly. At least I knew Solow loved me.

CHAPTER 16

I had successfully dodged most of David's questions about the raid on my house Wednesday, but Thursday morning I was bombarded with new questions from my friends at work. I could have refused to answer; but that would have been rude, so I gave them the short version I had given David the night before. Kyle and Chester gave me squinty-eyed looks and asked for names; but Alicia was silent, knowing I would eventually tell her everything. Chester finally gave up and went back to work upstairs.

"You guys did a great job on the mural yesterday," I said, still trying to lead them away from the "raid on my house" subject. By the time we sat down for lunch, I was ready to tell the truth except for the part about Jamie staying with Ben. Chester wasn't around and I had sent Kyle to the post office to mail a couple of my bills. I poured two cups of tea, sat down at the Formica table and accepted a tamale from Alicia's lunch. She usually packed extra food for Kyle because he was always hungry, and the soggy falafel he typically carried in his backpack was never enough. She watched me savor the first bite.

I told Alicia about Jamie finding his father's backpack and flight plan behind the desk at the nursery and answered half a dozen questions as I ate the last forkfuls of tender chicken and masa. When I turned my head, I saw Kyle standing at the door staring at my tamale crumbs.

"Like, did this Mo guy do the murder?" he asked.

"Maybe, but I haven't come up with a motive yet."

"So, like, is Jamie innocent?"

"Absolutely. Would I hide him if he wasn't? He's been investigating the murder on his own," I pointed out. Kyle looked at a sprinkler unit on the ceiling for a moment.

"But, like, how do you know he didn't do it?" He popped open a soda.

"I can tell," I said. But could I tell for sure? I had a few tiny doubts, but Clara was certain. "Aunt Clara thinks he's innocent too."

"Well that cinches it," Alicia focused on the sprinkler for a split-second. The discussion ended and the three of us walked back to our mural. We loaded our palettes with paint and began painting our interpretations of California history. Alicia asked me about my evening job. I described Clara's floral arrangements as I brushed in a tiny sailboat under the Golden Gate Bridge.

"Is she still stuck on Ben?" Alicia asked as she worked on Father Junipero Serra's robe on panel one.

"I don't exactly know. Aunt Clara told me she would hold out for a real bathroom if he asked her to marry him. But that's just talk. I think she's crazy about him." Kyle excused himself to the restroom where he wouldn't have to listen to girl gossip.

"Who's crazy?" Chester asked as he walked up behind us, checking out the mural and the gossip.

"Oh, didn't see you there," I said. "My Aunt Clara is kinda' stuck on a guy she went to school with, Ben DeWald."

"I know Ben. Good man. He helped me get the hours and experience I needed to take the state test, you know, to get my contractor's license. I worked with him right up to when his sister got sick and needed full-time care. Ben retired and moved her into his place."

"How did he take care of Beverly by himself?" I asked, remembering her elegant penmanship in her messages to Joey.

"Ben had help," Chester said.

"What do you mean? Who helped?" I suddenly knew who had taken care of Beverly, but I waited for Chester's answer.

"I remember the last time I saw Ben. Ran into him over at Home Depot about five years ago, right after I got my contractor's license. Asked him about his sister and he said he had an old friend taking care of her up at his cabin in Boulder Creek." I imagined Joey giving up everything, his unfaithful wife, his two sons and

his airplane to take care of Beverly, with Ben's blessing. I was beginning to see that there was no time or age limit on love. It could
happen at any age. I thought of Aunt Clara and smiled.

"Chester, did you ever meet Joey, ah, Mr. Gianelli?"

"Who's that? Is that the murder you're looking into?" he joked.

"Yes, and I'm making lots of progress. I have a flight plan that
will prove...ah, never mind. How's the upstairs coming along?"

"Just fine if I can get my contractor back on the job," Atwater
said, standing behind all of us, arms crossed. Chester gave us a
low bow, turned and followed his boss across the room and up the
stairs. Their voices disappeared into the general noise created by
carpenters using power tools. My friends and I turned our attention back to our work, painting non-stop through the afternoon
and leaving the building a little before five.

I stepped outside and looked up at the impressively large
moon surrounded by a trillion stars. I scanned the parking lot out
of habit, but there was not one Crown Vic in sight. I drove north to
Santa Cruz and arrived at the florist shop at five-thirty sharp. Clara
met me at the back door.

"Dear, I'm so glad you're here. Maurie didn't feel well and
took the bus home hours ago. At first, I didn't know what to do so
I locked the doors. I took a few orders over the phone and tried to
make them up myself." She pointed to three arrangements lined
up on the counter. "Derangements" was more like it. "Maybe I
should try again tomorrow when I'm not so tired." She looked
ready to dump all the flowers in the trash.

"Sit down, Auntie. You've been working so hard and these
bouquets are just fine. Maybe we should take the verbena out of
this one and add something that's not orange. What do you
think?"

"I'm too tired to think. Do whatever you need to do, dear." I
replaced the verbena with a few sprigs of lilac, made a few minor
adjustments to the second bouquet and left the third intact. Clara
told me about her day as I fussed with the flowers. Gabe had accidentally backed his delivery truck into the outside faucet by the
back door. After the plumber left, the undercover policeman
slipped on the wet floor where a customer had spilled water from

her flowers as she was leaving the store.

"I didn't have time to mop up the water before that fool fell and hurt his back. Good thing he's a policeman. I hear they have good medical coverage."

"What did he say?"

"Oh, you don't want to know. He was so angry. That'll teach him to come prowling around here all the time."

"Auntie, what was Gabe doing here? Doesn't he deliver Tuesdays and Saturdays?"

"He just wanted to talk to Maurie, but she'd already gone home. He stops at the store almost every day. How's Jamie? Did Benny call?"

"Jamie's fine and no, Ben didn't call. Did you watch the news last night?" Clara shook her head and raised one eyebrow. "Never mind, everything's fine. I guess we should get started on the deliveries." I hugged two arrangements in my arms, set them in the back of the van and came back for the third botanical masterpiece. Clara stood up, letting the rocker rock a couple of times on its own. "Clara, why don't you stay here and rest…."

"I've seen enough of this place. Let's go." She followed me out the door and climbed into the passenger seat. I fired up the van, her head dropped back against the headrest, her mouth opened slightly and minutes later her snoring was louder than the radio. I was about to deliver the third bouquet when Clara snorted, opened one eye at a time and looked around in the dark.

"Where are we, Josephine? These dim streetlights aren't much help…but this street looks familiar."

"You wrote down the address. Didn't you know who ordered the flowers?" I chuckled.

"No, but I remember he said they were for someone's birthday."

"It says right here on the clipboard, 1550 Gross Avenue. Does that ring a bell?" We pulled to a stop at the curb. Clara whipped her head around, eyes bright.

"I remember this house. It's Darla and Wayne's." We clambered out of the van. I opened the back and gathered up the remaining bouquet, the one featuring lots of blooming lilac. We walked to the front door and Clara rang the bell. Piddy paddy footsteps stopped behind the peephole. Fortunately, I was holding the flowers in front of the peeper. Darla slowly opened the door, gulped some air and stepped back.

"Happy birthday to you, happy birthday to you...," Clara sang and then gave little Darla a bear hug. I handed the flowers to her as she stepped back several steps and landed in Wayne's recliner. She spoke through the flowers on her lap.

"My, I don't know what to say, achoo! You did this...for me? Achoo!" Darla finally leaned forward, set the arrangement on the coffee table and pulled a handkerchief from her pocket. She removed her glasses as tears rolled down her wrinkly cheeks just before she sneezed again. "Wayne isn't here. He bowls."

"Yes, dear, we know. He bowls on my brother-in-law's team. How have you been, Darla? Is today your actual birthday?" Clara asked. Darla nodded. "I made this flower arrangement myself, but it was Wayne who ordered it, of course. He ordered a little bitty, ah, anyway, I put lots of flowers in it. I like to make fuller bouquets. It's my style," she beamed.

"Darla," I said, "I just want you to know that we're helping Jamie, and he's going to be just fine. The police are way off track. I have Joey's last flight plan, and I think it will help to prove that Jamie's totally innocent." She looked nonplussed with her jaw hanging. I wondered if she had understood one word of my little speech. I reached over and patted her skinny white hand. She finally smiled, took a deep breath and sneezed.

"Is that lilac?" Darla pointed, blinking and sniffling, to the purple flowers in the bouquet.

"Yes, I believe it is," Clara said with authority. "Josephine added them, but I did all the rest by myself. I'm sort of an advanced intern, learning the trade, you know."

"Would you mind taking the flowers into the other room, Josephine?" Darla said. I grabbed the vase, marched it over to the dingy little kitchen and set it down next to a dried-up half-eaten TV dinner on the counter by the sink. I returned to the sofa as Clara was winding up her spiel on floral design.

"And you have to be careful with roses. The thorns really

hurt." Clara pulled up a sleeve and showed off her wounds.

My mind wandered away from the scratches to another question. "Excuse me, Darla. I was wondering if you could tell me what business Joey invested in when he mortgaged your house. It might help us to find his murderer."

"It was a Watsonville business, but I don't remember the name. Joey told me we would make lots of money and to sign on the line. I was such a fool. It cost me my home," she moaned, dabbing her eyes with the handkerchief. "A nice big check came every month until Joey, ah, disappeared." Clara looked sad and I was feeling like I had already spoiled the birthday spirit we had initiated.

"Darla, I have an idea," I said. "Why don't we take you to dinner for your birthday?" She looked at me as if I had just recited the Gettysburg Address in Chinese.

"What a nice idea," Clara said, hoisting herself up from the sofa and hooking a purse strap over her arm. "Go put your lipstick on, dear, I'm starving." She helped Darla out of her chair and sent her down the hall to her room before she could utter a word. Darla trundled back wearing a brown corduroy jacket over her rust-color polyester dress. Her wrinkled lips were blood red. She had smeared rouge over her cheeks, and her slippers had been exchanged for a pair of sensible brown oxfords over wrinkly stockings.

"Where are we going, Josephine?" Clara asked, taking Darla's arm and leading her outside.

"I don't know exactly where, but one of you will have to sit on the floor in the back of the van."

"I'll do it—after all, Darla is our guest," Clara said. Darla tried to say she should, but Clara cut her off and scrambled into the back. I boosted Darla into the passenger seat, and we headed back into Santa Cruz. I heard Clara bumping around in the back with every turn, but the plastic crates kept her from sliding very far. I parked in front of my favorite Chinese restaurant. Darla and I dragged Clara out of the van and held onto her until she was able to stand by herself. By the time we reached the front entrance, she was hobbling along just fine. The lady at the front desk greeted us with a wide grin.

"You want table for tree?"

"Yes, three," I said.

"You want boot?"

"Yes, a booth would be nice. We followed the lady to a corner table and scooted into our seats. "Isn't this fun, Darla?" She almost smiled for the second time that evening.

"When Wayne left for Sacramento this morning, I never dreamed I would be out celebrating my birthday with you two, ah, friends."

"When you hang out with Josephine, you learn to live by the seat of your pants."

"What does that mean?" I asked.

"I don't know," Clara said. "I think I saw it in a movie. I think it means that life is never dull...isn't that Angela over there with that young man? And he looks very familiar."

"He should," I said, "that's Robert from the grocery store." I leaned to one side, trying to get a better look, just as a busboy went by with a pitcher of ice water. "Hey! Be careful," I said. The boy turned red and offered to get a towel. I shooed him away. Darla was already halfway to Angela's table. Her granddaughter stood and wrapped her arms around her bony little grandmother.

Robert slouched down on his bench seat, ignoring our stares from across the room. Finally, he raised a feeble wave. Clara sidled out of her seat and crossed the room to say hello. I followed her, feeling it would be rude and awkward to stay sitting alone in the booth.

"Gram, I didn't know you knew Clara," Angela said.

"Yes, we know each other. Have I met your friend before?" Darla asked, eyeing Robert.

"I'm sorry, Gram, this is Duane's little brother, Robert." Darla shook hands with my young friend, who looked like he would rather be under a bus.

"Nice to meet you, Robert. Who's Duane, dear?"

"My boyfriend, the one Dad doesn't like, especially after he crashed my car. I guess you didn't hear about that," Angela mumbled, looking at Clara for help.

"At least Duane wasn't hurt too badly," Clara said. Darla whipped her head around.

"You knew about the accident?"

"It's a long story, Darla. Maybe we should order our dinner now," Clara said, biting her lip. We said our goodbyes, repaired to our table and opened the menus. Our red-faced busboy arrived with a pot of tea and three sets of chopsticks. Darla asked for a fork, and he promptly brought her one while Clara and I speculated about Robert. Was he Angela's new boyfriend, her confidant or a temporary substitute for Duane? Robert was obviously younger, shorter, rounder and fairer than his brother, but maybe Angela liked his poignantly pessimistic personality. I couldn't wait to corner Robert at the store and pull the truth out of his cute little brain.

"Darla, dear, do your friends call you, Darla?" Clara asked, swirling her ice water with a teaspoon. Darla nodded, keeping her eyes focused on her menu. "I'm ordering a big bowl of won ton soup," Clara said. "It fills me up and doesn't cost too much."

"Auntie, you know you can order whatever you want…and you too, Darla."

"The won ton soup sounds good," Darla said, closing her menu.

"Three bowls of won ton soup," I said to the waitress, "and some chili oil please." Before the soup arrived, Clara gave our guest a good grilling. She asked poor Darla a zillion questions, like, how long have you been married to Wayne? Where is your family from? Do you still have your gall bladder? Have you ever experienced gout? The soup arrived and the chatter continued.

I yawned when my bowl was empty. Oh, what I would have given for another quiet evening with David.

"It's getting late, ladies," I yawned again. "I'm going to pay at the desk. I'll meet you at the van." Angela and Robert walked outside right behind Clara and Darla. By the time I arrived, they had already stuffed my aunt into the back of the van; and Angela was helping her grandmother into the passenger seat. I would have gladly taken Clara's place on the floor, but I was the only licensed driver aboard. Besides, the trip back to Darla's was only a mile.

From Darla's house, we motored across town to Candy's shop, swapped the toasty warm van for my freezing cold truck and forged ahead to the hills of Aromas with the heat on "high." At the top of my driveway, I cut the engine and immediately heard a howl and some deep-throated barks from inside the house.

"That dog sure loves you, Josephine, and I can hardly wait to see my little Felix."

Solow met us at the door—his tail wagging so hard his body was doing the rumba. Clara scooped up her cat and held him under her chin. We loved our animals but even better than that was the note I found on my pillow from David. I read it and blushed, read it again and pushed it under my pillow for a night of sweet dreams.

CHAPTER 17

Early Friday morning, before my alarm had a chance to startle me, Clara bustled around the house trying not to make all the noise she was making. Was that a ladder being dragged across the kitchen floor? What kind of glass object fell and broke? Who did she call on the phone that made her laugh like a teenager? I knew the answer to that one. It had to be Ben. Her laughter was getting closer. Finally, Clara peeked into my room with a phone and a smile.

"Good morning, dear. Ben would like to say hello," she shrugged, handed me the phone and slowly walked out of the room. I waited until she was gone, cleared my throat and spoke.

"Everything OK, Ben? That's good. We're fine. Actually, Clara's more than fine."

I rolled out of bed and discovered Clara giving Solow an ear rub in the hall a couple of feet from my door. I handed her the phone and she chuckled at Ben's next comment. I headed for the shower and when I finished dressing, I made breakfast. Clara had finally hung up the phone and sat at the kitchen table reading the newspaper. We ate breakfast, gathered purses and coats, and climbed into my truck. She had not mentioned Jamie once.

"How's the mural coming along, Josephine?"

"Better than I had estimated. We're a little ahead of schedule." I dropped her at the bus depot and met up with Alicia and Kyle at the library. They stood at the back door shivering. Something about the parking garage was different. I looked around. There were no four-wheel-drive pickups adorned with mega toolboxes and ladder racks, just a few dried leaves and Atwater's chewing gum wrappers blowing across fifty empty parking spaces.

"So what's going on, you guys?"

"Like, the door's locked," Kyle said. Alicia nodded as a late-model Ford pickup pulled to a stop close enough for us to feel the heat from its engine. Chester leaned out the window wearing his usual killer smile.

"Atwater sent me down here to tell you we're not working today. Apparently your phone was busy this morning."

"Can you let us in?" I asked. He frowned and shook his head.

"Nope. Atwater's in charge. He's taking a stand and refuses to work without pay."

"What do you mean, without pay?" I shivered. "You're kidding."

Chester shook his head again. "Remember the old woman with the donated check for two million dollars to help build the new library?" We all nodded and said we had read about it in the paper. "Well, she didn't have any actual money and her mansion is way under water. The bank foreclosed on her yesterday and the council called a special session last night. Atwater got the call around midnight. The city wants him to finish the job without pay. You know, wait until money can be raised from the sale of the old library."

"So what are we supposed to do now?" I asked, shivering in the meager morning sun.

"Don't worry. Atwater thinks they'll come up with the money by next week. It just means you get a three-day weekend. Politicians can always find money if you put the pressure on," he winked. I wasn't so sure, and how would I pay my painters if I didn't get paid?

"Don't look so worried, Jo," Alicia said. "We can wait to get paid." But Kyle looked like a bully had just taken his lunch.

"See you guys later. Gotta get back to the wharf job." Chester fired up his truck and left us standing in the cold. Kyle didn't say a word, walked to his motorcycle and roared out the exit into traffic.

"He'll be all right, Jo…."

"I feel awful. Today should have been payday."

"Think about this, Clara's at work, you're not and David lives next door," she smiled. "I'm going to catch up on some shopping. Let me know when we go back to work."

"Sure, I'll call." I had a check for Alicia and one for Kyle in my purse, but not enough money in the bank to cover them. I drove through Watsonville thinking about the best way to spend my newfound free time. I decided to pick up some milk and eggs on the way home. Naturally, I drove to my favorite market where Robert greeted me cautiously.

"How was your Chinese food last night?" I asked, trying to keep my smile to a minimum.

"I didn't want to go. Angela tricked me. She told me Duane was in some kind of trouble and to meet her at the restaurant. Duane wasn't there and then she tells me they broke up. Angela expects me to talk to my brother about how nice she is. I'm no good at fiction."

"I take it you didn't enjoy your date with Angela." We stopped walking as someone on the speaker asked for help on aisle five. Robert turned to answer the call.

"It wasn't a date," he said over his shoulder, probably glad to get away from my teasing. I picked up a few items and paid with credit. Robert wasn't around so I carried my two bags to the truck.

Driving toward home on San Juan Road, I saw the sign for Marcos Canyon Road and made a quick decision to turn. One block later, I parked between two delivery trucks in front of the nursery and walked in the front door. I looked through the glass walls of Mo's empty office and then at the rest of the expansive warehouse full of pallets, stacks of empty pots, shipping and wrapping materials and a lone forklift. The door on my left, about thirty feet away, opened and a man wearing a yellow hardhat hastened toward me.

"Hello there. Can I help you?" Hardhat shouted.

"I'm looking for Gabe."

"He's outside," the young man said, thumbing the open door behind him as he walked to the forklift and climbed aboard. I quickly made my way to the side door and outside to a couple of acres of potted trees and shrubs. I searched for Gabe among the rows, looking for movement behind the evergreen trees. I finally zeroed in on a pair of green overalls.

"Gabe, it's Josephine." He peered around a Monterey pine, clippers in mid-clip.

"Josephine? What...I mean, how are you?"

"Surprised? I was in the neighborhood, and I've been wanting to talk to you about something." I was finally close enough to him to talk without shouting. "Is your uncle here?"

"No, you'll have to come back in an hour if you want...."

"That's OK, Gabe. I wanted to talk to you, not Morton. Jamie told me he found Joey's backpack. The pack should have been on the plane, so where is the plane?" Gabe shrugged and slipped the clippers into a pocket. "Have you seen the pack?"

"No. Jamie asked me to find it, but it disappeared after he got fired. I looked under the desk and all over," he put his hands forward, palms up and cocked his head.

"Can you take me on a tour of the building?" I smiled sweetly.

"Mo's coming back in an hour. Guess we could do a quick look around the place." Gabe headed for the side door I had just used, but I suggested we go in the opposite direction. I charged ahead, looking for other entrances into the building. Gabe tagged along.

"Are these doors for the trucks?" I pointed to eight-foot by twelve-foot double doors on hinges at the back of the building.

"No. Nobody uses those doors. They're always locked," he said. One small cloudy window was ensconced in the metal wall to the right of the doors. I stepped up to the window on tiptoes, cupped my hands around my eyes and tried to see inside, but the film covering the glass eclipsed my view.

We continued around the building, using the paved drive that eventually connected up with the modest parking lot at the front of the building where I had parked my truck. On the east side, we passed three extra-large metal garage doors and one little side door, which I opened.

"Let's go around to the front. Mo doesn't like anyone in his office," Gabe said, grabbing my sleeve.

"It's OK. You go to the front and I'll meet you there." The door slammed behind me, shaking the wall that hosted high shelves crammed with manuals, files and comic books. A cigar box tumbled off the edge, hit my head and landed on the concrete floor, scattering dozens of old baseball cards. I looked around the glass cubicle with no ceiling. Not seeing anyone around, not even hardhat, I quickly scooped the cards back into the box, placed it on the shelf and turned to see Gabe and hardhat walking toward the office. Gabe looked worried. He motioned for me to get out of the office so I opened the side door I had used earlier. Suddenly I was paralyzed, except for my racing heart.

"Josephine, I presume?" Morton said, hands on hips, eyes squinted. In less than a nanosecond, my face went from ultra pale to rosy red.

"Sorry," I said, stepping back into the office. "I was, ah, looking for the restroom."

"I'll show you where it is," he growled. "What's your business here?"

"My Aunt Clara was thinking about buying a palm tree...."

"We only sell wholesale," he snapped as we walked through his office, turned right, passed by the three garage doors and fast-walked to the far wall of the giant steel building. He opened a narrow door smudged with handprints. I entered the tiny restroom, pulled a chain for light and took several deep breaths. Minutes later, when I had finally collected myself, I strolled up to the front entrance where Gabe and his uncle were having a discussion.

"You're wasting time, Gabe. Get out of here," Mo said. Gabe retreated to the potted trees outside while I tried for the front door. "Where are you going?" Mo asked.

"I figured you were busy...and you only do wholesale...."

"Gabe's the one who's busy. He has to load up his truck and get on the road."

"Doesn't he go to school?"

"Got his G.E.D. last year. Smart kid."

"Smart enough to go to college?"

"He's working so he can go to college in a few years. No student loans for him," Mo said.

"Gabe told me he wants to be a Marine."

"So, you've been talking to my nephew a lot, it seems. I know what's best for Gabe, so don't you encourage him and his wild ideas." Mo turned, walked into his office and shut the door. I thought about Gabe's stub-nosed mealy-mouthed uncle all the way home. Was it tough love for his nephew or just cheap labor? I suspected that no matter what Mo did, Gabe would find his way in the world.

I dropped off the groceries and helped Solow into my pickup. We trucked over to David's house and parked beside his Miata. I knocked on the front door several times. Finally, I walked over to his garage and peeked in the window. The Jeep was gone.

"There goes my day off," I said to Solow as I climbed back into the truck. We sat awhile listening to music from the radio, hoping David would return. Finally I gave up and drove to the end of his driveway, automatically looked both ways and saw an empty car I hadn't seen in the neighborhood before, an older white compact parked on the opposite side of the road. I turned left and left again and up my own driveway.

"Guess I should throw some clothes in the washing machine and maybe I'll clean the furnace filter...sorry old boy, I'll spend time with you later, don't worry." Solow thumped his tail on the seat beside me. I rubbed his ears and talked about David and Fluffy. Finally, we climbed out of the truck. Solow sniffed the air, the ground, the front door and then barked fiercely as we entered the living room. Suddenly an astonishing pain sprung from the back of my head. I lost my air, my sight and my equilibrium. All became black and quiet as I drifted away.

CHAPTER 18

My head throbbed, my ears rang and something was crawling on my neck. I swatted it with my hand and flinched when I felt how big and wet it was. I tried to look at my hand to see what I had squashed, but everything was black except for one slim crack of light inches away from my ear. I painfully turned my body and rested an eyelid against cold metal. At first my eye refused to focus and something sharp was pressed against my back. I pushed the object away, causing a cacophony of falling metal on concrete. Instantly I recognized the sound of garden tools thundering to the floor.

Putting two and three together, the smell of paint thinner and fertilizer plus the sound of crashing shovel, rake and hoe, it was obvious I was sitting in my own metal shed in my own backyard. My muddled and hurting brain couldn't tell me how I got there, but it did tell me I should leave before I froze to death or was bitten by one of the black widow spiders that made their home in the ten-foot square shed, firmly bolted to a slab of concrete.

Marty had planned to replace the old rusty, windowless shed, but never got the chance. I didn't replace it because it wasn't broken. Besides, it was almost rainproof and quite handy. I kept my paints and ladders on one side and garden tools on the other but always hated to go inside and pull things out because of the cobwebs. There would always be at least one fat black widow in a corner clinging to her web, daring me to disturb her.

My mind fluxed between past and present, the space shuttle and earth, but I finally landed solidly in the scary present. Realizing my situation was urgent, I pressed one squinted eye against the miniscule strip of light coming from between two flimsy metal doors held together in the middle with a padlock. The jolt of light that hit my retina made my head throb like a watermelon being pounded by a jackhammer. But my hypothesis had been verified when I recognized the back corner of my house just five impossible yards away.

To the left of the back wall, a low, blinding sun made me pull back. I put a hand against the door and tried to stand. Halfway up my legs buckled and my tailbone hit the concrete. All I could do was try to clear my mind and stay out of the way of a zillion hungry spiders. Obviously, I had been ambushed and dumped in my own shed—but why? Did the ambusher plan to come back and finish me off?

I listened for Solow, but all I heard was ringing in my ears. I decided I should be quiet in case the thug or thugs were still on my property. I pulled my jacket tighter and prayed for a plan of escape. I must have blacked out for a while because the next time I looked for the narrow strip of light it was gone. Clearly, the sun had gone down. My teeth chattered like castanets. I found the crack with my fingers, ventured another look and saw only black. I started to turn away but a light flickered on in the little window in the loft, just fifteen feet away.

Two more windows lit up. A car door slammed and I heard muffled voices. I decided a thug would never turn on lights and make noise like that, so I made a fist and pounded on the metal door. A strangled call for help worked its way up my dry throat, over cracked lips and came out like a squeak. The next one was louder and still I pounded my half-frozen fists against the door. My calls for help turned into a scream and then I was quiet, listening to the crunch of feet on gravel and dry leaves. Jumbled voices and a bobbing light were coming closer and there was a familiar, sniffing noise just inches away from my feet. Solow let out one of his best ever howls, long and deep, like a basset with a broken heart. Tears ran down my cheeks as I tried to speak.

"Josephine...where are you?" David called.

"Here, David, in the shed," my voice was only a whisper, but somehow he heard me between Solow's howling and Clara calling my name.

"Clara, she's in the shed," David shouted. Clara told him to hurry, not to wait for her. David's reassuring voice sounded inches away and then Clara arrived.

"Dear, we're here. David's working on the lock. Hang on, honey," she sniffed between gulps of air.

"Someone locked my padlock? I've never locked it and I haven't seen the key in years."

"That's OK, dear, don't worry. David's running back to his house for some tools. That man can really run. He was so worried about you. Just make yourself comfortable...."

"How did David know I was missing?"

"You didn't show up at Candy's shop and you didn't answer your phone so I called Leola; but, of course, she's in Sacramento so Maurie called Gabe. He drives awfully fast, but maybe he was just worried like the rest of us. He picked us up around 6:30, took Maurie home and then drove me out here. He had to leave right away...you know that nasty uncle of his."

"And David...?"

"Oh, I called him as soon as I saw the mess."

"What mess?"

"Someone went through all your drawers and left the whole house in a big mess. David called the police and then Solow wanted to go outside. We heard him howl and followed him out here, and now we need to get you out of this horrible shed," she sighed as car doors slammed a short distance away.

"Officers, over here," Clara shouted. Moments later I heard footsteps and a couple of familiar voices. Flashlight beams bounced light all around.

"I'll get the jaws of life," a husky male voice said after Clara had explained the situation.

"Ma'am, are you injured?" the woman officer asked.

"I'm OK, unless I die from spider bites."

"Josephine, Officer Sayer is back with the jaws. He'll get you out," Clara said. "David, I don't think we'll need that hacksaw after all." Something snapped, the lock hit the ground and the door squeaked opened. Officer Lund and Officer Sayer each took a hand and pulled me to my feet. Clara brushed cobwebs off my shoulders with one hand and dabbed at her tears with the other. David put his arm around my back and helped me across the backyard. Solow's head was touching my ankle all the way to the front door. The pain in my head slipped into seclusion as my joy escalated. I was alive and David was helping me into a chair when I saw the mess.

"Oh my…" I felt like fainting, but I wasn't that lucky.

"Don't worry, Josie. Aunt Clara and I will clean it up for you." Clara nodded energetically.

"Ma'am, do you know what they were looking for?" Officer Sayer asked.

"Are you kidding? My computer's old, my jewelry's fake and I don't even own a Blueberry, Blackberry, iPod, whatever." I couldn't think of a single thing a burglar would want. Officer Lund asked if I needed medical assistance and I said I didn't. David looked at me carefully.

"Are you sure, Josie? Maybe I could take you in for a checkup?"

"I'm fine." I said as I focused on the sandwich and hot tea Clara had just set on the little side table next to me. After countless questions and lots of snooping around, the officers finally left. While I finished my sandwich and tea, Clara ran a bath for me. It was only nine, but I was exhausted. I sat in my hot bath until it became lukewarm, checking my body for bites and trying to think what I owned that someone would want to steal. I came up with zilch in both categories.

Finally, I pulled on my flannel pajamas and a robe and curled up on the sofa to watch TV with David. Clara leaned against the upstairs railing with the phone at her ear.

"Josephine, Ben wants to talk to you. Do you feel up to talking?" I nodded. She thumped down the stairs and handed me the phone.

"Hello, Ben?"

"Hi Josephine. Cat just told me what happened. Are you feeling better?"

"Yeah, I'm fine, mostly. Aunt Clara is a wonderful nurse."

"Jamie wants to talk to you, so make some excuse and go to

your room. He says it's important." I didn't like the sound of Ben's voice. It sounded way too serious. I carried the phone down the hall to my room, which looked like it had been turned upside down by a small herd of mischievous orangutans and listened for Jamie's voice.

"What's this all about, Jamie?"

"I hear someone roughed you up and searched your house," he said. "I guess you know what he was looking for."

"I think I walked in on a burglary, that's all."

"Maybe, maybe not. What did you do with that flight plan you found at my house?"

"I stuffed it in a book in my bedroom. Are you saying someone would do all this to get that one piece of paper? I find that very hard to be…."

"It's possible. I'd love to get it back. Did you happen to notice the number in the lower right-hand corner?" Jamie asked.

"No. Why?"

"Where it says, 'number aboard' there's a number two. Two people went up in that plane."

"Well, if it wasn't you or your brother, who was it?"

"I have no idea," he said. "That flight plan was the only proof I had that someone else was in the plane with my dad, and that Dad's backpack was found under Mo's desk at the nursery. I want you to keep your doors locked, OK?"

"Yeah, I can do that. In fact, I feel really creepy and violated from this attack. I'll lock the doors for sure."

"Anyone else know about the flight plan?" Jamie asked.

"Of course not…just Clara and Darla, oh, and Alicia. Maybe David, I can't remember. Oh yeah, Chester and I think Mr. Atwater was listening. Did I tell Gabe…? Who did you tell?"

"I haven't told anyone," he said, "and don't you tell anyone else. Now, where did you hide the flight plan? See if it's still there. I'll hang on." I put the receiver on the bed and took a couple of steps to the pile of books some jerk had thrown on the floor. Right on top of the pile was, "Computers for Dummies." I picked it up, heart racing, flipped through the pages and came up with nothing. I stepped back and sat on my bed, stunned. A voice shouted from the phone on the bed beside me. I picked up the receiver and told Jamie the bad news.

"Are you sure? Did you look under the bed? Try looking...."

"Jamie, I'm sorry. I don't see it, but I'll do a good search tomorrow. I really don't feel...."

"I'm sorry. I know you've been through a lot. Get some rest and call me in the morning." He hung up. My head pounded. Did someone actually take the flight plan? I could think of no other explanation. I heard footsteps coming down the hall. David peeked into the room.

"Are you all right, sweetie?"

"Sure. My head is hurting less than before," I smiled.

"Someone's here to see you. I called my friend, Dr. Padilla. She's a dentist, but I figured she might be able to tell if you have a concussion."

"She's here now?"

"Yeah, she's listening to Clara explain the difference between a good flower arrangement and one that makes you sneeze," he grinned. I rolled my eyes and followed him to the living room where a dark-eyed beauty sat on my sofa. Her hair was long and shiny black, she didn't have an ounce of extra fat anywhere and there was no wedding ring on her finger. I hated feeling jealous, but I couldn't help it. To me, this friend of David's looked more like a model than a doctor. She stood when I approached and shook my reluctant hand. David introduced us.

"I understand there was a break-in and you were injured," she said.

"Yes, but I'm feeling better now," I smiled at David, keeping track of his gaze.

"If you don't mind, I'll just shine this little light in your eyes." She pointed the light in one and then the other and then moved her hands all over my head, pressing gently now and then. When she found the sore spot in the back, tears came to my eyes.

"Quite a lump. I'm afraid you might have a slight concussion. A cold pack will help bring down the knot on your head. David, dear, maybe you should stay here for a couple of hours and make sure she's all right. If she becomes dizzy, disoriented or unconscious, take her to the hospital immediately." David said he would stay and gave me a wink.

"Thank you, Doctor," I said.

"Anything for a friend," she said and left my house like the perfect cloud disappearing over the horizon. David closed the door behind her and headed into the kitchen for a sack of frozen peas. He wrapped the bag in a tea towel and positioned it behind my head.

"How's that, Josie?"

"Perfect, and thanks for staying," David began surfing the channels. Solow cuddled up on my feet, and Clara rocked Felix in her lap. My head still hurt, but I finally felt almost safe.

CHAPTER 19

Saturday morning I heard voices. I opened one eye trying to sort out where I was, what planet, which country and was it summer or winter. Because of the pain in the back of my head, I imagined or dreamt I had been the losing contestant in a Friday night boxing match with a grizzly bear.

Slowly, as I moved in and out of light sleep, facts and images penetrated my sorry brain. Joey's flight plan fluttered through my mind and set my heart to a faster beat. Images of black widow spiders gave me the creepy-crawlies and thoughts of freezing limbs made me shudder under my sheet. But I could not conjure up an image of the perpetrator, the person or persons who hit me and locked me in the shed. Clara tapped on my bedroom door.

"Dear, are you awake?" she whispered.

"Um, sure, is David still here?" I opened the other eye and focused on a pile of books strewn on the floor. My bowling trophy and a framed photo of Mom and Dad topped the pile.

"He left around midnight, right after we put you to bed. It's almost ten o'clock now, and the weather is lovely. How are you feeling?"

"Like a snowplow mistook me for a pile of snow."

"Take your time and rest, dear. I made eggs and biscuits, but we can always warm them up later." Nothing scared me as much as Clara's cooking, but it was a sweet gesture on her part. I knew the food would be much worse reheated so I let her help me into my robe and slippers. She steadied me as we trundled down the hall to the kitchen. After two cups of thick coffee, a couple of rock-hard biscuits and a mess of dry scrambled eggs, I felt stronger and my ears stopped ringing.

"Auntie, the living room is all put back together. Thank you. I remember worrying about it last night. I'll clean my room today and everything will be back to normal," I smiled.

"You don't think they'll come back, do you?" she asked, biting her lower lip.

"No, they won't be back." I knew the thugs wouldn't be back. They had what they came for. I speculated on who knew about the flight plan and would have the audacity to break into my home. Alicia…no. Darla…no. Clara? David? Gabe? No way. And then it occurred to me that one of my friends might have told someone else.

"What's the matter, dear? Is your head hurting?"

"My head's fine. I'm trying to sort things out, like who hit me yesterday." I rubbed the knot on the back of my head as I shuffled down the hall to get dressed. When I came back to the kitchen, the dishes were in the dishwasher and Clara was sweeping the floor.

"Auntie, take a break, you've been working for hours. Besides, I want to tell you what the thief was after…what's that noise? Who's there?" I cringed and stepped away from the door as it swung open and David entered.

"You look like you just saw a ghost, Josie," he said and gave Clara a hug as they exchanged subtle worried looks. I took a couple of steps toward David and received a warm, snuggly bear hug. We all sat down at the kitchen table for another round of coffee, David at my right shoulder flipping through the newspaper and Clara across from us.

"I'm so glad the color is coming back to your face, dear," Clara smiled. "Now, what were you going to tell me about the thief?" David let his paper drop.

"It's nothing…."

"Come on, Josie. If you know something, tell us, please," David said. He put an arm around my shoulder.

"You two already know about the flight plan I found at Jamie's house…."

"I guess I do, now," David said.

"Well, I'm not supposed to tell, but I talked to Jamie on the phone last night. He thinks the burglar was after Joey's flight plan." I watched Clara's mouth drop open and heard David catch his breath. "It was hidden in a book in my bedroom, and it's gone."

"Are you sure?" Clara gulped, one hand covering her mouth.

"I'm sure. I put the books back on the shelf a few minutes ago and looked all around for it." We sat in silence until the phone jolted us back to the moment. Clara robotically picked it up.

"For you, Josephine," she said, handing me the receiver. David's head was a couple of inches from mine and I could almost feel his curiosity. I stood and walked to my room as Jamie asked me again about the flight plan.

"Can't find it. I looked everywhere."

"OK, we have to accept the fact it's been stolen and move on. I talked to Gabe on the phone this morning. He said his uncle rescinded the charges against me, and I don't need to turn myself in. I'm anxious to find the thief; but right now, I'm committed to helping Ben with a project. I'll try to get down to see you in the next few days so we can compare notes."

"I'm glad you're not a 'person of interest' anymore. Call me when we can get together." I hung up the phone and trotted back to the kitchen table. Two sets of eyes glommed onto me.

"I have some good news. Jamie isn't wanted by the police anymore."

"Isn't that wonderful?" Clara cooed as she cuddled Felix in her arms. David smiled briefly and said he had to leave. We hugged and he walked home.

"And Jamie was calling from where?" Clara asked.

"He's been staying at Ben's." Clara nodded as if she had suspected as much.

"Maybe we should pay them a visit," she said, brightly.

"Sure, if they invite us." I wasn't about to travel over forty miles to Boulder Creek unless it was for a good reason. "You mentioned Oakhurst a few days ago. We have time if you still want to go."

"I do need to check on my property, but I'll buy the gas. Are you sure you feel up to going, my dear?" I nodded and told her I needed a break from work.

"What's wrong at work, dear?"

"We're not getting paid. It seems the city doesn't have the money. I feel like I'm letting Alicia and Kyle down, especially Kyle. He needs every nickel to pay rent. He rode off in a huff yesterday, but I couldn't give him a check unless I got paid first." I took a sip of my bitter coffee and winced.

"Josephine, there's something I want to show you in my room." She set Felix on the floor. I followed her up to the loft where she opened her old-fashioned suitcase and pulled a large Zip-lock plastic bag out of an inside pocket. The bag was stuffed with twenty and hundred dollar bills. "Take what you need, dear. I have plenty more." My jaw hit the floor.

"I can't take your m...."

"Oh yes you can. I'm not a freeloader you know. I've been waiting for the right moment to give you this money. Candice squanders everything I give her, but you're different. Now pay your painters and keep some for yourself."

"Thank you, Auntie. I'll send my friends their checks and make a deposit at the bank. I feel better already." We hugged and then I called Alicia and Kyle, explaining that the checks were in the mail and Monday would be a day off. I dressed, put the checks in envelopes and walked to the mailbox at the end of the driveway. Solow stayed close to my heels like a good protector. He watched me put the mail in the box and position the red flag. We trudged up the driveway to the house. As we entered, Clara handed me the phone.

"Hi, Mom, how's the bowling? Are they winning?"

"I'm afraid not. Their best bowler couldn't make it."

"And that would be?"

"Wayne, of course."

"Something must have happened at the last minute," I said. "Aunt Clara and I went to dinner with Darla Thursday night. She said Wayne had already gone to Sacramento. And it was her birthday, ta boot."

"That's peculiar. We haven't seen Wayne. Is Clara still working at Candy's shop?"

"Yes, but we'll be in Oakhurst Sunday and Monday. Aunt Clara needs to see her property. Information over the phone has been a bit sketchy."

"Have a lovely trip, dear. We'll be driving home from Sacramento Monday." She hung up. I decided to postpone the housework and run a few errands. We climbed into my truck and sailed down the road to the Watsonville bank where I deposited the money Clara had loaned me.

"Wouldn't it be fun to see Sal again?" Clara asked.

"What's on your mind, Auntie?"

"I feel he's holding information back from us. It's just a hunch."

"What do you think he's not telling us?

"If I knew that, I wouldn't need to drag anything out of him," she said, folding her arms.

"How do we get him to open up?" I pictured a scene from an old detective movie where one officer directs a bright light at the suspect's eyes and a second detective badgers him for answers. "We're almost there, Auntie. Have you come up with anything?"

"There's the turn. Better get in the right lane, dear. OK, now park behind the Mercedes." I stopped at the curb and we made our way to the front door. I rang the bell and Angela opened the door wearing black leotards and a gray knee-length cable-knit sweater. She didn't cringe or back away from us, so I figured we were finally getting to know each other. Clara stepped up and gave her a hug.

"Is your dad home?"

"Actually, he's busy with a, ah…client."

"We can wait," Clara said as she walked into the living room and plopped down on the sofa. "We have all day," she smiled. I sat beside her and Angela hurried upstairs to find her father. We heard voices and finally Sal thumped down the stairs wearing a weak smile.

"Ladies, I'm working with a client today, but I guess I can give you a few minutes." He turned his head to glare at Angela standing at the top of the stairs. "What can I do for you?"

"Did you know Jamie isn't wanted by the law anymore? Morton dropped the charges," I said. "And we found out that your, ah, father had a passenger in his plane the day he disappeared." Sal sat down in a large high-back chair facing the sofa.

"I knew about my brother. But what's this about someone being in the plane with my dad?"

"I had the flight plan for the day he, ah, flew…away. The box at the bottom of the form had the number two written in it which means two people were in the plane." I was nervous and couldn't think of anything else to say, and Clara was no help. "I'm wondering who that other person could have been. You told us it wasn't you…."

"It wasn't me, or Jamie, or Ben." Sal scratched his head as he paced the room. I was ready to give up and go home, when he finally cleared his throat to speak. "I'm thinking it could have been this old man Dad met at the VFW. He called the guy, Curly. I remember him as skinny and bald, and he had no family. Dad used to invite him over for dinner once in awhile, but Mom finally put a stop to that. Said the man smelled like old cabbage. I was a teenager and thought he smelled like a sweaty athlete. Didn't bother me."

"Do you remember his last name?" I asked. Sal shook his head.

"Just Curly. That's all I remember. Sorry. Do you think he had something to do with Dad's accident?"

"It's a long shot, but we'll try to find him," I said and Clara nodded. "Can you think of anyone else who might have gone for a ride in the plane that day?"

"No, but Ben might know of someone."

"We'll check that out too. Thanks for taking time from your work." I glanced at Clara as she did a magnificent eye roll. "We'll be going now." Sal stood up just before my aunt and I pushed up from the leather sofa. "We can let ourselves out, thank you." He walked us to the door anyway.

Clara and I stepped outside and Sal closed the front door behind us. Everybody knew the Veterans of Foreign Wars Hall was located on Front Street in downtown Santa Cruz. There was no discussion about going there—we just went.

"Oh my, there's no parking here. Try the parking structure on the next block, dear. That's right, now turn right. Dark in this garage, isn't it?" We clambered out of the truck and beat a path across the street to the hall. The door wasn't locked so we entered. Ahead of us, at the back end of a long, dimly lit, high-ceilinged room, a handful of cronies were bent over their drinks at the bar. One of them looked up.

"Sir," Clara smiled, "we're looking for a friend of a friend...."

"His name?" the closest guy asked.

"They call him Curly," Clara said. "He was a friend of Joey Gianelli." An octogenarian at the other end of the bar straightened up and looked our way.

"Sounds like the Curly what died of exposure 'bout five, six years ago. Too bad 'bout Joey," he said. Another man agreed and another nodded his head and raised his glass. Then all the glasses were up as the guys said their praises to the ancient twelve-foot ceiling.

"Excuse me. Sir, did Curly have a last name...or any relatives...friends?" I asked. The man shook his head and then emptied his glass.

"See, the deal is, Joey brought Curly here on Friday nights 'cause we have a buffet. Guess he felt sorry for the guy. The man looked and smelled like he was one of them homeless people." Clara and I had heard enough. We left the building and after a chilly walk to the parking garage, we climbed aboard my truck.

"Seems we found Curly and lost Curly in one sad minute," Clara said.

"Yeah, I'd sure like to know how he died. Something about it doesn't set right with me."

"Careful, dear, there's a big white car behind you."

"Not again." I twisted my upper body and looked out the rear window. It was a big white Ford all right. Probably the same undercover cop, but I couldn't see his face. For safety's sake, I decided to head over to Candy's shop instead of leading the cop to my house again.

"You missed the turn, Jo."

"Not really. We're going to surprise Maurie since we're in the neighborhood," I said, unconsciously rubbing the back of my neck. I pulled into the back lot, parked next to an old Nissan and watched the Crown Victoria wiz down the street. We found Maurie and a new employee hustling to fill orders. The new girl looked startled to see us enter from the back door. Or maybe her spiked hair always shot straight up. Maurie introduced us.

"Molly, have you done this kind of work before?" Clara asked.

"I helped my grandmother pick and arrange her flowers when I was a little girl." So that was the sum total of her resume. At least she had a car and could drive Maurie home. I stood beside Maurie and watched her deftly fill a vase with roses, ferns and baby's breath.

"Maurie, you've lived in Santa Cruz a long time, right?

"All my life."

"Did you ever run into a homeless guy named Curly?"

"Huh? Are you joking?"

"No," I said. "It would have been five or six years ago that Curly died from exposure...."

"Oh, that Curly. I remember reading about him. Wasn't he found dead in an empty boxcar? It was winter and there was something weird, like the door on the boxcar wouldn't open. Wasn't even wearing a jacket." Suddenly my skin prickled. I looked at Clara's big eyes, grabbed her arm and eased her into the rocker.

"Do you remember where the train car was located?" I asked Maurie. She searched the ceiling for a minute.

"I remember. It was Watsonville. They showed a picture of the boxcar in the middle of a lettuce field on the front page of the Sentinel." Maurie went back to her arrangement as we hurried outside and clamored into my truck.

Without a word between us, Clara and I knew where we were going next. The Sentinel building was only a few blocks away, and I managed to find the one-in-a-million empty parking space. Clara dropped a quarter in the meter, and we entered one of the oldest and most reputable buildings in Santa Cruz. Only one out of the four front desks was occupied.

"How can I help you?" a young gal asked, stepping up to the window separating us. I leaned closer to the little "teller-window" and explained that we needed to see a front-page article from five or six years ago. She twisted her lips thoughtfully and asked for the subject of the article. I told her about Curly and she pushed a buzzer. An impeccably dressed older gentleman appeared and asked me the same question.

"The story was on the front page, had a picture of the box-car...."

"Yes, yes, it's coming back to me. Excuse me, ma'am. I'll do a quick search for you." He settled into a roller chair at the next desk and fired up the computer. A couple of minutes later, he handed over a copy of the story, fresh from the printer. I felt like my last name should be Holmes. Clara looked pretty happy too. We mumbled our sincere thanks as we made our way to the front door.

"What's that note doing on your windshield, Jo?"

"Good grief! I got a parking ticket," I kicked the front tire. "I can't believe this. We were only in there a few minutes."

"I guess a quarter doesn't go as far as it used to," Clara sighed, shaking her head. I stuffed the ticket in the glove box. Clara read the Curly article aloud as I drove a few blocks to my favorite café on Walnut Avenue. It was 1:30, we were starving and the place was packed. Clara finished reading the article as we sat on a bench waiting for our table.

"The deceased was identified as Griswold Stanton, Jr., known by his friends as, Curly."

"At least his name was impressive. I wonder how he ended up in the boxcar." I was having a hard time with the whole story— like the fact that the man had been dead in the train car for two weeks before he was found. The dates listed meant he had died around the time Joey took his last flight.

"Exposure was the 'cause of death.' Mr. Stanton was found lying in a boxcar with an empty whiskey bottle and no jacket."

"Does it say if this case was investigated as a murder?" I asked. Clara wagged her head and said she didn't know but kept reading. Finally, she folded the paper on her lap.

"I finished the article and they never once mentioned an investigation," she said. "He had no family and no permanent address. I think no one cared enough to look into the matter, poor soul. I think someone gave him a bottle, took his jacket and put him in the boxcar."

I agreed with my aunt and thought about where I would start

if I were investigating Curly's demise. The boxcar, of course. I hurried through my lunch and watched Clara fiddle with her chicken salad.

"I think we should check out the boxcars in Watsonville. What do you think, Auntie?"

"I think I'm ready to go. Where's the check?" She waved to our waitress. The girl plucked our bill from her pocket. Clara paid and we headed south to the lettuce fields of Watsonville.

We had commented many times on the long string of boxcars plastered with graffiti, parked on a third rail. The collection of cars was surrounded by lettuce fields and positioned halfway between the foothills and San Juan Road. Mo's building was two miles east and the ocean about ten miles west.

"Josephine, look—a dirt road leading to the tracks. Turn right, turn," Clara squealed, leaning into the dash. The long, narrow road separated one field from another.

"The sprinklers are on, Auntie." After two car-lengths of mud, I put on the brakes. "Look, the road is a mess. It's so narrow we'll be lucky to get out of here." Clara didn't protest. I carefully backed up twenty feet, cranked the wheel to the left, moved onto the side of San Juan Road and then shot forward into light traffic, mud clods flying. I knew we would be back to try again.

CHAPTER 20

Our Sunday plan was to go to Oakhurst and see for ourselves why Clara's house was not ready for habitation. She didn't seem anxious to leave Aromas, but she wanted answers from her contractor. If he were smart, he would stop asking for more money and get out of town before Clara showed up.

"Auntie, it's only seven and you're dressed, packed and ready to go?" I yawned my way into the kitchen, wrapped my robe a little tighter and turned up the furnace. I poured myself a cup of Clara's thick coffee and settled into a chair at the table.

Clara circled the table, biting her nails. She let Solow in the back door and dumped kibble in his bowl.

"Looks like you're ready to go home. Are you in a hurry?"

"I'm glad you asked, dear. Actually, Joey and Curly were on my mind half the night. I barely got any sleep. I thought we might check out those boxcars on our way to Oakhurst. What do you think?"

"Fine, but give me a little time to wake up and get dressed. What shall we have for breakfast?" I took a sip of java.

"We could stop and have a nice breakfast on the way, you know, Casa De Fruita or some place like that." She smiled as she cradled Felix and tickled his bald tummy. I couldn't believe my ears. Clara hadn't suggested eggs in a taco, bacon burritos or drive-through egg burgers. Maybe her fast food craze was wearing down.

"Wherever you want to go, Auntie. I'll be ready at eight." I dragged myself into a hot shower; and at 7:52, I bounced back to the kitchen dressed in Levis and a pink mohair sweater, carrying an overnight bag and a fake fur-lined rain jacket. I had already arranged for David to feed Solow and Felix while we were gone. Clara set Felix on the floor, pulled on her clear plastic rain boots and grabbed her suitcase. We stowed our bags in the truck bed and climbed into our seats.

"I hope it doesn't rain," I said as I backed down the driveway.

Our boxcar destination happened to be in the opposite direction as breakfast and Oakhurst. Clara interrupted my thoughts of breakfast by mentioning a white car behind us. I figured the detective was watching us again, and then I forgot all about him. After all, I had to worry about muddy roads and impossible parking.

We passed up the muddy road with my truck tire prints embedded in it. Half a mile further we found a slightly wider dirt road cutting straight across the fields to the railroad tracks and beyond. I parked behind a maroon minivan. We trudged down the road past a dozen or more parked cars. Even though it was Sunday, men and women wearing hooded sweatshirts and warm clothing were bent over in the fields, hacking the dirt with hoes between rows of young lettuce plants. I glanced over my shoulder and noticed a nondescript white car pulling to a stop behind my truck. Might be a fieldworker who forgot to set the alarm and woke up late.

"I felt a drop on my...oh great, it's raining," I growled. More drops hit my face as Clara pulled a clear plastic bonnet out of her purse. "Why did you bring your purse?"

"Just habit, I suppose," Clara said, tying the strings on her bonnet. I slipped a hand in my pocket to make sure I had my keys. They were there.

"Once we get to the tracks, we only have a few hundred feet to go," I said, feeling like we would be there in no time. Clara began to slow her pace, which slowed mine.

When the farm workers behind us looked the size of bumblebees, we made a right turn at the tracks. Clara and I tramped along between the rails, thunking on wood, then crunching on gravel. We thunk-crunched about a hundred yards until we finally reached our first boxcar.

"Not that one, dear, the brown car over there. It looks more like the one in the picture," Clara said, swerving around the first boxcar and heading for the fourth. It was big and brown with two-foot high swirly white scribbles, words and initials across two sides. I figured it wasn't worth deciphering. Like a few of the other cars, the door was wide open.

Suddenly the piddly shower turned into honest rain. Clara's upper half leaned into the boxcar. She asked me for a hike. I gave her a boost from behind.

"Why do you want to be in that dirty old boxcar?" I asked as a clap of thunder drowned out my voice. Clara snooped around the inside while I stood outside, examining the locking system on the doors. It was a series of long levers. Finally, I couldn't put up with any more rain and climbed into the boxcar. Clara yanked on one door, dragging it toward the middle.

"Call me silly, but I just want to know how it was for poor Curly," she said. "I won't close it all the way. That would be spooky." She reached for the second door and pushed hard. When the doors had only ten inches between them, she let go. "There's not much to look at in here, except for those dead bugs on the floor. Maybe Curly was drunk and didn't care about the dirty floor."

"Dead drunk is more like it. Did you hear something, Auntie?" Clara shook her head. "What I want to know is…why wasn't Curly wearing a jacket? It was winter. Nobody takes their jacket off on a cold winter night."

"Honey, someone probably stole his jacket. Maybe a hobo needed a new shabby coat, or a fieldworker took it…Josephine, did you hear something?" We turned to look through the ten inches between the doors. Bam! The doors came together and daylight was gone. Metal scraped against metal until the locking system was in place.

I sucked air like a guppy out of water. Clara backed up, leaned against the wall and slid to the floor. I heard pounding footsteps moving farther away. I leaned against the door and screamed.

"Come back! Let us out! There are people in this car. I'll report you to the police if you don't open this door right now…help!" I kicked the door and pounded it with my fists.

"We wanted to know what it was like for Curly," Clara sighed, "and now we know. At least they didn't take our jackets."

My eyes finally adjusted to the dark. Tiny cracks in the flat roof gave the equivalent of a five-watt bulb lighting the Oakland Coliseum—enough light to almost see one's own hand. At first, I felt like I was back in the shed with the spiders but remembered that all the bugs were dead. Why were they dead? Too much pesticide from the nearby fields?

"Are you OK, Auntie?"

"Yes, dear…I'm truly sorry…."

"It wasn't your fault. How could you know someone was out there?"

"Who would do this…and why?" she moaned.

"I don't believe in coincidences, Auntie. Curly died in a boxcar similar to this one. We're looking into his murder and this happens."

"Well, I know the wind didn't blow the doors closed. It took all my strength to pull those doors. Now I wish I hadn't touched them," Clara sighed.

"Don't worry, someone will find us," I said, trying to sound confident.

"Everyone thinks we're going to Oakhurst. No one's going to notice an old red pickup parked on a dirt road with the farm workers cars and trucks. I just wish we had your purse instead of mine. At least yours has a phone in it." I started laughing.

"Auntie, just imagine if we had the phone and I called David." Clara wasn't laughing.

"David, could you please come and get us right away? I'm sorry you're busy replacing the transmission in your Jeep, but we're cold and want to go home now. Just drive down San Juan Road until you see the long string of boxcars off to your left. We're in the fourth one down. It's brown and the door's locked. Please hurry, David. It's dark in here." Clara actually giggled. The more we giggled, the warmer we felt.

"Or I could call your mother. Leola, dear, I know you and Bob like to go rollerblading on Sundays after church, but Josephine and I would like to see you right away. Oh, it's not far, just a couple of miles south of Watsonville. Just look for the row of empty boxcars.

We're in the rusty brown one decorated with fancy white lettering. You can't miss it." We were howling by that time.

"Any food in that purse of yours?"

"Throat lozenges, that's all. I guess we should have had breakfast before we came out here. Maybe we shouldn't have come here at all," she whispered.

"I'll have a lozenge, please." Clara dug one out of her purse and put it in my hand. Minutes later my tongue was numb and my stomach felt as empty as ever. Oh what I would have given for an egg and bacon burrito.

"At least Solow and Felix will be fine," Clara said. "David's a wonderful guy."

"Yeah, and Ben's a great guy too. Why haven't you called him lately?"

"I miss him. I just don't know how he feels about me. I don't want to be too forward."

"It's the twenty-first century, Auntie. Be as forward as you want."

"Oh? And what's holding you back, dear?" We sat shoulder-to-shoulder on the plank floor with our jackets pulled tight. I didn't have a good answer to Clara's question. It was getting colder and I worried about her. After all, she was seventy-five years old.

"Mom is going to be so upset with us. She already thinks we're crazy, you know."

"Leola never understood my curiosity, but I don't let it bother me."

"Auntie, are you shivering?"

"Just a little. I think I'll take a walk." She leaned forward, balanced on her knees and I pulled her up from there. We each put a hand on the wall and began circling the rectangular prison. Rain pounded on the roof. I imagined the farm workers going home and my little truck being left all alone in the middle of a thousand acres of lettuce, unnoticed.

"Can you see your watch, Josephine?"

"Only if I push the light button...oh, light, isn't it wonderful? It's almost noon. Time for...never mind." French toast and hot cocoa crossed my mind. We huddled around the tiny watch light for a minute and then continued our walk.

For a while, we pretended we were bird watching and took turns describing all the birds we could remember seeing. When we ran out of birds, we described various gardens we had been to. I described some of the beautiful homes where I had painted murals, and Clara told me about the paintings displayed in the Oakhurst galleries. Eventually we felt warmer and sat down on the padding nature provided voluptuous women.

"Do you hear that, Auntie?"

"Yes, kind of a roar, and I feel a vibration." The roar became louder and the vibration stronger. "Oh my, what's…?"

"It's a train," I shouted. But the thundering noise was so loud I doubt she heard me. I felt twenty-two cars clickity-clack in a westerly direction.

"It's gone," Clara said. "I counted twenty-two cars."

"You too? Do you find yourself counting things you don't need to count?" I asked.

"Yes, is that something else we have in common?"

"Yeah, I count all kinds of silly things. Like, when I go to the doctor's office, I sit in the waiting room counting all the crayon drawings on the wall. Dr. Carr is very proud of his grandchildren and hangs their artwork on the walls. Fourteen masterpieces at last count."

"I counted the patches on Ben's patchwork quilt. Fifteen rows across and twenty rows down. Three hundred patches. He said his mother made the quilt."

"Sounds like we have too much time on our hands," I said, feeling a shiver coming on. Time passed slowly. I checked my watch periodically mainly to enjoy its light, a mystical light that seemed to comfort us and give us hope.

"Josephine, dear, I want to tell you something important. If I have to be stranded in a boxcar, there isn't anyone I'd rather be with…do you hear that? And the vibrating…oh my."

"Trains coming back. I think they run once daily each way, but I didn't know they ran on Sundays. Here it comes," I shouted, bracing myself against the wall. Each car had its own clickity-clack pounding roar that turned into a rumble and finally faded away.

"Only four cars," Clara said.

"Yeah, I counted four, heading east. Sure is quiet. I think the rain stopped." I pushed the light button on my watch. It was dinnertime. I imagined David feeding Solow and Felix, then, settling onto my sofa for a movie. I felt warmer just thinking about him.

"Josephine, remember the dead bugs?"

"Yeah."

"One of them just bit my ankle."

CHAPTER 21

A noisy earthquake shook me so hard I lost my balance and fell into a giant puddle of chocolate syrup. I was hungry and wanted to sample the chocolate, but the chocolate was alive with hundreds of black beetles doing the backstroke all around me. I finally pulled out of the nightmare and opened my eyes. I saw nothing but black. The warm shoulder next to me moved. When my memory cleared, I realized I was propped up against my Aunt Clara on the floor of a moving boxcar.

"Auntie, wake up!" I shouted over the clickety-clack roar. "We're moving!"

"Oh dear, I thought it was another nightmare. Burr! It's so cold in here. Where do you think we're going, Josephine?"

"I think we're headed east. After Aromas the tracks will turn south."

Clara laughed. "I always wanted to take a train ride to LA and see my old chum…but never mind that, dear." She put an arm around my shoulder. "We'll think of it as a free ticket to a surprise destination." Our former discomfort multiplied as we swayed and bounced to the rhythm of the rails. Once we became accustomed to the jerky motion and loud noise, we dropped back into our dreams and nightmares. Several hours later, it was the absence of noise and motion that woke us. Dim light filtered into our boxcar. We looked at each other.

"I think it must be morning, dear."

"Yeah, and I hope today turns out better than yesterday." I hadn't had my coffee, and I was ready to pitch a fit; but I couldn't be angry with Clara. I just hated the person who locked the doors to the boxcar. I was cold and hungry, and my bum was numb.

"Help me up, Josephine. I need to stretch my legs." I pulled myself up first and then grabbed Clara's hand. Even though our stomachs were hollow pits, our bodies moved like heavy slugs. We marched back and forth until the blood began to circulate.

"Auntie, stop! I think I heard voices." We held our breath. Suddenly she grabbed her purse and slammed it against the door, screaming like a crazed banshee. I stood beside her, yelling.

"Quiet, Auntie...listen!" We each put an ear to the door and then started hollering again. "Help! We're locked inside!" I screamed. I heard a voice and then someone tinkering with the lock outside. I held my breath again, ready to suck in some fresh air and sunshine and then be hauled off to jail for trespassing. Clara backed away. Before I could follow her, one door parted a few inches from the other. Tears ran down my cheeks as a blinding stream of sunlight poured through the opening.

"Hello. Who's in there?" It was obviously a man's voice—maybe the train engineer or police with handcuffs just our size. I pulled on the door and looked into a young man's face. He was black as coal and outlined from behind by a halo of sunshine. He wore a black leather jacket and a red bandana around his forehead. A backpack hung from his shoulder and a beautiful brown-skinned woman stood several feet behind him. Her mouth dropped open when Clara and I poked our faces out the open door.

"Hey, Coco, look what I found...two ladies." Coco moved closer to the man pushing the door open.

"Now I've seen everything," she laughed. The young woman had a contagious laugh. My eyes were still tearing as I began laughing with relief. Clara wept into her handkerchief. Coco quickly climbed into the boxcar and hugged her tight. Soon we were in a three-way girl-hug, giggling and telling our stories.

I finally became aware of the fact that the young man had loaded several bulky items into the boxcar. He climbed in with us and pulled the door closed.

"What are you doing?" I screamed. He sat down on the floor, resting his forearms on his knees.

"Catching a train ride," he said, as if it was a regular thing that happened everyday.

"Ladies, this is my associate, Moses T. Hyman," Coco said as the floor jerked. "I think we'll ride north with you...if that's OK."

"Of course you can ride with us, dear," Clara said. "But how do you know we will be going north?"

"We've made the trip a few times before," Moses said. "The train stops here in Santa Maria, drops some cars, adds some cars, circles around and heads back up the coast to Santa Cruz."

"We should be in Santa Cruz by Tuesday afternoon," Coco added.

"Do we have to have the door closed?" I asked.

"For a while," Coco laughed, "unless you have a ticket."

"No, we don't have a ticket," Clara said. "By the way, my name is Clara Ramsey and this is my niece, Josephine Stuart. We were locked in this boxcar yesterday with no food or water, and left to freeze to death." Coco's jaw dropped.

"Someone did that to you?" she asked. Clara nodded.

"We have no idea who did it," I said. The boxcar was quiet except for metal on metal, slowly gaining speed. The four of us sat in a circle near the one-inch crack in the door. Coco opened her backpack and pulled out two plastic bottles of water. She handed each of us a bottle and placed a package of date nut bars on the floor.

"Aren't you the sweetest girl, Coco, and this bar is divine," Clara said. In record time, she was working on a second bar. Mine tasted like heaven and the water was way overdue. Our friends had no interest in food or water as they watched us stuffing our faces. When we had eaten enough to squelch our hunger pains, Clara asked Coco why they were going to Santa Cruz.

"We have a gig...a concert, Tuesday evening at the Catalyst. We live in Santa Maria but spend a lot of time with our friends in Santa Cruz. We met in Santa Cruz at the university. But we like Santa Maria, too." She pulled a guitar out of one of the large bundles and handed it to Moses, and then pulled out a second guitar for herself.

"Hope you don't mind if we practice," Moses said as he shoved one of the doors open.

"We feel privileged," Clara swooned. "Do you know Moon

River?" Moses shook his head and began to strum. Coco joined in. The rhythm was fast—somewhere between Cajun and country. They had written their own songs and sang one after another with plenty of heart and soul. The clickety-clack of the train added another dimension to their "sound."

Several hours passed. The sun had disappeared behind black clouds. Moses pulled on the door until the opening was only a few inches wide. Coco shared apples and cheese with us and then we napped using their blankets. I woke up to Clara's snoring, and Coco and Moses quietly discussing a job opportunity in Santa Maria. I kept still, eyes closed. I was just one hard cold floor away from feeling comfortable. The porta-potty Coco had unpacked (a plastic bucket) sure helped. Clara stopped snoring and sat up.

"Josephine, are you awake?"

"Sure. Why?"

"I had the most disturbing dream. I dreamt Darla was in the backseat of a run-away car, heading straight for a cliff. She called my name. I was standing near the cliff waving my arms, trying to stop the car, but the driver aimed the car at me. That's when I woke up. It was awful." I put my arm around Clara. "Sometimes my dreams seem so real," she said.

Coco picked up her guitar and began singing "Ninety-nine Bottles of Beer on the Wall." Clara and I joined in. We laughed as we went through several old Girl Scout songs and a catchy car commercial. The only thing missing was the campfire. I checked my watch, but it was the growl in my stomach that told me it was dinnertime. Moses rummaged around in his backpack and pulled out a plastic bag full of walnuts. The shells were not clean like store-bought nuts.

"We gathered these in an orchard on our way to the train," he said. "Help yourself."

"How do we open them?" Clara asked. Moses reached out, took a nut from her and squeezed it hard between his thumb and two fingers. The veins in his forearm bulged. The walnut shell cracked into a dozen pieces. Over time, Moses cracked the whole bag of nuts for us, one-by-one. We spent a couple of hours prying meat out with our fingers. But we had plenty of time.

As daylight faded into twilight, Coco brought out a bottle of red wine and a short stack of paper cups. Clara shook her head at the offer; but on the second round, she let Coco pour half a cup. We ate corn chips with bean dip and sipped wine. I tried not to eat too much too fast because Coco had obviously brought food enough for two people, not four. Clara held back even though she was hungry, but Coco encouraged her to have more.

"Are you gals going to make a report to the police when you get home?" Moses asked.

"If we do, we won't mention you guys," I said. "We're just thankful you came along."

"It's nothing," Coco said. "We like having company. Especially interesting people like you. Tell us about this murder mystery you said you're looking into." Like a greyhound at the starting gate, Clara leaped into an extensive account of the murders and all the facts and incidentals surrounding them. When she finally paused, Coco had a few questions.

"OK, if Joey flew away, where is his airplane? Did anyone see him fly away? And why did he leave in the first place?"

"I think he was having marital problems," Clara said. "His second son isn't even his biological son. He's Wayne's son. Seems Darla was seeing Wayne long before Joey disappeared. Maybe Joey just got tired of her being unfaithful."

"And he wanted to help Ben take care of his sister who had Alzheimer's," I said. Actually, I think Joey was sweet on Beverly."

"So where's the plane?" Moses asked.

"We haven't found it yet, but I would love to get into the back half of Mo's nursery," I said. "Unfortunately it's locked up tight."

"I've been thinking the same thing, Josephine. Why didn't you tell me your thoughts?"

"It wasn't so much a thought as a nagging feeling. Why didn't you tell me what you thought?" Clara shrugged and pulled her blanket up to her chin. Moses closed the door another couple of inches. Outside, the sky was almost as dark as our humble quarters.

"Who followed you to the boxcar?" Moses asked.

"We don't know...but I remember Clara saying there was a

white car following us. I just assumed it was the detective who had been following us around for days."

"Dear, the car was smaller and older."

"Now you tell me." I rolled my eyes in the dark. "Who drives an old white car? Anyone we know?" Clara didn't answer.

"I hate to say it," Moses said, "but in most cases you need to 'follow the money.'"

"That's the funny thing," Clara said. "Darla isn't getting the investment money that Joey set up for her. She doesn't even know what business he invested in. She actually lost her home because Joey mortgaged the house and invested the money somewhere before he left."

"But you said Darla married Wayne. Maybe he knows where the money was invested," Coco said. "Darla sounds like she's awfully forgetful."

"Yes she is," Clara said. "Poor dear."

"Is she forgetful or is she hiding something?" Moses asked. "What about the two sons? Are they on the level?"

"Jamie's a dear," Clara said. "He lost part of his leg in a motorcycle accident...."

"Why didn't you tell me it was Jamie Gianelli?" Moses said. "I worked for him one summer making cabinets. That was the summer he lost his leg, his wife and his cabinet business. We saw Jamie at the Catalyst last week. He heard we were playing the Club and just wanted to say 'hi' and then he had to run."

"Run is the right word. He was considered a 'person of interest' by the police, for a while. But Mo finally changed his story and Jamie's off the hook," I said. "What a small world."

"What about the backpack Jamie found in his uncle's office?" Coco asked.

"What about it? It's gone and someone stole the flight plan," I added. "The person who stole the flight plan...oh my God! I remember seeing an older white compact car parked on Otis. I didn't think anything of it at the time. Whoever locked me in the shed is probably the same person who locked us in the boxcar."

"Well, I'd hate to think there were two people with a bad attitude, running around locking people up," Clara sniped.

"I'm still following the money," Moses said. "I think the investment money is the key. How much was it? Who has the money? Who needed the money? Who would kill for the money? At least we can eliminate Jamie. He's a great guy...and a good musician."

"You said Joey's wife didn't get any life insurance. I wonder if he had any, and if he did, who got it." Coco said. "Guess I'm following the money, too. And what about Maureen? You said she hid Jamie in her apartment. Why would she do that?"

"Maureen is Gabe's great aunt and Mo's mother's sister, I believe," Clara yawned. "Maurie eventually threw Jamie out." Her words sounded far away and complicated. I put my heavy head down, pulled up the blanket and lost myself in the rhythm of wheels on rails.

CHAPTER 22

I checked my watch. Six o'clock, and I was the only one awake. I stared at the two-inch space between the boxcar doors as telephone poles whipped by. Miles of emerald foothills, flecked with dark green oaks, rested under a soft pink sky. Unfortunately, the boxcar smelled like a porta-potty. I scooted closer to the doors and sucked in some fresh air. Clara mumbled in her sleep.

"Did you sleep well?" Coco whispered as she scooted closer. I nodded, wishing I had a toothbrush and toothpaste. Coco's pleasant personality had transformed our sad drama into an adventure. She made us laugh, soothed us with song and shared everything she had packed for their journey to Santa Cruz.

Coco and I watched the scene outside as it whooshed by at about fifty miles per hour. I was transfixed. It was like watching a beautiful movie without a plot. No worries. I hardly noticed the clickety-clack anymore. We chugged along the backside of small towns at a much slower speed. It was the side of life one never sees from the highway, the real Americana, and I couldn't take my eyes off of it. By seven, everyone was awake.

"Oh my, I had the loveliest dream," Clara said. "Ben and I...ah, how was your sleep, dear?"

"Better than last night. Coco and I have been enjoying the scenery."

Coco stood up and stretched. "I think I'll put all the leftover food out and we can nibble till it's gone." Moses, the hulk, looked hungry but didn't complain. After a few bites of this and that, everything was gone. We would have a long wait for our next meal. Moses pulled a deck of cards out of his backpack, and Clara and I taught Coco and Moses how to play Hearts. When we tired of Hearts, Moses taught us how to play poker using dead beetles for poker chips.

"Raise you five beetles," Clara said, excitedly. Everyone folded, thinking she had a great hand. She finally showed us her pathetic cards and laughed out loud, adding more beetles to her pile. After the games, Coco and Moses played a few tunes for us.

"Coco, dear, do you know 'She'll be Coming Round the Mountain When She Comes'?"

"I'm afraid I don't. But here's one you'll like." Coco sang, "Daydream Believer." We were captivated, and then "Miss Coco Cruise Director" led us in a series of yoga poses while Moses took a nap. The poses were extra difficult because the train continuously lurched and swayed. We finally gave up and settled down for an afternoon nap.

Clara began snoring, and the train slowed to a fast walk. I looked outside and recognized Mo's nursery building and a couple of minutes later my red truck parked in a sea of lettuce. I ached to be home, to be warm and fed and to be with David and Solow. But the train didn't stop. It chugged along at about ten miles an hour all the way into Pajaro and then angled north, between fields of artichokes. The Pacific Ocean glinted and crashed nearby.

"Coco, the train's not stopping!"

"Sometimes it doesn't. We'll have to jump."

"What?! You've got to be kidding."

"I'll help you down," Moses said as he pushed his packs closer to the crack in the door, and then pushed the door until the gap was four feet wide. Air rushed in, waking Clara. She pulled herself up on wobbly legs and leaned against the metal wall.

"Did someone say we're going to jump?" she asked. "Why don't we see if the train will stop in Santa Cruz?"

"It might," Moses said. "I just thought you wanted to be in Watsonville."

"Santa Cruz would be fine. My sister, Leola, lives there."

"Do you think they'll be home?" I asked. Clara shrugged and Moses pushed the door closed except for the usual two inches. The train slowed to five miles per hour as we passed through Aptos and Capitola and finally chugged into Santa Cruz an hour later.

Moses opened the door.

"The station!" Clara pointed. "This is where the old train sta-tion used to be, and Leola's house is just a few blocks away from here." Moses quickly pushed his bundles close to the edge.

"Ladies, you say the word and we're out the door. This train might not stop again until it reaches Davenport." Clara opened her mouth and pointed. Moses took her hands, dangled her out the door as if she weighed eight pounds and dropped her gently on the ground. Before I had time for second thoughts, he grabbed my hands and out I went. Coco jumped out on her own. Moses tossed the gear and took a leap, landing on his feet a few yards down the tracks. We closed ranks and headed for Walnut Avenue.

We must have looked like four bedraggled street people when Mom opened the front door. Her open mouth and wide eyes said it all. I had never known a time when she didn't have something to say about something. Words never stuck in her throat, but they were definitely stuck. Finally she motioned with her fingers for us to come inside. Moses looked apprehensive. I assured him my par-ents wouldn't bite. Dad looked dumbstruck as he joined us in the kitchen.

"Is that banana bread I smell?" Clara asked. Mom nodded. Dad cleared his throat.

"Are you hungry?" he asked. Clara nodded her head and peeked in the oven.

"Looks done. Mind if we sample it?" She had already slipped her hand into an oven mitt. Dad pulled two extra chairs up to the breakfast bar to accommodate all six of us. Mom stood in the cor-ner watching Clara slice hot bread with a knife. Finally she came out of her stupor and placed six dessert plates on the counter. Clara served up the bread and Dad made fresh coffee.

"Mom, Dad, I want you to meet our friends, Coco and Moses." Dad stepped up for a couple of handshakes.

"Moses, remember the night you sang to Coco on her birth-day and she cried?"

"Yes, Sir. You must have been at the Catalyst last November," Moses smiled. Mom put a hand to her mouth.

"Now I know why you two look so familiar. We love your

music. Here, have some more bread. Do you take cream in your coffee?" From that point on, she pulled out all the stops. No amount of home cooking was too much. We told our boxcar story; and Mom heated, carved and served more food than we could eat in a month. Dad was especially intrigued with our adventure.

"You say it was a white compact? An older car?" he asked.

"Yeah, possibly the same car I saw in my neighborhood just before I was thrown in the shed." Mom's jaw went slack.

"Shed? Thrown in a shed?" Mom made eye contact with Aunt Clara, but Clara was staring into space, half asleep.

"It's a long story, Mom. But don't worry, everything is OK."

"Did you call the police, honey?" Dad asked.

"No. I've been thinking about it for three days, and I still wouldn't know what to tell them. In the first place, we were trespassing in the boxcar. We didn't see who locked the doors, and what have the police done to find Joey's murderer so far? I decided not to call." Clara listened and nodded her approval. I quickly excused myself from the afternoon feast before Dad could make an argument. I called David from the hall phone.

"Hi, Josie. I thought you two would be home Monday night. How did it go? Is Clara's house going to be all right?"

"We didn't go to Oakhurst. Something came up."

"Something came up? For three days? What's going on, sweetie?"

"Aunt Clara and I were curious about Curly being locked in a boxcar six years ago. One thing led to another and all of a sudden, we were locked in a boxcar traveling to Santa Maria. Luckily we met Coco and Moses, and they rode back to Santa Cruz with us. Actually, we're at Mom's eating everything in sight. She keeps pushing food at us, trying to save us from starvation. I think my button's going to pop if I eat another bite."

"So what you're saying is...everything is all right?"

"We're fine. That's why I called, to tell you not to worry. How's Solow?"

"Fine. I think he has adopted Fluffy as his little sister. He hasn't chased her once since you've been gone. Will we see you tonight?"

"Sure, whenever we can get a ride home," I said. "Bye for

now." We hung up and I turned to go back to the kitchen. Mom was waiting at the end of the hall.

"Honey, you know I don't like to criticize, but you don't look very clean and what's that smell? Were you riding in a cattle car?"

"No. I guess we're pretty gross. Three days in a boxcar will do that to you."

"Why don't you take a shower, and I'll find something clean for you to wear." She was already pulling towels out of the linen closet. I finally warmed up to the idea and ran the water. Once I was in the shower, I didn't want to get out. The water felt so good. Civilization was a wonderful thing, unless you were young, restless singers like our new friends. They seemed to handle hardship gracefully.

Dad's burgundy sweat suit was designed for a taller person, but it was warm and the tie-string at the waist was a big help. Mom loaned me clean socks and underwear. She had already laid out more of Dad's clothes for Clara. I stepped into the kitchen to tell her the shower was available. Clara sat alone at the breakfast bar, sipping a cup of tea.

"Where did everyone go?" I asked.

"Bob's driving the kids to their friend's house on the east side of town."

"I didn't get a chance to say goodbye, and I wanted to thank them. They were so good to us."

"Yes, that's why Leola invited them over for dinner next week. They were delighted."

"The bathroom's empty if you want to take a shower or bath." I handed her a fresh towel. It was two-thirty and I felt so relaxed. I stretched out on the sofa and didn't wake up until Dad slammed the front door.

"Sorry, honey, I didn't know you were napping."

"No problem, Dad. I was feeling so relaxed and happy to be here...and just fell asleep." I sat up and looked around. Mom and Aunt Clara were in the kitchen talking quietly. Dad sat down on the sofa next to me.

"Honey, I hope you don't go looking for this white compact you thought you saw."

"Oh, Dad, would I do that?" I laughed and he rolled his eyes to the ceiling.

"Your outfit looks familiar," he said, eyeing the burgundy sweat suit. Mom and Clara joined us in the living room. He quietly stared at Clara who was wearing his gray sweatshirt and pants. Mom probably thought we would pop a seam if we tried on her clothes. She announced we would all take a drive to Aromas after dinner.

"Bob, let's not forget to stop at Wayne's on the way," Mom said. "He borrowed the big coffeemaker for the VFW reunion, and I need to take it back to the Garden Club for tomorrow's meeting." Dad nodded dutifully. Mom's rose bushes were less than spectacular, but her club meetings were the best. The sun went down and we polished off another home cooked meal. The four of us piled into Mom's Subaru; and ten minutes later, we stood at the Bracken's front door pushing the doorbell over and over. The door finally opened slowly.

"I'm sorry, Wayne isn't here." Darla said, slamming the door on my foot. She stepped back and I pushed the door open a few inches. Mom stuck her head inside.

"Darla, it's Leola, dear."

"I'm sorry...I can't find my glasses. People usually want to see Wayne...." Darla muttered. "Who else is out there? Is that you, Bob?"

"Yes, I'm here and so are Jo and Clara. By the way, can you locate the big coffeemaker Wayne borrowed last month?" Dad asked.

"The what-maker?"

"The...coffee...maker," Mom said slowly. Darla found her glasses, but seemed disoriented just the same. Clara took her by the arm and helped her into the old wingback chair.

"You're welcome to look around in the kitchen," Darla said. "If that coffee thingy isn't in the kitchen, it might be in Wayne's trunk."

"Do you mean a trunk in the bedroom, dear?" Mom asked. Darla shook her head.

"No, the trunk of his car," she said. Clara brought her a glass of water and asked when Wayne would be coming home.

"Maybe tomorrow. I never know for sure," Darla said. Clara frowned as we made eye contact for a second. Dad opened all the cupboard doors in the tiny kitchen and came up empty-handed. I made a quick inspection, noticing a stack of empty TV dinner containers in the sink. I checked the freezer. There was only one dinner left. If Wayne didn't come home the next day, she would be eating catsup and soda crackers.

We said our goodbyes and clambered into Mom's car. Halfway home, Clara and I decided we would stop by Darla's the next day and take her to dinner if Wayne wasn't home yet. The four of us speculated on where an old retired locksmith goes for so long and why. And why would he go off and leave Darla alone when she was obviously not doing very well.

"I think Wayne has a bad case of wanderlust," Dad said. "He's a good bowler, but you never know if he'll show up."

Mom talked about changing her plans. She said she would use her everyday Mr. Coffee, pull her old coffee pot out of storage and borrow Myrtle's percolator. Three small pots might be enough.

Even though it was eight o'clock at night and pitch dark outside, my eyes automatically strained to inspect every passing car. I was looking for a certain white compact but didn't know the make or model. I told myself I would recognize it if I saw it. Dad pulled the Subaru to a stop in front of my house.

"Where's your truck, dear?" Mom asked.

"It's a few miles from here. We'll pick it up tomorrow," I said, hoping my folks wouldn't insist on taking us to it. Driving into a muddy lettuce patch at night would not be the best idea.

"So, Mom, how many people are you expecting tomorrow for your club meeting?"

"Twenty-something. Now, dear, tell me how you're going to get to your truck."

"That's no problem, Leola," Clara said. "David will drive us there in the morning." She winked at me. Clara and I climbed out of the Subaru, said our thank you's and goodbyes as Dad put the car in reverse.

I crashed on the sofa and called David while Clara banged

around in the kitchen. Minutes later David and Solow joined us for popcorn and hot chocolate. I asked David to give us a ride to Pajaro in the morning, which triggered a rush of questions and a long story on our part. Clara told most of it. Around ten we were all yawning.

"I'll see you girls at eight tomorrow morning," David yawned. "Can't wait to hear the real story," he rolled his eyes as if the whole trip to Santa Maria had been made up. Solow followed him to the door, torn between two masters—the kindly muralist and her handsome neighbor.

CHAPTER 23

Ready for work, Clara and I waited for David to pick us up. My aunt's hair billowed softly and her complexion looked rosy. She had called Ben the night before and they talked half the night. She should have been tired in the morning, but she was feeling fine and looking forward to lunch with Ben. David honked his horn and we scurried outside. He opened the rear door for Clara and helped her into the jeep. I had already settled into the front passenger seat.

"At least it's not raining," Clara said, brightly.

"Hope we aren't interrupting your plans for today," I said to David. He stared at the road ahead, but I saw a twitch of a smile cross his clean-shaven face.

"Nothing that can't wait," he said without explanation. "Is that your truck out there in the lettuce patch?" Clara said it was. He made a sharp left onto the one-lane dirt road separating one field from another. At least twenty cars were parked in a line behind my truck. David parked behind the last dusty car, and watched us walk the distance.

My truck looked the same as always, lots of character, but no new dents or scratches. We drove about a hundred yards forward, crossed the railroad tracks, hooked a U-turn and headed back to San Juan Road. Clara waved to David as we put two wheels into the lettuce field in order to pass by his jeep. Five minutes later, we were in Watsonville.

"Hurry, Auntie. Your bus is here." Clara climbed out of the pickup, hustled down the sidewalk and joined a pack of high school students funneling onto a city bus. I pulled back into traffic and a minute later entered the library parking lot. I was relieved to see all the regular cars and trucks plus Kyle's motorcycle parked there, and I was elated when I saw the progress Alicia and Kyle had made on the murals. They had put the final touches on the first mural, and started taping off the wall on the opposite side for the children's mural. Three ladders were in position, and Kyle was mixing batches of paint to match the colors in my sketch.

"There's our lost leader," Alicia said.

"Like, where ya been, Jo?" Kyle chimed in.

"Aunt Clara and I were riding the rails." Alicia rolled her eyes. "Really, we were trapped in a boxcar heading for L.A." Kyle laughed, but Alicia cocked her head, wanting to hear more. As soon as we finished measuring and drawing the preliminary lines of the mural, I gave them the full story.

"You're not going to go looking for the white car, Jo, are you?" Alicia said.

"Would I do that?"

"The Josephine I know would," Chester said, strolling into the children's reading room. "You guys have an extra level we can borrow?"

"Sure. Help yourself," I said, pointing to the three-footer we had just finished using.

"Thanks, and I hope you find that little white car before it finds you," he laughed. I didn't think Chester's comment was funny. In fact, it sent a shiver up my spine. If the culprit somehow found out Clara and I were not rotting away in the boxcar, he might try to harm us again. And the worst part was, he knew that we knew that he knew what we were up to, and "he" was most likely Joey's killer. I racked my brain for a motive, but all that came to mind was the phrase, "follow the money."

"Jo, shall I mix the blues?" Alicia asked. I nodded. "How many shades do you want?"

"Three." It was getting close to lunchtime so I decided we would paint the sky after a visit to the Mexican restaurant down the street. We finished our prep chores and followed the aroma of spicy food. A very handsome-looking gentleman happened to be sitting alone at a table near the front entrance.

"David, what are you doing here?" He smiled, Alicia laughed

and I suddenly realized they were in cahoots with each other. I sat in the booth seat with David, and Alicia and Kyle sat across from us. Alicia concentrated on her menu.

"What's going on, you guys?" I asked. Kyle snickered, knowingly.

"It's our tenth anniversary," David said. "Exactly ten years ago today, during a torrential winter storm, you found me trapped in my jeep on Otis Road. A fallen tree rested across the roof of my car, and live electrical wires dangled down to the street. You drove to the fire department and told them what happened." He smiled sweetly. "Now you're the one always needing to be rescued."

"I don't need to be rescued," I said, blushing like a schoolgirl. Alicia, Kyle and David roared with laughter. I had no defense. After a delicious lunch, David walked us back to the library and inspected the entry wall mural. He didn't stay long, probably sensing that we had a lot of work ahead of us.

By five o'clock, the three of us had created a twenty-foot stretch of blue, peppered with Alicia's wispy clouds. The sky paled as it came to rest on a pink chalk line, marking the tops of faraway hills. We would paint the hills and fields another day. It was time to vacate the library. I wondered if Molly would be delivering the orders, or would it be me. I thought about all these things as I drove to Santa Cruz, shading my eyes from the red sun just before it vanished.

I parked behind Candy's store. Stars were strewn across the darkening sky like sugar sprinkles. I entered the building. Clara sat in the dim green light of a neon FTD sign.

"Hi. You look relaxed."

"Done-in is more like it," Clara said with a dreamy smile. "Molly took Maurie home, and now she's out delivering our arrangements. How was lunch?"

"You knew about David's surprise?" She nodded.

"I had a nice lunch too, on the wharf with Ben. The ocean was choppy and deep blue…and his eyes looked tired but sweet. We talked about everything. He and Jamie are working on a construction project in Boulder Creek. That's why he's been too busy to see me." Still smiling, her eyes searched the ceiling, trying to recall every magical moment. Finally she floated out the back door and I helped her into my truck.

"You'll feel better after we have some dinner," I laughed, glad to see her so happy.

"Dear, don't forget to stop at Darla's."

"Right after I trade cars with Mom."

"I see what you mean. This little truck of yours barely holds the two of us." We had planned to use the Subaru, but Mom wasn't home and Dad told us to take the old Buick. I had no qualms with retro-luxury. In no time, we were across town heading for the freeway.

"Dear, don't forget to change lanes...." I quickly turned the car to the right, ignoring the honking behind us. Darla's street was quiet and her house looked dark. I knocked on the door a few times and Clara peeked through the front window.

"She must be gone. All the lights are out...oh, she turned on a lamp. Here she comes."

"Is that you, Wayne?"

"Darla, it's Clara and Josephine," I said. We waited a while before she decided to open the door and peek out. Clara quickly stepped inside and gave the frail little lady a hug. I buzzed around them over to the kitchen to see if Darla had eaten the last TV dinner. It was still in the freezer. The poor lady was already skin and bones.

"Darla, is Wayne home?" Clara asked.

"No," she said, looking at the floor.

"Did you know that it's Josephine's birthday today?" Clara gave me a wink so I wouldn't expose her prevarication. I kept still, guessing her intent. Darla shook her head and looked at me. "And since it's her fiftieth birthday," Clara chirped, "I wanted to take her out to dinner...you know, celebrate. If we had one more person it would be more like a party, don't you think?" Darla nodded and sat down in her chair in a way that suggested she might not want to get up and go somewhere. "Dear, let me help you find your coat."

Darla didn't budge so I checked the coat closet near the front door and came back with an old corduroy coat with a frayed collar.

Clara took Darla's arm and helped her up. We bundled her into the coat and walked her to the door.

"Where would you like to have dinner, Darla?" I asked as we helped her into the backseat. There was a long silence. Clara and I settled into our seats. Clara wrenched her neck around, looked at Darla and waited for an answer.

"We used to have a favorite...."

"Come on, dear. Tell us where you'd like to go," Clara said. My stomach growled.

"Wayne and I used to go to Slick's, on the wharf."

"I don't remember a Slick's on the wharf," Clara said.

"I do. But it's not on the Santa Cruz Wharf, it's the Monterey Wharf."

"Yes, yes, that's where it is. Such a lovely place," Darla cooed. My stomach growled.

"OK, Monterey it is." I put the Buick in drive, and we headed for the other side of the bay. Forty minutes later, I parked the car according to Clara's instructions, and we walked down to the wharf. Slick's was the only restaurant decked out in tacky neon advertisements, flashing and not flashing. We stepped inside. The greeter said she would have a table in a minute or two, never mind that the place was practically empty except for the bar.

I glanced at the swarm of people at the bar, talking, laughing and indulging in adult beverages. One older fellow caught my eye. I looked at Clara's shocked expression and realized I really had seen Wayne with his arm around a younger woman. She was not a day over sixty and fairly well preserved.

The greeter came back and led Darla toward the dining room. Clara and I hurried to catch up. As we made a right turn into the main dining area, I looked back over my shoulder in time to see Wayne and the shapely redhead exiting the place. Darla didn't have a clue.

"How do you like it? Wayne used to bring me here...." her voice evaporated into the ether of old memories.

"It's, ah, lovely, dear," Clara sputtered. "When was the last time you were here?"

"The night he proposed to me, five years ago," she sighed. I wondered what Wayne saw in Darla. Next to the trollop in the bar, Darla looked old and used up. More often than not, her eyes had a vacant stare. The poor lady's wrinkles had wrinkles, and her smile hadn't been used in a long time. I leaned toward her and gave her cold bony hand a little squeeze.

"Isn't this place the greatest? Aunt Clara is so thoughtful, giving me this birthday party. Order whatever you want." I hoped Darla would order at least two thousand calories worth. Slick's restaurant seemed to have touched a happy spot in her memory, but the spark died quickly as her shoulders caved and her thin lips gave in to gravity.

"Darla, dear, it's time for you to order your dinner," Clara said as the waitress hovered with pen and pad. Darla skimmed across the menu for the tenth time.

"Do you sell fish here?" she asked. Clara and I made eye contact. Darla was having a bad day, or else she was in worse shape than we thought. The gal with the apron rattled off six or eight kinds of fish, leaving the poor lady in a blur with her mouth hanging open. Desperate, Darla repeated the last choice. When the meal arrived, she looked surprised.

"Is your lobster OK, dear?" Clara asked. Darla stared at her plate. "Here, I'll help you break into that old rascal." Clara reached over, ripped off a claw and used it to pull meat out of the body. When most of the meat was out, she poured butter over everything. Darla sampled a bite, looking like she was tasting food for the first time. She went from sampling to porking it all down, including the baked potato and vegetables.

Our plates were cleared and a piece of chocolate cake with one flickering candle arrived.

"I almost forgot it was my birthday. Help me eat this cake." I passed it to Clara who carved out a big bite. She passed it to Darla who thought it was hers to keep and ate the whole thing.

"This is a wonderful party. Happy birthday, Clara," Darla said. That was the moment I realized she was running on a forty-watt bulb in a hundred-watt world, and Wayne wasn't around to lend a hand.

"Darla, I had lunch with my friend, Ben DeWald today." Clara paused. Darla thought for a moment.

"Yes, I know Ben. He and Joey were good friends."

"Ben told me he remembered something about a business you and Joey invested in. He said it was a large nursery. He couldn't remember the name. Do you remember the name of the business, or where it was located?" Darla shook her head slowly.

"Whose birthday did you say it was?" Clara pointed to me and then paid the bill with cash. We exited the building and climbed into Dad's Buick, feeling stuffed and ready to be home. Clara's head relaxed against the headrest, and soon she was snorting and puffing air to the beat of "Hit the Road Jack." Darla's head bobbed to the same rhythm in my rearview mirror. I parked in front of the Bracken house. Clara woke up with a start and looked around.

"Oh my, that was a quick trip." She cranked her head around and said, "Goodnight, my dear." Darla started to climb out of the car but stopped mid-step.

"His name was, Morton something."

"Who?"

"The man Joey gave money to. It was a man named Morton," Darla said as she stepped up to the sidewalk. I took her arm and walked her to the front door. The house was dark inside, but it didn't feel empty. I clicked on the two living room lamps and cranked up the heater. Darla settled into her wing chair, and I draped a ragged afghan over her legs. I thought I heard something and glanced down the hall. Nothing there.

"I'll be going now. Here's my card. Call me if you need anything, OK?" Darla nodded.

I wished I could have done more, but I was tired and needed to get home. I drove while Clara mulled over the fact that Joey had invested in Mo's nursery and was coincidentally murdered nearby. We agreed that we needed to check out the Pajaro nursery business and its owner, but we would save that for another day. We had a Buick to return.

I ran in and handed the keys to Dad, and Clara and I climbed into my ice-cold truck. I flipped on the heater and headed for home. Clara was wide awake and chatty.

"I'm going to let Jamie know that Darla isn't well, and Wayne isn't taking very good care of her," Clara said. I agreed. If something wasn't done soon, the poor lady would end up strapped in a wheelchair, droopy and slobbering in a rest home.

As soon as we entered my house, Clara said, "Goodnight," and climbed the stairs to the loft. I was glad to have her staying with me again and wished I had a nicer bed for her to sleep in. But she never complained, so I settled into my bed and fell asleep listening to Solow's heavy breathing.

I dreamt about a man wearing a wax mask and a frizzy red wig. We were trudging along, side-by-side, across a giant desert, desperate for a drink of soda pop. We saw a mirage up ahead and hurried toward it. The vision turned out to be a lake of sparkling orange soda pop. I looked down into the sweet liquid and saw the man's reflection. He reached into the air and grabbed a passing raven. As he rung the bird's neck, I had a feeling I knew who the man was.

CHAPTER 24

The week was flying by. It was already Wednesday and we had barely started the second mural. Alicia, Kyle and I worked hard painting huge stretches of hills and fields. Details would be added later. I tried to concentrate but my mind wandered away from the mural, back to the birthday dinner with Darla and Clara in Monterey. Darla had confirmed our suspicions, but how could we finagle a look at Mo's books? Create a diversion?

I imagined blowing up the dumpster in back of Mo's nursery. As soon as Mo and his employees ran to put out the flames, Clara and I would dash in the front door, snag a big book of records from the office and jump in the truck before Mo knew what happened. I experimented with a few more ideas, but finally gave up on breaking into Mo's place and turned my attention to Wayne. How could the man leave his wife cold and hungry, and who was the floozy on his arm?

"Jo, you look like your mind is a thousand miles away," Alicia said. "What goes up here?" She pointed to the upper right side of the mural wall.

"Wayne...I mean, a faraway redwood forest." Alicia cocked her head.

"Wayne? Who's that?"

"Darla's low-life husband." Alicia kept staring at me. I ended up giving her a full account of our faux birthday dinner party in Monterey.

"Like, is it really your birthday?" Kyle asked. I rolled my eyes.

"Alicia, I just had an idea. Would you like to help me solve a murder or two?" She shook her head. "You wouldn't have to paint these boring hills any more." She shook her head again and kept her eyes on her work. "You love plants, don't you?" She shook her head and dipped her brush in the green paint. "Wouldn't you like a temporary job at a big nursery?"

"What in the world are you up to, Jo?"

"The information we're looking for is out of reach. I desperately need to see Mo's books, and that's where you can help," I said, cheerfully. Alicia squinted and shook her head again. "Poor Darla is supposed to be getting money from an investment in Mo's nursery. She barely has enough to eat and her house is so cold." Alicia took a deep breath as she looked at the ceiling.

"You really think we can pull this off?"

"Sure. You know your way around a computer and you know about plants. All we have to do is create a need for a new employee. Mo hates me, but he would hire you in a minute."

"Couldn't you ask Gabe to do the dirty work?" Alicia asked.

"Gabe's walking on eggs as it is. His uncle is pretty hard on him."

"And you want me to work for this monster?" Alicia laughed. "You know I'll do it, Jo. We always help each other. Besides, I'm tired of painting hills."

"And the bad news is…I lied. You get a job with Mo after the hills are finished." Alicia tried to look disgusted as her brush deftly fashioned another set of rolling hills. The three of us chattered on, covering several subjects by the end of the day. Talking or thinking, it didn't matter. We painted out of habit. By five o'clock, we had a sunny sky, wispy clouds, lovely hills on the horizon and a redwood forest.

Alicia and Kyle went home, and I stayed behind to clean brushes. The building was quiet except for footsteps coming closer. I looked up from my work. Chester stopped in front of the mural and admired the clouds. After a little chitchat, I gathered up my purse and jacket and walked with him to the back door.

"You're here pretty late for a carpenter," I said, eyeing his thumb wrapped in gauze.

"Yeah, I smashed my thumb with a hammer and went home early. I got bored and decided to come back and see if the guys finished today's work. We only have one more week to finish everything, so I keep pushing them."

"Yeah, my people keep pushing me." He stopped and looked at me. "I'm easily side-tracked," I said. He scratched his head and opened the door for me.

"Think you'll be done by the end of next week?"

"Hope so," I answered as I pulled on my jacket. "Haven't seen Atwater around."

"Yeah, we have a deadline on the wharf project coming up soon." I wondered if we would make our deadline as I climbed into my truck.

By the time I reached Candy's shop in Santa Cruz, I had convinced myself Alicia was our answer. She was not only beautiful; she was smart and efficient. The perfect employee for Mo, if only he needed one. If he suddenly had an increase in business or a decrease in his workforce, would he hire Alicia? It was almost six when I knocked on the back door of Candy's shop. Clara finally opened it, rubbing one sleepy eye.

"I must have dozed off," she yawned. "Everything is locked and Maurie went home ages ago. All we have to do is deliver one bouquet on our way home." I followed her into the work area and examined the delivery item. I recognized the pink hollyhocks, yellow daffodils, red carnations and big silver bow as a "Clara Creation."

"Where's Molly?"

"She had a date. Her friend is taking her to dinner and then to the Catalyst to see Coco and Moses. They call themselves, 'Chocolate Sunday,'" Clara laughed. I grabbed the arrangement and followed Clara to the pickup. Once she was settled in her seat, I handed over the bouquet, fired up the engine, and we cruised through town dodging jaywalkers, musicians, bums and dogs. I told Clara about my plan for Alicia to work in Mo's office. She laughed as if I were joking.

"Oops, almost missed Broadway," I mumbled to myself. I cranked the wheel and someone honked. Clara jumped in her seat. "It's OK, Auntie, just an oversensitive driver. This looks like the right neighborhood...."

"Right there, see the big old white house with the numbers, three zero, zero over the door?" she said. "I remember this old house. A friend of mine used to live here. We went to school together. Park over there, dear. Not too close to the hydrant." We clambered out of our seats. Clara led the way, proudly holding the flower-stuffed vase with both hands.

My stomach growled in unison with five creaky stairs. I crossed the front porch and pushed the doorbell. I stepped back and looked up at a sky full of stars, wondering what David was doing at that moment. We heard footsteps. The door opened and a senior citizen poked her head out.

"Oh, my! For me?" she thundered as if we were deaf. She took a moment to crank up her hearing aid, causing it to squeal. I cringed but Clara was busy passing the flowers to the hunched little lady. The old woman looked up and studied Clara's face through thick lenses.

"Is that you, Cat?" she asked. Clara leaned closer and squinted.

"Yes. Is that you, Abigail?"

"Hold this," Abigail said, handing the flowers to me. The ladies hugged. "You haven't changed a bit, Clara."

"You haven't changed either, Abby. Have you lived in this house all these years?"

"Oh, no. I inherited the house and moved in a few years ago. It's cold out there. Please come inside." We followed Abigail into the front room and settled our weary bodies on antique chairs that felt like old-fashioned horsehair implements of torture. She quickly suggested a softer sofa in the corner. We melted into it, hoping to be able to climb out later.

Clara and Abigail poured over the last fifty years of their lives. They laughed and chatted for over an hour while I emptied the candy bowl and thought about dinner.

"Abigail, you said your husband went to school here in Santa Cruz," I said. "Did he know Joey Gianelli and Ben DeWald and Beverly?"

"Oh, yes, and like all the other boys, my Gilbert had his eye on Beverly. I think she was sweet on Joey...maybe not. Funny how things turned out. Gilbert and Joey used to get together now and then. Joey's boy, Jamie, worked with my husband. Poor boy lost a leg in a terrible motorcycle accident." Once Abigail started to talk, there was no shutting her down.

"My husband passed away the same year Mother died. I moved into her house hoping for a fresh start. I'm very happy here, surrounded by loved ones." About thirty black and white family photos in fancy old frames hung on the wall opposite the sofa.

"Looks like you come from a big family," I said.

"Oh, yes. Most of them call on me from time to time." Abigail smiled as her eyes circled the room. I glanced at Clara. She cocked her head and frowned. "They're usually here by now, but they're shy around strangers," Abby giggled. I wondered about Abigail's visitors.

"Abigail, how did Gilbert feel about his boss, Morton?" I asked.

"He admired the man's ability to make money but hated working for him. Mo usually wanted Gilbert to stay late, but my husband didn't want full-time work. He had retired from the army and worked part-time at the nursery until he, ah, had an accident. He was run over by a forklift. Broke his hip and had to go to a nursing home. It was downhill from there."

"Abby, dear, was Gilbert working at the nursery six years ago?"

"Yes he was. I think that was the year we lost Joey. It was so sad. Gilbert was devastated, wouldn't even talk about the accident. Shortly after that, Gilbert was hit by the forklift and Jamie lost his leg in a motorcycle accident. Ben moved to Boulder Creek while my husband was in the convalescent hospital and they lost touch. It was a terrible year, just terrible."

"Abigail," I said, "what do you think about Joey's train accident?" She shook her head.

"Tut, tut, people come and go from this world all the time." She ran her eyes around the room as if looking for her ghostly friends. I suddenly felt a cold draft and shivered. By that time, I was starving and whispered to Clara that we needed to be on our way. With much effort, she pulled herself up from the super soft seat.

"Abby, I'm afraid we have to leave now," Clara said. "It's been lovely catching up on old times." They hugged and promised to keep in touch.

Five minutes and ten blocks later we were horsing-down tacos and sucking up iced tea at the local Taco Bell. I thought about how well preserved Mom and Aunt Clara were compared to Abigail, Darla and Maurie. I hoped I had inherited the same youthful genes. Clara gurgled up the last of her iced tea.

"It was nice to see my old friend again, but I probably won't be back for awhile."

"What's the matter, Auntie, afraid of ghosts?"

"No, not exactly, I was just thinking about the way Abby acted. I think she thought the flowers were from me. Sometimes I think she's running on half a burner. The flowers were from Pierre. It said so right there on the card." Clara smiled and blew air at her fingers as if they were on fire. "I wonder who Pierre is. You look so serious, dear. What's on your mind?"

"I was thinking about Joey's accident. I think we're not seeing the forest for the trees. We really need to get Alicia hired at the nursery so she can look at the forest—I mean the books. I'm worried about Darla, and Wayne sure isn't any help."

"Dear, be serious. How do we get Alicia hired at the nursery?"

"Alicia will convince Morton." I was sure of it.

"Why would Mo hire her? Does he need more help? He seems like a penny-pincher to me."

"We need to talk to Gabe," I said. Twenty minutes later, I parked the pickup beside a delivery truck in front of Mo's nursery. Everything was dark except for a couple of outdoor lights and the cab of the delivery truck. Gabe sat in the driver's seat writing on a pad. He heard us, turned his head and opened the window.

"What are you ladies doing out here in the dark?"

"We need to talk to you, dear," Clara said as he opened the door and slid down from his seat.

"What's up?"

"We think your uncle might know something about Joey's investment," I said. "Apparently Joey invested a large sum of money here, in your uncle's nursery business. Apparently Joey's widow isn't getting any return on the money. We want to check the books and, ah, make sure Mo is doing the right thing."

"My uncle can be a jerk, but he wouldn't cheat anyone."

"We know that, dear. We just want to see that Darla receives her money every month. Would you mind if we went inside and looked around?"

"I wouldn't mind, but you can't go in. Mo sets the alarm when he goes home. I can't even go in there. That's why I do my paperwork out here."

"Do you know if he needs a new employee?" I asked.

"Don't think so."

"Maybe you would like to take a little vacation?" Clara said. Gabe scratched his head.

"Why would I do that?"

"You could tell Mo you signed up for the Marines," I said. He smiled as he shook his head, obviously conflicted on the Marine idea.

"Hey, I just thought of something. Uncle Mo said he needed to get hold of an accountant to straighten out his books. He said it again today. He was thumbing through the ledgers between phone calls. I left when his face turned red."

"Does he hit you?" Clara asked.

"Only that one time…when I had the black eye."

"OK, I think we have a plan," I said. "Gabe, we're going to send Alicia over here to do some accounting. You don't know anything and you don't know Alicia, OK?"

"Sure, I guess."

"Gabe, dear, I know you were only eleven when Joey's plane disappeared, but do you remember how your uncle took the news?"

"No. Not really. But I remember Uncle Mo was mad because Jamie didn't come back to work for a long, long time. While Jamie was gone, Gilbert was injured on the job and they needed more help. When Jamie finally came back, he was like a zombie. No fun anymore."

We said goodnight and Gabe climbed back into the delivery truck. I backed up the pickup, dropped it into drive and pointed it toward the foothills. Clara asked about the details of our plan.

"You heard it, Auntie. We get Mo to hire Alicia for a few days to straighten out his books, simple as that." I glanced in the side mirror. "How long have those headlights been following us?"

"Dear, there are other cars on the road. You need to relax." She took a quick peek at the mirror on her side. I made a left turn into Aromas, circled through town and made another left on to highway 129.

"Where are we going? Did you forget something?"

"The headlights are still there. Hang on." I cranked the wheel hard. We bumped over a small ditch, spun a u-ie and headed back to Aromas at high speed for an old truck. Clara finally caught her breath.

"Oh, my!"

"At least the headlights are gone." I took a breath and smiled in the dark.

"Dear, the lights are back, and there's a red light too." I glanced at the rearview mirror.

"Good grief!" I slowed the truck, pulled off the road and stopped. Clara was already searching the glove compartment for license and insurance papers. Burger Box napkins, forks and packets of mustard tumbled out on their own, unleashing more treasure. A flashlight rolled onto Clara's lap along with a tennis ball, screwdriver and a roll of masking tape. I rolled down my window.

"Ma'am, your driver's license."

"Got it right here…oops, that's not it. I dropped the library card into my purse and fished around some more, vowing to organize my purse as soon as I had time. I found the license and handed it to the highway patrolman.

"Did you know your right taillight is out?"

"Oh, is that why you pulled me over?"

"That little stunt you pulled back there wasn't very smart, but it wasn't illegal. I'll need proof of ownership and insurance…."

"I have it," Clara said. The officer seemed satisfied with the paperwork and let me off with a warning to get the light fixed or get a fix-it ticket. I drove home with one eye on the road and one on the speedometer—when I wasn't checking the mirrors. A pair of headlights followed us into Aromas and disappeared when I turned up my driveway.

CHAPTER 25

Thursday morning was nothing new, no big deal. Clara and I ate breakfast, fussed over Solow and Felix and then left for work. I dropped my aunt in front of the bus station, drove two blocks to the library and parked. Inside the building, I found Kyle sitting on the floor, bent at the waist, brushing in the "bigger than life" leaves and strawberries. Creating depth was simple. We had painted strawberry plants in rows that narrowed and angled toward a vanishing point at the horizon, becoming softer and less distinct as they went.

"Good morning. Berries are looking good, Kyle." I found a pallet, brush and a piece of cold concrete floor to sit on. By noon, we had completed the berries, right down to the highlights on the seeds covering their delicate skins. No wonder I was hungry, stiff and sore. Kyle stood up and stretched. I slowly pulled my body to a standing position.

"Did I tell you, like, Alicia is meeting us for lunch?"

"No, but I already talked to her about it. I can't wait to find out how she's doing." Alicia and I had been on the phone for over an hour the night before, plotting Alicia's installation into the nursery business. But it all came down to the fact that Mo was a man, and would probably hire a beautiful woman even if all she knew were how to buy pretty shoes. But I worried about Alicia and the risky business she was up to.

I drove Kyle to Pajaro and parked in front of the Milagro Mexican food restaurant. It was a colorful, noisy place where the smell of good food made my mouth water. I was relieved to see Alicia seated and waiting for us. She looked fabulous in a dark blue suit I had never seen before.

"Have you ordered yet?" I sat down. She shook her head.

"I was waiting for you guys. I told Mo I had an important meeting to go to. He would have had me working straight through to five o'clock without a break."

"Like, you have another job?" Kyle looked devastated.

"Just some part-time bookkeeping. Don't worry, Kyle, I'll be back at the library in a day or two." His brow relaxed. Alicia looked at me. "The man's books are a disaster, and he hangs over my shoulder most of the time. Every time I start to look for the Gianelli file, he finds another reason to be in the office."

"So you really do know how to straighten up his books?"

"His books will never be the same," she laughed. "I hope I'm helping. After all, he's paying me twelve dollars an hour."

"What a cheap guy. He couldn't hire a babysitter for that," I said and Kyle nodded. We ordered our lunches and then Alicia told me about Mo's filing system and what a mess it was. She said she would try to find Joey's file later in the afternoon.

"Was Gabe around?"

"He loaded his truck early this morning and hasn't been back. I didn't talk to him, and he didn't even look in my direction. I hope we don't get Gabe in trouble with his uncle." Alicia finished her burrito and said she had to get back to work.

"Can't you relax for a few more minutes?"

"Actually, I'm hoping to get a crack at the files before Mo gets back from lunch. See you later." I stifled an urge to tell her not to go. She slipped out the door, leaving me with an uneasy feeling. Alicia was my friend and employee, and I felt responsible for her safety. Kyle and I ate quietly while music blasted and people around us laughed and talked.

I battled an ugly mood all afternoon. Kyle worked in silence, probably not wanting to be involved in female underhanded schemes. We drew life-size outlines of several local historical icons right over the top of the strawberry field. The first figure was Father Junipero Serra. Then came Robert Lewis Stevenson, John Steinbeck, Walt Disney and Ronald Reagan. In time we would outline the drawings with thin black lines, letting the fields show through like a living, growing texture.

"Kyle, let's call it a day. We'll start the black lines tomorrow."
He seemed happy to be leaving. I know I was. I drove to Candy's
shop and burst in the back door. Maurie stood at the sink clipping
rose stems.

"Josephine…is Clara with you?"

"No. She isn't here?" Maurie shook her head and dropped the
roses into a vase. She pulled her rubber gloves off and sighed.

"I'm sure she's fine. A fellow came to see her, and they left
about an hour ago."

"Who was he?"

"Clara didn't introduce him. He seemed to be in a hurry. They
were going to visit someone in the hospital."

"What did he look like?" I asked, feeling a pinch in the back of
my neck.

"I don't know. He knocked on the back door, Clara opened it
and they talked for a couple of minutes outside. She came back in
and told me she was going to the hospital. That's all I know. Can
you drop me at my apartment, Josephine?"

"Sure, did you see the car?"

"No, I was busy right here." She pointed at the sink. "Molly already left…she's delivering flowers. I'm sorry, Josephine. That's
all I know. Can you take me home now?"

"Sure." Maurie locked the back door and hobbled over to my
truck. "When do you think Aunt Clara will be back?" Maurie
shrugged. I dropped her at her apartment, circled around the
downtown Santa Cruz area and parked behind Candy's shop. I
left the radio on for entertainment, hoping Clara would arrive
soon. A half hour passed. I was cold and my mood was going
south of miserable. I pulled my phone out of the cup holder.

"Hi, David, would you mind feeding Solow?"

"Not a problem. Are you working late?"

"Not really. I'm sitting in my truck behind the florist shop
waiting for Aunt Clara. Apparently, she rode off with a man to visit
someone in the hospital. If I knew who the someone was, or the
name of the hospital, I would feel a lot better. Not that I think anything is wrong." I rambled on until David assured me Clara would
be fine. I agreed, and dialed Alicia's number.

"Hi, Josephine," Ernie said. "I'm sorry, but Alicia hasn't come home yet. Anything I can help you with?" I told him I would call back later and dialed Mom.

"Hello, dear. What's on your mind?"

"I'm waiting for Aunt Clara to get back from the hospital...."

"What happened? Is she...."

"It's OK, Mom. She's just visiting someone at the hospital. Trouble is I don't know who she's with and when they will be back. I'm sitting in the truck in Candy's parking lot, afraid to leave, but I'm hungry and cold."

"It's six-thirty and we were going to have dinner soon. I made a lovely batch of curry chicken. I'll drive over there after dinner and give you some leftovers."

"Thanks, Mom. I've been trying to think who she's with. Who would be in the hospital?"

"Actually, Bob mentioned that Wayne's wife, ah, Darla is in the hospital. She stepped outside for the mail this morning and fainted right in front of the next-door neighbor. Wayne wasn't home at the time." I rolled my eyes.

"Do they know what's wrong with her?"

"That's all I know, dear." We hung up and I began counting the minutes until my chicken curry arrived. The minutes dragged and my imagination raced. Did Darla fall and break something? Was she weak from not eating enough, or did she have a disease? Was it a faint or a heart attack? I fired up the engine and put the heater on about every ten minutes. I was toasty warm when Dad parked the Buick next to my truck. Mom came to the window.

"Hi, honey. Here's your dinner." Mom lifted a foil-wrapped plate up to the window, and I pulled it inside. The savory aroma was beyond imagination. My stomach did a happy dance. Dad handed me a mug of hot coffee.

"Thanks. I'll stay another half hour or so." They wished me luck and left. Halfway into my dinner, the cell phone rang.

"Hi, Mom."

"Honey, I called Dominican Hospital. Darla's in room 204." There was a silence. "I asked about Clara, but the nurse I talked to hadn't seen her."

"Guess I'll wait a little bit longer...and then stop by the hospital, but first I'll call the house. Clara is probably home waiting for me right now." We hung up. I called home and let the phone ring a long time. I finally gave up and called David.

"What do you mean, Josie? She has to be somewhere. Maybe you should ask around at the hospital. Let me know when you find her."

"Talk to you later, David." We hung up. My stomach was full but my legs were turning into popsicles so I fired up the engine again to keep warm. It was almost eight o'clock when I gave up and drove across town to Dominican Hospital. I sat in the shadowy parking lot for a few minutes, scanning the area for a sweet old woman with billowy white hair. After living with Clara for three weeks, I felt we were more like sisters than aunt and niece. Of course there was the age gap, but it didn't seem to matter to either of us.

I marched up to the hospital information desk and asked the ancient, half-asleep volunteer if he had seen an older woman with white hair and a pretty face. I mentioned that she was close to my height and might be in the company of a sturdy-looking older fellow named Mr. Bracken. The old gent shook his head.

"That's OK, I'll ask Darla...that is, the patient." I hurried up the stairs and searched the second floor for room 204. The door was ajar so I stepped in. Darla was lying on her back with a tube up her nose and another dripping into one arm. Her skin color matched the sheets. I leaned over her and called her name. One eye opened slowly.

"Darla, how are you feeling?"

"Who are you?"

"Josephine, Clara's niece." Darla's other eye opened. "Have you seen my Aunt Clara?"

"Jamie was here...and Sal and Angela...and...." Her eyes closed and the door flew open behind me. I twirled around and faced an angry nurse pushing a cart full of needles and other scary medical supplies. I felt nauseous just looking at the stuff.

"What are you doing in here? This patient shouldn't be disturbed," the nurse said. I looked at her collection of needles and medicines and cocked my head. If anyone was guilty of disturbing someone, it was the nurse with the tray full of scary stuff. I squeezed past her and beat it down the hall to the first nurses' station.

"Can I help you ma'am?" a kindly nurse, wearing a green smock, asked.

"Yes. Can you tell me what's wrong with the patient in 204, Darla Bracken?"

"Are you family?" I shook my head. "I'm sorry...."

"I have another question." The middle-aged nurse frowned. "I'm looking for my aunt. She's about my height, seventy-five years old with fluffy white hair and pretty green eyes."

"I'm sorry...."

"She was with a gentleman, Darla's husband, actually, Wayne Bracken." The nurse's eyes rolled to the ceiling. When they dropped back to look at me, she wasn't smiling.

"Yes, Mr. Bracken was here when my shift started, but I don't remember seeing the woman." I thanked the nurse and left the building. My truck was cold again, or was it a chill brought on by irrational thoughts and conjectures? It would take more than chicken curry to ease my nerves. My stomach felt crampy for a moment.

From the hospital parking lot, I called Mom, David and then my home phone. Where could Clara be? I decided to check the flower shop one more time, but it turned out to be a waste of time and gas. Candy's parking lot was empty, except for the delivery van. My stomach felt tight and crampy again. I decided to drive the few blocks to Mom and Dad's house.

"Josephine, did you find Clara?" Mom asked, shivering at the front door. I shook my head. "Come in, honey, it's freezing out there." Dad was asleep on the couch so we went into the kitchen and sat at the breakfast bar. Mom said she was glad that Clara was with Wayne and maybe they were out getting a bite to eat.

"Mom, it's nine o'clock. I was supposed to pick her up no later than five-thirty. Aunt Clara has never done anything irresponsible like this before." I gulped some air as a couple of spasms tore through my mid-section followed by a heat wave and perspiration.

"I know, honey. I'm a little concerned myself."

"I think I'll stop by the Bracken's house on the way home. Maybe that's where she is." I bent down and brushed imaginary dust off my shoe, trying not to groan out loud.

"That's probably where she is," Mom said as she walked to the den and came back with a book I had wanted to borrow. She handed it to me and then poured two cups of tea. "Are you feeling all right, honey?" I started to tell her I was fine, but a cramp caught me by surprise. I groaned and hugged the countertop.

"You don't look well. That's how your father looked before he fell asleep on the couch."

"Did his stomach hurt?"

"I think so. He was twisting all around and perspiring."

"What did you put in the chicken dish?"

"Chicken…it's the same old recipe I always use. The chicken came from Mrs. Hawkins up the street who gave it to Myrtle, but Myrtle had no room in her freezer so she gave it to me." Mom took a sip of tea.

"Mom, you seem to be feeling fine…but you don't like chicken. You didn't eat it, did you?" She shook her head.

"You can never trust poultry. I guess that's why I never liked it. But your dad loves my curry chicken, poor dear. Drink your tea, honey, you'll feel better."

I slid off my stool and stumbled down the hall to the bathroom, hugging my ribs with both arms. When I had finally purged everything painful out of my body, I staggered, weak as a wet sandwich, over to the guest room and crawled into bed. The last thing I remembered was Mom tucking me in. I would have smiled but I didn't have the strength.

I slept through a hailstorm; but when thunder rattled the windows, I rolled over and fell off the narrow bed. I sat on an old braided rug looking around the dark bedroom that used to be mine, forty years ago. A plug-in ballerina nightlight added a spooky effect to a castle painted on the opposite wall. At fourteen years old, it was my first mural attempt. I was quite proud of the picture and added new features now and then, like a garden, an orchard and a prince and princess riding short-legged horses.

My legs quivered as I pulled myself up onto the bed. I had experienced chicken pox, flu, a sprained ankle and several cases of food poisoning in that bed. I crossed the room and looked down the dark hall as rain pelted the roof and blew against the windows. It was two o'clock in the morning when I grabbed my purse, stole out of my parent's house and drove through blinding rain to Darla's house. I rushed to the door and rang the bell non-stop for a long time. No one came to the door. Maybe Wayne had gone back to the hospital, but where was Clara?

I wasn't ready to give up. I unlatched a garden gate at the side of the house and sloshed along the wet walkway to the tiny backyard. I pressed my face against the window in the back of the attached one-car garage, but all I saw was a black abyss. I tried the back door. It was locked, so I sloshed back around the house to my truck, climbed in and a minute later, the driver's seat was as wet as I was. I cranked up the heater, creating a lot of unwanted steam. The defroster was periodically overwhelmed, and I had to wipe the windshield with a wet sleeve as I drove.

It was three o'clock in the morning when I finally crawled into my own bed, full of worry and dread. In my dreams, I heard Clara's voice. I stared into a dark, scary place, pleading for her to come home with me. Her voice sounded miles away. I turned to leave, but a door slammed in front of me.

CHAPTER 26

All the sunshine in the world couldn't brighten my outlook on life. Life had given me the shaft, ripped my heart out and stomped on my worthless brain. It was a "Black Friday," in the worst sense of the word. I ignored annoying streaks of sunlight streaming into my bedroom from half-closed blinds. Birds chirped sarcastically outside and Solow wasn't in his bed. I told myself it was all a bad dream—Clara wasn't missing; she was busy making breakfast in the kitchen. I almost believed my own lie and got up to check out the kitchen.

"OK, Solow, out you go." Who knows how long he had been standing by the door, waiting to be let outside for another Fluffy encounter. I opened the door and watched Solow bound through knee-high wet grass all the way to the base of Fluffy's perch, a fencepost. The lone post was the only thing remaining from a fence long ago dissolved by decades of weather. I could almost see Fluffy's lip curl into a smile as my exasperated dog howled at the sun. I thought about smiling, but it would have hurt too much. The phone rang.

"Hello?"

"Hi, Josie. Are you sick...or something?"

"Oh, David, I can't (sob) find Aunt Clara. I don't know where to look."

"I'll be right over." He hung up. I hurried to the bathroom, splashed water on my red hot eyes, quickly brushed a glob of toothpaste back and forth over my teeth a few times, rinsed and ran a brush through my hair. David knocked on the back door. I let him in and sobbed my heart out on his soft, baby blue sweater. He held me for a long time.

"Have you called…?"

"No, I just got up." Like he couldn't tell I was wearing pajamas?

"How about a cup of coffee?" he asked, already running water into Mr. Coffee's glass pot. "Are you going to work today?" I shook my head. "Sit down and tell me all about it."

"Darla's in the hospital, but I still don't know why; and her two sons, granddaughter and Wayne all came to see her. At least that's what Darla said. Her mind is usually a little muddled."

"I take it you didn't see these people?"

"No, and I asked three people about Aunt Clara and no one had seen her there." (Sniff)

"Have you called Ben yet?" I shook my head.

"That's a good idea…and maybe I can talk to Jamie too." I fumbled through the junk drawer, pulled out my personal little phone book and a minute later had Ben on the phone.

"Josephine, I don't understand what you're telling me. Who did Clara go with?"

"That's the problem, I don't know. All Maurie knew was that it was a man. He stayed outside and she never saw him. Aunt Clara told Maurie she was going to the hospital to see a friend. Mom and I figured it must be Darla. We don't know anyone else in the hospital. Is Jamie there?"

"Actually, he borrowed my truck yesterday afternoon to go see his mother and hasn't come back yet. Let me know if you find out where Clara is. I worry about that ol' gal." His voice sounded full of concern. We hung up and I called Sal. Angela answered the phone in a thick voice.

"Hi, Angela. How are you?"

"Is this Josephine?"

"Yeah, is your dad home?"

"I don't think so. I just woke up…I'll look around." I sipped my coffee and waited. Finally Angela came back. "Nope, he's gone." She hung up the phone. I immediately called back.

"Yeah?"

"Angela, I just wanted to know if you visited your grandmother in the hospital last night."

"Yeah."

"Was my Aunt Clara there?"

"No."

"Was Jamie there…and your dad and Wayne?"

"Dad and Uncle Jamie were there."

"What is wrong with your grandma?"

"Dad said she was dehydrated and anemic."

"OK, thank you, Angela." We hung up. David read my face and knew I was disappointed. "It sounds like Darla was right about Sal, Angela, and Jamie," I said. "I guess that means she was probably right about Clara not being there."

"Take it easy, honey. We'll find out, but in the meantime I think we should call the authorities." I nodded. He picked up the phone and dialed.

We waited an eternity for the sheriff's deputies to show up. I had time to shower and dress while David fed Solow and Felix and served up some great waffles and fruit. I took a small portion, not trusting my stomach. David cocked his head.

"Not hungry?"

"Just being careful. Mom poisoned me last night. Not on purpose, of course. She accidentally got a hold of an old chicken." David nodded as if he knew exactly what I was talking about and could feel my pain. The doorbell rang. Solow began barking, Felix hid in the loft and David opened the front door.

"Deputy Lund, Deputy Sayer, come in and sit down," David said. The officers sat on the sofa and glared at us as if we were breathing too much of their valuable air. I sat in the rocker and David sat on the bottom step leading to the loft.

"How can we help you folks today?" Deputy Lund said in her usual flat tone.

"My Aunt Clara is missing. Her boss said she left work yesterday with a man."

"How old is your aunt, ma'am?"

"Seventy-five. I know, she's old enough to take care of herself, but she would never leave without telling me where she was going. See, I was supposed to pick her up after work and supposedly she went to the hospital, but no one saw her there and she didn't come back to Candy's shop and she wasn't at Wayne's house…."

"Do you have a picture of your aunt?" Deputy Sayer asked.

"I'm not sure…maybe an old one."

"You can drop it off at the Salinas office on Aguajito Road," Sayer said.

"Ma'am, how long has she been missing?" Officer Lund asked as Sayer scribbled on his notepad. I counted on my fingers and thought a moment.

"Seventeen hours." The deputies stood up.

"If it hasn't been twenty-four hours, there's not much we can do. We'll put her on the list. If she's not back by four o'clock, give us a call." They darted out the door before I could say another word.

"She would never go with a stranger…so it has to be someone she knows," I said, more to myself than David. I found a pen and paper and began writing a list of Clara's male friends. I started with Jamie, then Sal, Patrick, Ben, Wayne, Mo, Gabe, Robert, and Moses. If she had more male acquaintances, I didn't know about them—and my dad didn't count.

"What was she wearing?" David asked. I closed my eyes and tried to remember Thursday morning.

"Navy blue sweat suit, gray jacket, red scarf and clear plastic galoshes."

"Did she seem stressed or anything?"

"I don't think so. It was an ordinary morning. She made coffee and burnt toast. I dropped her at the bus station…and that's the last time I saw…." (Sniff) David put an arm around my shoulder. "We have to do something," I choked. The phone rang and I jumped. I was wound way too tight. It was Dad.

"What's the matter, Dad?"

"Your mother thinks you're mad at her. Actually, she thinks I am, too. I told her it was nothing. My stomach is fine today. How is yours, honey?"

"My stomach is OK. All I can think about is Aunt Clara. I'm so worried. According to the deputy sheriff, she's not an official 'missing person' until twenty-four hours go by. They put her on a list of missing persons, but won't actually look for her until four o'clock this afternoon."

"I know, honey. Your mother tried to contact Candy, but we think she's out of town. If there's anything else we can do, give us a call." We hung up. I was pretty sure Mom was more worried than all of us, but she would never show it. She typically made a big fuss over little things but didn't come unhinged over serious problems. I suspected she kept them bottled up inside. I watched David pacing the room.

"I know...let's go for a drive. It'll take your mind off...your aunt."

"Yeah, let's go. We can visit a few people while we're out." I grabbed my list and a coat. "I'll drive." David frowned, but followed me out the door. He seemed to relax once we turned onto San Juan Road. "I think Sal should be our first stop." I handed him the list.

Traffic was light as we sailed through Watsonville and then north to Santa Cruz. I took the Morrissey exit and two minutes later, we were parked in front of the impressive Gianelli home.

David helped me down from my seat, probably realizing I felt a little weak from my exposure to bad chicken. His hand was warm and I took it gladly.

"So this is where Sal lives. Nice digs."

"Yeah, he really fell into it, didn't he? It belonged to his mom and dad." I led the way to the front door and rang the bell. Angela opened the door wearing a UCSC t-shirt and pink pajama bottoms.

"Ah, you want my dad?"

"Yes, please. May we come in?" Angela stepped back and we entered.

"I'll get him." She dragged herself upstairs. David and I made ourselves comfortable on the sofa and waited. Sal thundered down the stairs and into the living room.

"Josephine, what a surprise." He looked surprised all right.

"Sal, I'd like you to meet my friend, David Galaz." They shook hands and sat down.

"Your timing is very good. I just got back from the hospital. Mom's feeling a little better."

"Yes, I saw Darla last night. Angela told me she was dehydrated and anemic."

"That's right. So what is it you want to know?" he asked.

"My Aunt Clara is missing. We think someone took her to the hospital to see Darla, but we don't know who. The authorities are on the case as we speak. Did you happen see my aunt last night?" Sal squirmed in his seat.

"I'm afraid we didn't see your aunt last night. Angela and I were the first ones to visit my mother. We were in the parking lot getting ready to leave when my brother drove up."

"Did you talk to Jamie?"

"Yeah, for a minute, but I had called him at Ben's place as soon as I found out about Mom. He said he would drive down right away. We didn't talk much at the hospital. He was in a hurry to see Mom."

"Here's my card. Please call if you hear anything…anything at all about Clara."

"No problem. Hope you find her." Sal walked us to the door and stood watching as we approached the pickup and climbed in. Angela watched from a second-story dormer. I fired up the engine and wedged my way into lunch hour traffic.

"Where to?" I asked David, hoping he would somehow sense something I had missed. "I've been thinking. Why would Aunt Clara be invited to visit Darla at the hospital? She isn't family. This is a Gianelli family affair," I said. David studied the list.

"While we're in Santa Cruz, I think we should see if Wayne is home."

"Yeah, I guess we should, although the guy is never home. He's the one I told you about with his arm around the younger woman. Thank goodness Darla didn't see him." I changed lanes, crossed over the freeway and made a left turn onto Gross Avenue. The neighborhood was "old folks quiet" as I parked at the curb. We marched up to the door and I knocked. I was ready to give up when the door opened. Wayne poked his head out.

"Josephine, what are you doing here…I mean, come in."

"Wayne, this is my friend, David Galaz. We're looking for…."

"Here, sit down. Would you like a cup of coffee?" It smelled fresh-perked.

"Ah, that would be nice. I...." Wayne was already in the kitchen rattling cups and asking if we wanted cream or sugar. He set our steaming mugs on the coffee table and went back for his. He sat down in Darla's chair and gave us an update on her condition, saying he would be able to bring her home the next day if she kept improving.

"Wayne, I'm glad Darla is going to be OK, but the reason we're here is my Aunt Clara is missing. We were wondering if you saw her last night at the hospital." He tilted his head as his eyes searched the wall thoughtfully. Finally, he turned his eyes to me and frowned.

"No, Josephine. I've been so busy taking care of Darla...I haven't been anywhere else, and I didn't see Clara at the hospital. What do you think happened to her?" He calmly sipped his coffee while I bit my lip and concentrated on not screaming at him for being the biggest phony and worst husband alive. After we left, I wished I had screamed at him. David helped me into the truck.

"I'm so angry I could...." I sputtered as my truck roared up the highway.

"I know, sweetie. You're afraid he will abandon his wife whenever he feels like it."

"You took the words right out of my mouth, and since he lies about being a good husband, maybe he lies about other things. I'm so scared we won't find Clara."

"Where do you want to go next?" David asked, his eyes wandering over to the speedometer. I let off the gas and concentrated on traffic. "How about lunch?"

"Wayne makes me sick, but I could eat a few bites of something light."

"If you take the second Watsonville exit we can eat at Cilantros." He knew I loved Mexican food. Wayne had left a bad taste in my mouth, but I forced myself to eat. I polished off a large burrito with beans and rice. It was almost as good as Alicia's cooking. We sipped hot tea and reviewed the list. David pointed to Gabe's name.

"Gabe? You've got to be kidding. Clara came this close to

adopting him." I held up my forefinger positioned half an inch from my thumb. David laughed. "But we could stop at Alicia's and see if she was able to inspect Mo's books."

"Huh?"

"Oh, I forgot to tell you. Mo hired Alicia to reorganize his books at the nursery." I ignored David's intense stare. "We're trying to help Darla get her investment money, and we wanted to know if Mo has been paying her like he's supposed to." I smiled. David shook his head slowly.

"Is Alicia trained as an accountant?"

"No, but she's smart. She'll figure it out," I said, confidently.

"What makes you think Darla is being cheated?"

"She's so poor. No food. Her clothes are rags…."

"Maybe she's eccentric or feeble-minded. How do you know that she's poor?"

"Well, I don't know for sure, but we'll find out when Alicia studies the books." Actually, I had never questioned Darla's poverty. We finished our tea, David paid the bill and we scrambled back into my truck. Alicia's house was only five minutes away, but I was questioned by David the whole way. The Quintana home was a welcome refuge. I rang the doorbell. Trigger greeted us and led us to the kitchen where the family was finishing their lunch at the breakfast bar. Alicia stood up and stared at me.

"You're not working today?" I shook my head. "I should talk. I called in sick at the nursery. I'm exhausted."

"Ernie, don't get up." David pulled up a barstool and the guys began a discussion about basketball, the last thing in the world I was interested in. Alicia carried her plate to the sink and then we went to the living room for comfort and privacy. Trigger followed.

"Trigger, would you mind getting my coat from the truck?" He scooped up his little sheltie, ran to the front door and slammed it behind him.

"I'm exhausted, Jo. Morton had me working non-stop until seven last night. He kept asking me to finish one more thing and one more until I finally walked out. I'm making thirty-two dollars an hour now. Every time he asks me to stay longer, he adds five more dollars. What's the matter, Jo? You look worse than I feel."

"Clara's missing...." All of a sudden, tears were streaming down my cheeks. Alicia leaned closer and we hugged which made for even more tears. I managed to tell Alicia the whole story between sobs and hiccups. "It's been close to twenty-four hours. In another hour, I have to call the Sheriff. I really thought we would have found her by now."

"I'll help you any way I can," Alicia said.

"I have no idea what to do...how to find her. Clara and I usually think a lot alike, but she really has me stumped. If only Maurie had seen the car."

"I'll be praying for her," Alicia said.

"Thank you. What about Mo's books?" I sniffed.

"Nothing yet. He's always around, showing me more work to do. If I could just be alone for awhile." Trigger handed me my coat and then headed outside to play in the backyard. "I'll work for Mo one more day. Why don't you question him Monday? Maybe that will give me enough time to check out the Gianelli file." Monday was a faraway place that I immediately put out of my mind. But I went through the motions of normalcy, as if the world still spun on its axis and sweet old ladies were not in danger.

"Good idea, Allie." David and Ernie entered the room. "We have to go—more places to look, more people to talk to," I said.

"Don't worry, Josie, we'll find Clara," David said as he helped me into my coat. I couldn't look Allie in the face without a flood of tears, so I stared at my feet all the way to the truck. David helped me into the passenger seat. I didn't object. He drove while I tried to plan the next step.

"Since you're heading back to Aromas, we might as well stop at the nursery and talk to Mo." David agreed and parked beside a delivery truck in front of Mo's building. I pointed to a young man cornering the building pushing a dolly loaded with sacks of fertilizer. We climbed out of the truck and met him halfway.

"Hi, Gabe."

"What's new with you guys?" he asked.

"My Aunt Clara is missing. Have you seen her in the last twenty-four hours?"

"Actually, the last time I saw her was when I made a delivery at the florist shop yesterday around four. I asked Maurie where Clara was going. She said something about going to the hospital, but she didn't even know who the guy was." A kettledrum pulsed in my ears.

"What did he look like?"

"I only got a quick glance. He wore a baseball hat and sunglasses. They were leaving the parking lot as I was pulling in. I guess he was kinda big, sort of average looking...old, sixties or seventies maybe."

"Gabe, take your time, try to remember. What did the car look like?"

"White, kind of old, but not real old. Compact, I'd say." He scratched his head and looked at my truck. "Yeah, it was a compact four-door...something."

"Thanks, Gabe. If you remember any more details, call me." I handed him my card.

CHAPTER 27

L ife was not fair, but Friday had been unfair times ten. I had to report my own lovable aunt "missing." After much self-analysis, while lying in bed staring at the ceiling, I came to the conclusion that everything was my fault. I should have stopped looking for Joey's murderer long ago. Clara would have stopped looking if I had refused to drive her around, snooping into people's affairs. I had put her in harm's way and would do anything to get her back. If a ransom note came, I would sell my house to get Aunt Clara back.

Solow looked at me from across the room and groaned—my feelings exactly. It was Saturday and I was in no hurry to leave my warm bed. I had not come up with a plan for finding Clara. I wanted to stay in bed all day and pretend nothing was wrong, but someone was pounding on the front door. I pulled on my robe, hurried through the house and opened the door.

"Al, I mean, Jamie, ah, what...?"

"My brother said your aunt is missing. We want to help you find her." Jamie moved inside as Ben stepped up to the door and gave me a hug. He smelled like clean air and soap with a hint of wood smoke. No wonder Clara was crazy about him.

"That's really great. Thank you, but I don't have a clue where to look. David and I talked to Sal and Wayne yesterday. Actually, Gabe saw the car and the man but his description wasn't very good. I'm hoping he'll remember something and call me."

"That's a start, right there," Ben said. "Do you have a picture of Clara?"

"Somewhere. Make yourselves comfortable. I'll get dressed and then I'll look for the picture." I remembered a nice picture of

Dad and Clara from last thanksgiving. They were laughing as they pulled on the wishbone. Mom took the picture, and then Dad was showing off and pulled extra hard on the bone. The bone broke and he fell off the stool. It cost him several chiropractic visits.

From my bedroom, I heard the front door. David was talking to Jamie and Ben. We would have a sizable search party.

David had driven his Jeep to my house, prepared to continue the search for Clara. He took over the kitchen and made breakfast for everyone, including Solow. All I had to do was eat a few bites, grab the photo of Clara and climb into the Jeep. Jamie and Ben sat in the back. I forced myself to ride along on the hopeless search. Two miles from home my cell phone rang.

"Hi, Mom, what's the matter?"

"I didn't go to Garden Club this morning, and I canceled my dentist appointment for this afternoon. Now I wish I hadn't canceled because I'm going crazy with worry, just sitting around with nothing to do." I had never heard my mother talk this way.

"Take it easy, Mom. I talked to Gabe yesterday and he saw Clara leaving Candy's shop. He described the car and the man."

"So who was it?"

"Actually the description wasn't very good. The man was pretty old, kind of big and looked average." I could feel her disappointment over the phone. I told her we were already out looking for Clara and to keep her spirits up. First time I ever had to tell her that!

David asked where I wanted to go first.

"First we need to stop and make copies of this photo," I said. He pulled in at Staples. I erased Dad from the picture and blew Clara up. Minutes later we had a stack of flyers featuring Clara, and a stubborn wishbone with my two phone numbers under it.

"Where to?" David asked.

"I think we should stop at the Watsonville Market and talk to Robert," I said over the noisy Jeep engine. Jamie and Ben grunted their approval as air whistled through cracks in the canvas top. Minutes later David parked his four-wheel-drive refrigerator at the market. I went inside with Ben, glad for a chance to warm up, not that grocery stores are very warm.

"Where is Robert when we need him?" I mumbled to myself.

"You sound a bit grumpy, Jo," Robert said as he pushed a loaded dolly behind us. He parked it and asked who died.

"No one died...but my Aunt Clara is missing."

"Gosh, I'm sorry. I didn't mean anything...."

"Don't worry about it Robert, just be on the lookout for her. Keep your ears open too. Can you post these for us?" I handed him three posters.

"Oh, sure, I'll get right on it."

"Thanks...." The words stuck in my throat. I turned and quickly led Ben out of the store before my emotions went out of control. David drove through town, stopping at various stores, gas stations and restaurants. Ben and I took turns jumping out of the car to post the "missing person" signs.

"Let's post a couple at the bus terminal. No telling how many friends she made over there," I said. Ben and I each took posters into the crowd of transit customers. We asked people if they had seen the woman in the picture. One pale zombie-girl, dressed in black, smiled and said she remembered Clara—the nice lady who talked to her about sunshine and vitamin D. She said she had not seen my aunt in several days. I posted my flyers and Ben did the same.

"Any luck?" David asked as I hopped into my seat.

"Not exactly, but Clara definitely made some friends." The zombie had given me a spark of hope. If she remembered my aunt, maybe other people would too. David drove one block and stopped at a crosswalk. I jumped out of the Jeep and quickly posted a sign on a telephone pole a couple of inches above a missing poodle flyer. I saw a policeman standing on the sidewalk shaking his head at me.

"There's already a missing dog flyer." I pointed to the picture of a little white dog. "Mine is a missing, PERSON...." But he wasn't going to budge on the matter. I had been caught in the act. I yanked the sign and jumped into the car. David drove on. Two blocks later, I posted a flyer on a telephone pole and felt better. We papered the town and then sat at a table by the window of the local diner waiting for my cell phone to ring. It was so quiet I could hear the skin cells on my forehead discussing configurations for new worry lines. David had a few of his own.

"Don't worry, Josie. It's going to be all right." He laid his hand on mine. I wished I could believe him. Was Clara hungry or cold or hurt? Not knowing was the hardest part.

"What are you guys going to do now?" I asked, looking at Jamie and Ben.

"Guess we'll head back to Boulder Creek," Ben said.

"We'll stop in Santa Cruz and put up more posters," Jamie added.

"Thanks for helping me today. I think I need to go comfort my mom." David nodded.

"I'll post some flyers while you're gone," he said. David drove us back to my house. Jamie and Ben left in Ben's truck and I drove to Santa Cruz alone. I parked at the curb in front of Mom and Dad's house and rested my head on the steering wheel for a couple of minutes. I tried to think happy thoughts, but happy was far, far away. I finally dragged myself up to the front door and knocked. Dad opened the door looking like his best friend had died. Mom looked worse.

"I came over to cheer you up," I said. Mom took my jacket and Dad made me a hot cup of cocoa. We played a quiet game of hearts and then watched a mystery on TV. Jessica solved the latest murder in Cabot Cove with her usual finesse. I had worked with Clara for weeks on Joey's murder and still didn't have a clue. My cell phone jolted me out of my lethargic mood.

"Hello?"

"Hi, Jo, it's Alicia. How is the search going?"

"We did the best we could."

"I wish I could help somehow. I'm praying you'll find her. Don't give up."

"Thank you, Allie."

"Mo called a minute ago and asked if I would work a few hours tomorrow. He said he won't be able to be there very long, but he has some work for me that can't wait. This is my chance. He won't be hanging over me all day. I'll let you know what I find. Good luck, Jo. I know you'll find her." We hung up. The five o'clock news came on.

"I remember taking that picture," Mom said when Clara's face filled the TV screen.

"I'm glad she's on the news," I choked on the words. "Maybe someone will call." I crossed my fingers on both hands. I stayed with Mom and Dad through dinner, figuring the odds of being poisoned twice in a row were slim, and as depressed as I was, it didn't matter anyway. The pot roast sunk to the bottom of my belly like a rock. There was no joy in eating—no joy anywhere. My cell phone rang. I jumped.

"Hello?"

"It's me, David. I was wondering if you would like to watch a movie with me tonight."

"Sure. I'll be home in a couple of hours." I hung up. I was no comfort to Mom and Dad, so why not go home?

On my way out of town, I decided to stop at Abigail's. Maybe she would have some psychic news vibes about Aunt Clara. I climbed the creaky stairs to her front porch and knocked on the door. A full moon hovered over the house as cold air rustled nearby tree branches. Time passed. I knocked again. I heard creaky footsteps on the steps behind me. I bristled and turned.

"Oh, it's you."

"Hello. This is my house. Can I help you?" Abigail asked.

"Remember me? I'm Josephine, Clara's niece…remember, we were here…." She moved closer to me and studied my face.

"It's cold out here. Let's go inside." She led me through the foyer into the front room and pointed to the "sink at your own risk" sofa. I sunk into it feeling glad to be out of the frigid night air. I wondered if Clara was warm enough.

"Now, tell me why you didn't bring Clara along with you. Is she mad at me?"

"No, of course not. I would have brought her but she's missing. No one has seen her in two days and I'm worried sick. I thought maybe you could, ah, ask your friends where she is…or something."

"Excuse me. I'll heat up the teakettle." She hustled into the kitchen. I followed. She made a quick turn and I ran into her.

"I'm so sorry, Abigail. I just wanted to help you."

"Call me Abby. Hand me a match and we'll get the water boiling in no time." I handed her a match and she lit a burner on the massive gas stove from the Stone Age. We sat at the kitchen table and waited for the pot to whistle. "Now, dear, why did you say you were here?"

"I'm trying to find Aunt Clara. Don't you have a Ouija board or something?"

"Why would I have one of those things? I don't believe in things like that. Oh, my, there goes the teakettle." She jumped up and poured the hot water into a teapot. "It's best to live in the real world, don't you think?" I nodded, feeling like a fool. "Now, you should tell the police to get busy and find your aunt." I nodded again and told her I had already called the authorities. She poured two cups of tea and set out a bowl of gumdrops.

"Did you see Clara's picture on the news tonight?" I asked. She shook her head and smiled.

"I was at Pierre's house. He lives next door."

"Oh." I finished my tea and told Abigail I needed to go home because my neighbor was waiting for me. She smiled knowingly. "Thank you for the tea. Here's my card. Call me if you hear from Clara." We walked to the front room and paused.

"I'll see if my friends have seen Clara." Abigail ran her gaze around the room, up the dark staircase and back to me.

"They don't seem to know anything, but I'll keep after them." She walked me to the door and said goodbye. I took a breath of cold air, thanked God for my sanity and hurried to the truck. It was almost nine. We hadn't found Clara and my heart was breaking. I asked myself over and over, what more could I do to find her. Halfway home I turned on the wipers due to a light sprinkle. I imagined angels crying tiny teardrops as I drove up my driveway, parked next to David's Jeep and rested my head on the steering wheel until I was forced inside by the cold.

"Hi, Josie, honey. You're just in time for a good movie. David stood up and took my coat while Solow circled my legs, wagging his tail.

"I don't know if...."

"Come on, Josie, sit down. I made some popcorn…just relax."

"Did anyone call? Are there any messages?"

"I'm afraid not. How about a cup of tea?" He was standing again, ready to race to the kitchen to make tea or coffee or something to make me happy. But happy wasn't going to happen.

"My phone didn't ring either." My words sounded bitterly sad.

"How are your folks?"

"Upset." I sat down beside David and pretended to watch "Sleepless in Seattle," one of my favorite movies. I usually cried at the end, but this time my eyes were dry. I was all cried out. If only I would feel sleepy and fall asleep with my head on David's shoulder, but sleepy wasn't happening either. My mind raced from one grave scenario to another. Finally, I imagined Clara stranded, alone, in a broken down fishing boat off the coast. Giant waves tossed the boat against a rocky shore.

"Josie, now that the movie's over, is there anything you need before I go home?"

"It's over? Goodnight, David…and thank you." I heard the Jeep fire up and then tires crunching on gravel. I wished I could have been better company for my friend. I tried reading. I read each sentence five times and still didn't know what they said. Finally, I gave up the book and turned the TV to an old Perry Mason show. Ten minutes into it, with heavy eyelids, I succumbed.

A terrible nightmare held me hostage as I slept on the couch. Clara was crying and pleading for help. I couldn't see her in the dark prison. I tried to stand up to help her, but my legs were tied in knots and my hands were glued to the floor. Bugs crawled over my fingers as I called out for help.

CHAPTER 28

Sunday, two in the morning, I shot up to a sitting position and looked around. Solow was lying next to the couch looking up at me in the semi-darkness. My body felt wet and then cold after sloughing off a quilted lap blanket. I urgently tried to bring back the nightmare, even though it scared the bejesus out of me. I tried and tried to identify Clara's prison. I saw bugs walk over my hands, Clara was crying, the Beatles were singing "A Hard Day's Night" in the background…and the bugs were beetles!

"Oh, my God! Solow, I know where she is! I raced to the kitchen, threw several bottles of water, a block of cheese and a bag of apples into a shopping bag. I topped it off with a jar of peanut butter and a bag of chips. I pulled on a jacket, grabbed my purse, Solow's leash and the quilt on the way out. Solow followed me out the door. I put the bag in the back of the truck and hiked Solow into his seat. I ran back and grabbed Clara's good coat with the fake-fur collar and silky tassel on the zipper.

"OK, Solow, we're going to bring our auntie home." I fired up the engine and Solow howled. We swerved onto Otis, flew through town and then I put the pedal to the metal when we entered San Juan Road. The old Mazda truck rattled, bounced and picked up speed. My heart was racing as we tore through the dark night. There was not one car on the road, except for the one coming up fast behind us. Did I mention the red light?

"Think we can outrun him?" I asked Solow. I braked and pulled onto the shoulder, tears streaming down my cheeks. I opened the window and looked up at the Highway Patrol officer.

"Ma'am, your taillight is out…how fast do you think you were going?"

"Officer, I'm sorry. But my aunt's life is in danger. I was driv-ing fast because she's been hungry and cold for almost three days…locked in a boxcar!" Solow howled, adding a plea of his own.

"Ma'am, I need to see your driver's license and registration."

"Please, Officer, I beg you. Come with me and you'll see for yourself. It's only about a mile from here. She'll die out there if we don't hurry. Please!" I handed him my library card and he handed it back.

"Sorry, here's my license, insurance and registration. Normally I'm a very good driver, but my aunt is locked in a boxcar. We have to save her."

"How do you know your aunt is in a boxcar?" He smiled. I burst into tears.

"Officer, I don't care about the ticket…we have to save her. Can we go in your car?" He looked stunned.

"Ma'am, please step out of the truck." His smile was gone. I did as I was told. I even walked the stupid line he drew with his boot in the dirt. He finished writing the ticket and handed it to me. "If I see you out here again tonight, I'll have to notify the sheriff. Get that light fixed." He turned and walked to his car. I watched him get in and wait for me to leave. I turned the key and headed down San Juan Road at a conservative speed. After two turns in the road, I pushed the gas pedal to the floor. Solow went back against the seat, lifted his head and howled mournfully.

"Don't worry, we'll find her." Solow turned his head and licked my cheek. "This looks like the dirt road. I remember the 'no trespassing' sign." I made a sharp left and cruised straight to the railroad tracks. We crossed the tracks. I turned right and drove with the right wheels on gravel and the left wheels in mud and let-tuce leaves. I parked just short of the first boxcar, set the brake and held Clara's coat to Solow's nose for a moment. We climbed out of the truck.

"Stay with me, Solow." As we walked toward the first boxcar, I noticed the door was wide open. The next car was the same. In all, there were only seven boxcars and they all had their doors open. I looked down the empty tracks, wondering what to do next.

I had been so sure, positive, actually, that she was locked in a box-car. I remembered what it was like to be locked up, and then we woke up in Santa Maria.

"Solow, I know where she is!" I ran to the truck with Solow galloping along behind. I hoisted him into his seat, circled the truck and climbed in. Backing up in the dark for two blocks was not easy, but we finally arrived at the little road I was looking for. We crossed the railroad tracks and motored in a straight line between lettuce fields toward San Juan Road where a parked sheriff's car with circling red lights had a spotlight trained on us. I stopped twenty feet short of the cruiser and rolled down the window. A deputy plodded through the mud to greet me.

"Ma'am, step out of the vehicle please." Another officer aimed her flashlight at me.

"Deputy Sayer, I'm so glad to see you. I can explain...and I need your help with something."

"Ma'am, I need to see some ID." I rolled my eyes. He was treating me like a stranger. I decided to play the game. After all, they had their rules to follow.

"Sure, it's right here in my purse." I pulled out the paperwork and handed it over. "I came here to find my aunt. You remember Aunt Clara. You took the missing person report. She's been missing almost three days, and I figured she was locked in a boxcar."

"Right. Have you been drinking tonight?"

"No, just ask the highway patrol officer down the road."

"Anything in the back?" He pushed up on the bed-top and peeked inside. "Your groceries?"

"Of course they're...I mean, yes sir." Time was ticking by and the deputies asked the stupidest questions, like, "Any lettuce in there?" Yeah, I thought, I love to shop for my lettuce at two-thirty in the morning. But I played along, realizing it was the only way to get back to my objective, finding Clara.

"Any chance you can help me find...."

Deputy Lund took a call from a phone on the dash. She waved to Sayer that a two-eleven was in progress in Watsonville. They scrambled into the cruiser as if I didn't exist. I was left in the dark leaning against a "no trespassing" sign while Solow snored in the passenger seat. Another wave of panic temporarily paralyzed me. I was alone. How could I possibly save Clara?

It was almost three o'clock. The train would arrive in Santa Maria about six and leave at six-thirty, according to my personal experience. I decided to give it my best shot and to heck with speed limits. I leaped into the truck. Mud clods sprayed behind us. Solow woke up and howled.

"Don't worry, we'll find her," I whispered as we roared back to Aromas at twice the speed limit. Fortunately, there was not one other vehicle on the road, not even a certain highway patrol car. I turned up David's driveway, screeched to a halt beside his Jeep and pounded my horn. I jumped out and ran to the door, triggering the automatic security light. I raised a frantic fist, but before I could make contact, David opened the door wearing a t-shirt and a slack-jaw smile.

"Josie...."

"David, I need your help!" I gulped some air. "I know where Clara is...."

"That's great. Come inside and we'll call the police." I was already shaking my head.

"They don't believe me. I have already tried. They think I'm crazy."

"Slow down, sweetie, and tell me where she is."

"A boxcar in Santa Maria...."

"Whoa. Now, you think she's in a...."

"Boxcar!" I snapped.

"Ok, let's say she's in a boxcar, but Santa Maria?" he yawned. I pulled and pushed his sturdy frame through the house to his bedroom and handed him a pair of jeans. "You want me to get dressed?"

"Yes, and hurry." I checked my watch. "It's three and we have to be in Santa Maria by six." I closed the door and let him dress. "Where are your maps?" I yelled through the door.

"Kitchen drawer—first on the right." I opened the drawer and took out a pile of neatly folded maps. The only map covering Santa Maria was a California map. I had hoped for something more detailed, but it would have to do. I stuffed the map in my jacket pocket and went outside to check on Solow. He had gone back to sleep. I quickly transferred him to the backseat of the Jeep, along with the groceries and Clara's coat. I went back to the house for David.

We collided in the entry hall. He pulled on a jacket and we hurried to the Jeep. David seemed more awake and cooperative as he fired up the engine. He backed carefully down the driveway. We motored down Otis and cruised through Aromas in silence.

"OK, David, we're on the highway now, let's hurry!"

"I'm already going the speed limit…."

"Let me put it this way, Aunt Clara has been in an ice-cold box-car for almost three days and nights and her last meal was Thursday." Suddenly my head jerked back as he put on the gas. "And don't worry about getting a ticket. I'll treat."

"I take it you know where you're going," he muttered.

"I've been there before, but I'm not exactly sure about the details, and all I have is a California map." I sighed. "Looks like it's around two hundred miles." I turned my head away and watched the stars.

"Would you mind telling me how you found out where Clara is?" I felt his eyes on me as I pretended to be asleep. David would never understand how strong my dream had been. How it stayed with me, haunted me and made my skin prickle. Eventually, I was able to fall asleep for real. I woke up and looked around as we pulled into a gas station in King City.

"Can I help?" I asked, hoping to hurry up the process.

"I got it." He jumped out and filled the tank. I pulled Clara's coat up to my chin, glad to have it as a lap blanket. I pulled out my cell phone and dialed Alicia's number. A grumpy Ernie answered. I had never heard him like that. But at four in the morning, I had to give him some slack. He handed the phone to Alicia.

"Allie, it's me. I need your help on something very important."

"Jo, do you know what time…?"

"Like I said—very important. Call the Santa Maria police and ask them to hold the six-thirty train to Santa Cruz."

"But…."

"Clara's on that train. David is driving me down there, but we might not get there before the train is scheduled to leave. Can you do that for me? Call the police and ask them to search the boxcars." David jumped in the car and I hung up the phone.

"Did you call the police?"

"Indirectly. I asked Alicia to call. The authorities never take me seriously." David nodded as we entered the freeway. "It's almost four, we need to make up some time," I pressed. He turned and scowled at me.

"So how were the Quintanas when you woke them up?"

"Ernie was actually grumpy, and Alicia had a hard time understanding me." I shrugged. By five, we were passing by Atascadero, two-thirds of the way to Santa Maria. The eastern sky had a faint pink glow that became brighter by the minute. In my mind, the minutes ticked by at the speed of light, but the miles passed slowly. I offered to drive for a while. David said he'd rather be thrown into a pit full of live snakes. I saw his point. I was a nervous wreck and would have driven like one. I chewed my nails instead.

We were listening to the news on the radio about thirty miles north of Santa Maria when a large recreational vehicle with multiple bicycles strapped to the back, swerved into our lane. David cranked the wheel and slammed on the brakes. The RV straightened out in the right lane. David took the left lane and sped up. We were almost past the cumbersome vehicle when it drifted into our lane again and forced us off the road into the center divide. We came to a quick stop, but the motor home drove on.

"Holy moly, they're going to kill somebody!" I said. David nodded. He looked pale in the morning light. Once he caught his breath, he pulled back onto the highway.

A couple of miles later, I had my eyes on Pismo Beach, while David had his on a puff of smoke ahead. He slowed the Jeep as we approached a crash involving an RV and the center guardrail. Lined up against the rail was a mom carrying a baby, trying to keep track of little twin girls and one frightened boy. The dad was putting out flames in the front seat with a fire extinguisher. David jumped out to see if he could help while I called 911.

The back half of the RV stuck out, blocking the left lane. Traffic was light, but began to thicken as all vehicles funneled into the right lane. The fire was extinguished and warning cones were set in place. I held the baby while the mom corralled the older children. I wiped curdled milk slobber from my coat and checked my watch. The sun had already popped up from behind the hills. Time was ticking.

David was waving traffic into the right lane when two fire trucks arrived followed by the highway patrol. We quickly handed over our duties to professionals. David saw the panic on my face as we hurried to his Jeep and climbed in. Solow groaned in the backseat.

David eased the Jeep over to the right lane, skirted around a couple of lookiloos and forged ahead at commuter speed. After a few miles and a lot of perspiration, traffic thinned and the pace quickened.

"If the train doesn't leave until six-thirty, we'll probably make it," David said. "Just show me where the tracks are."

"I don't exactly know...wait, isn't that a train behind us?" I cranked my head around for another look. Two sets of tracks paralleled the highway and a freight train was chugging along about three blocks behind us. I was thrilled and scared all at the same time. What if we couldn't find the train yard?

"Looks like we're moving away from the tracks," David said. "We'll probably pick them up again later." No one, not even David, could have assured me of anything at that point, but I kept still. The train went straight, paralleling the coast as the highway swung inland to the left, around hilly, populated areas, but eventually curved back to the tracks. We lost sight of the train several times, but my heart leaped every time we closed in on it again. I had to remember to breath.

"There's the sign for Highway One," I pointed to an off-ramp coming up fast. David exited 101 onto Highway One, the coast highway. It was a much slower drive with only two lanes and fabulous views of the Pacific Ocean. I studied the map and decided that Guadalupe, a small town three miles west of Santa Maria, was the most likely place to have a train yard. Highway One and the railroad tracks both headed inland slightly, enough for us to loose sight of the water.

"OK, there's Guadalupe," David said as we passed a sign for the Guadalupe Motel.

"David, turn right. I see trains over there." I pointed to an area with many rows of tracks, boxcars, flatcars and train engines. We followed a little road that bump-bumped over six sets of tracks as it circled the area. David parked on the far side of the circle.

"Look, there's an engineer in that engine," David pointed to a big noisy orange engine attached to at least twenty-five cars. Half of them were boxcars. He waved to the engineer and the man waved back. I watched David run across three sets of rails, making his way to the engineer. I pulled Solow out of the Jeep, attached his leash and ran Clara's coat under his nose several times. He sneezed, so I used the other end of the coat one more time for good luck.

Solow and I hurried over a series of iron rails, up and down and over gravel and wood until we came to the yellow engine. We ran past two flatcars and a boxcar where the doors didn't quite touch, obviously not locked. We quickly went to the next boxcar where the doors were closed but not bolted. My heart pounded in my ears, and my hands trembled.

"Aunt Clara, are you in there?" I pushed one door with all my strength, creating a space I could insert my face into. The boxcar was empty. I hurried over to the next car, but the doors were already open with two feet of space between them. I peeked in just to make sure she wasn't there, and then went to the next car. Solow was already three cars ahead of me.

"Solow, what are you doing way down there? Come back here." He looked at me, lifted his muzzle and howled at the boxcar in front of him. "Solow, are you trying to tell me something?" I was already running full speed toward the seventh boxcar from the engine. Crazy things ran through my mind. Was seven a lucky number? Aunt Clara would have counted the cars too. It seemed I had inherited the counting gene from her. I stopped in front of car number seven.

The sliding doors were closed and bolted. I reached up over my head to the rusty peg and worked it up and out of its cradle. With all my strength, I began pushing one door away from the other as I called to Clara. Solow howled.

I poked my head inside. The car had an unhealthy smell. I saw a clear plastic rain boot. I felt like my heart would burst. I could barely see through my tears as I hoisted my mature body onto the floor of the boxcar, swiveled and scooted over a couple of feet. Clara was lying on her back near the door, her head turned, eyes closed. I saw no movement. I leaned down and put an arm across her belly. Her dusty sweat suit felt cold. I touched her hand. It was cold.

CHAPTER 29

Amazed, elated and terrified, Solow and I did our best to roust Clara from her boxcar nightmare. He kept up a steady whine as I tried my best to bring my aunt back from the edge.

"Clara, it's me, Josephine. Wake up, please wake up!" I tried to find a pulse on her neck, but didn't have the patience. I leaned out the door and saw David and the engineer two cars away, walking toward Solow. I waved and screamed. They broke into a run. I turned back to Clara and wrapped myself over her body, wishing for a hot flash to help warm her up.

"You found her!" David looked flabbergasted. "Well, I never...." He shook his head slowly. The engineer looked surprised.

"David, drive the Jeep over here...." He spun around and was already on his way back to the car. The engineer scratched his head.

"Anything I can do for you, ma'am?"

"Your jacket, I need your jacket." Mine was already over Clara's torso. "Help me sit her up." He immediately climbed into the boxcar and helped me pull Clara up to a floppy sitting position. Mr. Engineer held her while I draped his jacket over her legs. I thought I heard something just before Solow howled again. Maybe it was the howl that penetrated Clara's frozen receptors and prompted her eyes to flutter. They opened halfway for a second, just a flash of green, and closed as if the lids were too heavy.

"Auntie, you're alive!" I rearranged the jackets, trying to create more warmth. I rubbed her hands, dropping tears all over them. "Wake up, Auntie!" Her left eye twitched.

The Jeep screeched to a halt outside, and David appeared at

the door with the bag of food. I grabbed a bottle of water, opened it and held it to Clara's blue lips. A few drops might have gone in, I couldn't tell for sure. David called 911 and then climbed into the boxcar and took over for the engineer. He sat with his back to Clara's back, keeping her upright and sharing his body warmth.

"I have hot coffee in the cab," the engineer offered. I nodded. He jumped down from the boxcar and hoofed it to the giant engine eight cars away.

I pushed Clara's head up and tried the water again, managing to get another drop or two down her throat. I opened the peanut butter jar, scooped peanut butter with my finger and stuck it in Clara's mouth. She grunted and bit down on my finger.

"Good, Auntie! That hurt…you're doing great. Can you open your eyes?" I pushed her chin up and tried more water. Most of it ran down the side of her mouth, and I began to despair. She was pale, her breathing shallow, her body limp. Finally the hot coffee arrived in a thermos. The engineer poured black liquid into the cap, which served as a cup. I added a splash of cold water, lifted her chin and held the brew under Clara's nose. Her eyelids moved slightly, but her mouth stayed closed.

"Auntie, please take a swallow. Open your mouth. Can you hear me?" Her lids twitched.

"Josie, honey, I don't think she has the strength. She's lucky to be alive."

"I know." But I kept trying and a few drops of coffee hit the mark.

"Would you like your dog up there with you?" the engineer asked.

"That would be nice…thank you." The man was big and muscular and lifted Solow with ease. Solow put his nose to the floor and sniffed every inch of the boxcar. When he was finished, he whimpered and pushed his body against my thigh, causing the coffee to splash on Clara's neck and run down her shirt. I was so busy mopping up the coffee I didn't see her open her eyes. When I finally looked up, she was staring at me.

"Auntie, oh, Auntie!" I hugged her. She felt like a marble statue, but at least her eyes were open for brief periods. I gave her a small sip of the remaining coffee. Her eyes closed and her head dropped down. Solow paced nervously. Time passed slowly.

"Josie, do you hear sirens?"

Solow lifted his head and howled as sirens grew louder and then ceased. The engineer waved to a team of EMTs running toward us, one carrying a stretcher and the other medical supplies. Another fire engine arrived along with a highway patrol car and an ambulance. David and I stepped back as the uniforms took over. One paramedic pointed a light at Clara's eyes. He sniffed, turned to look at me and wrinkled his nose.

"Peanut butter," I said. He nodded and went back to work. In no time Clara was hooked up to an IV, placed on the stretcher and sent out the door. Two firemen stood outside. They grabbed the litter and took off with my aunt. We followed the EMTs as they jumped down from the boxcar. Solow whined. David reached inside, pulled Solow into his arms and set him down on the gravel. We hurried to catch up to the stretcher.

I was thrilled to be allowed to ride in the ambulance with Clara. I hoped to be able to talk to her, but the paramedic had the best seat. It didn't really matter because Clara was in her own world, resting. We arrived at the hospital, and I followed my aunt and her entourage into an emergency room cubicle where I was told to leave. I found my way through a maze of halls and doors to a large room featuring a small TV hanging near the ceiling and dozens of chairs filled with people waiting to see their loved ones. I spotted David holding a cup of coffee.

"How's she doing, sweetie?" He patted the chair next to him. I sat down, melting into the upholstery.

"Her face looks peaceful, but her eyes didn't open. I think she's sleeping."

"I had a heck of a time following the ambulance," David said. "I don't know anything about Santa Maria. I'm glad the hospital was close," he yawned. "Would you like a cup of coffee?" I nodded, suddenly realizing how tired I was. I vowed not to sleep until I knew Clara was all right, determined to stay awake in case she needed me.

Next thing I knew, David was shaking my shoulder. Two

hours had passed and a nurse needed my help. I forced myself awake. A plump nurse sat next to me with a clipboard and checklist of questions on her lap. If Clara had any diseases or ailments, I didn't know about them. All I could do was answer the questions to the best of my knowledge. My aunt never complained about her health, and I had never seen her take a pill of any kind. The nurse looked at me and cocked her head.

"Ma'am, this is very important. Are you sure your aunt hasn't been taking pills, ah, drugs?"

"Of course not—she's seventy-five years old. She wouldn't touch drugs."

"She tested positive for a drug. It would help the doctor if you could explain her lifestyle."

"You tell the doctor what I just told you. Better yet, where is this doctor?" I stood up, ready to meet the doctor and rearrange his over-educated brain cells. The nurse stood up and asked me to come with her. We stormed down the hall, made a right, a left and another left into a small room where Clara was lying, surrounded by beeping, spiking, ringing medical equipment. A pretty young doctor, her dark hair pulled into a banana clip, stood at the end of the bed studying Clara's test results. After quick introductions, the nurse left. Dr. Banana Clip asked me if my aunt took drugs. I bit my lip.

"No."

"Does she have a home?"

"Of course she has a home…but she's living with me right now because…."

"If she has a place to live, why was she found in a boxcar without a jacket in the winter?"

"Someone did this to her, but I can't figure out how they got her into the boxcar. She would have fought back. What if someone drugged her?" Of course, how else would she end up in a boxcar? The doctor's dark eyes met mine. "That's it," I said. "That explains everything." I had the answer to my own question.

"Do you know who did this?" the doctor asked. I shook my head.

"That's why I want to talk to her as soon as she wakes up."

The doctor didn't look up. She turned and hurried out of the room. I was sure she had many other patients relying on her, but it was all I could do to keep from calling her back. The room hummed with electronics as Clara slept, quiet as snow in Boulder Creek. I wanted to wake her and ask the question that begged to be asked. But more than that, I wanted her to rest and recover her strength. I pushed a chair close to the bed and sat for a long time with my hand resting on Clara's, willing my energy to enter her body.

"Sorry, ma'am, you'll have to leave now," a male nurse said, carrying a tray of needles, vials and such. I instantly snapped out of my daydreams, gave Clara's hand a gentle squeeze and hustled down to the waiting room. David wasn't there. I pulled my phone from my purse and called Mom.

"Hi, Mom, we found her...."

"Bob, Bob...they found Clara," she half laughed, half cried. I heard Dad in the background, probably giving her high-fives or something. "Honey, that's wonderful...I mean, is she all right?"

"I really don't know. She's been through a lot, but she's safe now." I went on to explain where we were and how we got there, but saved the dream for another time. Mom was not a big believer in things like that. She put Dad on the phone, and I repeated my story. We hung up just before David appeared with wrapped hospital sandwiches in his jacket pockets.

"Tuna was the only choice. Solow loved his." He sat next to me and handed over a sandwich.

"Thanks for watching after my little porch potato."

"No problem. How's Clara?" He unwrapped his tuna on white bread.

"About the same. The doctor thought she was homeless and taking drugs. Can you imagine?"

"No, I can't imagine, but maybe someone drugged her."

"That's what I think too. If only I could ask Clara who did it." In my mind, I concentrated on the list of my aunt's acquaintances as I masticated yesterday's tuna special. I tried to think what day it was and finally realized it was still Sunday morning. I wouldn't go to work Monday, but Alicia and Kyle knew what to paint and how to paint it.

I washed down my last bite of tuna with a swig of lukewarm coffee and looked up at a belt full of deadly weapons attached to a dark blue uniform. The officer asked me to follow him. I glanced at David and stood up. My friend said he would go outside and check on Solow. The policeman took me to a small backroom where we sat with a table between us. I could have easily rested my head on the table top but resisted the urge.

"I'm sorry, ma'am, but the department has a few questions regarding your aunt's condition."

"Do you know what her condition is...?"

"Doctor says she's going to be fine, ma'am." He pulled out a pencil and pad of paper. I think I might have floated above my chair for a moment. I felt like leaping in the air, shouting to the moon and crying my eyes out as I thanked God for sparing my dear aunt. But I sat still and waited for the first question. The officer's questions sounded familiar—obviously designed to look for elder abuse in my home. What a rotten job, I thought, always trying to uncover ugly deeds.

For half an hour, I answered Officer Casey's questions. My answers needed more explanation. But no matter how hard I tried to explain things, he would cut me off and then throw out another ridiculous question, like, do you kick your dog? A door opened behind me and an older police officer stepped into the little room. He stood against the wall, rubbing his chin.

"Ma'am, how did you know where to find your aunt?" the second officer asked.

"I had a nightmare." Officer Casey looked at the ceiling. "There were clues in the dream, like beetles crawling on my hands and Beatles music in the background, and it was cold and dark...." The second officer actually listened to me. I began to trust the older man who allowed me to go full-steam into my tale of woe, beginning with Joey's murder. The man asked questions now and then as I told him about waking up in my backyard shed full of spiders and later being locked in a boxcar with dead beetles on the floor.

"If you don't believe me, there are Sheriff's reports...."

"Now, why wouldn't we believe you?" Casey smirked. The older cop finally told Casey he could leave and took over his chair.

Was he really interested in my story, or was he tired and needed to sit?

"I'll make a few calls and get back to you," the older cop said. "Stay in the waiting room."

"Sure." I meandered through the maze of hallways to the waiting room and sat down next to David. "One of the officers I talked to said Aunt Clara is going to be fine," I grinned. David put his hand on mine and smiled his first smile in three days.

"Were you able to talk to her?"

"No. I just watched her sleep. They had cleaned her face and she looks fairly good. The color was back in her cheeks and her hands felt warm. David, thank you for trusting me. Some people would have thought I was crazy driving two hundred miles all because of a dream."

"A dream? Is that how you got your information?" David looked ready to bite me and laugh all at the same time. Once he started laughing, we both couldn't stop. It was like letting out the steam from an overheated radiator. The pinched feeling in the back of my neck disappeared, until I looked up into Casey's face. He motioned for me to follow him. Back in the interrogation room, the older officer took charge.

"Ma'am, we found no police report on your alleged trip to Santa Maria locked in a boxcar."

"It really happened but we didn't report it because we made it home safely; and besides, the deputies only believed half the stuff we told them about the shed incident. Let's just say, we weren't on the best of terms...."

"Ma'am, I don't care about your feelings toward the deputies. I just want the facts." I stared at my shoelaces for a moment.

"I would be happy to go over the information...."

"That won't be necessary. If you remember anything else about the white car, let us know. You can go now." I slipped out the door and made a few wrong turns until I ended up in Clara's room. She was alone, so I sat with her until a nurse asked me to leave.

I walked the halls and eventually entered the waiting room. David was on his cell phone.

"She says she…ah, had a dream," he said, looking up at me. I sat down in the chair he had saved for me. "Yeah, I guess she saw Clara in a boxcar. I better go. My battery is getting low." He dropped the phone in his breast pocket. "That was Alicia."

"Thanks, I should have called her."

"She understands. I asked her to call Ben. I hope his number's in the phone book."

"It is. That's how Aunt Clara and I found him. Did Allie call the police like I asked her to?"

"She said she did. The police gave her a hard time because she didn't know which train she was talking about. They asked her how she got her information, and that's when things started breaking down. She thinks they thought she was a nutcase, and probably didn't follow up. When I talked to the train engineer, he said he hadn't seen any police around."

David's voice trailed off. I wasn't actually listening. Time felt like it had stopped for me and probably wouldn't start again until Aunt Clara was back in my little house in Aromas. I would look forward to her bitter coffee and black toast, I would praise her artistic floral creations and I would encourage her to follow her dreams—including Ben. Funny how bad things put good things into perspective.

CHAPTER 30

hecking my watch periodically, I noticed that time had lost its momentum. In fact, each hour felt like five. Hospital life and waiting rooms were a real pain. My derriere was asleep, and I couldn't handle one more minute of CNN News. Unfortunately, my head had been conditioned over the years to automatically swivel and point itself at any and all TV screens. The news never took time off and neither did I, not even on Sundays. But through it all, my heart was smiling because my aunt was going to be OK. I heard a familiar voice talking to David. He was asking about Aunt Clara. Suddenly alert, I realized the voice was close by. I looked up at a grey-haired man with clear blue eyes. He smiled, took my hand and pulled me up for a hug.

"David says she's going to be OK." Ben's voice quavered.

"That's what they say," I beamed. "That's her doctor over there talking to the nurse. Let's see if we can learn a little more about her condition." The three of us were quick to corner the doctor before she had time to escape to her other patients.

"Ms. Stuart, I was about to look you up. Your aunt is responding to treatment and should be able to leave the hospital in two or three days." I nodded and thanked her as I thought about making the long trip home and then back to Santa Maria to pick her up. But whatever it took, we would be there for Aunt Clara. Ben had to introduce himself to the doctor since I was busy trying to visualize the two-hundred-mile drive back and forth and back again.

"Mr. DeWald, come with me please." Ben took off with the doctor, leaving me standing there with my mouth open, ready to ask the next question. David made a coffee run while I sat down and watched the news without really seeing it. Twenty minutes later, our coffee cups were empty and Ben entered the room. I jumped up to ask about Clara.

"Seems Cat mentioned my name in her sleep, so the doctor thought I should be allowed to see her for a minute. I told the doc I'm staying in Santa Maria until Clara is discharged."

"That's great. She'll mend even faster with you around," I said, feeling relieved that we would not be making another trip to Santa Maria. "Do you have a cell phone, Ben?"

"No. I'll call you from my motel room if there's any news. Would you two like to join me for an early dinner?"

"Sure, all we've had today was yesterday's tuna. I'm starved." David said he was hungry too. We traipsed through the hospital, halfway across the parking lot, and climbed into the Jeep, making Solow a very happy boy.

"I noticed a restaurant about a mile from here," Ben said, and gave directions to David. He said he had never been to Santa Maria and would spend the next couple of days looking it over.

"If Clara tells you who did this to her, you'll tell us right away?" I asked. He nodded.

"How did you two find her in the first place?" Ben asked. David rolled his eyes.

"You really want to know?" David laughed. "Josephine had a dream, or maybe it was a nightmare. Anyway, she saw her aunt in a boxcar. Isn't that how it was, Josie?"

"Close enough," I yawned. "Is this the restaurant, Ben?"

"Yeah, order whatever you want, my treat." We charged into the Chinese restaurant like three starving refugees and came out like overstuffed slugs. Streetlights reflected in scattered puddles. We sloshed across the parking lot to David's Jeep and climbed in. A steady drizzle was in full swing. Solow smelled leftovers and pressed his nose against the doggie bag I handed back to Ben. He fed pieces of sweet and sour pork to Solow making them blood brothers, at least in Solow's mind. Minutes later, David parked the Jeep near the entrance to the hospital.

"Josie, we should get going right away if we want to get home before I'm too sleepy to drive." I agreed. We said goodbye to Ben and reminded him to call. Ben crawled out of the backseat, stretched his long arms and sucked in some damp winter air. I opened my window and handed him my cell phone. He tried to refuse it, but I insisted. I desperately needed to know how Clara was doing. My good night's sleep depended on it.

As we headed north up Highway 101, I listened to Solow snoring in the backseat until I drifted off. The next thing I knew, a half hour had passed and David was stopping the car in front of a 7-Eleven. He asked if I wanted anything. I said no. He came back with steaming coffee, and I held his cup while he started the car.

"David, I can drive. I had a stick shift, um, about thirty years ago. I remember how to do it."

"I'm fine, Josie. This coffee will do the trick." I was beginning to feel like we were an old married couple, compatible and content, cruising up the highway of life. We talked about all things other than Aunt Clara.

"I wonder if Allie has any news for me," I said without thinking.

"What kind of news?"

"The accounting project." I turned and looked at Solow in the backseat.

"Isn't he the cutest thing?"

"I guess you don't want to tell me about it," David pouted.

"I wasn't going to worry you, but if you insist…Allie took on an accounting job at Mo's nursery. We're trying to find out why Joey's investment money isn't supporting Darla like it should. The poor lady is barely surviving, and then she lands in the hospital. I'm going to check on her from time to time. Someone has to."

"I'll help you check on her," David said, "but I don't like you two sneaking around the nursery. How much do you know about this Mo character? What if he harms Alicia?"

"I never thought of him as dangerous, just kind of mean to Gabe sometimes." I remembered Gabe's black eye and winced. Cold air circulated through the old Jeep. I shivered. "I changed my mind. I need a cup of coffee and something sweet."

"I'm sweet," he laughed as he took the Pismo exit. We stopped at the first mini-mart gas station. David topped off the tank while

I went inside.

"Mom? What are you doing here?" I was flabbergasted until I realized she was on her way to see her sister. We hugged. "Where's Dad?"

"Pumping gas, of course." I had never seen my mother with dark circles under red-rimmed eyes before. We carried our drinks and pastries outside. The men had already discovered each other and were chatting while they waited for us. Dad stood next to Myrtle's RV. He grinned when he saw me.

"Hi, honey. David tells me you two are headed home. We have Myrtle's camper. Why don't you ride with us—that way you can be around for Clara."

"I can take Solow home with me," David offered. I tried to imagine living in an RV with my parents for two or three days. Despite that vision, I desperately wanted to be at Clara's side when she spoke her first words.

"Thank you, David. I think I'll take you up on that offer. Solow won't mind. Sometimes I think he loves you more than me." David laughed. We embraced and he drove away with my long-eared basset in the front seat. I watched the taillights disappear into traffic, wishing for one more kiss. The rain had petered out and a trillion stars owned the sky. We climbed into the mammoth, black recreational vehicle—Mom and Dad in the front and me on the couch.

"Are you comfortable, honey?" Dad asked.

"Yes, but where's the seatbelt?" I had looked all around and ended up in a very comfortable horizontal position with a throw pillow under my head. Dad said a belt was not required. Half an hour later, we pulled into the hospital's main parking area.

"You two go ahead," I said. "I'll meet you in the waiting room a little later." They took off toward the main entrance, and I curled up for a nap. There was just one problem. I couldn't fall asleep. I clicked on the overhead light, picked up a copy of the Sunday Sentinel and turned to the front page. Clara's picture was on that page with a plea to the public for help in finding her. "Old news," I said to myself and smiled. When I finished skimming over the newspaper, front to back, I joined Mom and Dad in the waiting room.

"Did you guys meet up with Ben yet?" Mom shook her head. "I wonder where he is." I felt restless, excused myself and walked the halls. Without thinking, I ended up at Clara's side. She slept peacefully or was it my imagination. I hoped she was comfortable. I leaned down and whispered her name.

"Ma'am," a nurse at the door said, "she won't wake up tonight. The medication will let her sleep." She bustled around taking Clara's pulse, checking this and that. It was time for me to leave. I walked the halls and finally returned to the waiting room where Mom and Dad sat reading their books. Dad looked up.

"Did you talk to Clara, honey?"

"I talked to her, but she's asleep."

"We peeked into her room, but the nurse told us to come back in the morning," Mom said. Ben finally appeared and sat down next to me. Mom introduced him to Dad.

"I thought you were going home, Josephine," Ben said, handing my phone back to me.

"Yeah, I did too. We happened to stop at a mini-mart and there was Mom and Dad!" Eventually Ben changed seats to be next to Bob. They talked fishing, baseball and all things male while I gave Mom the details of Clara's rescue.

"Dear, do you normally have these interesting dreams?"

"No, but I'm glad I had this one." Interesting was a word she always used for anything outside her "irreproachable world." Around eleven o'clock, Ben stood up and announced he was going to his motel room. We all decided it was time to hit the sack and followed Ben outside. We trundled over to the RV under a peaceful sky. Dad ran the RV engine until the place warmed up. They had the big bed in the back, and I had the sofa bed near the front. It was the first camping trip with my folks since I was fifteen, the year that Aunt Clara and Uncle Roger tagged along.

We had camped in tents by a river on the valley floor of Yosemite Park. My cousin, Candy, was there too. I wondered if anyone had thought to call her about her mother.

The days were hot in the Yosemite Valley but the icy river was too cold to swim in, unless you were younger than fifteen. Actually, I was more interested in a cute guy working the ice cream concession.

After work, he walked with me to Bridalveil Fall. I'm sure I looked at the waterfall, but all I remember was the boy with his cool shades and Smokey the Bear sweatshirt. After a moment of minor reverie, my mind let go of the boy and latched onto David. I wondered if he had reached home yet. Did he miss me?

My bed wasn't too bad. It had been a long and emotional day. I finally dozed off and dreamt that someone threw me into a dark, smelly boxcar and slammed the door. I woke up with a start, perspiring and trying to remember where I was. Once I recognized the RV's interior, I calmed my pounding heart, sat up and ran fingers through unruly hair. I decided not to worry about my rumpled appearance and quietly walked away from Myrtle's pride and joy.

At first, the hospital lighting seemed bright and bothered my eyes. I quickly got used to it as I tramped up and down the halls, trying to get a little exercise. Eventually I ended up at Clara's door. It was open a crack, enough for me to hear someone talking inside. I listened to a man opening his heart to the woman he loved.

I decided not to interrupt and moved on as tears streamed down my cheeks. I roamed the halls, ending up in front of the TV with a couple of dozen other people, their eyes glued to the tube. I checked my watch. Two a.m. Ben saw me and sat down.

"Josephine, what are you doing out so late?"

"You're asking me?" I laughed.

"Yeah, I couldn't sleep either."

"Ben, what do you know about Mo, I mean, Morton?"

"Not much. Jamie told me he's a real jerk, bad temper and all that."

"What did Joey think about him?"

"They had a business deal—guess I can tell you now," Ben rubbed his chin. "I didn't want to say too much before…ah, because I had been harboring Joey for six years. Could have gotten in some trouble…."

"Aside from all that, there's a murderer still running around loose. Maybe you know something that can help the police figure out who it is."

"OK, six years ago, Joey landed his plane between a lettuce

field and the railroad tracks, close to the nursery. He and Mo and I cooked up the plan. Mo hid the plane and I hid Joey, but you probably already knew that."

Actually, I had only suspected Mo of being involved. Ben went on to say that he had kept the whole thing quiet for six years. When Joey was run over by a train, he was still afraid to talk about it. But the barn door was open and Ben let everything out.

"A couple of weeks after he moved in with me, Joey read the newspapers and found out his friend, Curly, had died of exposure. I think he suspected foul play. It really bothered him that he couldn't go to Curly's funeral."

"Was Curly in the plane?" Ben nodded.

"How did you know?"

"Clara and I have our sources."

"What else do you need to know?"

"Does Mo still have the plane?"

"I don't know…probably. You know that Joey took care of my sister…."

"Yes, I figured out that part from a photo I found in your truck." Ben nodded thoughtfully, staring at the TV but not really seeing it. "They were in love, weren't they?" He nodded.

"Why didn't Darla and Joey get a divorce?"

"Darla didn't want a divorce. She threatened to tell Sal that Joey wasn't his biological father. Joey thought he was protecting his son by not getting a divorce and faking his death instead, but Sal had figured out the truth a long time ago. All he had to do was look in the mirror."

"When did Darla marry Wayne?"

"Wayne moved into the Morrissey house right after Joey disappeared. They married about a year later. After awhile her money dried up, and Sal and his family moved in and took over the house payments. Darla then moved into Wayne's place."

"Well, she's still broke. She was nearly starving to death—that's probably why she ended up in the hospital." I looked at Ben's tired eyes and remembered how sleepy I was. My watch showed four-thirty. "I'm going back to the RV and try to sleep before the sun comes up." I stood up and Ben walked to the front entrance with me.

"Yeah, it's been a long day and night," he said, heading for his truck.

CHAPTER 31

I woke up to the clanging of pots and pans. Sunlight shot through every window as Dad opened the blinds. Mom flipped bacon and I sat up to watch. My two hours of sleep had left me in a state of fuzziness. All I wanted was more sleep but that was impossible. I rolled off the couch, stood up and stretched carefully, trying not to accidentally elbow another person sharing the small quarters.

"How many eggs, dear?" Mom asked. I grunted and she repeated the question. Half an hour later, I helped her clear away the breakfast dishes and scrub down the tiny kitchen. We made up the beds and then marched over to the hospital. Dad bought a local paper on the way inside. With just a quick glance, I knew what the headline story was about—a woman found in a boxcar. Mom asked the information person on duty where Clara was. We found her new room but weren't allowed inside because a nurse was giving Clara a sponge bath. On the way back to the waiting room, we met up with Ben coming the other way.

"Good morning, Ben. I'm afraid Clara is indisposed right now," I said. He wheeled around and walked with us to the waiting room. I was settling into my seat in front of the TV I didn't care to watch when my phone rang. It was Alicia.

"Hi, Allie, what's up?"

"Jo, David called me yesterday. He said Clara is doing pretty well."

"Yeah, that's all we know so far."

"I called to tell you about my snooping, I mean accounting job. I finally had a chance to go through the files without Mo hanging around. Guess what—there is no Gianelli file."

"What?"

"That's what I said. I looked through all the cabinets and all the files. Nothing! I was so disgusted that when he came back to the office I told him I found another job, collected my check and walked out. He didn't take it very well. Personally, I think he got his money's worth."

"So why would he hide the file?" I asked.

"I don't know, but it makes him look guilty of something. How is Clara doing?"

"They have her sedated so far. We haven't actually seen her today, but the doctor said she could go home in a couple of days. Mom and Dad are here, and David and Solow went home last night. Oh, and Ben's here too."

"What do you do all day, Jo?"

"Not much. I feel like my hands are tied—I can't wait to go after the person who did this to my aunt."

"If you find out who did it, you'll report it to the police, right?"

"Sure. Is today Monday?" I asked, feeling disconnected in the absence of my normal routine.

"Sure is. I'm getting ready to go to work as we speak. I called Kyle to make sure he'll be there. Maybe we can finish the mural before you get back."

"I'll be back to work in a couple of days. Take your time, we're still ahead of schedule," I said, not worried at all.

"I'll talk to you this evening. Take care, Jo." We hung up. I called David.

"David, you sound like you just woke up."

"Yeah."

"What time did you get home last night?"

"After midnight. How's Clara today?" I explained why we hadn't seen her yet and then let David go back to sleep. My phone showed one last bar. I knew it would be gone soon and the charger was at home. Mom had a cell phone she kept in her Subaru for emergencies, and Dad and Ben didn't believe in them. I noticed Ben was missing and figured he was with Clara. I smiled, remembering the time Clara took Mom and me shopping because she wanted to buy something pretty to wear for Ben.

"Ben's coming back. Do you want to go next, honey?" Dad asked. I nodded. Ben sat down next to me and whispered in my ear.

"Clara said something. I think she said, Mo...." I knew the guy was no good. I wasn't surprised at all and I couldn't wait to sic the police on him.

"Are you sure?" I asked. Ben tilted his head to one side.

"Yeah." I stood up and hurried down the hall to Clara's room. I peeked in. She was all alone and sound asleep.

"Dang!" I hung around for a few minutes and then went back to the waiting room. I picked up my cell phone and speed-dialed David.

"Hi, Josie. What's up?"

"Clara told us who did it. It was...." My phone chose that moment to die. "Double dang!"

"What's the matter, dear?" Mom asked.

"Ben said that Clara said that Mo did it." Mom raised one brow.

"Did what, dear?"

"Drugged her and put her in the boxcar."

"And Mo is Gabe's uncle?"

"Yes, Mom. He's a mean, creepy rat. I had a feeling it was him all along." Mom leaned over and told Dad and he took off down the hall. When he finally returned, he said he had found a public phone and called the police. Two officers arrived within the hour wanting a statement. I gave them my impression of Morton, but that didn't seem to be good enough for the police. Ben gave his statement, and then we all went with the officers to talk to Clara. She looked up at the half dozen people crammed into her room.

"Lovely day," Clara whispered. Her face looked pale and gaunt, but the smile warmed my heart.

"Aunt Clara, you're awake! How do you feel?" I asked, as Mom crowded in behind me.

"OK, dear," she said. I stepped back as one of the officers worked his way to the bed and leaned closer to Clara.

"Ma'am, can you identify the person who assaulted you?" She made a slight nod, not wishing to accidentally yank the tube out of her nose. I leaned in as close as possible.

"Mo...ron," she whispered. Wayne's a moron...and mean...."

"Is he the one? This, Wayne fellow?" he asked, bent at the waist and face to face with her. She gave a little nod and closed her eyes. We left the room, realizing that she needed to rest. Everyone was expressing their surprise at Clara's statement when the morning nurse bustled past us, pushing a cart full of breakfast into Clara's room. We moseyed down to the waiting room and then answered the officer's questions. Most of the questions came to me. An hour later, the officer had a full report beginning with Joey's disappearance.

"I hope he gets the word out fast and they snag that terrible man," I said to Ben.

"If they don't get him, I will."

"I know how you feel," I said, wondering why Wayne would try to kill my aunt. But the more I thought about it, the clearer it became. "Follow the money" ran through my head. The money had to be Darla's money, the missing money. Maybe Wayne gave Clara and me more credit than we deserved. Maybe he thought we knew enough about the money and other things to point a finger at him.

"Ben, do you think Wayne killed Joey?"

"If he did this to Cat, he could do anything."

"Did Wayne meet up with Joey the night of the train accident?"

"Maybe. He might have overheard Jamie on the phone. See, a couple of weeks after my sister passed away, Joey asked me to talk to Jamie, sort of test the waters and find out if he would forgive his dad for the big charade. Jamie was visiting his mother when his cell phone rang. He took the phone outside, and before I could tell him about his father, he told me how his mother was living in poverty. He was angry, yelling like a mad man, asking me why she wasn't getting the investment money."

"What did you tell Jamie?"

"I said I didn't know why Darla wasn't receiving the money. I still don't know why. I told him to meet with Mo that evening, but I don't think he showed up." Ben shook his head slowly. "When I told Joey, he came unglued. He said he would go to the nursery and kill Mo, after he got his money."

"Wow! So Joey talked to Mo at the nursery?"

"Who knows," Ben shrugged. "Maybe Wayne overheard Jamie on the phone and showed up at the nursery."

"Do you think Wayne was involved in the money problem—maybe keeping it for himself?" I had already seen for myself that Wayne was a horrible, deceitful husband.

"Maybe if we check Mo's books...."

"I already had Alicia check them out. She worked at the nursery for three days and found nothing—no records, no Gianelli file. Weird. So you never got a chance to tell Jamie that his dad was alive?"

"Nope. The climate wasn't right."

"Ben, do you think the cops will catch Wayne?"

"Sure, I mean, I guess so, why?"

"I know where he hangs out. I could find him easily." The image of Wayne and the redhead was a permanent fixture in my brain. "I won't soon forget my time locked in the spider-infested shed or the cold ride in a boxcar to Santa Maria, and I'll never forget what he did to Aunt Clara. Wayne must have thought we knew more than we did. Aunt Clara and I snooped around, but we never put two and two together." I thought about Moses saying we should follow the money. Seems he was singing the smartest tune in the songbook.

Knowing what I knew, I could barely sit still. I paced the halls, checked on Clara at regular intervals, chewed my nails to the nub and stared at the newspaper without really seeing it. Mom and Dad explored Santa Maria and took in a movie. They came back to the hospital hours later looking refreshed. They had asked me to go, but I declined. I wasn't ready to participate in normal activities.

Ben entered the waiting room balancing a tray with four coffees. We each took one.

"Josephine," Ben leaned closer to my ear and whispered, "I've been thinking. Clara is going to be all right. If you know how to find Wayne, we should get busy and do it." My heart thumped one big thump at the thought of actually going after Joey's murderer, but I was ready. Being idle was taking a toll on my nerves.

It was time to put words into action, and I felt sure Clara would have approved.

"Are you saying we should go now?" I gulped the last of my coffee.

"Yep. Just say you need to go to work tomorrow," he whispered. I nodded and broke the news to Mom and Dad. They were OK with it and said they would drive Clara home as soon as she was discharged from the hospital.

It was five o'clock in the evening when Ben and I finally climbed aboard his truck and joined commuter traffic heading north. I looked at Ben, trying to decide if he was bigger or smaller than Wayne. It was a tie. They were around the same age and both men were physically fit. They were the opposite sides of the same coin—the good side and the bad seed.

After two and a half hours of driving, we finally stopped for dinner in King City. When our plates were empty, I suggested we go to Slick's in Monterey. Ben said it would be nine before we got there.

"Are you too tired to go tonight?"

"Nope. Let's go." He paid the bill and we climbed back in the truck. Since there wasn't much to look at except oncoming headlights, I closed my eyes and drifted off. About an hour later, I felt Ben's hand pushing my shoulder. I blinked and stared at the scene in front of me. He had parked the truck on a bluff overlooking the Monterey wharf. Hoards of people walked to and from the wooden structure. The historic wharf was home to some very nice shops, restaurants, and Slick's.

"Just show me where Slick's is," Ben said as he helped me down from my seat. We followed the wide concrete walkway down to the wharf and entered the least attractive restaurant. We moved through the entry, made a right into the bar area and found a little table in the far corner. We ordered glasses of Perrier and began our vigil.

"I don't see Wayne, but the redhead at the bar looks familiar," I whispered.

"All we can do is wait." Ben leaned back in his chair, crossed his arms and fell asleep.

"Ben, wake up. You were snoring." He gulped some air and straightened up in his chair.

"Sorry, Josephine, I'm a little tired. Didn't sleep much last night."

"Ben, I'm curious. Did Joey ever leave your property in six years?"

"Nope, not until the night he went to the nursery. I should have gone with him. I told him not to go, but he was angry and took off on his own, hitchhiking. Hey, isn't that Wayne over there?" Sure enough, Wayne entered the bar and walked up behind Ms. Redhead. She turned in her seat for a kiss.

"Now what?" Ben asked.

"I was leaving that up to you. Hope he doesn't see us." I held a drink menu up to my face. "Stay here, I'll call the police."

"Where are you going?" he asked.

"My cell phone isn't charged. I need to find a phone." I sidled across the room with my body turned away from the bar as best I could. I turned the corner and looked around the foyer, no phone. I went to the greeter and asked if I could use a phone. She pointed to a narrow staircase. I climbed the stairs to a second floor with two smelly restrooms, a broken window and a dead phone dangling from its cord. I dropped in coin after coin—not a sound, except for cold air whistling through the window. I clambered down the stairs and snuck into the bar. Ben had a menu held to his chin.

"What's the matter? Did you call?"

"No!" I whispered. "The stupid phone was broken. Look, I think they're going to leave."

Wayne was lifting a coat over his friend's shoulders. We lowered our gaze and raised the menus.

"I thought you had a phone," Ben said.

"Sorry. I did my best. They're outside by now. We better follow." Ben left money on the table. We rounded the corner and crossed the entry. I cautiously moved closer to the glass doors and peeked out. I felt eyes on my back. I turned and looked up the stairs.

"Ben, look up there!" Wayne and his girl were looking down at us. Ben galloped up the narrow staircase, taking the steps three at a time. A roar came out of his mouth as he closed in on his prey. Slick as snot, Wayne turned and threw one leg over and out the window. His body and other leg followed, disappearing into the dark. I watched Ben lean out the window trying to see where Wayne had gone. He eventually gave up, plodded down the stairs and walked me to his truck.

"We gave it a good try, Ben. Don't worry, we'll get him later." Ben shook his head.

"I'm not so sure. He's pretty quick for an old guy, and he probably won't come back to this place again."

"You're right. We need to work up a plan. Why don't you stay at my house tonight? Clara's bed is empty," I yawned. "Or you could stay with David...."

"I think Clara's bed will be fine. Hope you have a razor."

"No problem." We stopped at David's to pick up Solow. My poor sweetie answered the door wearing pajamas. Solow whined and howled as he circled my knees.

"Thanks, David, for taking care of Solow. We'll see you tomorrow," I yawned.

"Yeah, tomorrow."

CHAPTER 32

Tuesday morning, five days after Clara went missing, I was lying in bed thinking. The good news was that I knew she would recover and be home soon. The bad news was that Wayne was still around…somewhere. The real question was how would the police find him? He was hardly ever home and probably would not show up at Slick's any time soon.

I crawled out of bed, pulled on my robe and found Ben at the kitchen table reading the newspaper to Solow. Why did everyone think my dog cared about the editorials?

"Good morning, Josephine."

"Ah,…morning, Ben. I've been thinking. We need to get some information from Mo. He probably won't talk to me…unless you make him talk."

"Josephine, I'm not a tough guy…."

"Just help me out. You don't have to hurt him, just act like you might," I purred. "Put your hand in your coat pocket and act like you have a gun. It works in the movies all the time." Ben rolled his eyes. We ate breakfast and then hiked the uneven path to David's house with Solow leading the way. David answered my knock on the back door, dressed and looking rested.

"Josie, Ben, what's up?"

"Ben and I want you to join us," I smiled. "We're going to the nursery to talk to Mo."

"What do you need me for?"

"We need more muscle." Ben laughed and David joined in. "Laugh all you want," I said, "but we can do this. We can find out if Wayne is taking Darla's money and, hopefully, that will give us some leads. It's all we have, unless you have a better idea."

"Sorry, Josie, I do want to help. I have a couple of things I need to do first. I'll meet you at your house in a few minutes." Ben and I trudged back to my house while Solow chased Fluffy through wet grass.

"That crazy dog of yours never learns," Ben laughed. We entered my house through the back door, and minutes later David knocked on the front door. Solow was panting at his side.

"I brought the Jeep."

"I'll take my truck and meet you two at the nursery," Ben said. "I need to get home right after I use my muscle on Mo." Ten minutes later we all met up at the Evergreen Nursery with Solow sound asleep in the backseat of the Jeep. I marched into the building and straight to the "fishbowl" office where Mo sat at his desk, yelling into the telephone with a red face. My loyal thugs lined up behind me. Mo finally put the receiver down and leaned his head out the door.

"What do you want?"

"Nice to see you too. These are my friends, David and Ben."

"Right, what's on your mind?" Mo grumbled.

"Are you sending money to Darla Bracken?" Mo cleared his throat.

"Is that any of your business?"

"I happen to know that Joey made a big investment in your nursery…" Mo tried to slam the door, but David's foot was already there. "You were sending a nice check to him every month. At some point the money stopped, Darla lost her house and last week she almost lost her life because she couldn't afford to buy food."

"So what?" Mo turned and headed for the back door to his office. He opened the door to find Ben standing there. Red faced and tongue-tied, he turned back to David and me. "Get out of my office. I'll call the police…."

"Good idea. Call the police," I smiled. Mo sputtered a few ugly words and finally fell into his chair, ready to talk.

"Now, who's getting Joey's money?" I asked. David and Ben stood behind Mo's chair.

"Joey came to see me about a plan he had. He wanted to disappear. His wife was unfaithful, and he had some other stuff going on in his life. He asked if he could hide his plane here. I said he could for a slight rental fee. He agreed. I agreed to send his regular checks, minus the rental fee, to his wife, Darla."

"Who's getting the money?" I asked again.

"I'm getting to that. About six months after Joey disappeared, Wayne showed up. He said he was living with Darla and planned to marry her. He said Darla wasn't very good with money and I should send the checks to a Post Office Box...that's all I know. Now, get out."

"Wait a minute. Was there a certain day of the month that you sent the checks?"

"First of the month," he grumbled. "I just mailed one yesterday. Now, get out of here."

"Right after you give me the box number and address." Mo reached for a Rolodex on the desktop and thumbed through the cards. He ripped a card loose and handed it to me. I snatched it and we left. I was still smiling as we regrouped outside next to Ben's truck.

"Thank you, Ben. You've been wonderful," I said.

"Hey, I have a thoroughbred in this race too," he smiled and climbed into his truck. "Stay safe, and keep me posted." He fired up the truck and left for home. David helped me into the Jeep, not that I needed help.

"Where are we going, Josie?"

"Aromas. Can you believe it? Mo sends the money to Aromas. No wonder Wayne knows our area and my house. Do you think the check would be at the post office now?"

"Probably not. Everything goes to San Jose to be sorted and then it's all trucked back here. No wonder they have to keep raising stamp prices," he said as he parked the Jeep in front of the tiny Aromas post office. We walked into the room with a couple hundred of little cubbies all over the walls. Each cubby had a tiny window and a lock. We found 3350 and took turns peeking inside. The box was empty. We decided to ask questions in the next room.

David and I had used the Aromas post office for many years and knew the two ladies who worked at the counter. Robby was weighing a package for an elderly gentleman, the only customer in the room. She looked up and smiled. The man paid Robby and tipped his cap as he passed by us. I waited until he was outside before speaking.

"What can I do for you, Jo, David?"

"If a person in Watsonville mailed a letter to a person in Aromas, how many days until the letter arrives?" I asked.

"You make it sound very mysterious. When was it mailed?"

"Yesterday."

"Should be here tomorrow or Thursday."

"What time of the day does the mail arrive?"

"Between nine and ten in the morning."

"Thanks, Robby." Like the gentleman he was, David opened two post office doors and a Jeep door for me. Solow whined and banged his tail on the backseat as I climbed into the front seat. David fired up the engine and drove us to his house for a great lunch he put together with minimal effort. It was a lovely afternoon with nothing to complain about—nothing I could put my finger on. Feeling restless, I finally walked Solow home over David's objections. I put clothes in the washing machine, vacuumed, swept, scrubbed and dusted, but I still felt antsy.

"Want to go for a ride, Solow?" He suddenly came out of a dead sleep and galloped to the door. I grabbed a coat and purse and helped Solow into my truck. I had felt guilty all day for not going to work. I decided to check on the library job. Alicia's car was still in the parking lot at five o'clock. The sun was down, leaving a faded half moon to traverse the purple sky. I shivered and entered the nearly finished building. I heard voices and smiled.

"Hey, you guys still working?" I asked as I came closer to Alicia and Kyle. They stopped talking and painting when they saw me.

"Jo, how are you? Is Clara OK?" Alicia asked.

"She's going to be fine. Mom called this afternoon to say they will be bringing her home tomorrow. I can't wait to see her." I scanned the wall and my mouth dropped open. "You two have done a beautiful job. It looks almost finished."

"Like, tomorrow we finish," Kyle crowed. I gave him a pat on the back.

"I'll be here with you when we cross the finish line," I laughed. "That way I can sign my name next to yours. Sorry I wasn't here…."

"Jo, we understand." Alicia began cleaning brushes.

"Kyle, I didn't see your motorcycle in the parking lot."

"Yeah, like, it's not running. Allie picked me up this morning."

"I'll drive you home. There's something I need to do in Santa Cruz anyway." Alicia left first. Kyle and I walked to the parking lot. I unlocked the door; and he stared at Solow, not knowing what to do next.

"You'll have to put Solow on your lap," I said. Kyle carefully lifted Solow, shoved one long leg into the cab under the dog. He hoisted the rest of his lanky body onto the seat. I don't know who looked the most uncomfortable, but a free ride is a free ride. Except for a couple of speed bumps, the boys managed pretty well.

I dropped Kyle at his apartment and headed across town to Darla's house. I curbed the truck. Her porch light blinked on and a curtain parted for a second. After three rings of the doorbell, she answered the door looking slightly better than the last time I had seen her. I entered the house as the back door to the garage clicked shut. I asked Darla if she had company.

"No, I don't have any company, just you. What did you say your name was?"

"Josephine. You remember my Aunt Clara, don't you?" She nodded her head. I heard a muffled noise coming from the garage. I stepped back a few feet, opened the front door and leaned out. A white compact car roared out of the garage straight into oncoming headlights. A driver honked and braked. Solow howled as the white car turned and tore down the road.

"Was Wayne in that car?" I asked Darla.

"I hope so. It's his car. Come in and sit down." She pointed to the sofa. I wished I could have followed the jerk, but it was too late. He was gone. Besides, David and I had a plan.

"Darla, have you had dinner yet?"

"Wayne gave me a bowl of applesauce," she smiled. I toured the kitchen and found the half-eaten applesauce. Some dinner! I checked the fridge—almost empty and the freezer housed one pathetic TV dinner.

"I'm hungry," I said. "Let's go out for dinner." Darla didn't budge. "My treat." I found her coat and purse in the closet by the front door. After a bit more coaxing, she stood up and walked out the door. I opened the truck door for her and Solow howled. Darla squealed and stepped back.

"Don't worry, he likes you. Solow, quiet old boy." I pulled him down to the floor by his collar. "There now, Darla, I'll help you up to the seat." She was light as a feather. When she was settled in her seat, I reached down, pulled off her loafers and set her feet on Solow's back. They both seemed content as we headed into town for Chinese food.

"Are we going to Slick's?"

"No, not tonight." I parked the truck and helped Darla into her shoes and down from her seat. Solow whined, but I told him he had to stay in the truck. The greeter walked us to an empty table in the far corner next to a table where an elderly couple were happily clinking their wine glasses together. The woman looked up.

"Aren't you Clara's niece? Pierre, this is the woman I told you about...wanted to know if I had a Ouija board." His thick white eyebrows twitched up and down as smiling lips peaked out from under a meticulously manicured mustache.

"My name is Josephine, and this is my friend, Darla."

"Would you like to sit with us...?"

"We would love to sit with you." Pierre pulled a chair out for Darla. His eyebrows twitched vigorously. I sat next to Abigail.

"Are you two celebrating something?" I asked. They shook their heads and smiled.

"We don't need a reason to celebrate," Abigail said. "Were you able to get Clara out of the boxcar?" My mouth dropped open. I was stunned.

"Who told you she was in a boxcar?"

"My friends told me." Abigail winked at Pierre and he reached for her hand.

"Ah, we ah, found her...and got her out...." I stammered. "She's going to be fine."

"That's nice," Abigail smiled. The whole conversation seemed to be going right over Darla's head. She hadn't said a word and neither had Pierre. I wondered if he spoke English. Abby and I ordered a family-style dinner for four, and Pierre pointed to an expensive Bordeaux on the wine list. I wondered who would be paying the bill.

Pierre looked clean and neat, but his clothes were "eighties disco" and he hadn't had a haircut in months, by the looks of his snowy locks. I gave up trying to figure him out and concentrated on eating. Darla was eating everything in sight. When we were completely stuffed, I had the leftovers boxed. I gathered the three boxes in front of my empty plate. Abigail reached over and pulled a box toward her plate. I picked up the two remaining boxes and balanced them on my lap.

Pierre examined the check and dug out exactly half the total. I put the other half on his money and resigned myself to paying for half of the expensive wine Darla and I didn't drink. We walked outside to our vehicles and said goodnight. Pierre's late model Lexus sat beside my dumpy little truck. But I loved my truck and the sleepy hound inside it.

I opened the door for Darla. She leaned forward and I gave her a push onto the seat. Solow sniffed the air, squirmed around under the dash and finally rested his head on Darla's feet. I put the two boxes of leftovers behind my seat, hoping the smell wouldn't drive Solow crazy. After a short drive, Darla perked up and looked around.

"This looks like my house," she said.

"It is your house. I'll walk you to the door." I helped her down from her seat and held onto her arm, carrying the boxes with the other hand. She unlocked the front door and turned on the lights. I took the food to the fridge.

"Now, Darla, when you get hungry, just heat up this food."

Minutes later, Solow and I were flying down the highway toward Aromas. We pulled up David's driveway and found him in the garage, changing the oil in his riding mower.

"Josie, what have you been up to?"

"Let's go inside and I'll tell you the whole story." He cleaned his hands and we went into the kitchen. He grabbed a couple of sodas from the fridge, and we curled up on the couch with Solow at our feet. "I was thirty feet from Wayne tonight, but he got away. At first, I was so mad at myself but then I remembered our plan. We're going to get him tomorrow, right?"

"We're going to notify the Sheriff." He snuggled closer.

"Yeah, right. But if they can't be there all day and night...."

"They will be there. It's not our worry," he said as he flipped through the channels. I rolled my eyes. "In fact, I called the deputies today, right after you left. They will have a patrol car pass by the post office every half hour for as long as it takes."

"What if Wayne shows up during the eighteen minutes when the cops aren't there?" I stiffened and sat up. "If we don't get him tomorrow, we might never get him. He knows he's wanted. When he gets the money, he might head for the border." David looked at the ceiling and then shook his head.

"You watch too many movies, Josie. It's going to be all right." David was content to watch Jessica solve another murder on TV. I was feeling antsy again and took Solow home before the show was over.

I fed Solow and went to bed. After much tossing and turning, I fell asleep and dreamt about a masked robber holding up our local post office. The ladies behind the counter ducked and ran out the back door. I wanted to run, but my feet wouldn't move. The robber came toward me. I tried to open my mouth to scream, but nothing came out.

Clara rushed into the building and whacked the robber with her umbrella. Suddenly her feet were stuck to the floor and the man crawled away like an ugly worm.

CHAPTER 33

Wednesday, I woke up at five o'clock to pounding rain on the roof and could not go back to sleep. I gave up and rolled out of bed. Solow groaned from his comfy bed across the room. I imagined he was rolling his eyes in the dark. I pulled on a robe and shuffled down the hall to the kitchen. Mr. Coffee was more than happy to perk up a pot of coffee for me.

I sipped my coffee and plotted Wayne's capture in my head. First, I would call Alicia and tell her not to expect me at work until later in the day. (Not until after I captured Wayne.) I planned to spend time at the Aromas Library, seated at the window facing the post office. I would wait for Wayne to arrive, call 911, run outside to my truck and quickly slam it into his car. On second thought, maybe I would just park it in his way so he couldn't drive away.

Solow finally entered the kitchen. I fed him and then read the highlights from yesterday's newspaper. If everyone else could read to him aloud….but my mind eventually wandered back to Wayne's capture. I planned to quick charge my cell phone and carry it on my person at all times. I dug the phone out of my purse and plugged it into the charger in my bedroom. In my nightstand I found an old can of pepper spray Dad had given me for protection and dropped it into my purse. I took a quick shower and pulled on jeans, a sweater and UGG boots.

I went back to the kitchen for a bowl of cereal. Time ticked by slowly. I poured coffee in a thermos and wrapped up a takeout tuna sandwich for later. Finally, the clock read eight o'clock. I called Alicia.

"Hi, Jo. What's up?"

"Allie, I have something I need to do today. I'll join you guys this afternoon."

"No problem. See you later." We hung up. I called the Santa Maria Hospital for an update on Clara. The woman on the phone said Clara would be checking out around ten o'clock, which meant she would be home by two or three in the afternoon. Solow finally woke up from his morning nap.

"I'll miss you today, old boy, but I have something I need to do." The rain had turned to mist with patches of blue sky here and there. Solow howled at the door, probably imagining a different outcome with Fluffy. I let him out. My nerves were raw. I wanted to sprint down to the post office and carry out my plan, but the mail wouldn't be there for another hour, and who could predict when Wayne would arrive.

I cleaned the kitchen and then the bathroom, ironed a basket full of clothes and stared at the clock. Finally, the clock read nine. I called Solow into the house, grabbed my provisions, a coat and purse, and climbed into my Mazda. The air was cold and damp. I shivered as I pushed on the gas pedal and roared down Otis into town. I parked behind the old library located across the street and kitty-corner from the post office.

I pulled a chair next to the window with the best view of the street, two stories below, and planted myself there. The librarian paid no attention to me as she read story after story to a group of preschoolers in the far corner of the large room. I peered through eighty-year-old imperfect panes of glass, straining to see people's features as they walked up to the post office.

I watched a man climb out of his white compact car wearing shorts and t-shirt. My heart raced for a moment until I realized he was too young and too short to be Wayne. After half an hour on the job, I was already tired of the hard-back chair.

I was standing, leaning up to the glass, when another white car parked near the post office. This time an older woman carrying a stack of packages entered the post office. If she had been a he with Wayne's build, I was afraid I still wouldn't have been able to make a conclusive identification. I finally made an executive decision to call David. He answered on the first ring.

"David, I need a favor. I need to borrow your binoculars."

"You're on a stakeout, right?" He sounded less than happy.

"You could call it that. How soon can you come down to the library?"

"I'll be right down, and don't approach Wayne if he shows up!" He slammed the phone down and arrived with binoculars minutes later. He looked handsome as ever wearing his old work-in-the-orchard clothes. "Looks like you're all set with food and coffee…and now you have my binoculars. Guess I'll have to stay here with you so you don't do something foolish."

"I'm prepared to do whatever it takes. Care for a cup of coffee?" He shook his head. I tried out the glasses. They were powerful, bringing people so close I felt I could reach out and touch someone. "Actually, this is good. We can cover for each other when we need a break. Oh, there goes a sheriff's car." I checked my watch. It was ten o'clock sharp. His next trip through town was ten-thirty. I aimed the binoculars at the cruiser and discovered my old friend, Deputy Sayer at the wheel.

David paced the library, pulling out various books, but always shoving them back in place after a quick look. I didn't dare take my eyes off the post office. Anything could happen in the twenty-eight minutes between deputy visits. David pulled up a chair and sat beside me.

"Anything interesting out there?" he scratched his head.

"Not really, but I did see Old Man Mercer flirting with a woman who looks just like Myrtle. Want to share a sandwich?"

"It's only eleven o'clock," he said. I polished off a tuna sandwich and washed it down with coffee. I was still chewing when the librarian advised me to eat outside. I forced the last bite down my throat and promised her I would eat outside next time. She marched over to her desk, sat down and watched me as I casually observed the people of Aromas.

"Josie, what happens if Wayne doesn't come here during the day? That part of the post office is open all night."

"It will be dark, so I'll sit in my truck across the street. Don't look at me like that. I have to do this. Can you watch for a minute while I go to the lady's room?" He nodded. I left for the back of the building. As I walked by the north-facing windows, I glanced down at my truck and a white compact Toyota. It looked like the car Wayne drove out of his garage the night before. Millions of people owned cars like it. I continued my walk to the restroom. When I came back, I checked the lot. The Toyota was still there.

By the time I ran down to the market, scoured every aisle and finally returned to my spy window, David was acting nervous. I caught him pacing back and forth as he watched the street below. He saw me and smiled.

"I thought you might have done something crazy like running after Wayne."

"Would I do that?" I smiled. "I did see a car like his in the back lot."

An hour later, David took a break and bought himself a sandwich at the market. Time dragged. My derrière felt numb on the hard seat, my arms ached from holding the binoculars and I wished I could be home when Clara arrived. But not everything was bad. David was keeping me company, and good old Deputy Sayer cruised the street every half-hour.

Two more hours crawled by. I watched neighbors, friends and strangers march into the Aromas post office and minutes later reappear in the parking area. They went about their business, never suspecting they were being spied upon.

The winter sun was heading for a dip in the Pacific Ocean, shining its afternoon light directly into my west-facing window. David had finally settled into a mystery novel. My phone rang. The librarian frowned. I answered the call with a whisper.

"Jo, why are you whispering?"

"I'm at the Aromas Library. What's going on, Allie?"

"I was just about to ask the same question. It's almost three o'clock. Will we see you today?"

"Gee, I'm sorry." I checked my watch. It was two fifty-five. "I'm all tied up here...oh my God! A white...gotta' go." I dropped the phone, leaped out of my chair and scrambled around David's long legs. "Hurry, I think it's him!" I ran to my truck and fired up the engine, knowing I only had a minute or two before Wayne would come out of the building and drive away. I peeled out, not waiting for David to climb aboard. I screeched to a stop at the main road and waited for a large RV to turn right. My jaw dropped when I saw my mom in the passenger seat.

Dad took the turn unusually fast. Clara stood behind his seat waving her arms frantically and pointing as the vehicle leaned and then righted itself. I pulled up behind them, blasting my horn. Dad paid no attention. He roared down the block, crossed the center line and clipped the white Toyota's back bumper as Wayne tried to back into the street. Dad slammed on the brakes, letting the back half of the RV block Wayne's car.

Everything happened in slow motion. Out of the corner of my eye, I saw flashing red lights on a sheriff's cruiser charging up the street toward me. Seconds later, Deputy Sayer cranked his car to the right and screeched to a halt near Wayne's passenger door.

Quickly, I cranked my truck to the left, barely missing the back of the RV, and made a quick right, skimming Wayne's door as I braked.

Wayne pulled his head up from the steering wheel and looked at me. His eyes widened. He growled something mean and then looked to his right where Deputy Sayer was parked. Wayne dropped his head back down on the wheel.

David arrived, breathing hard, still holding the phone I had dropped when I left the library like a chicken running from the ax. He had decided to hoof it rather than drive since it was only one block. He helped my trembling body climb out of the truck. We hugged in the street where traffic was temporarily stalled. I laughed out loud and clung to David, letting go of my pent-up nervous tension. Clara was almost home, and Wayne was no longer a threat.

Another sheriff's car pulled up next to Sayer's vehicle. Deputy Sayer held a gun in his hand as he opened the passenger door for Wayne. The minute I heard the cuffs snap on Wayne's wrists, I climbed up the steps into the RV for a raucous reunion with my family. The hugs were long and strong and tears fell freely. I motioned for David to climb aboard. He took a couple of steps up, looked around and backed down to the street. A third sheriff's car arrived as half the town gathered for a look at the heavy-set man wearing handcuffs who had climbed over the gearshift to get out the passenger door. But the best part was seeing my smiling aunt.

"Auntie, why were you waving your arms?" I asked.

"I saw Wayne in his white Toyota turning off the highway. I told your dad to follow him, but not too close. Actually, we almost lost him. We stopped at the corner, and I saw his car in front of the post office. I guess I got a little excited. Bob did a great job, don't you think?"

"Any better and he could be hired as a stunt man in the movies." I really was proud of him. Dad beamed.

"That was quite a tricky maneuver you pulled out there, sweetie. I hope your truck is OK."

"Probably no worse than Myrtle's RV—just a few scratches," I laughed. Deputy Sayer poked his head in the door.

"I need to take statements from you folks."

"Come up, Deputy, and be comfortable," Mom said, motioning with her hand for Sayer to enter. He climbed the three little silver steps and stood in front of the two bench seats where we were sitting. I explained that Clara had just been discharged from the hospital after Wayne locked her in an ice-cold boxcar for three days. Clara nodded. Her cheeks were rosy and her eyes sparkled.

"Yes, I read the report," he said, flipping to an empty page in his notepad. "I want to know how you folks coordinated this attack on Mr. Bracken." The four of us took turns answering Sayer's questions enthusiastically, still high from the capture. Then it was Clara's turn.

"Ms. Ramsey, do you know why Mr. Bracken drugged you and forced you into a boxcar?"

"Because he thought I knew too much. You see, his wife, Darla, told him about my questions and how Josephine was snooping around their kitchen. He thought we knew that he killed Joey. He told me it was an accident. He said he went to the nursery that night to make sure Joey didn't talk to Mo about the investment money. But when he got there, Joey and Mo were in a fistfight. Wayne jumped on the forklift and impaled Joey with it. Joey was dead, so Wayne drove the lift out to the train tracks and let the train…sniff, do the rest." Clara sighed and Mom paled.

"How did Mr. Bracken drug you?" Sayer asked.

"He held a cloth over my face. That's all I remember, but my doctor said Wayne had injected choloral hydrate into my arm. I woke up sometime later, freezing cold, all alone, in a dark smelly boxcar."

"I'm glad you are all right, ma'am. We'll be in touch." Closing his booklet, he looked shaken and climbed down to the street.

I watched the other two deputies drive away with Wayne in the backseat of their cruiser.

I looked around for David but didn't see him in the crowd as I approached my truck. Deputy Sayer told me to remove my vehicle. I backed up a few feet, revealing a minor dent in Wayne's door. Dad revved up the RV and backed away from the Toyota, making room for an idling tow truck. Wayne's crumpled bumper lay on the road looking like road kill. The RV had suffered very minor scrapes—badges of honor, really.

I yelled to Dad that I would see them at my house. We drove slowly as people parted and made room for us. The party was just about over. But the inhabitants of Aromas would talk about the four-car pileup for years to come.

CHAPTER 34

Thursday morning was a stunner. The sky was blue, the birds were singing and Ben called.

Clara cuddled Felix in one arm and took the receiver with her free hand. She beamed when she heard his voice inviting her to come for a visit. She paused, pretending to think about the invitation for a minute, and then accepted. She hung up the phone, put Felix down and danced into the kitchen where I had eggs and waffles waiting. She couldn't turn off the smile.

"You really like that old man, don't you." She took a bite of waffle and nodded. "When you were unconscious in the hospital, Ben sat next to the bed telling you how much he cares. He's a real keeper, don't you think?" Solow groaned at my feet.

"He's a wonderful man. Is that what you wanted to hear? Believe me...I thought about him a lot when I was in the boxcar. It was probably the thing that kept me alive. He wants us to come up to his place for lunch, including David and Solow. Are you ready for beans?" Another groan from Solow.

"He makes a good tuna sandwich," I said. "It doesn't matter because we're going. I'll call David after breakfast."

"Don't you have to work today?"

"Allie called this morning. She said they finished the second mural yesterday. I feel kind of bad that I didn't cross the finish line with them, but I wouldn't have missed Wayne's capture and your homecoming for anything. My house feels like a real home now that you're in it."

"Thank you, dear. What would I do without you?"

"Actually, you would probably stay out of trouble," I laughed. "But catching Wayne was more fun than I've had in a long time."

"It was fun, wasn't it?" she leaned back and smiled. "It feels good knowing he isn't lurking around the corner ready to grab us. Dear, what do you think happened to Curly?"

"I think he enjoyed his last ride in Joey's plane and then wandered down the tracks to a boxcar where he became inebriated, fell asleep and froze to death."

"Yeah, that's what I thought too, poor dear. Would you mind doing a little something to my hair today? I think I'll wear the lavender pantsuit you and your mother helped me pick out."

"Is that really you, Auntie? Are you sure they didn't do a brain or heart transplant on you in Santa Maria?"

"It's me, all the way. When I was in that dirty old boxcar, I decided if I lived, I would sell my house and move closer to Candy, Leola and you…and Ben, of course. You made me realize how important family is and how unimportant my cranky old neighbor in Oakhurst was. He wants my property and I'm going to sell it to him." She took a last bite of waffle as a lump formed in my throat.

"Auntie, you've taught me so much. I feel very close to you." We didn't say another word for a long time. We cleared the table, cleaned the kitchen and prepared ourselves for a trip to the mountains. I called David and he volunteered the Jeep so there would be room for all of us, including Solow. We left early because I had a couple of stops to make on the way to Ben's.

David was in high spirits as we sailed down San Juan Road. Solow had his head out the rear window, ears flying. Clara sat quietly next to him with a Mona Lisa smile on her lips. I sat next to David feeling like it was the natural place to be. Pajaro and Watsonville whizzed by. We entered Santa Cruz city limits and exited the freeway. A couple of turns and we were parked in front of Darla's house.

"Are you sure you're OK with this, Auntie?"

"Of course, Darla wasn't trying to be mean to us. Wayne probably pressured her to talk." We walked up to the front door and knocked. Someone kah-thunk, kah-thunked and opened the door.

"Jamie, dear, it's wonderful to see you," Clara said, giving him a bear hug.

"Nice to see you, too," he mumbled, grinning. We moved

through the front room and found Darla at the kitchen table eating a late breakfast. The room smelled like bacon and fresh perked coffee.

"Darla, dear, you remember Josephine, and this is her friend, David Galaz. How are you feeling? I heard you were in the hospital last week." Clara leaned down and gave Darla a peck on the cheek.

"Yes, I was. This is my son, Jamie," Darla said, sounding stronger and more coherent than before. Jamie stepped closer to his mother.

"I moved in with Mom. I think it will be good for both of us."

"Yes, I think you're right."

"Have you been up to see Ben yet?" he asked with a crooked smile tugging at his lips.

"Actually, we're on our way to his house," I said. "We just stopped here to check on Darla." I pulled Jamie aside and whispered in his ear. "If you don't get your mother's checks on time, just let me know. I know how to deal with Mo," I said. David heard me and laughed. I think he had fun playing the tough guy. We exited the room and let Darla and Jamie finish their breakfast. Solow pounded the backseat with his tail as we climbed into the noisy, breezy old Jeep.

Clara helped David navigate highway traffic, like merging, exiting and making all the right turns. Her invaluable instructions brought us to Ben's door. He stepped outside looking fit in a denim shirt tucked into Levis. He invited us into the house, but Clara peeled off to the left, taking the path to the outhouse. Ben caught up to her and persuaded her to come inside the house first, saying he wanted to show her something. Solow followed them into the house.

The kitchen and living room held no surprises except for the heavenly lasagna aroma coming from the oven. Ben led us down the hall, past the two bedrooms, to a new room at the back of the house. He opened the door. My mouth dropped open.

We all crowded together, staring at the white porcelain toilet as if it were a royal throne. An antique four-legged tub with claws sat to the left of the tiled shower stall, and a pedestal sink was planted in the corner, to the right of the toilet. Two east windows pulled in light that sparkled on black and white checked linoleum.

Clara looked ready to faint. Ben took her arm and steadied her. Solow squeezed through our legs and sniffed the new room wall-to-wall.

"Stand back, everyone," Ben said, holding onto my aunt. "This is Clara's room." Clara opened her mouth, but nothing came out. We backed up and made our way back to the living room while Ben showed Clara the bathroom's special features. Minutes later, he joined us.

"Ben, how did you accomplish all that work so fast?" I asked.

"I had the plans and permits and materials for years. The foundation was already poured. I should have done this years ago, but it took Clara to inspire me. I started the project right after your last visit. Jamie was a big help. He's a hard worker and very skilled."

We heard the bathroom door open and turned our heads to watch Clara practically float down the hall. She deftly sat down on the sofa, still wearing the Mona Lisa smile. David, Ben and Dad discussed the building project as Clara stared into space.

"Nice bathroom, don't you think?" I asked Clara. Her lips quivered. David squeezed my hand.

"Lovely," she said.

I watched Ben round the corner into the kitchen. The oven door thunked as he checked on our lunch. He came back looking scared. I figured he had burned something, but I was wrong. He pulled something small out of his pocket, walked over to Clara and slowly, carefully, put his knees to the floor. He looked up and handed her a tiny velvet box. Everyone held their breath.

"Thank you, dear. What is it?" She flipped the top up and pulled out a diamond ring. "It's...it's lovely! You didn't have to do this, Ben. The bathroom was enough." Everyone laughed as Clara and Ben embraced. "The minute I saw the powder room, I knew you loved me. But when I was locked in that dirty old boxcar, I knew I loved you whether you had a bathroom or not."

Acknowledgements

I wish to give sincere thanks to Tomi Edmiston, my friend and editor, for a fabulous job.

Thanks also to the wonderful ladies with the red pencils — daughter, Wendy Carter, and friend, Marlene Sherwin — for their diligence, and to John Bush for educating me about boxcars.

Many thanks also go to my super tech team, Avery and Michael Laurin and Jeff Holmbeck.

And thank you, Mom, for your enthusiasm and encouragement; and loving thanks to the guy who always has my back — author and husband, Arthur C. Oroz.

Made in the USA
Charleston, SC
17 February 2014